TALES OF THE OUTLAW MAGES
Book Four

AMY CAMPBELL

Published in the United States by Amy Campbell

Cover design by Anna Spies, Atra Luna Cover & Logo Art

Edited by Vicky Brewster

Author photograph by Kim Routon Photography

Map by Amy Campbell, designed in Wonderdraft

Pegasus chapter heading art © Depositphotos.com

ISBN-13: 978-1-7361418-7-8 (paperback), 978-1-7361418-8-5 (ebook)

First edition: May 2023

10 9 8 7 6 5 4 3 2 1

v031423

For Rose, the best doggo.

Author's Note

Fantasy books take us to another world, but that doesn't keep them from serving as a mirror to our own. Because of that, there are topics in this story that may prove difficult for some readers— and if that's you, please be gentle with yourself. *Persuader* includes blood, death, drinking, kidnapping, forced captivity, guns, murder, PTSD, mention of suicide, violence, abusive relationship, anxiety, profanity, stalking, physical abuse, and weapons.

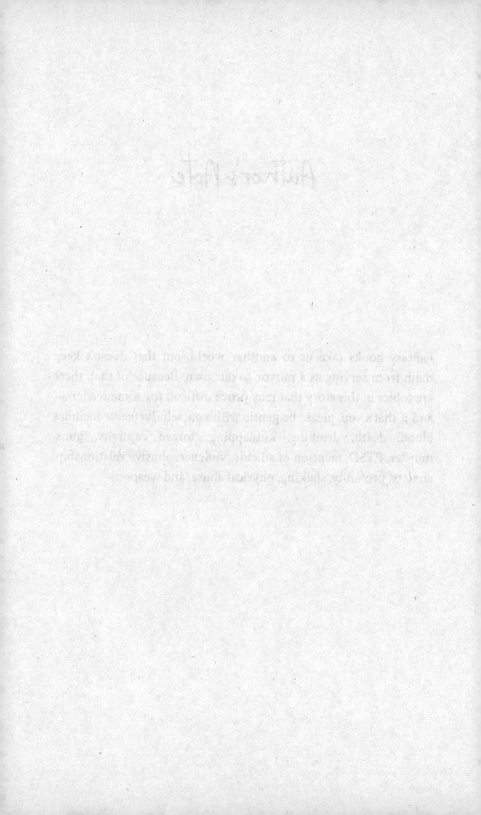

Previously...

While struggling with the knowledge that his alchemist mother transmuted him into a mage, Blaise Hawthorne also grapples with traumatic nightmares triggered by his previous imprisonment. Free to return to the outlaw town of Fortitude with Jefferson Cole, a man he's come to love, at his side, Blaise is slowly on the road to recovery.

But duty calls, and Jefferson is tapped to lead a diplomatic delegation to seek recognition for the new nation of outlaws. Along with Pyromancer Kittie Dewitt, Jefferson strikes out for his home country, Ganland, hoping his political connections will make their task easier.

With Jefferson away, Blaise considers reconciling with his alchemist mother. He rejects the idea, despite cantankerous outlaw mage Jack Dewitt, husband to Kittie, spurring him on. It isn't until Blaise receives the dire news of an attack upon his family that he takes action. But it's too late—his father is dead, his siblings terrified though unhurt, and his mother kidnapped. With Jack and the outlaw's daughter, Emmaline, by his side, Blaise pursues the desperadoes responsible.

Meanwhile, Jefferson makes a brief but necessary stop in his old home town. The purpose: to attend the funeral of his alter ego, Malcolm Wells. Jefferson is eager to put his grim family history and old life behind him. But his nemesis Gregor Gaitwood is in attendance as well, and after being tormented by nightmares, he knows Jefferson's secret.

With the funeral and his encounter with Gaitwood behind him, Jefferson and his team continue to the capital of Ganland. They're welcomed by the leader, but soon they realize the recognition they seek won't be easy to attain. A group of politicians is fiercely against their nation allying with outlaws, and they'll do anything to prevent it.

As Jefferson tangles with the politicians, Blaise, Jack, and Emmaline traverse the vast Untamed Territory. They endure a wild animal attack, glean new information from an old associate for a high price, and weather a fierce storm that would have killed them if not for a powerful display of Blaise's strange magic. The outlaws approach the town of Thorn, where they hope to find Blaise's mother. Blaise and Emmaline wait outside of town at an abandoned farm while Jack scouts ahead. But while he's away, their enemy strikes, taking Blaise and Emmaline prisoner.

Back in Ganland, Jefferson and his friends have problems of their own. After a treacherous dinner party where Jefferson runs afoul of an old beau, their lodging catches fire. As Kittie uses her magic to battle the flames and save the day, Jefferson is overwhelmed and stolen away.

When he awakes, Jefferson finds himself in the clutches of a shadowy cabal called the Quiet Ones. And they know *all* of his secrets. Without the enchanted ring that changes his appearance, Jefferson's only option is to take up the mantle of Malcolm Wells once more—a prospect that fills him with dread.

Unable to escape the warded residence, Jefferson's only chance for help comes through a tenuous link of power between him and Blaise. He uses the bond to visit Blaise in a dream.

Blaise vows to help Jefferson—as soon as he's taken care of his own dilemma. He's confirmed that the desperadoes have his mother, and their goal is to sell her—and *him*—at a one-of-a-kind auction.

On the evening of the auction, Blaise allows the desperadoes to take him to the block. But as the bids come in, the other auction creatures—magical creatures of all varieties—break loose from their cages, causing chaos. Blaise frees himself and searches for his mother. He almost reaches her when a mysterious mage sneaks up from behind and uses magic to transport Blaise hundreds of miles across the continent with his angry pegasus in tow.

After a struggle, Blaise bests his attacker and finds himself in Ganland. With Emrys, he makes his way to Jefferson's home and comes across the rest of the delegation, who believe Jefferson dead. Blaise reveals that Malcolm Wells, who had recently made his miraculous return from the dead to the world of politics, is truly Jefferson. And a new enemy has blackmailed him into a no-win situation.

Meanwhile, across the continent, Jack and Emmaline rescue Blaise's mother. They discover that Blaise was sent to Ganland—and there's no way they can catch up. Blaise's mother presents an audacious option: Jack or Emmaline can open a portal. Jack repudiates the idea, but she insists that with an alchemical potion of her creation, it's possible. To Jack's annoyance, Emmaline volunteers, and before long, the young mage opens a portal across the continent.

Reunited with his friends, Blaise plots to recover Jefferson's enchanted ring and free him from the web of the Quiet Ones. On the eve of Ganland recognizing the outlaw nation, they launch their plan. Blaise and a small group infiltrate the Quiet One compound to find the ring while Jefferson distracts them with an elaborate party. Blaise locates the ring, and they return with it in time for Jefferson to declare that he's done with secrets. He puts on his ring, announcing that he's Jefferson Cole, an outlaw mage —and Malcolm Wells is no more.

In the confusion that follows, Jefferson escapes with Blaise. But the damage is done. Because of his lies, few trust Jefferson anymore—except for Blaise. They return to the outlaw town of Fortitude, where they decide how they'll get through this strange new existence together.

Pronunciation Guide

Words are fun. Below is a rough guide to the pronunciation for words you'll find in this book. If your brain disagrees, that's fine. Language is malleable, so you do you!

Argor – ARR-gor
Asaphenia – Ass-uh-FEE-nee-yuh
Blaise – BLAY-z
Canen – KAY-nun
Chupacabra – CHOO-puh-cah-bruh
Desina – Dess-EE-nuh
Effigest – Eff-IH-jest
Emmaline – Em-uh-LINE
Emrys – Em-RISS
Faedra – FAY-druh
Faedran – FAY-drun
Ganland – Gan-LUND
Garus – Gair-USS
Garusian – Gair-OO-shee-un
Geasa – GESH-uh
Hospitalier — Hoss-pih-tal-yer

Itude – Ih-TOOD
Izhadell – Iz-UH-dell
Knossan – NOSS-uhn
Knossas – NOSS-us
Kur Agur – Kur Ah-GRR
Leonora – LEE-oh-nor-uh
Lucienne – Loo-SEE-ann
Marian – Mayr-EE-uhn
Marta – Mahr-tuh
Mella – Mell-UH
Mellan – Mell-UHN
Nadine – Nay-DEEN
Nera – NEER-uh
Nexarae – Nex-UH-ray
Oberidon – Oh-BEAR-uh-don (alternate: Oby – Oh-BEE)
Ondin – Onn-dihn
Oscen – Oss-KIN
Petria – Pet-RIA
Phinora – Fin-OR-uh
Ravance – Ruh-VAN-s
Ravanchen – Ruh-VAN-chen
Reuben – Roo-ben
Rhys – Reess
Seledora – Sel-uh-DOR-uh
Seward – SOO-urd
Tabris – Tab-RISS
Theilia – Thee-LEE-uh
Theilian – Thee-LEE-uhn
Theurgist – THEE-ur-jest
Zepheus – Zeff-EE-us

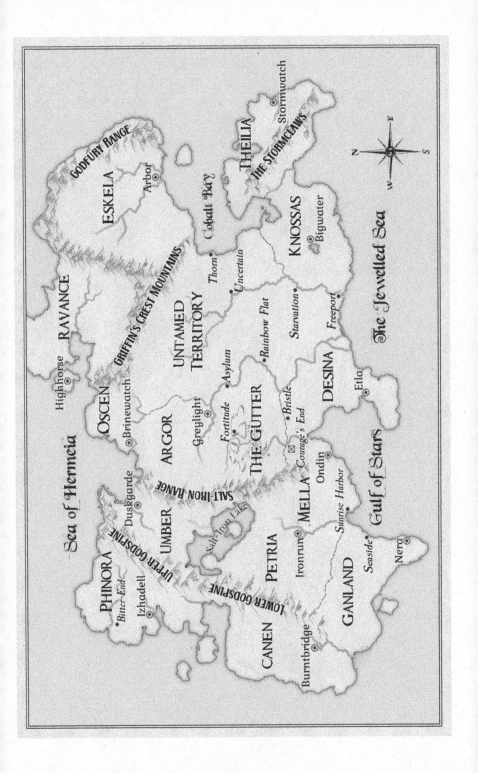

CHAPTER ONE

Piss-Poor Name Choice

Vixen

"You've been nursing that same drink for the past hour."

Vixen sighed as Clover slid down the bar closer to her. She should have known better than to linger at the Broken Horn, especially feeling as she did. But it had been comforting to come here, to be surrounded by the familiar sound of pool cues striking billiards balls, the slosh of whiskey being poured, the hum of voices and braying laughter.

Aside from Vixen's pegasus, Clover was the one who knew the most about her. Or at least hints about her. But some self-destructive behavior declared Vixen needed to be near those who would nudge her down the road she dared not tread of her own accord. "Got some things on my mind."

"Hmm." The Knossan flicked an ear, tilting her head. She was fishing for more information, and normally the Persuader would speak freely. But not about this. Not now. "I suppose I have to guess. Is it Raven?"

Vixen huffed out a breath. Raven. Things with him were

complicated, but that was tiny by comparison to what was currently on her mind. She shook her head. "Guess again, cowgirl."

Clover drummed her stubby fingers against the wood of the bar. Her fuzzy ears flipped forward. Newcomers to town who had never come across a Knossan before were often intimidated by the bovine race, but Vixen had known Clover for years. "I have heard rumors of problems with the Confederation."

That was closer to the target. But the problem went beyond that even. Vixen scraped a fleck of gunk from the top of the bar with a fingernail. "Not just problems. Odds are good, they're going to come knocking."

The Knossan snorted out an unhappy breath, understanding that *knocking* would involve battle and blood. Like Vixen, Clover was a survivor of the assault that had claimed so many lives in their town, formerly known as Itude. That attack had been orchestrated by one man with a grudge. What would happen if the entire might of the Confederation came at them? It was horrifying to even contemplate. And that didn't take into consideration the shadowy cabal Jefferson claimed was working behind the scenes. Vixen longed for the days when the most she had to worry about was if Jack would catch her cheating at cards.

"You do not have to stay, you know," Clover said, her voice gentle. "After what happened, no one would begrudge you."

Clover was giving her permission to turn tail and flee. Vixen rubbed absently at her cheek. If only it were that simple. Clover, and probably others, thought she was still traumatized over what had befallen her at Fort Courage. And while in a way that was true, that wasn't the sum of her issues. "I'm not turning my back on the Gutter. Not when I can do something about it."

"Ah," Clover murmured, though there was a wagonload of meaning in the single syllable. "Your magic, then?"

Vixen laughed, though she knew it held an edge of borderline hysteria. Yeah, her magic would play a role, no doubt. And it was still amazing she'd gotten it back. She chalked that up to the walking miracle that was their Breaker. "Sort of. I..." Vixen faltered. It had been a bad idea to come here. What was she thinking? "I gotta go, Clover. Add this to my tab?"

"Of course," Clover agreed, watching as she pushed up from the stool and headed for the door.

Vixen wove through the crowd of regulars, none of them paying her much mind. Her presence in the Broken Horn was a natural thing, and no one would blame her for leaving in a mood with the pall of current events hanging over them.

But there was one who would call her bluff. She heard the cadence of wingbeats announcing her pegasus's arrival. Alekon wheeled overhead and let out a trilling whinny—his way of catching her attention, the arrogant bastard. She watched him head for the stables, where he would no doubt alight in the area the pegasi dedicated to departures and arrivals.

<I may have been on patrol, but you know we pegasi gossip like old broodmares,> Alekon remarked as he trotted around the corner, dust roiling before him. He drew to a stiff-legged, snorting halt, his onyx mane tossing artfully around him. Alekon was a bright bay, his coat a rich red-brown with mane and tail like black satin. He lacked the flashy white markings some of the other pegasi bore, but made up for it with flair.

"Yeah, I'm well aware, you pest," Vixen complained, batting at his neck.

Alekon whacked her in return with his nose. <We should go for a flight.>

A flight. With her mind abuzz, that wasn't a bad idea. "Yeah, let's do that."

She pulled herself onto his back, unable to hide the surge of joy that flooded her. No matter how many times she rode a pegasus, she would always feel the same. There was freedom here. Freedom she wouldn't find anywhere else.

Alekon craned his neck to make certain she was secure before breaking into a fluid trot and then a lope. Vixen clung to his barrel with her legs, and her hands twined through his mane as he took to the air. She could count on one hand the number of outlaws willing to ride a pegasus bareback. It wasn't a safe endeavor by any means, but there was something in the act of defiance, in throwing caution to the wind, that she loved.

With a high-spirited snort, Alekon threaded through the network of canyons that made up the Gutter. His wings pumped with the effort, pouring on more and more speed until Vixen wished she'd remembered to swap her tinted glasses for her flight goggles as the wind whipped beneath the frames, making her eyes tear. But she wasn't going to let that stop her. She squeezed her eyes shut, whooping as she clung to her stallion's sleek back. The early summer sun's warmth offset the chill of the wind, further invigorating her.

She felt his wingbeats slow, evening out as he changed course. Vixen's eyes still stung, so she kept them closed when Alekon's hooves rang against stone as he landed atop the canyon rim. Vixen shoved a hank of hair out of her face, opening her eyes at last. They were several miles from Fortitude on a cliff overlooking the Deadwood River.

The sound of new hooves on stone drew her attention. Vixen twisted, looking behind her to find a familiar palomino pegasus pacing toward them, a rider on his back. She frowned. "Jack? What are you doing out here?"

The Effigest glanced at Alekon, then at her. "Wanted to talk to you, and I figured you'd want this discussion as far from town as possible." He stroked Zepheus's neck. "Keeps us away from so many busybodies."

Vixen froze, not liking where this was going at all. "Don't see any reason for that." Maybe she could bluff her way out of this conversation. What did the wily Effigest know about her? Too much, she feared.

"I think you do," Jack shot back, almost too quickly. "I'm downright ashamed at how long it took me to figure you out."

Damn it. Jack knew. Or he thought he knew something, at any rate. Didn't mean it was right, though with the way he prided himself on his web of information, the odds weren't in her favor. He had trapped her nicely—if she stormed off she would confirm his suspicions. Vixen lifted a hand, adjusting the fit of the glasses on her face, the ones that kept her magic from inadvertently affecting others. Jack met her gaze, his cool blue eyes almost daring her to try him. He knew what she could do.

But he had come on his pegasus, and Zepheus would know if she used her power on him. It was generally frowned upon for her to use her magic against friendly outlaws without good reason, and she doubted anyone else would agree this was a good reason. Vixen settled for crossing her arms. "What do you think you know?"

He chuckled, shaking his head. "Valerie ain't your last name. Ain't your first name, either."

She couldn't help but roll her eyes at that. "You already practice these lines on Jefferson?"

At the mention of the Gannish ambassador, Jack's eyes narrowed with keen calculation. "No, but I have a notion you got more in common with him than you let on."

Vixen had half a mind to use her persuasive magic on the Effigest to force him off the trail of her past. She licked her lips, peering at him over the top of her smoke-lensed glasses, hoping he read the warning. "I reckon you should let it go."

"Yeah, can't do that when I'm looking at every angle to keep our fat from the fire." He looked away, his gaze falling across the golden walls of the canyon. A hawk soared over the nearby rim, wings skimming the air as it gained altitude.

"I told you to *let it go*," Vixen hissed, brow furrowing with frustration. "You don't know a lick about me."

"I do." He turned, eyes snapping to her face, as if daring her to use her power. "I know you're Valoria Kildare, the Spark of Garus, second only to the Luminary." Jack's lips curled at the title. "And I'm the idiot who didn't connect Valerie and Valoria for years, despite your piss-poor name choice."

Vixen bristled. "I was only fourteen! I had to come up with something!"

Jack laughed, and belatedly she realized he'd baited her into the confirmation. Gods, he was insufferable. Beneath her, Alekon shifted uneasily. The pegasus was the only one in the entire Gutter who knew her secret. She hadn't even told Raven. Which, upon reflection, was one of the smarter things she'd done.

<I did not tell Jack,> Alekon said apologetically. <He only asked me if his suspicions were true and said it was important.>

Yeah, Jack would say just about anything was important. And what could Vixen say? She could argue, could say he was being ridiculous, that he was wrong. But he wasn't wrong. She swallowed. "And I guess it ain't a coincidence you're asking after me now."

He gave her a look that she couldn't quite discern. There was something almost sad about it, but she didn't know why. "Nah, it's not. You know what's at stake. You survived the Battle of Itude and Fort Courage." His voice hitched at the last sentence, confirming his strong feelings on the subject.

"What do you expect me to do, Jack? I can't just walk back to my old life and demand the Confederation stand down." She shook her head. "I'm a mage. An *outlaw mage.* I'm not what I was."

He looked away, gaze roaming the ruggedly beautiful lands around them once more. "There's still part of what you used to be buried deep. It's buried, not lost."

Buried. "The Spark is dead."

Jack snorted a laugh. "Yeah, so was Malcolm Wells." He tilted his head. "And then Jefferson Cole. And then he wasn't, and he's still a pain in the ass. If anyone can help you reclaim your old life, it's the peacock."

"What if I don't want to?"

He gave her a look. "Yeah, ain't that the question?"

Did Jack know how frustrating it was to talk to him sometimes? He surely knew because why else would he do it? "I'm sayin' I'm not keen on the idea."

To her surprise, he nodded. "That's fair."

She blinked. "What?"

"You heard me." He shifted in the saddle. Zepheus blew out a bored snort. "Vixen, I ain't gonna force you to do something you don't wanna do. Even if it's the best shot we got at keeping clear of war. Nobody should have to give up the life they wanna live."

Vixen pursed her lips. Damn, but he was a manipulative bastard. If she wanted to be selfish and stay hidden, others would suffer. But if she put herself out there and reclaimed her birthright...he was right. She would lose the life she loved. There was no way she could win this, no way that everyone ended up happy.

"Have you told anyone else?"

Jack clucked to Zepheus, and the stallion pivoted to move away. "Nope."

"Are you going to?" she called after him.

"Nope. That's on you."

Vixen huffed in annoyance. Bastard. Now she felt terrible about the whole thing. She buried her face in Alekon's ebony mane. "What do I do?"

Alekon arched his neck, eyeing her. <All you have to do is the next right thing.>

The next right thing. She sighed, ruffling her stallion's black mane. The feel of the coarse hair grounded her, made her feel as if she weren't adrift. Yes. She would have to talk to Jefferson.

CHAPTER TWO

As Serious as a Smoking Sixgun

Jefferson

That Vixen wanted to meet with him privately was both concerning and intriguing. Jefferson didn't know as much as he'd like about the flame-haired outlaw, aside from the fact that Blaise trusted her. Come to think of it, that said volumes about a person. Blaise was reserved and preferred to keep to himself.

What was strange about the whole thing was the way the pegasi conspired to make it happen. Seledora was the one who told him Vixen would like to meet, and the grey mare then made a point to fly him out to a distant precipice where the Persuader awaited him.

There wasn't much grazing to be had on this part of the rust-colored rim overlooking the Deadwood River, but Alekon made a show of pretending to browse on the stubby growth. Seledora rolled her eyes at his theatre and simply moved to the question-able shade of a scrubby mesquite, cocking a hind hoof in a stance of relaxation. The bay joined her a moment later, and they stood nose to rump, using wings and tail to swish flies from each other as they relaxed.

Vixen stood near the edge. Heights didn't scare Jefferson, but even he would have been hesitant to stand so close. She angled toward him, lips curling into a smile of greeting. "Thanks for coming."

Jefferson shrugged. "I don't think I had much say in the matter. Seledora seemed determined to bring me here. And anything that makes her so intent is intriguing to me."

Vixen's expression shifted, as if she didn't wish to be the source of any intrigue. "Yeah, *intriguing*. I suppose that's the word."

"May I ask why we're so far from town?" Jefferson asked, eyeing the gorge below. "You don't have plans to dump my body down there, do you?" He was only half-joking, though he knew there were people out there who would happily do exactly that.

<I would not have brought you in that case,> Seledora reminded him, mental voice drowsy.

The Persuader huffed. "I'm not *Jack*."

"Wait, has Jack actually done that to someone? And you think he might do that to me?" The thought was disturbing. And it did, in fact, seem like something the tempestuous outlaw might do.

"Not that I know of, but no telling with him," Vixen admitted. She licked her lips, and Jefferson realized she was nervous. She had neatly evaded explaining why they were so far from town.

Jefferson didn't have Flora out here—since their run-in with the Quiet Ones, he'd asked the half-knocker to keep an eye on Madame Boss Rachel Clayton, the leader of Ganland. Clayton knew about their enemies, which meant they might come for her. Blaise didn't know he was gone. Only Seledora was here. Was this a set-up of some sort? He took a step backward, readying his magic in case he needed it.

Vixen must have noticed his sudden tension. Her brows knit. "Oh, damn. You think I'm up to no good, don't you?"

Jefferson kept a firm hold on his dream magic. He was relatively certain he could use it on her if needed, but he didn't want to without reason. "The last year has been rough, so forgive me for being cautious." *Longer than that, honestly.*

Her shoulders slumped. "Sorry. Sometimes I forget I'm not the only one who's been through things that would make the demons of Perdition think twice." She gave him a rueful smile, gesturing to the nearby outcropping. "No, I didn't ask you out here to kill you and dump your body in the Deadwood. Alekon asked Seledora to bring you because out of all the people in Fortitude, you may understand what I'm about to tell you the most."

Why do I have the impression I'm going to regret this conversation? Jefferson walked over to a chunk of stone that looked like it would make a serviceable seat. As a bonus, it was a healthy distance from the edge. "I have my suspicions about why you think I'm the best person to come to. I'm listening."

Vixen blew out a breath, ambling closer to where he sat, though she didn't join him. "I'm not the person I appear to be."

Bullseye. As soon as she'd said he would understand, he had thought it might be something like this. He offered her an encouraging smile. "I suppose I do know a little something about that. Though I doubt it's any worse than being a Salt-Iron Council Doyen in an outlaw town."

Vixen laughed, a hollow sound. She flipped a lock of brilliant red hair out of her face. "That's a bet you would lose, Doyen."

"I prefer *Ambassador,*" Jefferson said mildly, if only to dampen the rising tension.

"Ambassador," Vixen agreed with a good-natured shake of her head. "I still don't know how you sweet-talked your way into that. You're not even a Persuader."

"I can be quite charming, but I was lucky," he admitted, since it was true enough. Odd that she was once again straying from the original topic.

<She's nervous,> Seledora told him privately, ears pricked in their direction. <This truth scares her.> Jefferson knew a thing or

two about that, too. Revealing the truth made a person vulnerable. He would always see falsehoods as armor, even if Blaise disagreed.

Vixen watched him as she mulled over whatever thoughts meandered through her mind. Jefferson let her, knowing better than to push. She picked at a thread in the seam of her trousers, as if it had suddenly become far more interesting than anything else. "This thing I'm going to tell you...I'm only telling you because it directly affects the Gutter. The threats against the Gutter, I mean."

Jefferson nodded at the earnestness in her voice. He noticed she'd dropped the drawl she often used. All a part of her act, he mused. "I understand."

"And I may need your help with it."

That sent a flash of shock through him. "My help?"

Vixen smiled. "You're our ambassador to a Salt-Iron nation. And you were a Doyen. You have connections and influence that may be necessary."

Jefferson cocked his head, uncertain. He wasn't sure if he liked where this was going. "I think you underestimate how royally I've burned bridges with my stunt in Nera."

"That'll change when you return to the Confederation with the Spark."

Jefferson stiffened, and even Seledora let out a whicker of surprise, proof that Alekon had left her in the dark, too. As an attorney, the mare knew a little more about the hierarchy of Confederation nations than the average pegasus. Garus was the patron god of Phinora, and the Luminary served as his vessel—with the Spark as an heir. Not only that, but the Luminary acted as the head of state. Vixen was *far* more important than Malcolm Wells had ever been. Jefferson swallowed. "Please tell me you're joking."

"I'm as serious as a smoking sixgun," Vixen said, rubbing her forehead.

Jefferson closed his eyes. He wished this was a nightmare—he could influence those. Change the outcome. This truth Vixen had revealed was dangerous. Not only to him but to every single person who called the Gutter home. There were zealots who would turn the Gutter into dust to get her back if they thought the outlaws were involved. Which raised the question…

"Lamar Gaitwood had you. How in Tabris's name did he not know who he had at the time?" Jefferson asked.

Vixen shook her head. "How would he know that Vixen Valerie, outlaw mage, was worth the time of day? The Spark is dead."

Assumed dead, Jefferson suddenly realized. He sighed. "I suppose we do have a lot in common, you and I."

"Unfortunately," she agreed.

"What are you proposing?" Jefferson asked.

"I need to go back. To Izhadell."

To Phinora. To the heart of the Salt-Iron Confederation. Vixen was asking him to help her get to a place that was dangerous to both of them. To use the gossamer-thin strings of his tenuous ambassadorship to ease the way there. "What do we gain by doing this?"

Vixen straightened her shoulders, as if donning a mantle of boldness. She met his gaze. "Come on, Ambassador. You're well aware that the Confederation's considering an attack on the Gutter."

The breeze rippled through Jefferson's hair as he grimaced at the dire reminder. "Yes, that's been keeping me busy with—*oh.*" He'd been almost too preoccupied to see what she was getting at, but now he did. "You could stop it."

"I could stop it." Vixen glanced back toward town, lips pursed.

Damn, it sounded far-fetched, but she was right. It might work. He tilted his head in a side-to-side rhythm, puzzling through how he could make this happen. "Very well. I'll help you."

"When we travel, my identity remains a secret," Vixen said, her tone sharp. "Until I can figure out the best way to let the Luminary know."

Jefferson shook his head. "I can't keep any more secrets from Blaise. Especially not one this big." And one that would put him in direct peril.

Vixen chewed on her lower lip, conflicted. Then she nodded. "I trust Blaise. He won't..." Her sentence died, unfinished.

Oh. This was deeper than Jefferson had thought, perhaps even a worse tangle than his own mess of identities had been. "Anyone who hates you for finding out your truth was never your friend to begin with."

She made a soft scoffing sound. "That works for simple things, yeah. But I'm the heir to the Luminary, the living avatar of Garus. Thanks to the Confederation's invocation of Garus, mages don't exactly like that god very much." Though the feeling was mutual. Followers of Garus hated mages just as much, happy to subjugate them as little more than tools.

Jefferson cocked his head, thinking. "But nothing has changed in the two minutes since you've told me. You're still the same person."

Vixen's smile was tight. "Because you understand. You've always been you, no matter if you were Malcolm Wells or Jefferson Cole."

He stepped closer, not invading her space, but near enough to be a firm presence. Proof that she had not alienated herself from him, at least. "Whether you are the Spark or Vixen Valerie, you're still you. The woman who cheats at cards and taught the Breaker how to wield his magic."

At the accusation of cheating, she pulled away. "I do *not*—" Vixen paused, then made a soft laugh. "Fine, I get it. You're saying even if I'm the Spark, I'm not so high and mighty to people who know me."

"Exactly," Jefferson agreed, pleased that she understood.

"So, what do we do now?" Vixen asked.

Ah, that was the question, wasn't it? A large part of Jefferson wanted to pretend this conversation had never happened. A tiny part of him wondered if hurtling himself off a cliff might be a cleaner fate than whatever might happen if he went to Izhadell as a liar and a mage—with the Spark in tow, no less. But he said none of those things. "I'll speak with Blaise, and once I've felt him out, we'll form a plan of action."

Vixen nodded, relaxing. She looked more like herself: the confident outlaw mage who knew her mind and took no guff. "There's one more thing you might help with..."

Tabris's sweet golden ass, what next? "And that is?"

Vixen sighed. "I need to hide my magic for as long as I can."

"Ah." He understood why she'd made that request. Word had spread about the unusual ring Blaise had gotten for him. Jefferson always carried it when he went out and about, not only because it could be useful, but because it was a reminder of Blaise's regard for him. The ring had cost the Breaker an enormous sum, and all to protect Jefferson. It was the next best thing to a proposal from the Breaker, which he knew was unlikely to come. He fished it out of his pocket, the inset nub of unicorn horn glinting in the light. "This infernal thing is rather precious to me, you know."

Vixen's gaze fell on the ring cupped in his palm. "Blaise gave it to you."

Jefferson nodded. "Yes. He gave it to me, to protect someone he holds dear." He extended his hand, the nullifying ring jostling with the movement. "But I also know he considers you a dear friend."

She reached out to take the offered ring, but paused. "We can wait and ask him, if you prefer."

Jefferson chuckled. "You and I both know Blaise's kindness. He would want you safe as well."

Vixen took the ring, holding it gingerly in her palm as she studied it. Then she slipped it on her finger, wincing at the sensation of her magic being cut off. Jefferson knew exactly how awful it felt, but it had come in handy before. "I can't believe you wore this for an extended time," she muttered as she shucked it off again.

He chuckled. "You get used to it after a bit. I suppose it wasn't as hard on me, since I haven't had magic for as long as you." But even in that short time, it had become an intrinsic part of his fiber. He hadn't felt whole without his magic.

"Do you want it back for now?" Vixen asked.

Jefferson shook his head. "No, hang on to it. I presume, since you've revealed your truth to me, you'll have to stay the course."

She rubbed the ring between her thumb and index finger, then stuck it in a pouch at her belt. "Thanks, Jefferson."

He was going to regret this, he just knew it. But if what Vixen had told him was true, then she was right. It might head off any aggressions if they handled the situation delicately. "Don't mention it."

CHAPTER THREE
Play to Win

Blaise

Blaise stared at Jefferson blankly. "She's what now?"

Jefferson sighed, running a hand through his hair, the scarlet gem on his precious cabochon ring winking with the motion. "Not a *what*, more of a *who*."

That didn't really help, as far as Blaise was concerned. Sometimes Jefferson forgot how little he knew about all things Confederation-related. And while he understood Jefferson was trying to explain something of great importance to him, he really had no concept of why there was any importance to it at all. "Again, Vixen being the Spark of Garus means about as much to me as declaring Emrys the Prime Minister of Pies."

Jefferson snorted a laugh at that, though he made it look elegant and charming. "Fair enough. I don't enjoy feeling as if I'm talking down to you."

Blaise shrugged. "You're not, since I really have no context for any of this." It wasn't as if, during his stint in Phinora, anyone had bothered to explain their favorite god or political structure. No one would stoop to explain such things to a prisoner.

"I suppose that's true," Jefferson mused. He stared at the board arrayed before them. The Dreamer had laid out a game of chess, though they hadn't begun gameplay. The pieces stood at the ready, like armies carved from wood. Jefferson picked up the white queen. "Imagine this is the Luminary."

"Now I see why you picked chess," Blaise remarked, studying the pieces. "The Luminary isn't the leader, then?" He pointed to the king piece. Honestly, Blaise had never connected the Luminary to Garus, but then again, he'd only ever heard the title and nothing more.

"Well, yes, though there's also a Clergy Council that makes decisions," Jefferson said. He set down the queen, exchanging it for a bishop that he waved around as he spoke. "What I'm getting at doesn't align with the rules of chess, though. Which of these pieces has more power?"

That was easy. "The queen."

Jefferson nodded. "That's the Luminary in a nutshell. She is not only the voice of a god but runs the theocracy, for the most part."

It had never occurred to Blaise that the gods and goddesses might be anything more than stories. He knew Jefferson was a follower of the Gannish god Tabris, but they hadn't discussed it much. "Um, do you think the Luminary really *is* an avatar?"

Jefferson smiled, setting the piece back on the board. "I suspect you really mean if I think Garus is real. That I can't answer." His face shifted to what Blaise thought of as his cunning expression, when Jefferson was looking to reap the highest rewards. "But I do know that belief is a powerful thing and might be something we can use to our advantage."

"How does Vixen factor into all of this?" That was what Blaise really didn't understand.

"Ah." Jefferson picked up a pawn from the board. "She's something like this. What happens when this pawn makes it across the board?" He gestured to the spread in front of them.

"It becomes a—oh." Blaise glanced from the pawn to the queen. "So you're saying Vixen will become the Luminary? The avatar of Garus?"

"She has the potential, yes," Jefferson agreed. "For the past few centuries, the Luminary position has been hereditary."

Blaise frowned. Vixen had kept a huge secret from all of them, though he suspected she had good reason. He still remembered talking to her what felt like ages ago, when he first realized he wasn't the only mage with a hard-luck story. Then the puzzle pieces fell into place in his mind—Vixen was a mage. She had been in an important position in Phinora, beholden to a god notorious for disliking mages. Or that was what Blaise understood, at any rate.

"No wonder she hasn't told anyone," he whispered.

Jefferson nodded, no doubt having already made all those connections. "I see you understand."

Blaise did, but now he had other questions. "She told you all this…why?"

The sudden tautness around Jefferson's eyes spoke volumes. "As the Spark, she'll be in a position of power. If I understand her correctly, she believes she can convince the Confederation to stand down from attacking the Gutter. Phinora always has the most say in the Confederation's actions."

Jefferson was evading the question, dancing around it as if he were back in his politicking days. Blaise crossed his arms. "And this involves you how?" He had an idea, but he wanted his beau to confirm it.

"She would like me to use my position and whatever's left of my influence to help her return to Izhadell for an audience with the Luminary." Jefferson watched him closely, as if waiting for Blaise to refuse the idea outright.

And Blaise wanted to—he really did. He didn't want Jefferson anywhere near Izhadell. Not after all they had been through there —or rather, what Blaise had been through. But the place was just as much a threat to Jefferson, possibly even more so now, since he had openly declared he was a mage. Blaise cocked his head. "The fact that you're telling me this leads me to believe you've already agreed to it."

Jefferson nodded. "Yes. I think Vixen has the right of it. That this is worth trying, for the sake of the Gutter and all the people here." He looked the gravest Blaise had ever seen him, his green eyes alight with a fire of determination. Jefferson believed in this, despite the potential for danger.

"Will your ambassadorship provide any buffer for you?" Blaise asked.

"Look at you, being strategic. Fair question," Jefferson mused, a tiny smile gracing his lips. "Technically, it should, but that entirely depends upon if the rest of the Confederation feesl like further poking Ganland. And they may, considering Ganland isn't on the best terms with the other nations at the moment."

"That's not really encouraging," Blaise commented, crossing his arms and hoping he gave Jefferson a look communicating how much he disliked this idea.

Jefferson shifted the game board, rising from his chair to move to Blaise's side of the table. His eyes were earnest as he gestured to Blaise's lap. "May I?"

"You think I'm going to be mad at you," Blaise guessed, though he nodded.

The Dreamer shot him a wounded look as he lowered himself to sit sideways on Blaise's lap, slinging an arm around the Breaker's shoulder. It was a comfortably intimate position; Jefferson's slender form nestled against his. "Not mad, no. Worried." Jefferson angled to plant an apologetic kiss on Blaise's forehead. "After my past mistakes, I have a better understanding of how I may accidentally make you mad versus what worries you."

Jefferson was right—everything about this worried him. He appreciated his beau's foresight in coming to him. Something about Jefferson grounded him, staved off the panic that constantly threatened. Blaise didn't know what to say. He knew Jefferson, knew that this man he loved would do what he could for the mages of the Gutter. And Blaise loved him even more for that, even as it terrified him.

"I'm not defenseless, you know," Jefferson murmured, peering down at him.

"Neither was I," Blaise reminded him, finding his words at last. "And you're vulnerable to salt-iron."

Jefferson's nose wrinkled in distaste. "An unfortunate allergy, like most mages."

Blaise licked his lips. Vixen would be vulnerable to it, too. Vixen was a friend, someone he cared about. And Jefferson was going.... There was only one response to any of this. "I'm going with you."

He felt Jefferson's shiver of surprise. The Dreamer shifted to straddle him, leaning in to rest his forehead against Blaise's. Jefferson tenderly lifted a hand to cup his cheek. "I can't ask that of you."

Blaise closed his eyes. "You're not. I'm asking this of *me*."

"I see," Jefferson murmured, looping his arms around Blaise's neck.

Blaise wasn't sure he did, though. He looked up at Jefferson, debating how he could explain his tangle of thoughts. How he wasn't willing to risk Jefferson going without him. And he wanted to go, wanted to defeat his fear of everything Phinora represented in his mind. But by the way Jefferson smiled down at him, maybe he did understand.

Blaise cleared his throat. "Besides, you'll need a place to stay while you're there. And it just so happens I have one."

Jefferson chuckled. "Oh, you don't say? I suppose we'd make poor guests to go calling there when the master is away."

"Can't have that," Blaise agreed. He had given little thought to the Wells estate that he'd inherited from Malcolm's alleged death. Now it was one of the few assets of Jefferson's that had evaded the machinations of the Quiet Ones, the shadowy cabal of elite pulling the strings within the Salt-Iron Confederation. He didn't mention that was his other motive for accompanying Jefferson. Blaise feared the Quiet Ones might move against Jefferson within the Confederation boundaries. He would not allow it.

"You're too kind," Jefferson said. "To tell you the truth, I'm happy that you want to go along for purely selfish reasons."

"And what are those selfish reasons?" Blaise asked.

Jefferson glanced away for a beat, blowing out a soft breath. "Ah..." His green eyes darted back to Blaise. "Because of how I feel about you."

"I don't think love is selfish."

"Perhaps not, but it feels like it sometimes," Jefferson admitted, canting his head. "And I know I can be a bit much." He brushed the fingers of his right hand along the ridge of Blaise's jaw, then rose to move to his own side of the table once more.

Blaise's gaze followed Jefferson. "Sometimes I like when you're a bit much."

"Do you?" Jefferson raised his eyebrows.

"You generally get that way over things you're passionate about," Blaise said, picking up a white pawn and tossing it from one hand to the other.

A smile softened Jefferson's face. "I do have strong feelings regarding you."

And I feel the same about you. Blaise held up the pawn. "If you win this match, you can be a bit much with me later."

Jefferson narrowed his eyes. "I hope you don't intend to lose on purpose to humor me." The skin between his eyes creased into a V of concern.

"First of all, I intend to play to win. But even if I didn't, it's not *humoring* you." Blaise placed the pawn back on the board. "I love you and like seeing you happy."

"I'll be happy with you regardless," Jefferson murmured.

Blaise smiled. "I know."

Jefferson

JEFFERSON SHOULD HAVE KNOWN THE MEETING WOULD GO SOUR. He'd been too optimistic after his pleasant evening with Blaise the previous night. Still, it had been nice to entertain the idea that everything would go smooth as silk.

"So, let me get this straight." Jack tilted his head, eyes darting from Jefferson to Vixen. "Not only do the both of you want to go to Phinora unannounced, but you want to take our Breaker with you."

"That's the long and short of it," Jefferson agreed, though there was something about the way the outlaw worded the statement that didn't sit right. As if it were some sort of bluff. Odd. Did he know about Vixen?

"It's not for nothin'," Vixen insisted, crossing her arms. Jefferson noticed she was careful not to meet Raven Dawson's gaze. Not because of her magic, no. She kept her tinted glasses firmly on the bridge of her nose. Jefferson knew they were old flames, though he didn't know how they'd parted ways.

Kur Agur, the wolfish Theilian, drummed his furry fingers against the table, claws clicking with each movement. His nostrils flared. "It seems like too great a risk. Why would we send you to the enemy's heart? Especially when there are whispers they may come to us." A growl rumbled in his throat.

"By then, it will be too late," Jefferson said. This argument, at least, he was prepared for. "When we get to Izhadell, we can get an audience with the Luminary. If we can convince her, the odds are good that the Salt-Iron Council will also scrub any potential thoughts of attack." He hoped no one planned to ask for the details on how he'd arrange an audience with the Luminary.

"Why the *Luminary?*" Raven asked, his emphasis on the word as sharp as the knives sheathed at his hip.

Vixen had an answer ready. "Garus represents wisdom. If we can convince his avatar that it would be wiser to work with us than fight us, we stand a chance."

Raven's eyes narrowed, clearly unconvinced by her response—but he didn't argue.

Jack was studying Vixen, his frigid blue eyes calculating. His lips pursed as he considered. Jefferson watched the outlaw closely. The more he saw, the more he was convinced the Effigest was play-acting. "You're planning to use magic, yeah?"

Vixen crossed her arms. "I reckon, if it's necessary."

Mindy looked uneasy about the plan. Jefferson knew the Hospitalier was no coward—she had been an integral part of their mission to Nera last year. "You think waltzing into Izhadell and using magic is a good idea? What makes you think it won't have them come after the Gutter even harder?" She swallowed. "And we wouldn't have any of you here if that happened."

Jefferson traded a look with Vixen. This was an uphill battle, and it was quickly becoming apparent the vote was going to go against them. If only he could figure out Jack's angle. Jefferson suspected that regardless of the outcome, Vixen was going to Phinora. Her mind was made up. *I'm going to have to put a spin on this—*

The door to the meeting room creaked open. "It's a show of strength," Blaise said, all eyes falling on him as he stood framed in the threshold. He leaned against the lintel as if all that attention didn't unnerve him. Jefferson knew different. The Breaker's gaze settled on him as if he were the only person in the room, a solid rock to grab onto amid a river of discomfort.

<I told him the discussion was not going well,> Seledora reported from outside. Ah, so his pegasus attorney had stuck her nose into the meeting. She was quite handy to have around.

The other Ringleaders frowned at the Breaker. "I thought that was the last place you would want to go, Blaise," Mindy pointed out, her voice gentle.

Out of reflex, Blaise rubbed the tender underside of his left arm. No one could see it beneath the blue-checked, long-sleeved shirt he wore, but all of them knew of the long scar that marred his skin. Jefferson knew it intimately. "I'm not the same man I was the last time I was in Izhadell. I was a victim then. A prisoner." The corners of his mouth tightened, and Jefferson knew Blaise was thinking of what else he had been considered. A criminal. A murderer. There were times he still grappled with the guilt of what happened at Fort Courage. He was quiet for a long moment before continuing. "I'm not those things now. And after the Inquiry, I have *standing* in Phinora." He shrugged. "At least that's what Jefferson tells me."

"And a lot of people there are gonna want you dead," Jack added amiably. "Or just want you." Jefferson arrowed a glare at the outlaw.

Blaise shook his head. "That's true no matter where I am." His voice held a note of sadness. Jefferson wished he could change that reality for Blaise, but he was right. They could pretend to have an idyllic life in Fortitude, but it would take very little for their bubble to not just burst, but shatter. "This is our best shot to protect the place and people I care about before it comes to that. If we let them march on the Gutter, innocents will die." His fists clenched at his sides, a sheen of silver wafting from his closed palms.

"You're not invulnerable," Kur Agur rumbled, flattening his ears.

Blaise pursed his lips. "I'll be the first to agree with that. But I think it's a chance worth taking. With Vixen's persuasion and Jefferson's..." He paused, and for a moment, Jefferson feared his love would inadvertently reveal his magic. "...diplomacy, I think we stand a good chance."

"What are you gonna do? Bake them a cake?" Jack asked, sounding amused. Jefferson continued to be perplexed by the outlaw's stance. What game was he playing?

Blaise smirked at that. Actually *smirked*. Jefferson couldn't hide his own smile. "Yeah, if it comes to it."

"I can't believe any of you are actually warming up to this idea," Raven said, his eyes dark with barely concealed anger. "It's reckless. It puts three of our mages hopelessly far into enemy territory with no assurance of their safety."

"We make our own assurances, thank you very much," Vixen shot back, arrowing an irritated look at her former beau.

"Vixen, you're a *Ringleader*," Raven growled, testy. "And despite his theatrics, Jefferson is an *ambassador*. You have responsibilities to the Gutter."

"And you can't just mosey into Phinora and claim to represent the Gutter without our say-so," Mindy agreed.

"We *do* have responsibilities to the Gutter," Vixen said. "Do you think we want to go to Izhadell for some sort of pleasure holiday? We know what's there."

"We're going because it's the right thing to do. The only way we see to stop an attack before it starts," Jefferson added.

Blaise's voice was soft when he spoke. "I wasn't here to help at the Battle of Itude. At the very least, I want to do something before this town is attacked again." His blue eyes raked the room, and for a moment, Jefferson feared old memories had reared up to capture the younger mage's attention. Then Blaise shook his head, as if flinging those memories away. "We should at least try."

"What's going to happen when the Confederation captures you?" Raven asked, voice tight as he fidgeted with a knife. *Damn him.* Jefferson's jaw tensed, too aware the Shadowstepper had asked to goad Blaise. His panic attacks were common knowledge among the Ringleaders.

"They won't." The Breaker's words were almost inaudible. There was a feral underlying growl, like a cornered wild animal. Blaise would not be held by the Confederation again, not without a significant cost. He would fight.

"Have a little faith in us," Vixen said, perching her hands on her hips. "None of us are greenhorns."

Kur scratched his chin. "As much as it pains me, I see the wisdom of their gambit. It is better to be the hunter than the prey."

Jack nodded at that. "We're outlaws. We ain't prey." He rapped his knuckles against the table, though there was a strange glint in his eyes. As if the Effigest knew something, but was keeping his cards to himself. "Y'all have my vote."

Mindy's gaze flicked between Raven and the other Ringleaders. The Hospitalier mage shifted in her seat, then nodded. "Faedra knows we've done more audacious things. I'll back it."

Raven hissed out a breath of frustrated dissent. Jefferson caught Blaise's eyes, aiming a grateful smile at the Breaker. *Majority rules.*

CHAPTER FOUR
Never Yours to Lose

Vixen

"What in Perdition was that about? You can't be serious about going to Izhadell!"

Vixen had known Raven would come after her, critical of their plan. She'd seen it in his eyes, in the set of his jaw. Even so, she was annoyed that he had. Better for him to just let them do it. Did he think he had the chance of a snowball in a dragon's maw of convincing her otherwise? She spun on her boot heel to face him. "You were at the meeting. I know you don't got cotton stuck in your ears."

She expected to see the same anger from the meeting lining his face, but it had been replaced with something else. Concern. Worry. Even a dash of defeat, if she was reading him right. "I only know the things you and Cole spoke aloud. But I know you. I know to read between the lines, and I can't." He swallowed, his dark eyebrows low, shadowing his eyes. "Let me start over. Can we talk?"

Vixen tilted her head. She appreciated he was trying, but it wouldn't change anything. Still, talking wouldn't hurt. "We can. I

was going to the shop. I've got some work to do." When Fortitude had been rebuilt, she'd cleaned up her ways—at least a little.
She'd taken up work that was more honest than cheating at
cards, opening her own tailoring shop. Through necessity, she'd
learned to mend and sometimes fashion her own clothing, and
over time had found that she was good at it—and enjoyed
doing it.

He nodded, falling into step beside her as they made their way
up the street. Raven wisely didn't speak as they walked, holding
his silence until they reached the shop. Vixen had flipped the sign
on the door to *closed* while she attended the Ringleader meeting
and now realized it would be closed for an extended time when
she left. In fact, she might never open it again. That bothered her
more than she'd thought it would. Vixen had become attached to
her little shop and understood a bit of why Blaise loved his
bakery.

Raven cast a glance around her shop, past her work table by
the massive windows that lined the front, to the organized
swathes of fabric, lace, and spools of thread. A mannequin bore an
almost-complete dress that Vixen had been working on for
herself—though it wasn't fully a dress. The skirt was much
shorter than any respectable woman would wear, reminiscent of a
saloon girl's. For good reason, that caught Raven's attention.

"What's that?"

"A little something I've been working on," Vixen said. She was
proud of it and thought it was going to be a lovely piece when she
was done.

"Isn't it a little...um, short?"

She scoffed. As if he had any say in what she did or wore. But
it was a valid question—it was shorter than what she usually
wore. Though, to be fair, she favored trousers. "If it were worn
alone, yes. But that's not it. Let me show you." She moved to the
worktable, picking up the other part of the outfit and holding it
up to reveal dark trousers that would be form-fitting, the hem at

the end of each leg edged with ornate black lace. "See, I was making something sensible that could be worn while riding."

Raven cocked his head. "I'm not sure how *sensible* it is."

"Says the man who's never had to consider riding in a dress," she shot back, earning a chagrined look. "Trust me. It's very sensible." She folded up the trousers and set them aside. "But we didn't come here to talk about my work."

"No," Raven agreed, taking another turn around the shop. Since it wasn't large, it didn't take him long at all. He blew out a breath. "Look, I know this is the last thing you want to hear from me, but..." The Shadowstepper paused, as if deciding on his next words. "I don't know what your history is in Phinora, but I know you have one. And I know you never wanted to tell me, so it must be painful. That's why it's a mystery to me why you'd want to go back."

Vixen weighed her options. With the trajectory she was on, her secret would come out and he would learn soon anyway. But that didn't mean she wanted everyone to know. Once word got out, no one would look at her the same. And Raven...well, he was the son of a theurgist. He wouldn't look kindly upon anyone from the upper echelons of the Confederation.

"I don't owe you an explanation."

Hurt registered on his face. "You don't. You made that pretty clear when you turned me down the day I proposed to you."

Her hackles raised at that. Vixen wished he hadn't brought it up. Turning him down had been one of the hardest things she'd done in her life, but she'd known it was the right thing for both their sakes. And not just because of her past, but because, while he loved her, she didn't feel the same for him. Two people bonding over the shared pain from Fort Courage didn't make them compatible in the long run. She saw that plain as day, but he didn't.

"Drop it, Raven," she advised him.

"Why can't Jefferson and Blaise go without you? Why is it so important for you to go?" he asked.

"Blaise is only going because Jefferson is. And this is something Jefferson can't do alone." For more reasons than she was willing to state aloud. They both knew Blaise was a good man, but he wasn't a diplomat. He was too anxious, and being the center of attention was one of his worst nightmares.

"Someone else could go," Raven suggested.

Vixen snorted, ticking off the options on her fingers. "Sure, we can send Jack. Wait, no we can't—his mug is still on wanted handbills all over the Confederation. Oh, we could send Kur. Never mind, we can't because the Phinorans would take offense at a wolf in their sheep-like presence. And while Mindy went to Nera with the delegation, she kept to the fringes for good reason. Who's left? You?" She knew her words were a challenge. Didn't care.

He scowled. "You know I can't. I meant someone like Kittie."

"I wanna see you suggest that to Jack. Makes me wonder if he has a poppet of you yet," Vixen drawled. From what she knew of Jack, there was no way in Perdition he'd keep his peace if Kittie went to Phinora for any reason. The fear of losing her again would be too much for the man.

Raven shook his head, unwilling to admit defeat. "Fine. It doesn't have to be Kittie. We've had lots of new arrivals. Might find someone suitable among them."

Vixen canted her head. "Do you think I'm such a poor choice for this?"

He blinked in surprise, then took a step back as if he only now realized what his suggestions sounded like. "No, but I don't want to lose you."

"I was never yours to lose, Raven." She couldn't help the annoyance that crept into her voice. She had told him no. How hard was that to get through his thick skull? "I could decide to up and move to Starvation tomorrow. Would you follow me across the Untamed Territory?"

The jut of his jaw proved he would consider it. He sighed. "I can't help how I feel about you, even after..."

"Yeah, well, I can't help it either," Vixen shot back. "And now, if you don't mind, I have work to do. With luck and time on my side, maybe I can finish this before I leave." She nodded to the almost-complete outfit.

Raven rubbed his forehead. He looked as if he wanted to say something else, but maybe he realized it was a lost cause. He gave her a final, wounded look and strode out the door.

Vixen huffed out a breath, shaking her head. Relationships were messy things. From here on out, it would just be her and Alekon. No more humans to pine after her. Pegasi were better than people.

Jefferson

"JEFFERSON! A MOMENT, PLEASE!"

He paused at the familiar voice, turning to see Kittie trotting toward him on a chestnut mare. Though the Firebrand's mount was no mare of flesh and blood—somehow, after their return to Fortitude, she'd come into possession of an equine fire elemental. Jefferson assumed Jack was likely involved, though he didn't know how. All the same, he had a great deal of respect for the mare. Even though she was horse-shaped, some instinct in the back of his brain held a healthy fear of the elemental. Didn't help that he had rather unpleasant memories of being kidnapped during a fire. He took a breath to compose himself. "Afternoon, Kittie."

The woman slipped out of the saddle. Like the pegasi of Fortitude, there was no need for Kittie's steed to wear a bridle in the town. The mare eased to the side, so she didn't crowd her rider, while staying protectively close.

"Do you have a moment to speak?" Kittie asked, her eyes

flicking to the nearby bakery.

She knew he was headed home and had intended to intercept him. Curious. But Jefferson liked Kittie a great deal after his work with her in Ganland. She had a good head on her shoulders—and she hadn't turned her back on him for his duplicity. He was rather thankful for any allies he had. "Absolutely. Would you like to come to the bakery? I'm certain there would be a treat we could enjoy." That was an unfair trick. Elemental she may be, but Kittie's mare loved Blaise's sweets as much as any of the pegasi. The mare's nostrils widened at the prospect, her head craning toward the bakery.

Brief annoyance crossed the Pyromancer's face, and she shook her head. "I was thinking perhaps a walk around the outskirts of town." The elemental heaved a disappointed sigh.

Poor mare. Jefferson hadn't meant to distress her. He paused, glancing at the creature. "I'd be happy to speak with you, Kittie. And if your mare would like a snack, I'm sure Blaise would see to it. She only has to go around to the back window."

The equine rocked on her heels, as if ready to bolt away. But she waited, lambent eyes on her rider. Kittie nodded. "Go on, girl. You deserve it." And with that, the mare whinnied and trotted to the bakery, tail swishing in her wake. The occasional spark flickered in the dust after her passage, but nothing caught fire, and that was what mattered.

Jefferson allowed Kittie to lead their stroll. She didn't speak for several minutes, until they were out of earshot of most anyone else, perhaps save a pegasus. "I've heard of your plans to travel to Izhadell."

It was a statement. Jefferson wasn't sure if she expected a response or if her intent was to add more. But after a few steps, when she made no additions, he said, "Yes, that's the goal."

Kittie frowned. "I don't believe for a moment that you're only going to convince Phinora to keep the Confederation from waging war against us."

Jefferson should have been insulted, but he wasn't. Partly because Kittie was right. And he was also impressed that she had picked up on facets of him that Blaise hadn't. "To be fair, that's most definitely part of why I'm going. The Gutter is my home now. And there are people here I care about." And it was more than Blaise. He liked Clover, the Knossan bartender, a great deal. And Flora's uncle, Jasper. And Blaise's family lived here now, too. They were all worthy of protection.

The Firebrand blew out a breath, a lock of hair flipping out of her face. "But that's not all, is it?"

He swung his hands behind his back, threading the fingers together as they continued to walk. "In truth, no. Flora hasn't been able to find out how deep the Quiet Ones have burrowed into the Confederation."

"Are you planning to use yourself as bait?"

Jefferson sighed. "Not as bait, exactly. But I'm hoping to flush them out. They've done all the damage they can to me from a distance." That was depressing to think about. His enemies had drained his vast fortune, stripping him of every fiscal advantage he had.

Kittie crossed her arms. "According to Jack, parts of the Confederation want you."

"Ah, that." That was nothing new. As soon as the truth of his dual personas had come to light, the Salt-Iron Confederation had become exceedingly interested in him. "And that is why my attorney will accompany me."

The Pyromancer scoffed. "Jefferson, this is *serious*." Worry reflected in her eyes. "You don't know what they do to mages."

"Actually, I do," Jefferson retorted, his voice suddenly frosty as his brows slammed down. He remembered only too well the things Blaise had revealed at the Inquiry. The way Gregor had stripped Jack's will and used the Effigest like a weapon. There wasn't a day that passed when he didn't reflect on the horrors visited upon mages in the Confederation. "I know many people think that everything I've ever done has been a sham. But I have always—*always*—fought for mages. Even before I became one." He ran a hand through his hair, turning to face her. "I know what they do to mages. And I know there is the potential it could happen to me." Gods, he hoped not. "I also know what will happen if we let the might of the Confederation rain down on the Gutter. That's not a fight we can win."

Kittie was quiet for a moment, thoughtful. As if she were calculating their own strength against the relentless Confederation onslaught. It would be a bloody, horrible thing all around. Jefferson knew without a doubt that they could inflict terrible losses on the Confederation. But magic, even power like Blaise's, had limits. The Confederation boasted multiple nations. Even if Ganland stood down—bloody Perdition, even if Ganland *helped*—it still wouldn't be enough.

"Do you believe the Quiet Ones would engineer this? I thought they supported the Gutter," Kittie said at last.

"That right there is the thousand golden eagle question," Jefferson murmured. "Whatever game they're playing, it's a long one." He grimaced. "And I believe I've scuttled some of their plans. I wonder how they're regrouping. And how deep their claws are into the upper echelons."

Kittie nodded. "You're risking a lot by going there."

Oh, he knew. And the thought of what he might walk into was enough to twist his stomach. "I won't be alone." That was the only thing that made him think he could do this. That he had half a chance.

Kittie cast him a side-eyed glance. "Does your beau know about this angle?"

"We haven't spoken of it, but Blaise has his concerns," Jefferson said, looking over his shoulder toward the distant bakery. "Unlike our trip to Nera, I have a better idea of what I'm getting into. They no longer have the advantage of surprise."

"I hope you're right," Kittie murmured.

CHAPTER FIVE
Family Fun

Blaise

"At least take this one." Marian Hawthorne shoved a potion into Blaise's hand, closing his fingers around the glass and its sloshing contents.

"Mom," he protested, freeing himself from her grasp. Blaise glanced down at the label on the bottle. His mother had been experimenting again, and he never knew what to expect. She was always happy to foist potions on him if he had plans to leave town for any reason. "*Polymorph*? Do I even want to know what this does?"

"Emptying the contents on a person will turn them into an animal. Temporarily." She smiled at him as if that were a completely normal thing to offer her son.

As a child, he hadn't thought twice about his mother's work. Now that he knew how uncommon alchemists were and how gifted his mother, in particular, was? It was a little frightening. Scratch that, it was terrifying. "How do you even know if it works?"

"Your brother wanted to be a dog."

Blaise rubbed his forehead. Maybe he was fortunate that his mother had made him a mage and not a dog.

"He got better," Marian said, frowning at him. "Do you honestly think I'd leave Brody as a dog?"

The question stung. And that wasn't how Blaise wanted to leave Fortitude, frustrated with his mother. He didn't know what to say, didn't know how to voice the words he feared would hurt her, either.

In the end, he didn't need to. She blinked, then made a soft hissing sound, her expression crumpling. "That was the wrong thing to say. I'm sorry, Blaise. I'm worried about you going to Izhadell, and I wasn't thinking." She was shorter than he was, and she closed the distance between them, reclaiming the potion in the same motion as she wrapped him in a hug. "I love you."

Blaise relaxed against her. "Love you, too. And I'll be okay." Nearby, Jefferson was speaking with Lucienne and Brody—and Blaise's younger brother was definitely not a dog. Brody laughed at something Jefferson said. "Can you maybe not experiment on family members, though?"

"That's part of being an alchemist," Marian said, her mouth close to his ear. Blaise realized she was revealing something that wasn't meant for others to hear. "We're able to experience the effects of our potions for a short time without suffering ill from them."

He made a soft, surprised sound. "I never realized..." Blaise licked his lips as he thought. Did that mean that for a brief time, long ago, his mother had Breaker magic like him? No wonder she had known his magic was dangerous, but not that it had other uses. Other possibilities.

"Alchemist's secret," she whispered.

Blaise tilted his head. "I'm not an alchemist."

"No, but you're my son. And I don't want you worrying about the things I'll be teaching Luci and Brody." Marian pulled back, her expression serious. "There's no one else to teach them, and though we live in a town surrounded by outlaw mages, they're alchemists by birth."

He didn't fully understand alchemy, but he understood that denying them the chance to learn it was akin to leaving a mage ignorant of their magic. And he knew what that felt like. Blaise smiled. "I'll take potions, but please only send normal ones. I don't want to explain to anyone why I'm a Breaker armed with offensive potions."

"Simple answer. Because you're *my son*," she said, sounding smug. "Give me a moment."

While she stepped into her apothecary shop, which was a stone's throw from the stables, Blaise ambled to join his siblings and Jefferson. When they turned to look at him, Blaise pointed at Brody. "A dog? *Really?*"

The boy grinned. "It was the best! I could pee on everything outside, and no one could be mad at me."

Jefferson's eyebrows flew up, a mix of curiosity and confusion. "Do I even want to know about this conversation?"

"Mom made a potion that turned Brody into a dog," Lucienne offered helpfully. Brody dropped down on hands and knees in the dirt, growling at his sister.

Blaise rubbed the bridge of his nose. "Temporarily, at least."

"Ah." Jefferson threaded his hands behind his back. "Remind me not to get on your mother's bad side."

"You'll be on my good side as long as you treat my son as he deserves," Marian said, coming up behind them. Jefferson jumped at her voice, though he did a good job of covering his surprise by pretending to adjust his cuffs.

"I wouldn't imagine treating him any other way," Jefferson said. The certainty of his own words must have put him back at ease, as he aimed a dashing smile at Blaise.

"Here." Marian shoved a leather bag into Blaise's arms. "Perfectly normal potions."

He frowned, freeing the laces to peer inside. "Please tell me

there's no Chill of Death or Faedra's Embrace." Blaise pulled out
one bottle, sighing when he saw the name of another unusual
potion. "Mom! This is *not normal*."

"There's no Chill of Death. I don't want to risk you with that
one again." Marian shook a finger at him. "You know better than
to administer potions to yourself when you're bad off."

She was trying to change the subject. He wasn't going to let
her. Blaise pulled the cobalt blue bottle out, pointing to the label.
"Incognito? Why?"

"Why not?" Marian asked, as if it were perfectly reasonable.

"What's it do?" Jefferson asked, curious. "I'm going to assume it
doesn't turn you into a dog, at the very least."

"Oh! Oh, can I show them?" Brody asked, bouncing to his feet.

Blaise sighed as his little brother snatched the potion from his
hand. "Why can't I have a normal family?"

"I don't think there is such a thing," Jefferson said with sympathy. Then more softly, he added, "But let me assure you, this is a
breath of fresh air."

Brody held the bottle in his hand, poised to open it. "Can I
show you? Pleeeeease?"

How could Blaise say no to that? It was good to see Brody
excited about something. "Go ahead."

The boy unstoppered the bottle, taking a sniff. "It smells and
tastes like peppermint." That was good to know. Too often,
alchemical potions tasted awful. Brody took a tiny swig, then
shoved the stopper in again. As he swallowed, an effect rippled
across him, reminiscent of when Jefferson's glamor fell into place.
A moment later, Brody no longer looked like the brown-haired,
fair-skinned child he had been, but now had bright red hair and a
generous smattering of freckles across his face.

"Oh, so it's like an alchemical glamor." Jefferson crouched
down to peer at the boy, appearing far too interested. He glanced
at Blaise. "We should take that."

"See?" Marian asked, grinning at the Dreamer.

"Fine, we'll take it," Blaise relented. "Better to look like another person than an animal, I guess." He accepted the bottle from Brody. "But how do you remove it?"

"The duration depends on how much you ingest," Marian said. "There's no reversal for it aside from time."

Blaise didn't like that, but he had an idea. "Brody, come here."

His brother cocked his head. It was odd to see him with such red hair. "Wait, why?"

"I want to see if my magic will work on it."

"No way, that's no fun!" Brody pulled something out of his pocket—another vial. He took a step backward.

"Brody Hawthorne, don't you dare," Marian warned.

He drank the potion, shrinking into an orange tabby. The bottle fell to the dirt with a clatter as the cat meowed and darted off, paws pattering against the dirt. Blaise sighed. "Really?"

"Well, you mentioned getting a cat for the bakery." Jefferson was far too jovial about the whole thing.

"He is so grounded." Marian put her hands on her hips, looking at her daughter. "Luci?"

"On it." Before Blaise could even ask what she was doing, his sister scooped up the bottle, grinning at him. She tapped her forehead. "Sometimes, to catch an alchemist, it takes an alchemist. Try to keep up." Then she sipped from the bottle as well, shifting into a fawn-colored hound.

"Your family is so much more fun than mine ever was," Jefferson observed. "Are they always like this?"

"Only when they're flaunting their alchemy," Blaise grumbled. He picked up the bottle and handed it to his mother. "We'll be back." Then he broke into a reluctant jog after Luci. The hound had already bolted after the cat, her nose low to the ground as she picked up the trail. She bayed, the sound so deep it rattled Blaise's teeth.

In her canine form, Luci was much faster than either of them. Blaise didn't even attempt to keep up. Attracted by the strange doings, Emrys came over to see what was going on. Like Jefferson, he was amused by the whole thing and took up the chase with them. That worked in Blaise's favor, allowing him to climb onto the stallion's back. Seledora joined them a moment later.

<I hear baying toward the eastern trail,> Emrys said, turning to trot in that direction.

"How far do you think a little cat can run?" Jefferson asked.

"When that little cat is an alchemist, there's no telling." Blaise shook his head.

Ten minutes later, the pegasi homed in on the hound, discovering that Luci had Brody treed. The orange cat clung to a branch, hissing at the dog. Luci's tail wagged with fiendish glee as she leaped up, snapping at the cat. She wasn't big enough to reach him, though.

Blaise eyed the tableau. "Brody, come down."

The cat meowed, digging his claws into the branch. Blaise assumed that was a no.

"What's the plan?" Jefferson asked. "I've never hunted an alchemist-turned-domestic cat before. This is out of my wheelhouse."

Blaise cocked his head, thinking. He wasn't about to climb the tree, and even aboard Emrys, he couldn't reach the branch. His magic was more than a match for the tree, but that move was too extreme. No, sometimes the simplest solution was the answer.

"If you come down from the tree and let me try my magic on the glamor, you can eat as many cookies as you want before dinner."

Luci whirled with a snarl, fangs bared.

Blaise shrugged at her. "I'll take it up with Mom later." He peered up at the cat. "Best I can do."

<I think the kid is getting the better end of the deal.> Emrys snorted, arching his neck.

Brody must have agreed. He eased toward the trunk with a mewl, ears flattening when Luci barked at him.

"Luci, let him down," Blaise called.

The hound backed off with a whine, moving beside the pegasi. Her whip-thin tail wagged as she watched the cat tentatively make his way down. When Brody hit the ground, his feline form rippled, and he returned to the shape of a boy with oddly red hair.

"Hey, how'd you do that?" Blaise asked. "Did the polymorph potion run out?"

"Nah." Brody shook his head. "I'm an alchemist. I ended it." He raised his brows. "You promise about the cookies?"

"Yes."

"I want in on the cookies, too!" Luci demanded, reclaiming her human shape. "It's not fair."

"Mom's going to kill me," Blaise muttered. "Fine. Cookies for you, too. Now, Brody, let me see you."

Blaise slipped down from Emrys's back. Brody obediently came over, though he still wore a mischievous smirk, and Blaise half expected him to bolt. But he held still as Blaise rested his palm on Brody's arm. This was where he needed a delicate touch with his magic—without control, he could just as easily shatter a bone as remove the potion's effect. But he was beyond that now. Taking a breath, he focused his magic, feeling out the layer of potion that overlaid Brody's skin.

He had to admit, the potion was intricate. It was almost impossible to find where the glamor ended and Brody began. Blaise persevered, though, and before long, he sent his magic into the thin shell of the glamor. His power ate away at it, and a moment later, brown-haired Brody grinned up at him.

"Is it cookie time?"

"Yes, I guess it is," Blaise agreed with a rueful shake of his head. "I'll meet you both at the bakery." With a whoop, the Hawthorne children dashed off. He turned back to Emrys. "Now it's time to go ruin everyone's dinner and face my mother's wrath."

<Can my dinner be ruined, too?> Emrys asked.

"I don't think it matters at this point." Blaise hoped he had enough leftover cookies in the bakery for this. He had a sinking feeling that his surplus inventory was about to take a hit.

Jefferson chuckled. "I do love your family."

Blaise couldn't help but smile. "Yeah. Me, too."

"Your mother can't be too angry, you know," Jefferson reasoned as they made their way back. "What with us leaving tomorrow and all. And she was the one who suggested the potions."

<Listen to Jefferson. He has a good defense,> Seledora agreed, easing into a trot.

<If she's too angry, just offer her cookies.> Emrys bobbed his head at the sage advice. <It's impossible to be mad in the face of cookies.>

Blaise chuckled. "I guess it's worth a try."

CHAPTER SIX

Nobody Here Likes Unicorns

Blaise

Traveling with Jefferson and Vixen was almost pleasant. For a little while, Blaise could pretend as if they weren't on the trail to head off another crisis. He didn't even mind that they had to dodge inclement weather that slowed their progress to Ondin, the capital city of Mella.

He knew everything would change once they reached Ondin, however. Jefferson had sent messages ahead, working with his connections in Ganland. Through Flora, he'd gotten in touch with someone who worked with Madame Boss Clayton to secure their passage on a train that would take them all the way to Izhadell.

"Are you looking forward to the train ride, Blaise?" Vixen asked as their pegasi approached the station.

He made a face at the question. "I'm not overly excited. But it'll be nice to dry out, at the very least," Blaise said, shaking the sleeves of his yellow rain slicker. It wasn't raining in Ondin, but they had come through another shower as they'd approached, and now they stuck out like sore thumbs in their bright raincoats. Well, he and Vixen did, at any rate. Jefferson's raincoat was a deep blue, and the raindrops beading on the fabric made him look as if he were garbed in bejeweled finery.

"What?" Jefferson asked, glancing back and noticing Blaise's eyes on him.

"I was just thinking you're the only one of us that doesn't look like a drowned rat."

The Dreamer grinned. "Oh, you think I look good, do you?"

"That's not what I said."

"But it's what you meant."

Vixen snickered at their banter. Blaise hissed out an exasperated sigh. Better to change the subject than let Jefferson continue to needle him. He wondered if Jefferson had made his flirtatious sally as a distraction. His beau knew he was nervous. "Where do we go?"

"We're going to be riding in a private car, or so Flora assured me." Jefferson pointed to a train hunkered down on the nearest set of tracks. Unlike some of the other iron behemoths, the engine and cars belonging to this train appeared to be freshly painted and in good repair. "And the pegasi will have a livestock car to themselves."

Seledora pinned her ears, snapping her teeth. <We are not livestock.>

Her rider was quick to stroke her neck. "No, you certainly aren't. I suppose we'll have to call it the pegasi car."

The train station was bustling with activity. That should have come as no surprise to Blaise—Ondin itself was a riot of people, as he supposed a capital city would be. It wasn't as busy a place as Nera in Ganland, but nonetheless, pedestrians, wagons, and riders clogged the streets. The calls of vendors selling wares rose above the din of voices and hooves on hard-packed ground. A rumbling blast from the train on the farthest rail split the air, giving Blaise a start, but all around him, the mass of people carried on as if nothing were amiss.

With Seledora and Jefferson leading the way, they threaded

through the crowd. The pegasi had their wings hidden, so aside from their rain gear, no one gave them a second look. Jefferson had Seledora pause every few steps as he scanned the area, seeking someone.

"Cole! Jefferson Cole!" a voice rang out. Seledora swung in the caller's direction. Blaise followed Jefferson's gaze to a woman standing on the stairs to the station, waving enthusiastically at them. "Over here!"

"And that would be our contact," Jefferson said, glancing back at Blaise and Vixen.

They followed him over to the woman, who looked a few years older than Jefferson. She was dressed in a black frock coat over a long striped skirt and gleaming ankle boots. Blaise didn't think she had the look of one of the elite but perhaps a bureaucrat. A man stood a few paces behind her, wearing a dark red wool coat with gold braiding over tan trousers. The colors of the Confederation. Blaise froze up when he saw the uniform.

Emrys balked, sensing his unease. <Do you want me to back away?>

Blaise swallowed. He noticed that Vixen's eyes had gone wide, and she was staring at the uniformed man, but not with the same gut-clenching fear that Blaise was experiencing. Jefferson seemed oblivious to the both of them, intent on connecting with the other diplomat.

"Monica Bremner, I was not expecting that you would be the one to meet us," Jefferson said, sliding out of the saddle to land on the balls of his feet with flawless ease. He flashed her a charming smile, only then seeming to note Blaise's unease.

The woman, Monica, returned the smile. "The Madame Boss isn't playing games. We don't want a war any more than you do."

"So she sends the best." Jefferson chuckled.

The uniformed man watched their exchange with polite interest and little more, though he hazarded the occasional furtive glance at Vixen. Not at Blaise—which was fine with him.

Monica spread her hands. "Let's just say she's trying to prevent a powder keg from going off. We're a little nervous about outlaw mages going to parley with Phinora."

Jefferson's eyes flicked to the Confederation man. "I see."

The Gannish woman's mouth tightened. "Allow me to introduce your escort. This is Tracker Rhys Kildare. It was thought prudent to send along additional security."

To protect us or to protect others from us? Blaise kept the thought to himself.

"A Tracker?" Jefferson's brow furrowed. He clearly had misgivings about this, too.

Rhys stepped forward, arms uncurling. "As Diplomat Bremner said, I'm here in the capacity of security. I'm not here to conscript you as theurgists or anything else you may think."

"I see." Jefferson paused. Blaise wondered for a moment if he was about to call the whole thing off. Being accompanied by a diplomat was one thing. But a Confederation Tracker? That was something they had not prepared for. It was almost a threat.

"It will be fine," Vixen said suddenly, her words confident. She glanced at Blaise and Jefferson, giving them both a nod.

<Alekon doesn't have specifics, but Vixen has reason to trust the Tracker,> Emrys advised Blaise. <He believes we do not need to worry.>

Blaise chewed on his bottom lip, forcing his shoulders to relax. He trusted the pegasi—and Vixen. He caught Jefferson's eye and nodded.

Jefferson studied him for a moment before turning back to the others. "Excellent. In that case, we should make our introductions."

Vixen

It was difficult to feign the coolness she showed, but Vixen had years of gambling experience to draw on. Alekon sensed her inner turmoil, though, and she knew he was assessing her rush of emotions. Rhys Kildare was the last person she had expected to run into upon her return to the Confederation.

She noticed that the sight of the Tracker distressed Blaise, and even with his impressive level of control, no one wanted an upset Breaker. Vixen was thankful Alekon had passed on a message to calm the others while she tried to decipher what this meant.

Monica showed them to the livestock car that was reserved for the pegasi. It was a fancy thing, painted a glossy red with the words *Bull's Eye Stables* painted in a swirl of letters.

"Is this car on loan from a racing stable?" Jefferson asked when he saw it, apparently recognizing the name.

Monica nodded. "Yes. The stalls in this car are wider than the standard livestock cars. I thought it might be necessary." She twined her thumbs together and wiggled her fingers, hinting at wings.

"Ah," Jefferson murmured.

The broad door to the boxcar was open, a long ramp leading the way inside. The pegasi paused at the base, ears flicking. Alekon tossed his head, uttering a loud snort. <There's a unicorn inside.>

Given Rhys's presence, that wasn't a surprise to Vixen at all. A unicorn was part of a Tracker's kit. But Emrys's last experience with unicorns had been traumatic, and the black stallion shied backward, his rider not even attempting to stop him. Since he'd likely told Blaise what manner of creature was inside the boxcar, the Breaker no doubt understood his response.

This wouldn't help their trip at all, though. Vixen jumped down from Alekon's back, springing over to Emrys and snatching the loose reins. The stallion rolled his eyes at her. "Emrys, shhh. You have reason to be upset, I know. But trust me. If this unicorn is who I think it is, it's okay." She kept her voice low, only carrying to the black stallion's ears.

Emrys's neck was slick with sweat from his anxiety. <I don't *like* unicorns.> He pawed at the ground, massive hoof scraping at gravel. <*Nobody* here likes unicorns.>

Vixen looked up at Blaise. They couldn't let old fears derail their mission. True, she and Jefferson could go on without Blaise, but she doubted either of the men would allow such a thing. "Can you do something?"

The reluctance on her friend's face was clear. With a sigh, Blaise slipped out of the saddle and moved to Emrys's other side. "You know what the unicorns did to him and Oby out in Thorn."

She glanced at the black stallion's hindquarters, his sleek hide pocked by scars. "This one is different," Vixen whispered, and she hoped she was right. But a gulf of years spanned between the last time she'd seen Rhys and his unicorn. Things could have changed.

Blaise nodded, placing a hand on Emrys's forehead. "Go along with this, and when we get to the house in Izhadell, I'll bake you whatever pie you want."

Emrys snorted, lowering his head as he considered the offer. <A pie *and* a cake.>

The Breaker chuckled, scratching beneath the stallion's forelock. "Deal."

<I would like a cheesecake,> Seledora added.

Blaise blew out a breath. "Okay."

Alekon twisted in Blaise's direction. <If you're taking orders, I'll have a tray of sugar cookies.>

Vixen rolled her eyes, turning back to her stallion. "The lot of you are ridiculous." But she was pleased that, once again, Blaise's baked goods would win the day for them.

Unaware of the bribery afoot, Rhys had already climbed the ramp and waited at the top, no doubt prepared to show them to their pegasi's accommodations. Vixen had so many things she wanted to ask, but this wasn't the time. All the same, she was the first to escort Alekon up the ramp, meeting Rhys's eyes when they stepped into the car. If he recognized her, he gave no sign.

Four large box stalls took up most of the livestock car, though there was a makeshift area that served as a tack room and storage for feed. A cot huddled along one wall in the small room, a blanket laid across it and a knapsack tucked beneath.

"Is there a groom staying here?" Vixen asked, glancing at the cot.

Rhys's expression was neutral. "That's where I'll be staying."

Well, that answered that. Whatever his purpose, the Confederation or Ganland hadn't ponied up the fare for him to have a proper stay on the train. Or maybe it was more pragmatic—it wasn't a bad idea to keep someone near the pegasi on a train full of unfamiliar people. Still, Vixen had mixed feelings about Rhys staying in such conditions.

An equine head Vixen hadn't seen in years thrust over the only currently occupied stall. The unicorn was a blue-grey that might be mistaken for a standard grey horse at a glance. But the spiraling silver horn on his forehead stamped him for what he was.

"Darby," Vixen whispered when the unicorn flared his nostrils in her direction. He made a huffing sound, almost an affirmation. Alekon bumped into her with his muzzle, feigning envy. "You have no reason to be jealous."

<You're the one making sugar-sweet eyes at the unicorn,> Alekon retorted, then pricked an ear at the open stall door. <Oh no. I'm going to be stabled next to him?>

"Grow up," Vixen muttered, urging the bay stallion into the stall. Better Alekon than Emrys, at any rate. As it was, she saw Blaise making sure the black stallion stayed as far from the unicorn as possible, which was wise. Then she set to removing his saddle and hackamore. She stowed the tack but kept her saddle-bags right outside the stall door, ready to take with her to their own accommodations.

That done, she regrouped with the others. Jefferson was chatting with Monica while Blaise hovered nearby, looking awkward and uncertain. Vixen very much wanted to find an excuse to talk to Rhys, but this didn't seem the time. But if he was staying in this car, she figured she'd have ample excuse to do so later. So, she focused on Blaise, slipping up beside him.

He relaxed slightly at her appearance. Blaise's saddlebags were perched over his shoulder, though he seemed unbothered by their weight. "Will Alekon be okay?"

Vixen nodded. "He'll behave." She hoped so, anyway. Wooden slats separated the stalls. If Darby was so inclined, he could poke his horn through it to annoy his neighbor. She didn't think Darby would do that—at least, she hoped he wouldn't. Such antics would give Alekon reason to respond, though.

Monica finished whatever she was telling Jefferson and turned to them, a bright smile on her face. "Well, now that the pegasi are settled, allow me to show you to your car!"

CHAPTER SEVEN

Respect the Name

Blaise

*B*laise was thankful that, while it appeared they were being given one of the more luxurious cars, their quarters were not at all reminiscent of his only previous train experience. Monica showed him and Jefferson to a master bedroom, a compartment with seating that folded out into beds. There was also a washstand and a toilet. Jefferson seemed pleased by the accommodations, so Blaise decided he was, too.

To his relief, Vixen would be nearby, so their group would stay together. She laid claim to the next compartment over with a similar set-up, though smaller and designed for a single person.

Jefferson had already unpacked his meager belongings. It was odd to see him travel so light, but he seemed to have adjusted to his new reality. Blaise still marveled at the way his beau had cobbled together a new wardrobe piece by piece after being decimated by the Quiet Ones. Jefferson was resourceful, though, so it really shouldn't have been a surprise. And fashion was one of his priorities.

"What do you think?" Jefferson asked, gesturing to their quarters.

Blaise raised his brows. "What's there to say? It's about the same size as the loft back home."

Jefferson chuckled. "I suppose so." He shifted closer, his green eyes going soft. "I'm glad you're coming with me."

Earlier, Blaise had felt like an afterthought while Jefferson chatted easily with Monica. Now, this admission eroded all of his anxiety. "Me, too."

Jefferson smiled—not his roguish smile, not the one that charmed so many. It was all warmth and love, a smile meant only for Blaise. The sort of smile that communicated a wealth of emotions. "I will admit, I've been hoping to take you on a proper train ride. The last one didn't count."

Blaise couldn't help but laugh. Jefferson had the worst of it the last time they'd been on a train, spending the entire trip paralyzed by Jack while Gregor Gaitwood taunted him. Blaise had spent most of it drugged and asleep, which upon reflection, he decided was preferable. "I guess we can scratch this off the list."

"Indeed." Jefferson pulled out a pamphlet he found tucked against the window, opening it to show a diagram of the train. "Here, this is the layout. In the normal configuration, there's an observation car, but that was removed because of the pegasi." He stabbed a finger to show the car at the end of the line. "Our quarters are here." Jefferson pointed to the car adjoining the pegasi car.

Blaise had figured that much out, at least. The boxcar for the pegasi had a door and connector that allowed them to travel between the pair of cars. He liked knowing the pegasi were nearby. "And these other cars?"

Jefferson traced a hand over them. "There are two more sleeper cars in front of this. There's also a lounge car and a dining car." He tapped the dining car. "I expect, aside from this car or the pegasi car, that is where we'll spend most of our time. Unless you'd care to socialize?"

He meant the lounge car, no doubt. Blaise made a face. "With people?"

"That answers that," Jefferson said, though his eyes danced with amusement. He'd known Blaise wouldn't enjoy the idea. "Sometimes, on a train such as this, the lounge car will have entertainment in the evenings."

"You want to go, don't you?" Blaise asked.

"Is it that obvious?"

He chuckled. "Only because I know you." Jefferson was a social butterfly, the polar opposite of Blaise. He still didn't know how they got along at all, considering their differences. "Find out more about it, and let me know."

Jefferson's brows shot up. "You'll go with me?"

"I'll consider it." Blaise figured it didn't hurt to needle his beau a little.

The Dreamer grinned, heartened by the statement. "In that case, I'll most definitely find out."

———————————

Vixen

THE TRAIN PULLED AWAY FROM THE STATION MID-AFTERNOON. Vixen discovered that their contact, Monica, didn't intend to travel with them, entrusting them to Rhys's care as she waved goodbye. Once they got underway, Jefferson and Blaise made their way to the dining car. Blaise wasn't as excited by the prospect as Jefferson but went along anyway.

That gave Vixen her chance. She told them she would check on the pegasi and make certain they were comfortable, then catch up.

She negotiated the accordion connector between the cars, the door to the pegasi car creaking as it opened. Snorts greeted her, along with the unmistakable sensation of Alekon touching her mind.

Emrys swung his head over the stall door, nostrils cupped to drink in the scents that wafted into the car. <Is Blaise coming?>

Vixen paused at his stall. "No, he went to the dining car. I'm sure he'll stop by later."

<Perhaps with treats,> Emrys commented, though Vixen knew a suggestion when she heard one. She'd have to remember to tell Blaise.

Rhys had come to the door of the tack room, leaning against the frame. He watched her, eyes intent. The Tracker looked as if he wanted to say something but was keeping it to himself.

Vixen had no such inclinations. She strode over. "Rhys Kildare, what in Garus's name are you *doing* here?"

At her use of his name, he blew out a breath. "I should ask you the same thing. I thought..." Rhys trailed off, glancing toward the unicorn's stall. "You said you would never come back."

She had said that, hadn't she? It felt like an eternity ago. "That's what I thought but..." Vixen turned to Alekon. The bay stallion craned his head toward her, and she closed the distance to stroke his forehead, smoothing his silky forelock. He sighed with contentment, though his dark eyes were watchful. "Things changed."

<Who is he to you?> Alekon asked, curious. <I know he is important, but you have not mentioned him before.>

Emrys and Seledora weren't watching, but she knew they were both eavesdropping. Besides, they would find out sooner or later. Might as well be sooner. "Rhys, allow me to introduce you to my pegasus, Alekon. Alekon, Rhys is my brother."

The pegasus blew out a breath of surprise. <You never told me you had a brother.> And to Rhys, he said, <I am pleased to meet you.>

Yeah, Vixen knew that at some point, she was going to have to explain their convoluted relationship. She wasn't looking forward to that. Life had been so much simpler when she only had to be an outlaw.

"I've never spoken to a pegasus. It's good to meet you, Alekon," Rhys replied, hesitant. He tilted his head as if Alekon were a puzzle to be deciphered.

<Then you're missing out. We're a treat.>

Vixen snorted at that, shaking her head. Time to get back on track while she had the chance. "How is it you're the one who came?" It seemed too contrived to be a coincidence. Vixen feared someone was positioning them like game pieces.

Rhys shook his head. "I was given orders. I didn't know it would be you. I was told to accompany three outlaw mages and their pegasi. The Breaker, the Traitor, and..." He gestured to her.

"The *Traitor*?" Vixen frowned.

He winced. "That's what Ambassador Cole is called in...certain circles."

It was also a testament to the fact that the Confederation didn't know what Jefferson's magic was. That probably scared them, so they sought to belittle him with a moniker like Traitor. Well, it wasn't Rhys's fault for repeating what he had been told, so she set that aside for now. "And all you're supposed to do is serve as security?"

Rhys nodded. "Yes. To protect the public from the outlaw mages, and the outlaw mages from anyone else."

If the Confederation had sent another Tracker in his stead, Vixen would have been concerned. Trackers had unique training that gave them the upper hand when dealing with mages. And all Trackers were immune to direct magical attacks—a closely guarded secret that Vixen only knew because of her relationship with Rhys. That ability, combined with combat training, made them more than capable of taking on most mages one-on-one. But as small a portion of the populace as mages were, Trackers were even smaller. Maybe it really was a coincidence.

She glanced at Darby. Trackers rode unicorns just as many

outlaw mages rode pegasi, but that was where the similarities ended. Some Trackers had a strong working relationship with their unicorns, but that was rare. Most unicorns were trained under cruel conditions and treated afterward just as poorly. But not Rhys's unicorn. In the past, she'd seen her brother treat the blue-grey stallion with the same regard she showed Alekon. Darby watched them with liquid brown eyes full of intelligence. Unicorns couldn't communicate in the same way as pegasi, but they were smart. Vixen didn't doubt that Rhys and the stallion were prepared to neutralize mages, if necessary.

Rhys was watching her. "And why are you here?" He paused, brow knitting. "What do I even call you?"

"Vixen," she said automatically, which earned an amused look.

"You must be kidding."

She made a face at him, and for a moment, it was like the gulf of years between them vanished. "I'm not. Respect the name—I'm rather fond of it." With a shake of her crimson hair, Vixen rubbed her forehead. "I'm here because I'm afraid I may be all that stands between the Gutter and an attack from the Confederation."

He raised his brows. "You're going back? To Izhadell?"

"Unless I'm on the wrong train."

"You know what I mean." Rhys blew out a breath. "When you left, it seemed pretty final. Besides, how are you going to even do that? You're..." He gestured to her, then paused. His eyes narrowed. "Except I don't feel your magic."

Ah, yes, the other, better-known ability of Trackers. They were sensitive to magic, able to detect when it was in use. A good Tracker knew when a mage was around, though it took a unicorn to pinpoint one in a crowd. Vixen pursed her lips, deciding if she should reveal the ring or not.

While she considered, Rhys spoke again, excitement growing with each word. "Are you not a mage? Was there some sort of mistake? Is that why you're coming back?"

Vixen ground her teeth. There it was, the old Confederation

bias that magic was wrong. In her heart, she knew Rhys hadn't meant it that way, but it galled her regardless. Worse, she realized with a sinking feeling that she could have come back after Lamar Gaitwood's forces had stripped her magic at Fort Courage. But she hadn't even entertained the idea. Why?

Because even on her worst day, she loved being an outlaw and living in the Gutter more than her best day as the Spark in Izhadell.

Decision made, she lifted her hand, rubbing her index finger over the curl of silver. "I'll never stop being a mage, any more than you can stop being a Tracker. It's part of my soul. This is hiding my magic, for now."

His expression crumpled at her declaration. Rhys leaned over to peer at the ring, then nodded. "I still don't understand why you're returning to Izhadell."

"There are innocent people back in the Gutter who deserve a chance at a peaceful life."

He relaxed at her words. "That's why you're coming back? Not to…usurp the Luminary's position?"

Vixen snorted at the very idea. "Gods, no. That sounds terrible. I don't know exactly how I'll handle things with mother, but that's not my goal." Ridiculous, that's what it was. Then she pointed to his cot. "Who'd you tick off to get stuck with this detail?"

His shoulders went rigid. "No one. I'm not important enough to warrant anything better."

She scowled. "I strongly disagree with that." It was unfortunate her room wasn't larger, or she would have invited him to sleep in comfort befitting his lineage. Though that wouldn't work, either —people would make the wrong assumption about them. And right now, she couldn't take such a risk.

Rhys sighed. "I'm just a Tracker."

"That's dragonshit." He blinked in surprise at her language. Oops. Vixen was going to have to remember to curb her outlaw tongue. "Do you get to go to the dining car, at least?" she asked, to distract from her slip.

"Only if there's someone here to keep tabs on them." He pointed to the equines.

Vixen figured, at the very least, Blaise would be happy for the excuse to come here later. "I think I can make that happen. Let me go catch up with the others, and I'll make sure there's relief for you here soon."

CHAPTER EIGHT

On Time is Late

Jack

Jack despised meetings, but they were part and parcel of his position as a Ringleader. He was glad that, aside from the times when something came up requiring an emergency meeting, they otherwise only met once a week. That was far too often, in his opinion.

He ambled over to his customary seat in the meeting room at HQ, eyeing the others who had already assembled. Mindy was there, chatting with Kur Agur. With Vixen on the mission to Izhadell, that meant all they were missing was Raven.

Jack frowned. It wasn't like Raven Dawson to be late. He was usually the first to arrive for all of their meetings. The Shadow-stepper assumed the unofficial role as the chair of their ragtag council. The outlaw pulled out his pocket watch, checking the time. Two minutes until the agreed-upon start time. Dawson wasn't officially late...yet.

The silver flash of Jack's watch snapping shut caught Kur's eye. The Theilian twitched an ear. "Do you need to be elsewhere?"

"Nah," the Effigest said with a shake of his head. "Was just thinking it's odd that Raven's last to arrive."

Mindy pursed her lips. "Come to think of it, he didn't eat at the Jitterbug last night like he normally does." She paused. "Though he might have gone to the Broken Horn instead."

That was reasonable, but Jack suddenly had a terrible feeling in his gut. And he'd been around long enough to know when he needed to trust his instincts. He couldn't remember the last time he'd seen Raven. Days ago, at the very least. "I'm gonna see if Zeph knows anything from Naureus."

Mindy raised her eyebrows. "Is that necessary? He's not late yet."

Jack was already at the door. "On time is late for Raven."

"I will go check his home," Kur volunteered. "Sniff around and see what I uncover."

"I'll stay here in case he comes and you miss him," Mindy said.

Jack nodded, hurrying out with the lupine close on his heels. Kur loped off in a cloud of dust as Jack broke into a jog, heading for the stable.

His first stop was the stall that housed Naureus, Raven's buckskin pegasus. It was empty, but that meant little. Most of the stalls were unoccupied at this time of day. Jack whirled, marching up the aisle on the hunt for any of the five grooms who worked at the stables. The pegasi paid the young humans to muck out the stalls, refill their buckets with sugar water, and feed them morning and evening. The youngsters had a good handle on the comings and goings of each pegasus.

A scrawny kid with dark, tousled hair hauled a water bucket into the stables, pausing at the sight of Jack. From what the outlaw recalled, the kid was one of the new arrivals, the son of a maverick mage. He stared and looked like he was ready to flee, but stood his ground as Jack stalked up to him.

"You know anything about Naureus?" Jack demanded, pointing toward the vacant stall.

The boy followed Jack's gesture, swallowing. "Um. He's not

here?"

Jack reined in his frustration. He tried to save his moments of intimidation for those who deserved it, and this greenhorn groom didn't. Taking a breath, he did his best to keep his voice reasonable. "What I mean is, has he been here recently?"

"Oh." The groom blinked. "It's been a couple of days. Why?"

Jack waved a hand in dismissal. That was what he wanted to know. It lined up with his own last sighting of Raven. "Thanks, kid."

A quick stop by Zepheus's stall revealed that, like most of the other pegasi, the stallion was out. Jack stopped by the tack room to review the posted sentry schedule. Yeah, Zepheus was out covering the northern canyons, so wouldn't be close.

He felt a sudden rush of warmth. He spun, knowing what that meant. Kittie's aethon steed stood uncomfortably close behind him, mane whipping like a windswept flame. The fire elemental looked like a horse most of the time, and though she was an embodiment of magic, she couldn't communicate with him the way a pegasus could. But she was intelligent in her own primal way.

She snorted in his face, acting far too much like a spiteful mare for his comfort. A spiteful mare who could turn everything around her to cinders if she chose.

Jack didn't have time for her drama. "What is it, Najaria?"

The aethon turned to the paper schedule on the door. For an instant, Jack feared she was going to burn it. But she didn't—she tapped it with her velvet-soft nose, then pawed the ground, her hooves sparking.

What in tarnation? "You got something I need to know?" Her red equine head bobbed in agreement. "Is it about Kittie?" A snort of disagreement. Jack paused, thinking. "You know something about Raven or Naureus?"

Najaria retreated a step, head rocking up and down in assent. She turned, ears pricked toward the exit.

It would be really helpful if she could communicate with him. Kittie could understand her in a limited way through their shared affinity for fire. Jack moved to follow the elemental. "Lead on."

The mare broke into a trot, showing him to a fire pit on the far side of town. The ashes in the pit were cold, and nothing about it looked unusual to Jack until the aethon adamantly nosed something stuck to a stone along the edge of the pit. It was a charred scrap of paper. He reached down and plucked it up, frowning. The remnant was no bigger than his thumb, and it was mostly scorched, though he knew there was some sort of writing on it.

He shook his head. "Sorry. I don't know what this clue means."

Najaria snorted in a manner that communicated she thought he was quite the stupid human. Which, yeah, that was true sometimes, but in this matter, it was hardly fair.

Jack tilted his head, considering. If the elemental knew something, he didn't want to miss out. "Would you be able to tell Kittie?"

The mare approved of the idea. She spun on a hind hoof and then moved like a living blaze. She was there one moment and gone the next, leaving only a charred hoof track. Wisps of smoke drifted from the imprint. Jack crouched down to study the fire pit while he waited.

That scrap wasn't the only paper. There were more tiny bits, though he assumed the bulk of the writing had become ash. Why had burned papers made the aethon suspicious?

Najaria jogged up a few moments later, Kittie astride her bareback. Jack had to admit, Kittie looked damn good on that mare. Though, if he were honest, it didn't take much for Kittie to look good in his eyes. She was the fire that warmed his heart. The Pyromancer raised her brows at her husband. "So, you must be why Najaria is riled up."

Jack snorted. "No, she's got *me* riled up. Trying to figure out where Raven is, and your horse dragged me over here."

Najaria made a dangerous, primal noise at being called a *horse*, reminiscent of the roar and crackle of a growing inferno. Jack raised his hands in apology.

Kittie rolled her eyes at the exchange, then slipped down from the mare's back. "You want me to translate, is that it?"

"Would be helpful, yeah."

Kittie pursed her lips, turning to the aethon. "What do you want Jack to know?" She laid a hand on Najaria's forehead.

As Jack watched, Najaria's eyes closed to a blissful, half-lidded state. A smile curled Kittie's lips as they communed. A small part of Jack was jealous, but he knew he had a similar relationship with Zepheus. Well, with a lot more snark and hard-headedness.

"Mostly, she just shows me simple images," Kittie relayed after a moment. "Raven was here, reading papers. Letters, maybe. Then he burned them." She paused, sorting through new information. "She says he was...hot? No, that's not the right word. Upset. Angry, perhaps. Elementals don't translate emotions very well."

Upset or angry. And then he had burned whatever might have inspired those feelings. He then didn't show up for a meeting. Letters from Vixen, perhaps? Jack knew the pair had parted ways, and the Shadowstepper hadn't been happy about it. But his gut didn't think it was anything from Vixen. That didn't feel right. "We need to find Raven." Jack feared they wouldn't find him in Fortitude. Or even in the Gutter.

WHEN JACK REGROUPED WITH THE OTHER RINGLEADERS, KUR reported that Raven's house was vacant, filled with only stale scents of the man. As expected, Mindy hadn't seen him come to HQ, either.

Zepheus returned from his patrol, trotting up at Jack's call. <What is wrong?>

"You heard anything from Naureus?"

The palomino shook his mane. <Regarding anything in

particular?>

"Yeah. His rider is missing."

The pegasus's head snapped up in startlement. <What?>

Jack gave him a brief run-down on their findings so far. Further inspection of the tack room revealed that Naureus's saddle and hackamore had been left behind. While it was normal to go without the hackamore around the Gutter, the saddle was a different issue. Jack couldn't imagine why anyone would go out without a saddle for an extended time—especially if they had made plans to skip town. He said as much to Zepheus.

<Perhaps he would not take a saddle if he didn't plan to stay with his pegasus,> Zepheus reasoned after considering the question. And Jack hated to admit it, but that made a level of sense. If that was the case, it meant Naureus might come back to Fortitude, unless Raven had asked him to keep a low profile. Either was a possibility.

Jack rubbed his forehead. "Yeah, the pegasi are gonna hate me, but this might be important. Ask all available sentries to go out and fly a grid pattern, searching for Naureus or Raven. If they find both, that's preferable. Have them work the grid in pairs."

Zepheus pricked an ear. <What do they do if they find them?>

The outlaw assumed Raven didn't want to be found. "One sentry tails them, the other passes the message to us with their last known location as soon as possible." He turned, another idea coming to mind. Yeah, he was going to use every resource at hand. "Can you get the sentries on that? I need to find Em."

<I will. You know this will require bonus pay.> Zepheus snorted. Jack waved a hand in agreement.

Jack found Emmaline at the bakery. The thing Jack liked about her work with the Breaker was that she stayed out of trouble, and he knew where to find her half the time. She, Reuben, and Hannah were cleaning up from their morning work. The bakery seemed somehow emptier without Blaise there—the Breaker wasn't an outgoing man by any definition, but he had a presence in the bakery. It was his domain, the one place in the world the young man never doubted himself. Even Jack had to admit he made damn good desserts.

The trio looked up at his entrance. Emmaline narrowed her eyes, no doubt immediately reading the tension that lined his face. "Daddy?"

"Need your magic, Em." He jerked his head toward the door, a silent command for her to come with him. Though she had the same flavor of magic that he did, Emmaline had different strengths. And right now, he could use them.

Emmaline glanced at the other two. Reuben had a healthy respect for Jack and made himself busy sweeping the floor, desperate to steer clear of the elder Effigest's attention. "We're fine. Go do what you need to do."

Emmaline blew out a breath. She didn't enjoy being ordered around by her father, and Jack realized he had misstepped by blustering in and making a demand. He cleared his throat, deciding he needed to correct that. With anyone else, he wouldn't give a damn. But he still walked a thin line when it came to Emmaline, and he didn't want to chase her away. "You can do something I can't, so I'd appreciate your help."

His daughter gave him an incredulous look but nodded and headed for the door. When they were on the porch, she said, "Sometimes you really *can* be a reasonable person."

Jack snorted at the comment. "We both know I'm a piss-goblin at heart." Then he sobered. "You got a spare poppet on you?"

"Yeah." Emmaline patted the back pocket of her trousers. "Small one. Does that matter?"

"Shouldn't," Jack said.

"Are we looking for someone?" Emmaline asked.

She knew very well her specialty and why he might come to her. "Yeah. Raven."

Emmaline sucked in a surprised breath and didn't speak as they headed for Raven's home. The door was unlocked—even though it was a town of outlaws, it was rare for them to steal from one another. Any outsiders who came in to do such a deed would soon discover that the outlaws defended their own swiftly and brutally. Jack tugged the door open, studying everything.

As far as homes in Fortitude went, it was tiny. Raven lived alone and had needed little—it was a single room with a bed, a rudimentary kitchen that would have given Blaise conniptions, and a table. A chest stood beside the bed. Jack stalked over to it, pulling open a drawer.

Emmaline watched him, brow furrowed. "What are you looking for?"

"Something for your poppet." Jack wanted to make certain whatever they used was tied to the missing Ringleader.

After a moment, he located a black bandanna that he knew for a fact the other outlaw had worn. Even better, since it covered his nose and mouth, it would have a deeper tie to Raven's essence. Silently, he handed it to Emmaline.

She accepted it, winding it around the poppet. Emmaline moved over to the bed and sat down on its edge, cupping the tiny doll in her hands as she whispered words not even Jack understood, activating the poppet. The air over the doll rippled with magic she began her spellwork.

Emmaline had tried to show him how to cast this spell, but it seemed the sort of magic one had to have a knack for. Jack couldn't do much with it—he could use a poppet to sense if someone was alive and well, but not where they were located. It was a potent ability, and one more reason to make sure the Confederation never got their hands on his daughter.

Ten minutes passed before she rolled her shoulders, which had surely grown stiff. Emmaline groaned. "He's west of here."

"Close?"

"No. I think...I think he's past the mountains."

"Which mountains?"

Emmaline met his gaze. "All of them."

CHAPTER NINE

She's Not My Girl

Raven

It had been a long, long time since Raven had willingly set foot on Confederation soil. Unlike Jack, he wasn't fool enough to constantly risk his neck. He might not have the bounty on his head that the Effigest did, but he was a wanted man. And yet, here he was in the back alley of a restaurant in Ondin, doing the unthinkable.

He sighed, glancing up at the stars that salted the velvet night sky overhead. Coming here was a risk, yes, but so was not coming here. Shadows surrounded him. As long as no one got the drop on him, he had the advantage. He brushed his fingertips against the knives sheathed at his belt, his preferred weapons. Sixguns got the job done, but so did a good blade. The greenhorn who coined the adage *don't bring a knife to a gunfight* had never come across a Shadowstepper.

"Come on, I don't have all night," he murmured, turning in a slow circle. Raven felt naked here by himself. Out of necessity, he'd left Naureus back on the farthest fringes of the Gutter.

Raven's insistence had displeased the buckskin stallion, even more so when Raven couldn't say when he'd be back.

Or *if* he'd be back. He just didn't know. There was too much at stake. And he wasn't willing to tangle Naureus in this web.

Somewhere nearby, a door opened with a chilling creak. Raven tensed, fighting the urge to leap into the safety of the nearest shadow to watch and wait. But he was expected here, and if he ran and hid every time his contact came to look for him, he'd get nowhere.

"Mr. Dawson?" Someone shuffled into the light. A middle-aged man, human. Dressed like a waiter from the stuffy restaurant, judging by the attire.

Raven took a step forward. "Yeah?"

"They'll see you now." The man ducked his head. Raven couldn't tell if it was a tic or deference. "Follow me, please."

The Shadowstepper frowned. "Not until I know who's summoned me."

His guide didn't look back, only shuffled over to the door. "I don't know. I was only told to come out back and fetch a gentleman by the name of Dawson."

Gentleman. Raven was the farthest thing from that descriptor, but he let it go. Full of mistrust, he followed the man inside. They entered through the kitchen, the staff bustling, busy at various stations. Raven didn't have time to goggle about and look, instead following his guide through into what looked like a pantry but opened into stairs that led down. A cellar, perhaps? Raven had no choice but to follow. He kept his magic at the ready—just in case.

His escort led him into a room flanked by so many mage-lights, it was almost as bright as day. Raven winced, his eyes still adjusting after being outside. When his vision cleared, he found a man and woman studying him.

They were well-dressed, the man in a fine greatcoat, crisp trousers, and polished shoes. The woman appeared to be similar in age to Raven, though her attire was more a match for the man accompanying her. She wore a burgundy ruffled blouse and smart black boots that disappeared beneath the voluminous floral skirt. *Confederation elite.* Raven stilled, heart thundering. He could magic himself away. It wasn't too late. "Who are you?"

The man was the older of the pair, his salt-and-pepper hair catching the light. "Consider us...potential benefactors, Mr. Dawson."

Raven frowned. "Benefactors?"

"Yes," the man continued. "We have quite an interest in the Gutter and the people who call it home."

Raven had sat through enough Ringleader meetings to know that any outsider expressing an interest in the Gutter usually meant trouble for the outlaws. He shifted his weight from one foot to the other. "Whatever you want with me, it's nothing I can give."

"I wouldn't be so certain. Wouldn't you agree, Tara?" The man smiled at his counterpart.

The woman, Tara, shrugged. "Depends if Mr. Dawson wants to spare his friends, Phillip." She moved to pick up something from the table that separated the pair, the move like a languid afterthought. At first, Raven thought the table held nothing of importance—maybe only mail or magazines—but he lost confidence in that as Tara flipped through a few pieces of paper. "Ah yes, there it is." She pulled out a slip. "This one, in particular."

Tara held the paper out for Raven. With misgivings, the Shadowstepper accepted it, swallowing when he realized it was a sketch of Vixen. The worst part was, he knew exactly what it was from. When they'd been taken to Fort Courage, sketches had been made of each imprisoned outlaw to go with their records. They knew about Vixen and had connected her to him. And while she might not love him, he didn't feel the same. He hated that this pair knew. Would use that as leverage.

"Like I said, whatever you want is probably not something I can give."

"That's too bad." Tara clucked her tongue, taking the sketch back and settling it among the other papers. Almost idly, she removed another one, shifting it into the light just so. It was an image of Raven himself. "You were at Fort Courage, were you not, Mr. Dawson?"

Raven bristled. His instinct told him to get out of there, but another part told him to stay. These elite were an implied threat against the Gutter and the people there. "I was."

Phillip whistled and shook his head. "Nasty business all around, that attack on the outlaw town and then the mess with Courage." He aimed a smirk at Raven. "It would be a shame if it happened again."

Raven gritted his teeth, suddenly glad Vixen, Jefferson, and Blaise were striking out to prevent that. "Not if we can stop it first."

Phillip nodded at that. "Oh yes. We know about Cole and the Breaker." Was it Raven's imagination, or did the man's voice grow sour when he spoke Jefferson's last name? *Definitely wasn't my imagination.* "Your girl is with them, too, hmm?"

"She's not my girl." The words hurt to say. They were true, but that didn't ease the pain. Gods, he loved Vixen, and the knowledge that she didn't feel the same way was almost a physical wound.

"No?" Phillip asked with an interested quirk of his brow.

"No," Raven confirmed through clenched teeth.

The well-dressed pair exchanged knowing glances. Phillip reached across to Tara's assortment of pictures, picking up Vixen's. He lifted it, his gaze flicking to Raven. "But you wish she was, don't you?"

Raven felt his cheeks warm, hating the man picking at a festering wound. He could just disappear into a shadow—that would be the safe thing to do. But how did they know so much about Vixen? There were many things she hadn't told *him*.

"He does," Tara confirmed with a soft laugh. Raven arrowed a glare at her. "Don't try to hide it. We can see it in your eyes."

"She could be yours, you know." Phillip's voice was a seductive whisper. He rose from his seat, hands behind his back as he walked in a circle around the room, as if the action helped him think aloud. "I know what it's like to love someone. To lose that person because of the machinations of others." His words became heated, leaving Raven to wonder who had come between this powerful man and his love.

Tara frowned, waving a hand to draw attention back to herself. "Your friends can't win. Surely you know this."

Raven swallowed. As much as he hadn't wanted Vixen to go, he understood their task was important. He read the undercurrents easily enough—this pair was determined to stop them. And for some reason, they'd set their sights on Raven. Maybe he could do something about it, though.

"What do you want with me?"

Phillip smiled, composed once more. "You have a special set of skills that would be useful to our cause."

They wanted to use him. He narrowed his eyes. "What makes you think I'd betray my friends? I'm a Ringleader, for Faedra's sake."

Tara smirked. "Because if you work with us, you can get your girl back. If those outlaw friends of yours succeed at their task, you'll lose her forever."

Raven stiffened. "She doesn't love me."

"But she *could*," Tara insisted, her voice almost a purr. "We have the means to make it happen."

That couldn't be true…could it? Indecision warred within. His need to have Vixen as his own pitted against the knowledge that she was a spitfire who knew her mind—and ultimately, that was what he loved about her. But he *loved* her.

As if sensing his conflict, the woman rose from her seat and crossed the room, moving to a collection of stoppered bottles. She made a contemplative sound, then selected one with a flourish. "Alchemy has progressed by leaps and bounds."

Alchemy. As a mage, he detested alchemy, but...what if it was true? Raven swallowed. It was tempting to refuse to work with these brash elites, but if they were plotting something, wouldn't it be better to be on the inside? Maybe he could scuttle their plans.

And if it meant he had a chance to win Vixen back, wouldn't it be worth it? Raven closed his eyes. "Tell me what I need to do."

CHAPTER TEN
Jefferson's Favorite Party Game

Vixen

Their train made an afternoon stop in the Gannish town of Aspenpoint two days later. Jefferson discovered it would be a longer stop than normal, allowing them a chance to let the unicorn and pegasi disembark to stretch their legs and graze.

The Godspine Mountains were visible in the distance, looming on the horizon like jagged teeth. The train depot at Aspenpoint bordered a verdant field, and their group appreciated the convenience as they accompanied the equines there. The sun glared overhead, making Vixen regret leaving her smoke-lensed glasses packed in her things. With the ring, she didn't need them to temper her magic, but they were handy against the sun.

<I wish we could fly,> Alekon lamented to Vixen, his liquid brown eyes on the fluffy clouds overhead, ears pricked. <I want to go fly in the mountains. Maybe startle some goats. It would be fun.>

"You're land-bound for the time being," she replied, patting his warm shoulder at the point where his wings would be, had he not shrouded them with the camouflaging magic unique to pegasi.

"But it's a lovely day, and there's nothing to stop you from flying with your hooves."

Alekon arched his neck, snorting at the sentiment. <That will have to do.> He swung his head away when she freed him from the halter—they had committed to the farce that the pegasi were horses, which meant all the normal equine trappings. As soon as she stepped back, he bolted across the turf to join the others, who had already been released.

Vixen watched, a smile curling her lips as Alekon raced alongside Seledora and Darby. Emrys rolled in the grass nearby, grunting and snorting his contentment. The pegasi had become more accepting of the unicorn, though Vixen wouldn't quite call them friends. They were tolerant but wary of each other, which was all they could ask under the circumstances.

"They're quite the sight, aren't they?"

Vixen turned at Rhys's voice. Darby's halter and lead rope were slung over his shoulder as he ambled over to lean against the fence.

"They are," she agreed, relaxing at the spectacle of the jubilant equines. While the train was luxurious, it was still a confining box of metal and wood. Vixen had grown far too accustomed to open skies and the freedom to do as she pleased. Her gaze skated over to where Blaise and Jefferson sat beneath a shady tree, relaxing. The Breaker's back rested against the bough, with Jefferson laying down, hands pillowing his head which rested in Blaise's lap as they spoke quietly.

Rhys followed her gaze. "You're rather fond of your friends."

She nodded. "Blaise has had some hard times. It's nice to see him happy. He's been a good friend."

The Tracker leaned over, plucked a flower, and twirled it between his index finger and thumb, thoughtful. "Everyone says he's dangerous."

Vixen scoffed, shaking her head. "The people who say that don't understand his magic. Folks are always going to think the things they don't understand are dangerous." She'd had a lot of time to think about that. Vixen thought this was why the Confederation felt as they did about magic in general. That, and also those without were desperate to grasp whatever power they could.

Rhys nodded. "That's true." He tossed the flower aside, bending to pick a new one. "Do you—?"

Darby interrupted him with a shrill cry. The unicorn skidded to a halt, grass flying beneath his cloven hooves. Seledora and Alekon continued to gallop, though they swung in a circle, coming around behind the unicorn, also on alert. Darby ignored them, moving into a high-action trot, nostrils flaring as he drank the scents on the wind. Every few paces, he swung his horn from one side to the other.

Rhys's brow furrowed. "I'll be back. He's signaling something."

A mage. Vixen knew that only too well. She watched as Rhys broke into a run, the halter flapping against his arm as he rushed to keep up with the unicorn. She shaded her eyes. Darby stopped at the edge of the field, allowing Rhys to catch up.

She wasn't sure what passed between them. Vixen scowled, straining to see what might have set off the unicorn. People were coming and going at the station house, with a few new passengers boarding their train. Were there unbound mages among the incoming passengers? Unicorns were trained to scent the difference between a maverick and a mage with a tattoo, whether or not they were geasa-bound.

Blaise and Jefferson ambled over to Vixen, their idyllic peace interrupted by the unicorn's alarm. "Do you think we need to be worried?" Blaise's voice was soft but laced with nerves, his shoulders tensing.

Vixen glanced at Jefferson. He edged closer to Blaise, subtly capturing the Breaker's pinky finger with his own. It was a sweet gesture, a kindness that made her smile. Like others, she'd been suspicious of Jefferson at first, but he was undeniably good for

Blaise. "No. Unicorns are extremely sensitive to the scent of magic, that's all." She twisted the ring on her finger, wondering how Darby would react if she removed it.

"Luckily, I know firsthand how well that lovely piece of jewelry works," Jefferson said with a smile, tipping his head toward her. Blaise had relaxed at her words and Jefferson's proximity.

Vixen nodded, shifting her gaze to the unicorn. Darby had his head slung over the distant fence, nostrils distended. "Sorry your quiet moment got interrupted."

"As am I," Jefferson murmured.

Blaise rubbed the back of his neck. "It was nice while it lasted."

A few minutes later, Rhys made his way back, though Darby kept pausing, twisting around to peer over his shoulder. The Tracker had a deep frown etched on his face.

"What was that all about?" Vixen asked.

Rhys shook his head. "I'm not sure. There must be a mage over there."

"A theurgist?" Blaise asked, not as schooled in the nuances of unicorns as Vixen was.

"No. A maverick or outlaw," Rhys said.

"Do you have to go after them?" Tension lined Blaise's eyes, and Vixen knew the Breaker was dangerously close to a resurgence of old memories. Jefferson must have known, too, since he brushed his fingers lightly against Blaise's arm.

Vixen didn't know if Rhys sensed Blaise's turmoil. He smiled and shook his head. "That's not my current job, so no." His easy words made Blaise relax almost immediately. Rhys slipped the halter back onto Darby's head. "I think I'll put this troublemaker back in his stall. He's going to be too distracted now." He gently smacked the velvet of the stallion's nose. "That's not the work we're doing right now, you great pest."

Jefferson consulted his pocket watch. "We'll follow shortly. We need to have the pegasi back aboard within the half-hour." Rhys and the unicorn headed toward the station. When they were out of earshot, Jefferson cleared his throat. "Care to share with us how you know the Tracker?"

Vixen spun at his question. Blaise had moved to lean against the fence, watching the pegasi. Jefferson climbed the fence to perch atop the rail, a behavior she wouldn't have expected of the dapper ambassador. Somehow, he made it work and looked good doing it. She was sure he knew that. "We have a history."

"And that is?" Jefferson asked, tone mild, as if he were making a polite inquiry at a dinner party.

Vixen watched as their pegasi settled back to grazing. Alekon stayed nearby, though, the hide at his shoulders twitched like a memory of his wings. "Rhys and Darby are the ones who figured out I was a mage."

Blaise made a soft sound of surprise. "So, he knows about you?"

"Yes, but he won't betray me." Vixen paused. "At least, I don't think so. He didn't when he had the opportunity years ago."

"How is it he's the one saddled with our group?" Jefferson asked.

She shrugged. "I asked him, and it sounds like it's just a coincidence."

"Hmm." Jefferson rubbed his chin, twisting to glance over his shoulder in the station's direction.

"You don't think it's a coincidence," Blaise guessed.

"I don't," Jefferson admitted. "After everything I've been through with the Quiet Ones, I wouldn't put it past them to manipulate his placement somehow. He might even be in their pay."

Vixen shook her head. "No! Rhys wouldn't." Jefferson aimed a cool look her way, which gave her pause. She frowned. "I mean, he wouldn't because…" She faltered. "Because it's complicated."

Jefferson cocked his head, reminding her of a hunting hound on the trail of a scent. "Were you lovers?"

"What? Ew, no," Vixen blurted, failing to hide the revulsion the very idea incited.

Her response only intrigued Jefferson further, though. He leaned over, and it was a surprise he didn't fall off the fence. "Oh? That's a shame. He looks like a treat."

"Hey," Blaise protested, jabbing his beau in the side. "Check yourself."

Jefferson chuckled, though he shot a fond look at Blaise. "I'm allowed to make observations, love. And the Tracker does have rugged good looks." His green eyes arrowed back to Vixen. "So what is he, then? I'm prepared to make more equally scandalous guesses. This is one of my favorite party games."

Vixen blew out a frustrated breath. "He's my brother. My twin."

"*Oh.*" Jefferson's eyes widened at that. "But you don't look alike."

Oh, how she knew. That was perhaps the most remarked-upon aspect of their family growing up, aside from their status. Rhys had hair that gleamed like oiled bronze in the sunlight, a sharp contrast to Vixen's red. And their eyes differed, too. Vixen's were a light grey like liquid silver. Rhys's were brown.

"He favors our father, and I take after our mother," Vixen explained.

Blaise raised his brows. "Then why is he a Tracker? Why isn't he...?" The Breaker stalled, licking his lips. He waved a hand in Vixen's general direction. "Whatever you are?"

Vixen fiddled with the ring on her finger. Though he hadn't been clear, she understood Blaise didn't mean a mage. "There was an uproar when we were born. Never in memory had the Luminary birthed twins." She stared off in the direction Rhys had gone. "Historically, the Luminary only has a single child, so we were quite the scandal."

Jefferson snapped his fingers. "Yes, now I recall! I had

forgotten that since the Spark was supposedly..." He cleared his throat with a look of sudden discomfort.

"Dead?" Vixen suggested.

"Well, yes." Jefferson studiously stared at the distant mountains, possibly to forget his own dalliances with alleged death.

"Doesn't explain much of anything to me," Blaise said, reminding them he had precious little context for their conversation. "Does this mean your father is a god or...?" He chewed on his bottom lip, brows furrowed with confusion.

"Oh, no," Vixen said with a shake of her head. "Our father was as mortal as anyone else." She swallowed the lump that suddenly formed in her throat. Her father hadn't crossed her mind in ages, and for that, she felt a pang of guilt. "He died when we were little, so I don't remember much about him."

Blaise's expression closed. He was thinking of his own father, Vixen suspected. "I'm sorry."

She waved a hand, deciding to refocus on the question Blaise had asked earlier. "The reason Rhys isn't the Spark is simple. Garus chose me." Vixen recalled the weighty sensation of a deity pressing into her skull. She had been twelve and, at first, hadn't understood what was happening. For most of her life, Garus had just been a big idea to which her mother dedicated most of her waking time. Things had changed when he made his presence known, wrapping her in a brilliant beam of golden light that not even the most skeptical of clerics could deny. All of that was why she'd been so confused when her magic manifested two years later.

"But shouldn't he be something else important?" Blaise asked.

"Trackers are important," Jefferson observed.

Vixen nodded. "At around the same time Garus chose me, we discovered..." She hesitated. Should she tell them? Perhaps she owed this knowledge to them—they were going into a dangerous situation. If Vixen was to serve Garus, then she would arm her friends with information. "I need you both to keep a secret."

"Oh, I'm good at keeping secrets." Jefferson grinned. Blaise elbowed him again. "I don't mean from *you*."

"I don't like secrets, but I know sometimes they're necessary," Blaise said, voice soft.

She trusted them. "This is particular to Trackers, and it's not common knowledge. Rhys is immune to magic—all Trackers are. They're also sensitive to when it's being used around them."

"I thought unicorns were needed to sniff out mages?" Blaise asked.

Vixen wiggled the fingers of one hand in an indecisive gesture. "A unicorn can pinpoint a mage in a crowd of people, or a mage who's not actively using their magic. That's why Trackers have them."

"Magic immunity," Jefferson mused. "That makes sense. I'd always assumed it was the unicorn and combat training that gave them the upper hand against a mage."

"That's what they want everyone to think." It was a fine bit of sleight of hand. Most maverick mages didn't have the training to fight someone, and when faced with a Tracker, they relied on their magic. The tactic fell apart quickly when faced with a Tracker immune to their power. Vixen wet her lips. "So anyway, that's the story of me and Rhys."

"The god of wisdom chose a Spark with magic." Jefferson's green eyes were on her, calculating. "He chose you. Why did you leave?"

"I ran away." Vixen decided this was a good time to look elsewhere. She reached down and snatched up a flower, methodically plucking the petals and flicking them away. "Rhys and Darby were the ones who discovered my magic. At first, we thought maybe I could hide it..." She ripped the head of the flower from the stem, tossing it aside. "It didn't take long for me to figure out I couldn't. I'd seen too many mages hang. I was scared."

She had fled. Not for a minute had Vixen even considered taking the new development to her mother. The Luminary despised mages because magic was an abomination of wisdom. Vixen had only seen all the ways she would be hated. Ostracized. Maybe even killed for something beyond her control. Garus had been absent from her life since he'd chosen her—she assumed he'd realized his mistake.

"Huh," Blaise murmured.

"Rhys helped me escape from Izhadell," Vixen whispered. "And that's how I know we can trust him."

Blaise's eyes softened at that. She knew he would understand, based on his own past. "I think, even if he weren't your brother, we could trust him."

"Why's that?" Jefferson peered at his beau, curious.

Blaise gestured to the pegasi. "Emrys said he takes good care of them. He doesn't treat them like horses."

<He does not,> Alekon confirmed, lifting his head. <He treats the unicorn well, and he makes certain our needs are met. Even talks to us.>

Vixen raised her brows at that. "That's good to hear. Rhys always had a way with the unicorns." Even better if he knew to treat the pegasi as more than a normal horse. The unaware often made that mistake.

Jefferson pulled his pocket watch out, consulting the time. "I think our break is at an end. We should make our way back before we miss our ride."

<I'd be happy to never get in that box again,> Alekon admitted with a snort, ambling over.

Vixen scratched him between the eyes. "Just a little longer. We'll be in Izhadell before you know it."

And then the real work would begin.

CHAPTER ELEVEN
The Accountant

Jefferson

The train was the luxurious sort that Jefferson was accustomed to on the occasions when he had taken this mode of transportation, all polished wood panels, ornate brocade draperies, and gleaming brass fittings. The other passengers were exactly the sort he would expect to see in such a setting—the Confederation elite, though he spied a few he suspected were high-class merchants on the cusp of elite status. They fluttered around the elite like moths to a flame.

That meant it was also the sort of setting where Blaise felt most awkward. This was exacerbated by the fact Jefferson wasn't comfortable giving out his name (or Blaise's) in their present company. As it was, there was always the chance someone might recognize Jefferson from his affluent past. He didn't mind adopting a temporary moniker, though Blaise certainly did. The Breaker had only grudgingly agreed to the idea.

The dining car boasted beautiful booths that were spacious enough to hold large parties. None of them were designed for intimate meals, but to accommodate as many people as possible.

They'd been fortunate so far and had been able to keep to themselves when they ate, but that didn't seem to be on the cards tonight. Every booth held at least two occupants, many of them completely full.

"We must have picked up additional passengers in Aspenpoint," Jefferson murmured.

"We have to sit with other people?" Blaise asked, voice soft as he took in the crowded car.

Jefferson gave his hand a surreptitious squeeze. "If you prefer, we can take a plate back to the room."

The Breaker eased, as if the option gave him more clarity of mind. He glanced at Jefferson. "We can eat here." There was something he left unsaid, but Jefferson suspected he knew. Blaise understood Jefferson would enjoy this, and he wanted him to be happy. It was no small thing, and it made him want to pull Blaise in for an appreciative kiss, but that would only embarrass his beau in their current situation. He settled for flashing Blaise a smile that he hoped communicated all that and more.

A group of four diners rose from a booth in the corner. Jefferson touched Blaise's elbow, and they moved to claim it. Blaise scooted in to sit beside the broad window—it would provide the Breaker a chance to focus on the scenery more than those around him. Jefferson sat comfortably close beside him.

A well-dressed man and woman approached, obviously on the hunt for seating. The gentlemen gestured to the empty bench opposite Blaise and Jefferson. "May we?"

Jefferson inclined his head. "Be our guest." He supposed Blaise would regret his concession, but they couldn't be rude and deny fellow passengers a seat. The Breaker nodded, but he didn't turn from the window to acknowledge them otherwise. Jefferson knew he would come around after a few minutes.

The newcomers bobbed their heads and made a show of taking their seats, expensive fabric rustling with their movements. It reminded Jefferson of a flock of birds preening. "Excellent.

Allow us to make introductions. I'm Barnabas Inman, and this is my lovely wife Antoinette." The man smiled. "We own a modest number of fish factories on the Canen coast. And you are?"

The Inmans. Jefferson had heard of them, but fortunately, didn't know them. But if he gave his name, this pair of elite would know exactly who he was. If they hadn't known him as a wealthy entrepreneur, they would most certainly know him after the mess at Nera. He was spared from having to come up with an immediate answer, however, as a new woman appeared. She was a brunette with close-cropped hair, and while she dressed respectably, she was a step down from the Inmans.

The woman gave them a bright smile. "Hello! The other tables are all filling up. Could I impose on you?"

Ah, bless her for the interruption. Jefferson met her smile with a brilliant one of his own. "We'd be delighted for your company. Please, have a seat. We were just introducing ourselves."

She bobbed her head as she sat. "Of course. I'm Holly Lewis, traveling home to Phinora." Holly's gaze swept over everyone at the table. Was it Jefferson's imagination, or did she linger on Blaise? Wonderful. As if he needed another person to worry about on this train.

The others were looking at him and Blaise for their own introductions. Jefferson could feel the discomfort radiating from his beau. Blaise, no doubt, was worried about what would happen if people knew who he was. That put Jefferson in a difficult position. Blaise also disliked deceptions. But sometimes, like now, they were necessary.

Jefferson cleared his throat. "I'm Jeffrey Hawthorne. An accountant." Blaise made a soft, surprised sound at the use of his last name, but Jefferson decided he rather liked it.

"Jeffrey the Accountant," Antoinette repeated, as if tasting the words. As if she were trying to decide if he could possibly be monied enough to be in their presence. It wasn't even a bald-faced lie. He did most of his own accounting these days, what little there was to be done. And he handled the books for the bakery, to Blaise's benefit. "And this is Blake Cole. He's a pastry chef."

Blaise shot him a look that was a mix of annoyance (probably at the last name) and optimistic joy. Jefferson had given him something he could have a level of proficiency about in conversation. Blaise murmured a greeting, then went back to looking out the window.

"An accountant and a pastry chef," Antoinette mused. "How quaint."

"I believe we saw you load the horses that are in the livestock transport," Barnabas commented, keen interest in his voice. "Are you somehow connected with Bull's Eye Stables, then?"

That was something Jefferson hadn't accounted for. His mind raced, seeking plausible connections. The current unicorn racing meets were taking place in western Ganland, but that wasn't their destination. He thought it likely Monica would secure a boxcar that wouldn't be too out-of-place going to Phinora, however. It was possible there was a stud or training stable there, though for the life of him, he couldn't recall. Time to bluff. "Indeed, we are."

At that, Blaise elbowed him. *Hard*. He didn't like lies, even needful ones. And he clearly didn't appreciate Jefferson including him. It was likely the Breaker would take the rest of his meals in their room after this. And perhaps that wasn't the worst idea.

Barnabas nodded. "So, you'll be working with Tara Woodrow, then. And you're escorting new bloodstock?"

"We are," Jefferson agreed without batting an eye. "It seemed expedient." But the name immediately put him on edge. Tara was one of the Quiet Ones. She must own Bull's Eye Stables. If so, that was worrisome for many reasons.

Holly had been quiet until that point, either polite or calculating. She fussed with her flatware, which was still rolled up in a linen napkin. "So, you're a pastry chef, Mr. Cole?"

Perhaps it had been a miscalculation to swap last names. Jefferson made the mistake of opening his mouth to speak before realizing the question was meant for Blaise. To his credit, the words *pastry chef* had snared Blaise's attention, and he nodded.

"I am," Blaise agreed, sounding confident. As he should, Jefferson thought with pride.

"I didn't know Woodrow would hire a no-name chef," Antoinette said with a sniff.

That was a flat-out insult. Jefferson wished he could argue against it. Blaise, however, simply shrugged. "I like to think that I'm up-and-coming."

The server came, bearing their meals, which gave them a much-needed break from conversation, allowing Jefferson a chance to mull over Woodrow's potential part in whatever plot was afoot. Perhaps it was merely a coincidence—Monica would have no way of knowing she was the enemy. But in this case, Jefferson didn't like coincidences.

Vixen's reappearance spared Jefferson from further contemplation. The Persuader paused when she saw the others seated at the table, her lips pressed together and silver eyes narrowed. It seemed she was making a threat assessment, too. She motioned for Blaise, and the Breaker squeezed out of the booth. She whispered something in his ear that Jefferson couldn't quite make out, then slipped in to claim the spot the young man had vacated.

Blaise smiled. "If you'll excuse me, there's been a..." He hesitated, eyebrows raised as he chose his words. "Pastry emergency."

"A pastry emergency?" Antoinette repeated, boggled. She glanced toward the kitchen compartment, as if expecting Blaise might venture there next.

Blaise laid out a linen napkin and scooped a handful of scones into its middle, creating a bundle. "Yep. And I always rise to the occasion."

Jefferson could barely conceal a chuckle at his beau's pun. He watched as Blaise beat a retreat out of the dining car, clutching the precious scones against his chest. Then Jefferson returned to his dining partners and did what he could to suss out any connections they might have to the Quiet Ones.

"BLAKE *COLE*? OF ALL THE POSSIBLE NAMES, *THAT'S* WHAT YOU choose?" Blaise crossed his arms, sitting on the couch that folded out into a bed. He had returned to the room before Jefferson and Vixen, and it appeared he had been planning his ambush for some time.

Vixen's lips pinched together as she fought back a laugh. Jefferson, meanwhile, shrugged. "What? I thought it had a very nice ring to it."

The Breaker blew out a breath. "At least you didn't make me an accountant."

Vixen's glance shifted between them. "Sounds like I missed out on some fun."

"It was not fun. It was mostly just awkward," Blaise muttered.

Jefferson sat down beside his love, so close their shoulders brushed. "If you'll forgive me, you know why I didn't offer our true names."

Blaise breathed out a long sigh, slouching back. "I understand why. I just don't *like* it."

At that, Jefferson smiled and patted Blaise's knee. "It's only for the duration of the train ride. Not much longer." Then he updated Vixen on their temporary personas.

When he finished, the Persuader nodded. "Yeah, that was the right thing to do." Her mouth twisted into a frown. "Though if they figure out who you are, I could probably use my magic to convince them otherwise."

And I could do similar. Jefferson didn't dare say it aloud. Instead, he said, "But we need to keep your magic hidden."

She made a face, fiddling with the ring. "If we need it, though, it's there."

Her words nudged a smile from Blaise. The Breaker reached over for the train's information pamphlet and unfolded it, scanning its pages. "You want to go to this?" He pointed at something on the schedule.

Jefferson leaned over to get a better look. "Oh. That's a recital." He raised his brows, hope stirring. "You would go to that with me? Even after how dinner went tonight?"

"As long as there's no music about *me*." Blaise's expression soured at the thought.

"You *do* recall me telling you that one of the songs in the musical about you won an award, yes?" Jefferson asked, almost unable to hold back a smile. Having his friend Lizzie Jennings pen a musical about Blaise's extraordinary life had ended up as quite the coup that had helped them gain favor during the Inquiry that would have otherwise spelled their doom.

"No songs about me," Blaise repeated, adamant. "Just because I didn't die of embarrassment before doesn't mean it won't happen now."

"If there are any songs about you, I promise to whisk you away to the confines of this room immediately," Jefferson said gravely, earning an amused snort from Vixen.

Blaise relented, his shoulders relaxing. "Okay, I'll go with you. But only because I figure there will be less chance for awkward introductions since, hopefully, I won't be the entertainment."

And because you know I would enjoy it. Jefferson smiled. He suspected Blaise would like it, too. Jefferson could count the number of concerts his beau had seen on one hand. Blaise had never really had the opportunity to enjoy them like a normal person.

"Yes, there is that," Jefferson agreed. He vowed to set aside his suspicions for the rest of the evening, if only to allow himself and Blaise the chance to be normal. Jefferson turned to Vixen. "Would you like to come along?"

She waved a hand. "Three's a crowd. I'm going to check on the pegasi and then explore the rest of the train. I've never been on one before." They all knew she really wanted to spend more time with her brother. Jefferson felt an age-old pang, the old scar that flared up whenever he wished he had a better relationship with his sister. Or a relationship at all.

"Have fun," Jefferson said instead. He pulled out his pocket watch to check the time. "As for us, we should head out soon, or we may not get a seat."

CHAPTER TWELVE

Outhouse Surprise

Jack

It was a full day before anyone came across Naureus, and even then, it was the elemental mare who ended up locating him. According to Zepheus, Najaria threatened to scorch the buckskin stallion's wings if he didn't return with her. Jack wasn't sure he wanted to know how the aethon had communicated such a threat.

Raven's pegasus alighted on the edge of town, the tips of his wings singed but otherwise intact. Jack studied the equine as he trotted up, head hanging. Naureus knew that none of this looked good for him or his rider.

Most of the human citizens suspected nothing, but the pegasi certainly knew. The Fortitude flight had grown over the past year and now boasted around fifty of the equines. Most of them lined the street leading to the stables, ears laid back because they didn't understand what would have made Naureus and his rider part ways. It made them fearful.

Jack glanced at the ranks of pegasi, then turned to Zepheus.

"They ain't gonna make this any easier. Can you get 'em out of here?"

The palomino bobbed his head in agreement. <Yes. Do not begin with Naureus until I am back, though.> With that said, he surged forward, ears flat against his skull, shrilling a cry that broke up the knots of pegasi. They bolted away, turning tail as Zepheus chased them off.

Naureus watched quietly, then ambled into the shade of the stable, heading to his stall as if he were an old plow horse. Jack frowned, having seen pegasi behave like this before. Naureus was worried about his rider, and when that happened, a pegasus often went off their feed and lost weight. It could lead to a whole mess of health problems that weren't easy to treat.

Zepheus returned, folding his wings as he quick-stepped over to where Jack waited outside Naureus's stall. With the palomino back, the outlaw nodded, giving the stud permission to lead the questioning. He figured it made sense, seeing as they were the same species.

Zepheus regarded Jack with surprise for a beat, then turned to the buckskin. <Where is your rider, Raven Dawson?>

Naureus sighed heavily, digging at the straw with a forehoof. <I do not know. He would not tell me where he was going, though I have my suspicions.>

Jack frowned. That made little sense. "But you took him somewhere." Then he winced, realizing he had intended for Zepheus to do most of the questioning.

<Only as far as Desina. Then he instructed me to stay away from Fortitude.> Naureus gave them a mournful look. <I told him I wanted to stay with him, but he said where he was going, it would be too dangerous for me. I tried to follow him but...> The stallion's black-tipped muzzle touched the ground. <When Raven wants to lose someone, it is easy for him.>

Jack nodded. Raven was one of the handiest sorts of Walkers, since shadows were everywhere. Small wonder Naureus wouldn't have been able to follow. He grunted in agreement.

<Do you know why he left?> Zepheus asked.

Naureus lifted his head. <No.>

"You think he might have gone after Vixen?" Jack figured it was a likely possibility.

The buckskin snorted. <Perhaps, but that is not the sum. He had become more distant over the last few months. Secretive.>

Jack and Zepheus traded looks. That wasn't a good sign. Jack loved his secrets, but Zepheus was privy to them. It was a foundation of their partnership. Outlaw and pegasus had to trust one another, or things went sour fast.

<Did you pick up anything unusual from him? Emotionally?> Zepheus asked.

Naureus blew out a breath. <His relationship with Vixen has been like a stone in his hoof. But that does not seem unreasonable when pursuing a mate.>

Yeah, that was true. But from what Jack understood, there was no more pursuing Vixen. Raven had proposed. She'd said no. Jack was one of the few in town privy to that bit of information. He rubbed his chin, thinking back to the fire pit. "Had he been communicating with anyone new?"

<There were letters he read, but that did not seem strange. Every human in town receives mail occasionally.> The buckskin paused. <Though Raven seldom received any previously.>

Jack pursed his lips. By itself, it wasn't strange. But with Najaria considering burned bits of paper suspicious, it took on a new light. "Letters from the post office or from elsewhere?"

Naureus arched his neck, suddenly thoughtful. <Not from the post office.>

That's what Jack had thought. Raven's only family were far, far away in Confederation lands. And from what the outlaw had gleaned, they were unaware of Raven's whereabouts. The odds of the letters being from a doting mother were low.

<Could it be from another mate?> Zepheus asked.

Naureus considered the question, then shook his inky mane. <No. I never picked up on any passionate emotions, nor scented any musk.>

Jack raised his brows at that. Naureus's statement left him wondering exactly how much Zepheus picked up from him when he was around Kittie. He didn't want his pesky pegasus sticking his nose where it didn't belong. But Zepheus's line of questioning inspired one of Jack's own. "Did he keep any of the letters, or burn 'em all? Do you know if Raven has any hidey-holes?"

The buckskin twitched an ear. <I don't know if he kept any. But yes, he has a stash.>

Zepheus traded looks with Jack. <Can you take us to it?>

Moments later, they were back at Raven's house with Naureus. Jack frowned—he thought he'd done a solid job of checking the inside for clues. The pegasus didn't lead them to the house, but instead around to the back, where an outhouse stood solitary vigil.

Jack wrinkled his nose. "You gotta be kidding me."

Naureus nudged the wood on one side of the outhouse. <There's a false wall. I have not seen inside, but from what I understand there is a latch that will open a compartment out here.>

Jack sighed. Of course, a damned pegasus had no need for an outhouse, which meant *he* had the privilege of exploring the interior. Silently cursing Raven, Jack entered. There was no magelight to brighten the inside, but ample light flooded the cracks in the walls. As Jack groped around, he wished he'd had the presence of mind to cast the working that would shield him from the stink.

Then his fingers brushed something to the left of the rough wooden seat. It was, in fact, a lever of some sort. Jack pulled it. "That do anything out there?"

<Yes. Naureus is right. There is a compartment, but it's in the eaves.> Zepheus's golden bulk was visible through the cracks.

Jack came out, sucking in a lungful of fresh air before peering up. With the false door open, the stash was quite obvious. But when it was closed, it was nearly invisible in the shadow of the eaves. Jack couldn't quite reach it, but climbing aboard Zepheus gave him the height to pull out a bound wad of envelopes.

<What are they?> Naureus asked, ears pricked forward with interest—and a hint of optimism, as if hoping that the contents might vindicate his rider.

"Let's find out," Jack murmured, slipping from Zepheus's back so that he'd have an easier time perusing the find.

The first few letters were ones Raven had written, but never sent. They were all addressed to Vixen; the contents ranging from anger at her dismissal to poems professing the depths of his love. Not very good poems, but poems, nonetheless. Jack scowled as he flipped through them, then froze when he came across half of a torn letter with crisp handwriting that didn't belong to Raven.

—last time we will make this offer. Meet us in Ondin on—

Ondin? Jack nearly crumpled the paper. Meet the author in Ondin *when?* That part was missing, but flipping the correspondence over showed a date from a little more than a month ago. He tried to make sense of the rest of the letter, searching for clues, but the closing had been torn away as well.

<Jack?> Zepheus nudged him. <We cannot read.>

Jack hissed out a breath. "Doesn't matter. This doesn't tell us shit."

<But you are still upset with my rider.> Naureus's ears flopped to the side.

The outlaw tilted his head, thinking of how to express his frustrations without hurting the buckskin any further. A good pegasus was loyal to their rider—even when that same rider had abandoned them. "Yeah. This mentions Ondin, and that has me on edge."

<Ondin. That is where Vixen's group got on the train.> Zepheus pawed at the ground, catching some of his rider's unease.

"Yeah. And I don't like coincidences."

<Perhaps we should go to Ondin and investigate?> Zepheus suggested.

Jack flipped to the next letter, eyes widening. "Nah, not Ondin. Izhadell." He traced Raven's precise scrawl with one finger.

Stay out of Phinora, Jack.

CHAPTER THIRTEEN
Colorful Past

Jefferson

The train pulled into the station outside Izhadell, hissing as it came to a stop. Jefferson watched as Blaise peered out the window, his face pinched with worry. Sinister memories had plagued Blaise's dreams the past two nights, and Jefferson didn't know how the younger man would have fared without Jefferson's magic to chase them away.

Maybe bringing Blaise along had been a mistake. Maybe they were wrong in thinking that coming back here would heal him. Jefferson feared that, if anything, it might make him worse. He didn't tell Blaise that, though. He didn't want his love to bear any more worries than he already carried.

"There's so many people. I don't remember there being this many people," Blaise murmured.

No, he wouldn't remember. Blaise had either been in the Golden Citadel, on Malcolm's estate, or ferried to the Salt-Iron Confederation Council building. In fact, once they had freed Blaise, Jefferson had made it a priority to shield the young man from the outside world however he could. He took Blaise's hand.

"There are. But here, you're just like a drop of water in a stream. No one will even think twice about you."

Blaise pressed his lips together, uncertain. His blue eyes were doubtful. "They will when they know who I am."

"Perhaps," Jefferson agreed, voice soft. "Though I suspect you'll be of much less interest than Vixen." *Or myself.*

The Breaker huffed out a breath. He looked as if he wanted to say something but didn't know how to put it into words. Jefferson slung an arm around him.

"Remember, you came of your own free will. This is not like last time. You decided this. *Your choice.*" Jefferson sank as much conviction into his words as he could, hoping it would ease Blaise's mind.

Blaise swallowed, then nodded. He sighed. "You're right. Sorry. I shouldn't borrow trouble, especially when I know we're bringing our own."

Jefferson raised his brows, noting the weak smile on his love's face. "Was that a joke?"

"A terrible one," Blaise said, though now his expression had bloomed into a genuine smile, as if he were feeling better.

"Not that bad." Jefferson chuckled. This was good. Perhaps he could keep Blaise in a positive frame of mind. "We'll disembark soon. We should make sure we have everything."

Really, it was just a distraction ploy—Jefferson knew they had everything packed. He'd triple-checked, in fact. But it was busy-work, which Blaise needed. Though it didn't stop Jefferson's mind from wandering. Their travels on the train had been mostly uneventful. Jefferson had only caught fleeting looks at the woman who'd shown interest in Blaise at the dinner. Perhaps she'd only found the Breaker comely. Jefferson couldn't fault her for that.

By the time they made their way back to the pegasi car, Blaise was calm, behaving as if nothing had bothered him. Their saddle-bags slung over their shoulders, they joined Vixen and Rhys with the pegasi and unicorn. Alekon and Darby were already saddled.

Blaise and Jefferson set to tacking up Emrys and Seledora—another diversion for the Breaker.

A few minutes later, the car door rolled open, afternoon sunlight streaming in. Rhys led Darby to the threshold, glancing back at them. "I'll go first."

They watched as Rhys and the unicorn made their way down the ramp. Someone called to the Tracker, and he turned in their direction. He strode over to a group of men wearing—oh, damn. That was not a good sign. Salt-Iron Confederation uniforms.

No need to worry. Not yet. Rhys is a Tracker, and nothing has gone amiss with his presence. Jefferson hoped his faith wasn't misplaced. He glanced at Blaise but found the Breaker was facing Emrys, murmuring to the stallion.

Rhys gestured, the lines of his body growing tense. Vixen slipped beside Jefferson. "This doesn't look good," she whispered.

"It doesn't," he agreed, voice just as soft. Jefferson had suspicions about what was afoot. Well, there was no sense in delaying the inevitable. He took a steadying breath, patting Seledora's shoulder before going down the ramp with her. "I may need you as legal counsel."

The mare's dark eye found his. <Not surprising. How lucky for you I'm here.>

When they reached the base, the soldiers were there to greet them. A man with a bushy mustache stepped forward. "Doyen Malcolm Wells, you are under arrest. You'll come with us."

The name made Jefferson freeze, a flash of shock racing through his veins. His breath hitched, but he recovered quickly and offered them a smile. "I beg your pardon, but you seem to have me confused with someone else."

"Malcolm Wells, alias Jefferson Cole," Mustache Man clarified, to Jefferson's dismay. He pulled a folded piece of paper from a pocket. "Our orders list both names, so it's all the same to us."

<On what charges?> Seledora asked. Jefferson was gratified that her mental speech startled the entire group, and they took a

step back as if someone had slapped them, glancing around to look for the speaker. The mare advanced, head high as her wings shimmered into view. <I am Counselor Seledora, and I represent Mr. Cole.>

Mustache Man swallowed, staring at the pegasus. For a moment, Jefferson thought he was too stunned to speak. Then he remembered himself, clearing his throat. "Identity fraud."

That was sadly unsurprising. The Quiet Ones loved to attack his identity, trying to force him back into the person he didn't wish to be. His brow furrowed. Jefferson opened his mouth to speak, but Seledora nonchalantly rammed her shoulder against him. <Say nothing to refute this. We both know it is the least of things they can hold you for.>

But Jefferson didn't *want* to go with the soldiers. He turned, staring up the ramp to where Blaise stood beside Emrys. The Breaker was watching the proceedings, and even from this distance, Jefferson read the emotions on his face: fear and worry. Damn it all, this might spiral Blaise into a panic attack.

It didn't look like a fate Jefferson could avoid, though. He took a breath, addressing the soldiers. "I need a moment."

"No, you—"

"Give him a moment." This demand came from Rhys, who had ambled over to stand with arms crossed. "He's not going to escape."

Ignoring the soldiers, Jefferson walked back up the ramp to Blaise. The Breaker was trembling, and his face had grown pale. He leaned heavily against Emrys.

"Blaise, I have to go with them," Jefferson said, voice soft.

The Breaker stared at him, his expression hollow. "You can't. What if...?" He swiped a hand at one eye.

"Listen to me." Jefferson wrapped his arms around his beau, pulling him into a tight embrace. He felt the tension in Blaise's body, like a tightly coiled spring ready to snap. Jefferson didn't fear the Breaker would lose control of his magic—but he didn't want those men to know exactly who Blaise was. *They* would fear a potential loss of control, and if they moved against Blaise, it very well could become a self-fulfilling prophecy. "I'll be okay. I suspected this might happen, and the charge they're bringing against me is one Seledora and I can easily fight."

At that, Blaise pulled back just enough to look at him. "You *knew* they might arrest you?"

Jefferson's face warmed with chagrin. "Well, considering my colorful past, yes."

"And you didn't tell me?" The Breaker's lips drew into a taut, pale line.

Blaise was mad, which meant it was in Jefferson's best interest to be honest. "No, because you would worry." *And we both know you've had enough on your mind.*

Blaise gave Jefferson a look that was all annoyance, which was preferable to him shutting down. "I hate that you're right."

Jefferson smiled, then reached up to cup Blaise's cheek. "I'm not defenseless, and neither are you. I promise they won't keep me."

"They'd better not," Blaise agreed. "I'll fight the entire Confederation for you if I must."

The words, a long-ago echo, struck Jefferson like an arrow. He had said nearly the very same to Blaise when the Breaker had been imprisoned at the Golden Citadel. Meeting his beau's eyes, he realized Blaise had intended it. It was the most heartfelt declaration anyone had ever made him, and it warmed Jefferson in ways he couldn't explain. Ways that cemented how he felt about Blaise.

"Malcolm Wells!" mustache man called.

"That's not your name," Blaise whispered, voice rough with slumbering anger.

"I know. They're being rather obtuse," Jefferson murmured, relieved that Blaise had traded his momentary fear for other emotions. While an angry Blaise was hazardous, it was better than when the mage was locked down by panic and the burden of memories. Anger granted Blaise renewed determination.

Vixen, who had been watching their interaction from beside Alekon a few yards away, said, "I'll be with Blaise. We'll be okay."

"I should go," Jefferson said with regret, though he flashed the Persuader a grateful look.

"Wait." Blaise's voice was so soft Jefferson almost didn't hear it. But that didn't matter as the Breaker lifted his chin, lips brushing against Jefferson's. *Oh.* Jefferson hadn't expected that, but it was easy to lean into the kiss, to lose himself to the sweetness of a blissful moment with Blaise.

But it was over far too soon. Jefferson smiled as he stepped back, then pivoted to start down the ramp. He paused midway down to call back, "You know, conjugal visits are a thing."

Blaise stared at him for a moment before the press of his lips showed further annoyance. "You're insufferable."

Privately, Jefferson counted that a victory. He'd calmed Blaise and succeeded in distracting him. Jefferson strode down the ramp, summoning up every bit of snootiness he possessed. He gave the soldiers a condescending look. "I suppose I'm ready to go with you."

Blaise

BLAISE'S MOOD DARKENED AFTER JEFFERSON'S ARREST. HE HAD BEEN naive to think they could travel to Phinora and everything would be fine. Gullible to believe it was as easy as Jefferson made it sound. He should have known that for them, nothing was ever easy.

Things didn't improve when they reached the estate. *His* estate. That didn't sit well with him, either. It felt wrong in a way he couldn't put his finger on, so it became one more thing bringing him down. Not even Emrys could stir him from his dour mood.

"Looks like the groundskeeping has been lacking," Vixen commented from beside him. She had made a point to take up Jefferson's place at his side. Blaise didn't like that, either, but he knew why she did it, and he valued her too much to snap at her for the imposition.

At her observation, Blaise frowned, his gaze sweeping the land before him. She was right. He hadn't noticed immediately because of his mood, but the garden was overgrown. A top rail of one of the fences had come loose, and the home's windows had a haze of grime. None of that had been in evidence when it had been Malcolm's estate. Jefferson had told Blaise funds had been set aside for the upkeep of the house and grounds. Something wasn't right.

Had the Quiet Ones gotten to this cache of money, too? The thought roused Blaise's fury even more. They were relentless in their campaign against Jefferson.

"Howdy to the house!" Vixen called when Blaise said nothing. He knew he was being uncharacteristically prickly, but he had good reason.

A moment later, a teenage boy ducked out of the barn, eyes widening when he saw them. He hurried over. "Mr. Hawthorne?"

<He means you.> Emrys prompted when Blaise made no response.

Oh. Right. Blaise had been so distracted he'd forgotten that he was an authority here. "Um, yes. That's me." Gods, would he ever be able to act like a normal person?

"We got the letter that you'd be coming. Didn't think you'd actually come," the boy remarked, then winced when he no doubt realized he'd spoken private thoughts aloud. Well, at least Blaise wasn't the only awkward one.

"*We?*" This from Rhys, who had been quiet as they traveled, seemingly lost in his own thoughts. Blaise had forgotten the Tracker was even there.

When the boy caught sight of the gleaming unicorn's horn, he faltered. Was it Blaise's imagination, or did he pale a shade or two? "Um, well, it's just me now. Everyone else is gone."

"What happened?" Blaise asked. Jefferson would have made certain the estate had adequate staff, of that Blaise was sure. That made him suspect something had happened here that his beau hadn't caught wind of yet.

The boy dug a toe into the dirt. "They all up and left. Better pay elsewhere, I suppose."

Blaise didn't believe that for an instant—unless someone had maliciously hired them away, which was a possibility. "Why did you stay?"

The boy hitched a thumb to the barn. "The horses here can't take care of themselves, sir."

That said something for the boy's character, and Blaise gave an approving nod. "What's your name?"

"Tristan, sir."

"You can call me Blaise."

Tristan goggled at him. "Yes, sir. I mean, Blaise. Sir."

Blaise sighed. He swung out of the saddle, Vixen following suit. Blaise looked at the Persuader's brother, who was still mounted. "There's enough rooms here if you'd like to stay." Whether they were suitable for habitation was a whole different issue.

Rhys shook his head. "I appreciate the offer, but I have my own place. I should get Darby back to the stables and make my reports."

Reports? Blaise didn't know if he liked the sound of that.

The Tracker's unicorn edged closer to Vixen as he continued to speak. "And I'll see what I can find out about your friend. I expect they'll have to bring him before a magistrate in the next day or two. I'll be in touch." Rhys smiled, and tapped two fingers to his forehead in a little salute before Darby turned and trotted off.

"Well, suppose we should see to the pegasi now," Vixen said.

"Pegasi?" Tristan squeaked. As he spoke, Emrys's purple-tinged wings shimmered into view, the feathers whispering against Blaise's arm. The boy looked torn between running for the hills and coming closer to stare with admiration. He split the difference by stumbling backward until his back rammed into the white fence surrounding a paddock.

<We're harmless to you,> Alekon advised the boy with a jaunty tilt of his head. He shook out his mane as his own wings swept into view.

Blaise studied the boy, the only person apparently still in his employ at Hawthorne House. "You've been taking care of everything here on your own?"

"Best I can," Tristan agreed, though he seemed worried that Blaise might reprimand him. "It's hard to do much with this place alone."

Blaise nodded. "Thank you for what you've done. I'll see to it you get paid extra for doing so much more than you were hired on for." It was the least he could do, and it seemed reasonable. Blaise would figure out how to make that happen later.

They took care of their pegasi, and he discovered that there were, indeed, horses. Two light grey carriage horses, though they were caked a muddy brown from a recent wallow. Blaise didn't remember them from his previous visit, though Emrys assured him they had been there.

Blaise moved alongside Tristan, who had been watching them with a high level of bemusement, as if he didn't know what to make of them. "Is the kitchen stocked?"

The boy cringed. "With only the most basic things, sir."

"It's *Blaise*. And if you had the funds, could you fetch more?"

Tristan blinked at him. "Yes, sir. I mean Blaise. Yes."

He arranged the matter of coin for the boy. While Tristan

headed off to the nearest market riding one of the carriage horses
bareback, Blaise and Vixen made their way into the house.

Blaise only had fleeting memories of the place. He remembered the master bedroom because…well, it wasn't the time to
think about that. His cheeks warmed at the pleasant memory. And
he remembered the kitchen—that was where he and Malcolm had
worked together on Blaise's plan to win public favor with baked
goods. His recollection of the rest of the house was murky.

"How are you doing?" Vixen asked.

His shoulders slumped at her question. "Jefferson said he'd be
okay, but I can't help it. I'm worried about him." He rubbed the
back of his neck. "He's a *mage*. Not just the politician he was the
last time he was here."

The Persuader settled a hand on his shoulder, her touch light.
"You know we're not going to let them keep him, right?"

Blaise nodded. He didn't want to say it, but if it came down to
it, he'd use his magic to free Jefferson. He'd tear the Golden
Citadel down to its foundations. Blaise huffed out a breath, feeling
tension pool at the base of his neck.

Vixen seemed to have her own thoughts on the matter. She
lifted her hand from his shoulder, fiddling with the ring on her
finger. "I know what you're thinking. It won't get to that. I can use
my magic or my name."

He frowned. "You'd show your cards so soon?"

She smiled. "Might be no better time to tip my hand. Besides,
what kind of friend would I be if I kept my magic hidden when it
was needed?"

Her words and friendship warmed him, doing much to
improve his mood. Blaise wondered if she knew how much it
helped him. Knowing Vixen, she did. She was good at reading
other people. "Thanks."

"You can repay me by whipping up something sweet once
Tristan gets back."

"That's the plan."

CHAPTER FOURTEEN
Straw Man

Jefferson

The Golden Citadel was the last place Jefferson wanted to see on his return trip to Izhadell. But he wasn't all that surprised to discover that was where his escort intended to leave him. He was a mage, after all.

Seledora followed for as long as she could, determined to represent him. But when they arrived at the Cit, he knew she would have no choice but to leave and rejoin the others. His guard had allowed him a moment to speak with her before she flew off.

Now Jefferson reclined on a lounger that was a decade out of fashion. He was lucky, or as lucky as anyone imprisoned in the Cit could be. Because of his former position as a Doyen, they'd jailed him in one of the more luxurious cells. That was fortunate, since it was a far cry from his memory of Blaise's cell—and the panic he'd felt when they'd arrived to free the Breaker and discovered it empty.

While the cell had comforts, that didn't mean it was comfortable. Like the rest of the complex, the walls had salt-iron incorporated into them. The metal didn't agree with Jefferson at all. He had the beginnings of a headache, and it would only get worse. If he was truly unlucky, it would turn his stomach.

"You've got a visitor!" The scrape of a key and click of a lock followed the announcement.

Jefferson straightened. He set aside the book he'd been reading, rising as a guard entered and motioned for him to come over.

"Who's visiting me?" Jefferson asked, then hissed in pain as the guard slapped salt-iron cuffs onto his wrists. "Blessed Tabris! Give a man some warning next time." He'd love to have Blaise's resistance to the vile metal.

The guard shook her head, saying nothing. She gestured for him to walk beside her.

With a resigned sigh, he did as she required, determined that he would be on his best behavior. He didn't want to give them any cause to mistreat him or otherwise find a reason to keep him there. Perhaps Blaise had somehow come to visit him? No, this would be too soon. Blaise and Vixen would be settling into the estate. At least, he hoped. Though a small part of him wished it was Blaise. While he'd only intended to shock Blaise out of making a mistake with his suggestion of conjugal visits, Jefferson desperately wished for a visit from the man he loved. As unrealistic as that was.

She showed him into a visitation cell. Like his own cell, it was a much nicer affair than anything Blaise had experienced during his stay. He sat down in the chair, waiting for his visitor to arrive.

The door opened a moment later, and another guard showed in a man who made Jefferson's hackles rise. Most definitely not Blaise. Jefferson's eyes narrowed as soon as he saw the well-dressed elite. His hands tightened into fists. "Phillip Dillon. You're quite far from Ganland. To what do I owe the displeasure?"

The Quiet One waited until the guards shut the door behind him, the locking mechanism grating. Phillip smiled, then ambled over to sit across from Jefferson. "I heard you came all the way to Phinora, and I thought I owed you a visit." He made a show of looking around the visitation cell, lip curling with disgust. "Though I certainly wasn't expecting to find you *here*."

Like Perdition you weren't. He was certain that Phillip had known exactly where he would end up. Most likely had orchestrated it. "Yes, well, these accommodations would be much more fitting for you, I'm sure."

Something dangerous flickered in Dillon's gaze. "Tread carefully, Malcolm."

"Do I look like Malcolm Wells?" Jefferson growled. He was so very tired of people calling him by that name.

"No, but underneath all this, you still are." Phillip gestured to him. He folded his hands in his lap. "You have seen how far our reach extends, haven't you?"

Jefferson scowled, knowing exactly what Phillip was referring to. The Quiet Ones had systematically eviscerated his persona as Jefferson Cole, destroying all of his years of hard work to establish himself. Then they drained his bank accounts and holdings, leaving him destitute. Without Blaise, he would have been lost. His pulse sped at the reminder.

"Yes, very impressive job of destroying a straw man," Jefferson said. "If you came to gloat about that, then your work here is done." But even as he said the words, he wished he hadn't. He had come to Phinora to root out information about the Quiet Ones, after all. And this meeting could unearth a few precious nuggets, though it wasn't something he'd prepared for.

Phillip smiled. "It's not time for me to take my leave. Not yet. I'm here for a purpose."

"I thought I'd made it quite clear I want nothing to do with any of you," Jefferson said, pulse racing.

The Quiet One leaned in, reminding Jefferson of a predator. "Rest assured that I want nothing to do with you as well. But I have a vested interest in you for other reasons."

That was puzzling. "If you didn't come to convince me to take up my father's mantle, then why *did* you come?" As much as he despised Phillip, maybe Jefferson could tease information from him. That might make this incarceration worth a damn.

"Because I want to know where *she* is," Phillip said, his voice a rumble.

Jefferson blinked. Of all the things the Quiet One might have said, that was not what he'd expected. Though, Jefferson realized with chagrin, perhaps that was an oversight on his part. Phillip was an enemy for more reasons than simply being a member of the shadowy group who'd taken so much from him. Dillon had *also* bought Jefferson's sister Alice as a bride, simply because she had developed magic.

"You think I know where Alice is?"

Phillip pressed his lips together so tightly they were pale. "You spoke to her at your own funeral."

As far as sentences went, it was certainly one that would have been nonsensical to nearly anyone else. Jefferson eased back in his seat, trying to act as if the blasted salt-iron shackles didn't chafe his wrists. "Correction: I, Jefferson Cole, spoke to Alice Wells at the funeral of Malcolm Wells. What makes you think she would have told me anything? She doesn't know me." That last bit stung to admit, but it was true. He wondered if word had reached her of his duplicitous nature.

Phillip stared at him. "Then you're useless to me."

"Even if I knew, what makes you think I would tell you?" Jefferson asked.

The older man studied him for a moment. "Because you have a softer heart than your father, Malcolm. And I have it on good authority that with the proper motivation, you have a tendency to make things happen."

A surge of fury washed through Jefferson. "Let me assure you that though my heart is soft, I can still be every bit as hard and cruel as Stafford Wells ever was." And even as he spoke the words that made his gut clench with dread, Jefferson wasn't about to back down from them. "Consider yourself warned."

Phillip made a dismissive gesture. "I appreciate it, but at the moment, I imagine you'd have a difficult time following through." He made a show of rising from his seat slowly, his gaze meeting Jefferson's. "I'll offer you something in good faith, however. Perhaps it will inspire you to help me find Alice."

"I don't want whatever you have to give." Jefferson didn't wish to be beholden to this man. It would only be trouble.

"It's advice." Phillip stood over him. Jefferson rose so that they were on equal footing. "Keep your nose out of Phinoran politics."

Damn it. Did this mean Phillip knew their purpose in coming —did he know who Vixen was? *Maybe I can squeeze an admission from him.* "That's like advising the sun to not rise in the morning."

Phillip shook his head. "I'm trying to help you. Stay clear of the politics. Cool your heels here until..." He gestured to the surrounding chamber, though his words faltered.

"Until what?" Oh, Jefferson was so close to an answer.

The older man gave him an assessing look, then heaved a sigh. "I'll see that you're released, in due time. Remain here. And I'll see if I can use my influence to protect your Breaker, too."

The reference to Blaise made Jefferson's pulse race. But not at Phillip's offer to shield him. No, Blaise wouldn't tolerate Jefferson staying in the Golden Citadel for very long, of that he was certain. And even if Blaise would allow such a thing, Jefferson didn't like the idea of relying on Dillon's charity. Not to mention, doing so would leave Vixen vulnerable.

The smart option would be to agree and perhaps go the route of malicious compliance. Jefferson considered it for a beat, but erred on the side of keeping clear of his enemies. "I don't need your protection."

Phillip pursed his lips, making a frustrated sound. "Let me put it plainly: the Quiet Ones have goals in Phinora. If you thwart us, you *will* regret it."

"Funny, I was about to say the same to you." Jefferson aimed a charming smile at him.

. The sour look on Phillip's face proved that even though Jefferson didn't feel confident inside, at least he sounded confident. Jefferson watched with disinterest as Dillon stalked to the door, rapping on it to get the guard's attention.

Well, that could have gone worse. Jefferson watched Phillip slip out, then took a moment to wince at the blisters on his wrist. *Blasted salt-iron shackles.*

CHAPTER FIFTEEN

Stolen Fair and Square

Jack

$\mathcal{J}$ack stared down at the paper in his hands. Most people thought he was impulsive and rash—and yeah, sometimes he was. But at times like this, when something big and important lay in the balance, he took his time to think about things. And he kept coming back to the problem that Raven Dawson was currently a wild card.

More than that, he'd suspected Jack would find his stash and had left a warning. There had been no mention of Vixen aside from the unsent letters that seemed to predate the other correspondence. Zepheus suggested that if Raven told Jack to stay clear of Phinora, it might be wise to heed the advice. Whatever was afoot had to be more than a scorned lover. And it spelled trouble that Raven mentioned Phinora when Vixen was headed there, too.

"What's that?"

Damn it. He had been so caught up in his own thoughts he'd not been paying attention and had missed Kittie slipping into their bedroom. She snugged an arm around him, resting her chin on his shoulder as she peered down at the paper.

He was tempted to snatch it away and hide it, but that would only make him look suspicious. Or guilty. And he was neither of those things, not right now. Besides, this was his wife. If there was anyone he should be honest with, it was her. "A copy of the portal spell Emmaline used."

Kittie made an interested sound, then rested one of her hands atop his. "And you have this why?"

Jack glanced at her. "'Cause the grimoire with the original is in the bakery. And I figured it didn't hurt to have a copy."

"Hmm." Kittie regarded it with a critical eye. "So, not only have we stolen grimoires from Ravance, we now have a copy of one of their spells."

Jack snorted. "I stole it from the Copperheads fair and square." It was splitting hairs, but it was true. She had a point, though. If the Ravanchens had a way to hunt down their missing grimoires, they'd be angry to discover them in the hands of an outlaw mage. Jack assumed that the former owner of Blaise's grimoire was likely dead, though. With a little luck, no one was missing it.

"I suppose the question I should have asked is why you're staring at it right now," Kittie clarified.

At that, he nodded. It was a better question. "Because Vixen, Blaise, and Jefferson don't know about Raven." Jack had revealed the information contained within Raven's stash to Kittie, as well as the other remaining Ringleaders.

Kittie narrowed her eyes. "Jack..." She looked away, her gaze falling on the porcelain doll with long, brown locks settled atop their dresser. "You're not considering portalling to Izhadell, are you?"

He grimaced at her tone. "It'll take Hank days to get there, if he even gets that far." And anyway, what would he even put in a letter? *Howdy Vixen, hate to send you this in the post, but your old flame is headed your way, and I suspect he's up to no good.* That wasn't the sort of thing to commit to paper.

The Pyromancer crossed her arms, moving to sit on the bed

beside him. "Why does it have to be you? Can't someone else do this? Someone else could go."

Jack shook his head. Few in town knew about the grimoires, and he was happy to keep it that way. The people who knew weren't ones to flap their jaws about it. Emmaline could cast the spell—she had done it before—but the thought of her in Izhadell again twisted his stomach in knots. Especially since the spell would leave her vulnerable.

"It ain't a simple spell. And I'm gonna have to ask Marian for a potion to even have a chance at casting it. Unless..." He paused, thinking back to the way Blaise had empowered him and Emmaline before. By Perdition, Blaise could probably cast the portal spell without breaking a sweat. Jack knew that some Ritualists worked in covens, combining their magic into something powerful. He wasn't one to work well with others, though. It was something to consider for later. A coven might be what they needed in the end. But that wasn't something to dally with now.

Kittie raised her eyebrows, waiting for him to continue. "Unless?"

Jack frowned. "Nothing. The alchemist can make what I need to pull this off."

The Pyromancer sighed. "Jack, *I* could help you do this."

The words struck him like a bullet. He shivered at her suggestion. How could he explain to her that this was his greatest fear? Kittie back in Phinora, falling into the hands of the Confederation again. It had been bad enough having her in Ganland with the ambassadorial delegation. But he knew he couldn't explain all that and have it make sense. She would think he didn't believe in her to do the task. But that was wrong—Jack knew she could do it. Kittie could do anything she put her mind to.

He bowed his head, almost crumpling the paper in his hands. "No." Jack swallowed, hating how raw his voice sounded. "You're one of Fortitude's strongest defenders, with Blaise gone. I'm good, but you're better."

She canted her head, giving him a skeptical look. "I don't believe for a second that's your reason."

Jack scowled. "It's reason enough."

Kittie sighed, moving in to press a kiss against his forehead. "You're scared of me going to Phinora."

"I ain't scared," he grumbled, but they both knew that was a lie. The Effigest closed his eyes, savoring her affection even as he dreaded what might happen to her.

He felt her hand move lightly along his shoulder to rest against the back of his neck. "How do you think I feel about you going there? Your handsome face is still on handbills."

Yeah, and he still had the same wanted posters tacked to the bedroom walls as proof. His humbling reminder. Jack's eyes opened. "What if we came to a compromise?"

Kittie made a soft sound of consideration. "What sort of compromise?"

"You cast the spell, and I go through."

She frowned. "It should be the other way around."

"Nope," he said, voice gravelly. "This is the best I'm gonna offer. That spell wipes out the caster. Ask Em about that. This will let me arrive in Izhadell without being an unconscious lump."

"You're insufferable," Kittie accused.

Jack chuckled. "Yep."

Kittie blew out a breath, pulling away from him. "Am I to assume that if I cast the spell and go through, you would just be a stubborn ass and go as well?"

He grinned. "What do you think?"

"You're a jackass."

Jack closed the distance between them again. "That's me. So you'll do it?"

Kittie rubbed her forehead. "I'll do it. I won't like it, and I'll worry about you as much as you'd worry about me, you know."

Jack knew, but there was no help for it. "I'd expect nothing less."

CHAPTER SIXTEEN
The Bread-Locomotive

Blaise

The kitchen was a chaotic mess of mixing bowls, pans, measuring cups and spoons, and a variety of other items. Blaise surveyed his domain, inhaling the calming aroma of cooling cookies and cake. Vixen had chipped in to help with his baking frenzy, but after a while, had withdrawn when it was clear she couldn't keep up with him. She'd stayed nearby to watch, though.

"Gotta check the quality," Vixen said as she pried a still-warm chocolate chip cookie from a nearby cooling rack.

"None of the work and all the reward. I think there's a children's fable about that." Blaise aimed a mock-stern look her way. They both knew it was bluster. He'd relaxed considerably since first descending into his baking frenzy.

Vixen hefted the crumbling cookie at him. She nimbly caught part of it in her free hand before it hit the floor, then shoved it into her mouth. "Right, but I *tried* to help. I just bowed out to give the master room to work."

He smiled, glad that he felt more like himself. Baking always served as a bulwark that offered him a literal sweet release from stress. But later would be an entirely different matter. He couldn't stay up all night and bake—well, he *could*, but it wouldn't be wise. He had to sleep sometime, and that was when he'd really feel Jefferson's absence.

Blaise swallowed, rising to collect a basket from a countertop. "I'm going to take some treats out to the pegasi." Then he forced himself to pretend that he would be okay. "I'll tell you what. Clean up the dishes and kitchen, and we'll call it even."

The Persuader eyed the mountain of dishes Blaise had left in his wake. "This seems about as fair as a one-legged donkey in an ass-kicking contest." Vixen grabbed a towel and moved to the sink. She was lucky—Doyen Malcolm Wells had been extravagant enough to install plumbing in the house before his untimely false demise.

Blaise slung the basket over his arm and made his way into the cool night air. A gentle breeze tousled his hair, and night insects sang nearby. Not the screaming cicadas from the Gutter, at least. That was a pleasant change.

<Seledora is coming,> Emrys informed him before Blaise even reached the stable. The stallion had his head over the stall door, ears pricked.

True to his word, the dapple grey mare landed with a musical ringing of hooves a moment later. She tossed her head, folding her wings to her sides before striding into the barn.

"How's Jefferson?" Blaise blurted as soon as the pegasus was near. Then he realized he was being rude and pulled a cookie out of the basket. "And welcome back, by the way." He offered the treat in apology.

The mare lipped it from his palm, her dark eyes assessing him. <They've jailed him in the elite wing of the Golden Citadel. All we can do is wait until he has his chance before a magistrate.>

Blaise's stomach clenched at her mention of the Golden Citadel. It brought back too many awful thoughts. He stumbled over to Emrys, his breath ragged as he rested his forehead against the stallion's neck.

<Breathe,> Emrys reminded him, blowing out a loud breath of his own. <Seledora would not have left her rider there if she thought he would come to harm. Right?> One of his ears flicked toward the mare, uncertain.

<I cannot just go in and take him out,> the mare replied, swishing her tail with agitation. <Not even as his attorney.> Then her mental tone softened. <But I do not believe he is in danger of being mistreated. Even as a mage, he is too high-profile.>

She had a point. Jefferson Cole—or Malcolm Wells—was both famous and infamous. Blaise sighed, relaxing a little again. And Emrys was right, too. Now that Seledora had declared Jefferson her rider, she wouldn't want him jailed for long. Pegasi bonded with their riders, and it was difficult to be parted for too long. Though there was no telling if that was the case with Seledora—she was unconventional.

Blaise distracted himself by doling out the basket of treats, having made certain Seledora was properly untacked. He checked to make sure her stall had fresh water and gave her a ration of sweet feed. He even spared a few cookies for the draft horses, who had been taking in the excitement with stoic calm.

<You will see him tonight in your dreams, will you not?> Emrys asked, crunching another cookie. Crumbs tumbled to the straw.

Blaise's hand was sticky with sugar and pegasus saliva. He needed to rinse it off in the water trough soon. "The Cit has salt-iron. I don't think his magic can get past that."

<Salt-iron does very little to *you*, though,> Emrys pointed out.

Blaise frowned at that. "But Jefferson is the one who has to reach out to me."

The stallion considered him with bright eyes, nosing him for another treat. <Your magic does not follow rules. I heard your mother say you can do almost anything with your power.>

Blaise blinked in surprise. Was Emrys insinuating that he might be able to use dream magic? His face scrunched as he considered that. He didn't know how Jefferson used his power, and had never thought to ask because it didn't feel similar to his at all. But Jefferson's magic had spawned from Blaise's. And more than that, they shared a bond that he didn't quite understand. Jefferson had used the thread that connected them, a sliver of Breaker magic, to get through a ward before. Blaise rubbed his forehead.

"You might be right."

<Of course I am. And now, am I right to think you have strawberry tarts?>

An hour later, after the trio of pegasi were sated and content with their sweet treats, he headed back to the house for bed. It was already late, and Blaise wondered if Jefferson had been trying to reach him. Or if he… No. Blaise shook his head. Jefferson was fine. He had to be fine. Seledora had said so.

Blaise climbed into the king-sized bed, gaze lingering on the empty spot beside him. The place Jefferson should have been. He whooshed out a breath to steady himself and then laid down.

Blaise always had a difficult time going to sleep unless he was flat-out exhausted. Too often, he would drift, only to be startled awake by the beginnings of a nightmare. Jefferson was the one who eased him past the nightmares and into sleep. But the Dreamer wasn't there. Blaise clenched his teeth, willing sleep to come. If he could just get to sleep, he had a hope of seeing his beau.

After tossing and turning for far too long, he finally drifted. At first, his mind took over, sending him into a strange dream. He was at the station in Ondin, waiting for their train to arrive. Blaise was alone, except for a black bird that hopped on the ground behind him. Every time he turned to look at the bird, it hopped behind something to obstruct his view. That was odd, but he didn't worry about it for long. A sound that reminded him of the jingle of the bell over his bakery door announced the train's arrival. The locomotive pulled into the station, though it looked more like a loaf of bread than a train—

Blaise frowned as something tickled his mind. A memory. He was missing someone.

Jack appeared out of nowhere. "You're missing a peacock." Then, with a grin, he vanished.

Jefferson. Right, he was supposed to reach the Dreamer, if he could.

He was dreaming, but was he in the actual dreamscape or his own mind? Or were they the same? Blaise didn't know. But he had to try before he lost this precarious grip on his slumbering mind. Already, he felt how easy it would be to flow back into a deeper sleep. He was in the grey area between wakefulness and slumber.

Blaise sought Jefferson, though he felt as if he were floundering in a vast ocean. Jack appeared again, reaching down to pick up a thread as thin as spider silk. "This what you're looking for, kid?"

"Why do I include your insults in my dreams?" Blaise asked as he plucked the thread from the outlaw's outstretched hand. Then he paused, a thought occurring to him. "Wait. Are you the real Jack, or...?"

The Effigest shook his head. "Nah. You ain't good enough to track down the real me, Breaker." He vanished again, leaving Blaise alone with the thread and the bird.

"I kind of prefer *my* magic to this confusion," Blaise muttered, focusing on the thread. Strangely enough, Dream Jack was right. This wisp led to Jefferson.

He turned, tugging on it with both hands. The thread widened in his grip until it was a rope. Blaise heard a confused exclamation, and Jefferson appeared.

The rope tangled around the other man's waist like a lassoed calf. Jefferson glanced down at it, then at Blaise. "Oh. That was *you?*"

"Yes," Blaise mumbled, though he felt the fist of deepening sleep tighten around him.

The bells of the bread-locomotive chimed again, claiming Jefferson's momentary attention. "Of course, you would have a train made of rye. I suppose I'd better do something before I lose you."

"Don't want to lose you," Blaise echoed with a yawn. The scenery flickered around him like a guttering candle.

"No, no, you can rest once I have control of this place," Jefferson murmured, slipping up beside Blaise and putting an arm around him.

Jefferson's touch roused him. Blaise shook his head. "Sorry. This is hard." So hard. And sleep was such a welcome temptation.

"I know. I'm going to use my power, so you don't have to do all this. But it's a challenge." Jefferson blew out a breath.

Blaise felt the brush of Dreamer magic against him, but it stuttered as if Jefferson were having difficulty. He heard Jefferson make a soft, pained sound and realized that somewhere far away, salt-iron was sapping his beau's magic. Blaise pulled him close and lent him power. Jefferson inhaled sharply, eyes widening as he broke free of the salt-iron drain. All around them, the dreamscape sharpened and gained a new semblance of order as Jefferson took command.

"Ah, that's better. Thank you." Jefferson straightened, composed once more. The gossamer rope hung at his waist like a fashionable belt. "Now you can rest."

The words had weight to them. Blaise felt the pressure of Jefferson's magic release him into a true sleep. He relaxed, though he stayed in the dreamscape. He no longer had to fight to remain in the liminal space between dreams and wakefulness. "That's really hard. I don't know how you manage it."

Jefferson chuckled. "Practice. Lots of annoying practice. How in Tabris's name did you do that? I didn't know you could."

"I didn't know I could either. Emrys suggested it." Blaise

watched as the rye train wavered, shifting into a locomotive of gleaming dark metal. "Don't think I'll be doing it again unless I really have to."

"I'm so glad you tried." Jefferson's voice was gentle. He touched Blaise's chin with one hand, as if he feared Blaise might vanish.

"Are you okay?" Blaise asked, deciding to move on to his chief concerns. The sooner he and Jefferson addressed them, the better. "Seledora came back."

"I was hoping she'd made it back to the estate without issue." Jefferson kept an arm around him, though he tugged Blaise a little closer. The Dreamer was a warm, solid presence and smelled lightly of peppermint. "Aside from the salt-iron, I'm fine. I have enough social standing that they've put me in a posh cell. If not for the bars on the windows and the fact that I can't leave when I wish, you'd think I'm a guest in a fine hotel."

That was good news to Blaise. "No one's hurt you?"

Jefferson made a soft sound of understanding. "No one has harmed me." He moved to sit on a nearby bench that looked like it was made of pretzels. Jefferson waved a hand, and it became polished wood. "I did, however, already merit a visit from a Quiet One."

"Already?" Blaise sat down beside him.

"Yes, they're not wasting any time." Jefferson sighed. "It comes as no surprise, though. It was Phillip Dillon." As he spoke the name, the atmosphere of the surrounding dreamscape darkened for a beat, a sign that the Dreamer was unsettled.

Blaise glanced at him. "What did he say?"

Jefferson's gaze fell on the black bird, which had persisted through the change of dreamscape management. It hopped closer, peering at them with glassy eyes. "To stay out of their affairs. He said if I behaved and stayed in the Cit, he would make certain I was released later."

"*No*," Blaise said without hesitation, his heartbeat racing.

"He promised protection for you as well, if I stay out of matters," Jefferson added, voice soft.

Blaise shook his head. He had come to terms with the idea that he might never be truly safe, and he wasn't willing to rely on the dubious *protection* of a member from the group that had damaged Jefferson's life. "No," he repeated, firm. He wanted to say more, but his throat constricted with emotion.

"That's what I told him, too." Jefferson put a hand on Blaise's knee, patting it.

Blaise hissed out a breath, relaxing. He should have known Jefferson would refuse. "Was that all he came to tell you?"

Jefferson squeezed Blaise's knee. "Oh, there was a bit of classic melodramatic villain drivel. I've heard more threatening lines at a third-rate play."

"I doubt you've ever seen a third-rate play."

The Dreamer grinned. "On that, I'm guilty as charged."

Blaise frowned. "Aren't you worried about what this means for you? For us?"

Jefferson pressed his lips together, quiet for a moment. "They want to take me out of play like a captured pawn. More than that, they want you to stay out of matters as well. They're afraid of us. We have the upper hand."

Blaise wasn't so certain that was what any of this meant, but who was he to dispute it? Jefferson had more experience with these adversaries than he did.

"Did you bake?"

Jefferson's question caught him off guard. It took Blaise a moment to catch up with the change of topic. "Um, yes. I am, in fact, that predictable." And that reminded him... "I think the Quiet Ones targeted the estate."

Jefferson tensed at the suggestion. He frowned. "What do you mean?"

"All the staff are gone. Well, except for one."

Jefferson swore softly, shaking his head. "Blast. I hoped that with the estate in your name, they'd keep their claws out of it. But they found another angle to attack."

Blaise rested his head against Jefferson's shoulder. "It'll be okay. It's dusty, and the garden would horrify you, but it's nothing that can't be fixed."

At that, Jefferson smiled. "You're right. We'll get past this."

Somehow, Blaise knew Jefferson meant more than just the issues with the house. He sighed, but this time with contentment. Jefferson might not be physically with him, but not even the Golden Citadel could keep them apart. And together, they could make things right.

CHAPTER SEVENTEEN

Magic Theory

Jack

The problem with Kittie casting the portal spell was that the locations she knew in Phinora differed from those Jack knew. Ideally, he would arrive straight at Hawthorne House, with no one the wiser to his appearance. But Kittie had never been there. Emmaline had also never been there, so it wasn't as if he could ask for her to assist with that, either.

Kittie crossed her arms as they mulled it over. "I should be the one to go."

"No," Jack snapped before he could stop himself.

"Why don't you cast it together?"

Jack growled, spinning to see Emmaline leaning against the door frame behind them. "How long have you been listening in?"

She grinned shamelessly. "Long enough to know what you're up to."

He glared at her, but he knew he had no one to blame but himself. It was exactly the sort of thing he'd do, after all.

"What do you mean, cast it together?" Kittie asked.

Emmaline became animated at the question. "I've been

thinking about this ever since I cast the portal spell back in Thorn. Daddy, remember the lightning rod spell?"

He pursed his lips. "Yeah. But what does that have to do with this?"

She moved closer, peering down at the paper. "You copied the spell? That was a good idea. Anyway, it has everything to do with this. That lightning rod spell I cast with you was modified from Rising Dread."

Jack frowned, uncertain. "That was a modification of a mage spell."

Emmaline's eyes were bright. "I don't think they're that different. Look, there are parts each of you could cast, and then you bring them together. Just like we did with the lightning rod."

Kittie looked thoughtful but not convinced. "You're both Effigests. That makes it easier for you to work together."

"*Blaise* worked with us, too," Emmaline added.

Yeah, because the Breaker can do impossible things with his magic when he puts his mind to it. Jack studied the spell. Was he being too close-minded about this? It was possible—sometimes, he got stuck on an idea and had a hard time getting beyond it. But what Emmaline suggested was awfully close to his earlier thoughts. "You think we can combine two disparate magics like a coven."

Emmaline nodded. "That's exactly what I think. If not you and Mom, then who?"

"She's got you there," Kittie said, failing to hide an amused smile.

Jack folded the paper and shoved it in his pocket. "Fine. You may be on to something. I can cast the location part of the spell while Kittie powers the travel portion."

"When do we try?" Kittie asked.

Jack rose from the bed. "As soon as I make sure I have enough ammunition and reagents."

Kittie's hand shot out, grabbing his upper arm in a firm grip. "Jack Arthur Dewitt, you are not haring off on this half-cocked."

Her voice was so harsh and earnest that Jack paused. If there was anyone who could get him to slow down, it was Kittie. "Yeah, fine. I get it. I'm just champing at the bit." He shook his head, itching to make his move. But Kittie would be involved in a spell —a wizard spell—she'd never cast before, which meant they needed to be careful. And they still required an Overwhelming Power potion from the alchemist. "I tell you what. You go talk to Marian Hawthorne and make arrangements. I'll make my own preparations, and we'll cast it tomorrow. How's that sound?"

"Realistic," Kittie said, and this time there was amusement in her eyes. "Was that so hard?"

Yes. It was incredibly hard. No one understood the urgency he felt, the drive to do what he could to protect Fortitude and the people he cared about—especially now that Kittie was here. But instead of admitting all that, he kissed her, pleased when she reciprocated.

"Guess it'll give me another night with you," he whispered.

"Ugh." Emmaline rolled her eyes. "Let me know when you're done mauling each other."

CHAPTER EIGHTEEN

One Headache at a Time

Blaise

"You're looking more chipper than I'd expect this morning," Vixen commented as Blaise joined her for breakfast—much later than he'd intended. Once he'd found Jefferson in the dreamscape, he'd given himself permission to rest and relax, which included sleeping past the time his body normally woke him to start a day of work at the bakery.

But Blaise couldn't tell her he felt better because he'd spent the night with Jefferson. Vixen didn't know about the Dreamer's magic, and it wasn't Blaise's place to tell her. He eyed the uninspiring spread of food. Dry toast and scrambled eggs. He brought over a tin of muffins he'd made in his flurry of baking last night and popped it open, offering Vixen one.

"A good night of sleep helps," Blaise finally said, which he decided was close enough to the truth. He nibbled on the muffin, deciding that the next batch needed some additional flavor. Blueberry? Maybe strawberry? "How soon do you think we'll hear something?"

Vixen sighed. "Hard to say. I assume Jefferson's high profile enough that he won't sit around very long."

And that could be good or bad. "But we'll find out in time because he needs his lawyer...right?"

She made a face. "I don't know. There's going to be a bias against him as a mage. And for..." Vixen waved her half-eaten muffin around. "All the other general lying he's done."

Blaise clamped his jaw. It wasn't lying, exactly. Though, he'd be the first to admit Jefferson had a habit of obscuring the truth. "What does this mean for what you came here to do?"

Vixen glanced away, momentarily evasive. "I won't approach the Luminary 'til we have things ironed out with Jefferson. One headache at a time, I think."

If it took too long to free Jefferson, they'd have to reconsider— Blaise didn't know how much time they had before the Confederation moved on the Gutter.

A clatter at the door interrupted his thoughts as Tristan came in, already rumpled from seeing to his work. "Thought you should know your Tracker from last night is coming up the drive." His face was pinched with worry.

Vixen's eyes widened. "Rhys." She dropped her mostly eaten muffin on a plate, rising to head for the door.

Blaise got up as well, but he paused, studying Tristan. The teen was more nervous around the Tracker than seemed normal for a Phinoran. Unless... "Tristan, are you a mage?"

The boy's eyes widened. "N-no," he stammered.

Another reason, then. "You have mages in the family?"

Tristan swallowed. "Something like that, sir—I mean, Mr. Hawthorne."

Blaise sighed. Maybe *sir* was better than *Mr. Hawthorne*. "You don't have to be scared of Rhys. He's on our side." At least, Blaise hoped that was the case. Would things change once Vixen presented herself as the Spark?

Tristan gave him a dubious look. "In my house, they taught us not to trust a Tracker. But if the Breaker does, then maybe I will."

Yeah, okay, Mr. Hawthorne *or* sir *is definitely better than* the Breaker. Blaise rubbed his cheek. "I'm going to go greet our visitor. Are you hungry?" He gestured to the remaining muffins.

"I'm always hungry." Tristan stared at the muffins with a covetous look.

"Enjoy," Blaise urged him, then hurried out to join Vixen.

The three pegasi were out of the stables, and predictably they had flown over the fence so they could join the conversation. Rhys dismounted from Darby as Blaise approached, looking only slightly bemused by their presence. The Tracker nodded a greeting to Blaise.

"Rhys found out when Jefferson's going before the magistrate," Vixen updated him.

Blaise licked his lips. "When?"

"At three this afternoon," Rhys said. He shook his head. "But he's going before one of the worst possible magistrates."

Of course. If the Quiet Ones were pulling the strings, nothing would go in their favor. "In what way?" Blaise asked.

The Tracker rubbed his forehead. "Magistrate Hooper is well known for his anti-mage stance. And he declared this morning that he wouldn't tolerate any *animals* in his court."

Seledora snorted at that, flattening her ears. <I am not an *animal!* I am an attorney.>

Blaise's heart sank. The mare was their best shot at helping Jefferson. His mind raced through other options. They could try to break Jefferson out. However, not only would that be difficult, but it would wreak havoc on their reason for coming to Izhadell in the first place. And Blaise didn't know if he could trust himself to set foot in the Golden Citadel without panicking. The very thought made his heart race and his breath hitch.

Vixen waved a hand in front of his face. "Blaise?"

He blinked, then cleared his throat. "Um, sorry. What?"

The Persuader's silver eyes flicked over him. "I was saying Seledora may not be able to go in, but we can."

Immediately, Blaise shook his head. "I can't." Not because he didn't want to. Though, to be honest, he didn't want to. There was no way he would do anything but stumble over his words in front of the magistrate. "Whether or not I like it, people know who I am. That won't help Jefferson."

Vixen nodded. "Yeah, that's true."

<He doesn't have my training, but with his background in politics, Jefferson stands a chance at defending himself,> Seledora suggested, thoughtful. Her ears twitched. <And if he is not bound by salt-iron, I might even offer him guidance.>

The mare had a good point. Jefferson stood a better chance than any of the rest of them—especially if the pegasus attorney could get through to him. "You think so?"

Seledora bobbed her head, then shifted to face the house. <Yes. But we need to prepare.> She trotted around the side of the manor. <Come along, Blaise. I'll need your hands.>

Vixen gave him a baffled look. "What's she going on about?"

He shook his head. "I don't know, but I'm going to find out." He followed the grey mare toward Hawthorne House.

CHAPTER NINETEEN
I'm Not Judging

Kittie

arian Hawthorne crossed her arms, pinning Kittie with a look as only a mother could. It was an expression Kittie understood all the way to her core. "Is my son in danger?"

"He's in *Izhadell*," Kittie said.

The alchemist snorted from her place behind the counter in her apothecary shop. Kittie wasn't sure why Marian continued with the farce that she was a simple apothecary. Everyone in town knew she was an alchemist. "Fine. Is my son in additional danger?"

That was more like it. Any mage traveling to Phinora was going to be in some level of danger. The remaining Ringleaders had kept Raven's disappearance quiet, and from what Kittie had observed, most of the citizens thought the Shadowstepper had simply left to follow Vixen like a lovesick puppy. She had Jack's blessing to explain more of the situation to Marian Hawthorne, and so she did.

When she'd finished, the alchemist's lips pinched into an unhappy line. "Their task was already hard enough without a rogue mage causing problems." She paused, arching a brow. "And I assume you're telling me this for a reason?"

Kittie nodded. "Jack wants to portal to Izhadell to nip any problems in the bud."

"Does he, now?" Marian's tone was somewhere between impressed and derisive. "Is that wise? Even I know he has quite a record. And he's been foolish enough to risk himself on Confederation land before."

"Multiple times," Kittie agreed. She wasn't going to comment on the wisdom of Jack's decision.

"Hmm." Marian turned, making a circuit around the interior of her shop. It wasn't large and took only a matter of seconds. "I suppose he wants Overwhelming Power, then. You know it will leave him as weak as a day-old kitten afterward, right?"

Kittie swallowed. "We're going to cast the spell together so that he can go through."

"Only him?" Marian arched a single brow, the other remaining firmly in place. Kittie wondered how she managed that. Her own brows kept a united front and only moved together.

"Well..." Now it was Kittie's turn to pause, studying one of the nearby bottles filled with an amber dust.

"I'm not judging." Marian came around the counter, clutching something in her hand. A vial, Kittie supposed, when she saw the slight bulge. "But all I'm saying is I've lost my husband. I know you've only recently reunited with yours, and it's not been easy."

Kittie nodded, thinking of her own travels to Ganland, which had kept her from her husband. Meanwhile, he'd hared off on another dangerous adventure, taking their daughter with him. Marian Hawthorne understood how fragile life and love could be. "I don't *want* him to go, but he's stubborn."

The alchemist extended her hand, a potion cupped in her

palm. "This one's on the house. So that you can go help my son and his friends." Marian smiled. "Your husband doesn't have to be the only stubborn one, you know."

Kittie met Marian's smile with one of her own. "He's not."

CHAPTER TWENTY

Exhibit A

Vixen

*A*lekon tossed his head, glancing back at his rider as they wove through the press of traffic. <This place stinks. I thought we were already in Izhadell at Blaise's house. Is the whole place this crowded?>

"That was well outside the city," Vixen murmured to the stallion's cocked ears. "And yes. Welcome to the city."

<Zepheus told me it stank. I didn't believe him.> Alekon blew out a snotty breath in disgust.

Izhadell was much as Vixen remembered it. Well, she didn't remember the landmarks all that much, but the press of people? That, she recalled. They had constructed new buildings since she'd left, and the streets almost seemed to have narrowed, but perhaps that was because she had grown.

"You really think this will work?" Rhys asked. He had traded his uniform for clothing that allowed him to blend in and had left Darby behind. Seledora had agreed to serve as his mount, which Vixen considered rather progressive for a pegasus. But Seledora prided herself on not being like other pegasi.

Vixen wet her lips. "It's worth a try. What other option do we have?"

He gave a long-suffering sigh. "I already told you the Luminary has the power to pardon someone like your friend."

She had the power, but would she do it? Jefferson was a mage. And more than that, many of the elite despised him. There was no guarantee that her mother would free the ambassador. Besides, Vixen didn't want her first act upon reuniting with her mother to be to beg her for a favor. That wouldn't do.

"I'm not running to mother with my tail between my legs."

"That's not even close to what I'm suggesting!" He shook his head. "It would be really helpful if either of you pegasi would back me up here."

Alekon angled his head to look at Rhys. <You must be new to how pegasi loyalty works. I will always side with my rider. Unless I have a better idea.>

<I remain unconvinced the Luminary would pardon Jefferson,> Seledora said, swishing her tail with agitation. <And I have a saddlebag full of evidence for our case.> As far as Vixen knew, this was true. She hadn't seen the contents of the folders Blaise had packed into the saddlebag, but she knew they'd found something.

Rhys rubbed the bridge of his nose. "This is the most ridiculous circus I've ever been a part of."

"You haven't been around outlaws long enough." Vixen couldn't help but laugh. With everything else going on around them, laughing felt good. She quickly sobered, though, as she caught sight of familiar architecture in the distance. The Asaphenia, the main cathedral built to honor Garus, towered above the other buildings on the horizon. She hadn't realized how close the courts would take her. She tore her gaze from it. "And you didn't have to come along with me."

"I'm your escort." Rhys bristled.

"Yeah, to Izhadell. We got here. Job done," she drawled. "Good work."

He sighed, shaking his head. "No. Your friend shouldn't have been arrested. So my job isn't done." Rhys swallowed. "And besides, you're *you*."

Vixen knew he was avoiding her real name and title, but all the same, his words annoyed her. "If you're going to treat me like a delicate flower, let me just stop you right there. Not interested."

He raised his brows at that, then, in a surprising move, laughed. Rhys nodded. "Your spirit hasn't changed from when we were kids." He gestured to the dour brick building to their right. "We're here. And I suspect your friend is already inside awaiting his turn."

Vixen followed his gaze to a jail wagon parked further up the street. Alekon flattened his ears. <Salt-iron bars on that monstrosity.>

There was a place to tether their *horses* off to one side of the building. As Vixen dismounted, she murmured to Alekon, "Give me a warning if you find any unicorns in the area."

The pegasus snorted, flicking an ear at her with curiosity. <Do I want to ask why?>

"You know me. I'll cheat if it'll give us a win," she whispered back, meaning every word. She rubbed the silver ring, hissing out a breath.

<I heard that,> Seledora said, sounding righteously insulted.

Vixen sighed. She hadn't meant it as an insult to the mare. Vixen didn't trust anyone they were dealing with in Izhadell, and she would much rather be prepared.

After Vixen collected the folders from Seledora's saddlebag, she followed Rhys inside. He walked with confidence, and she realized he must have come here before. She vaguely remembered that sometimes, Trackers brought mages accused of crimes before magistrates. That explained why he knew of this one's biases.

The court was in session with another case. Rhys found a bench to sit on, and she settled beside him, listening as the magistrate heard the defense of a man accused of using magic to kill his neighbor's orchard. The problem, as Vixen saw it, was that the accused wasn't even a mage. Though as the case progressed, she discovered that the man's teenage son had come into power. As the accused spoke, she realized that, while there was bad blood between the neighbors, the arboricide had been accidental as the young mage grappled with learning to control his magic while trying to stay hidden.

"The court orders you to pay the plaintiff ten thousand golden eagles for damages. In addition, the accused mage is indentured to the Salt-Iron Confederation immediately." Magistrate Hooper's eyes gleamed with malevolent glee at the declaration.

The father gasped at the mighty sum, but at the mention of his son, he wailed. "For how long? He's my only son—I need him to help with my—"

"Indefinitely." Hooper took great pleasure in cutting him off.

Vixen's heart sank. Murmurs arose from the gallery as the bailiff led the dejected father out. She had known that this magistrate was unfriendly to mages, but she had forgotten how cold many in the Confederation were towards her kind. She took a deep breath. That was why she was here. To do something about that.

Rhys nudged her. Vixen shook her head, having missed the introduction to Jefferson's trial. The Ambassador strode into the courtroom, his head high. He scanned the assembly, no doubt looking for a familiar face. His gaze settled on her and Rhys, and she didn't miss the disappointed crinkle tug at the corner of his eyes when he realized Blaise wasn't there.

Jefferson

IT HAD BEEN UNREALISTIC TO EXPECT BLAISE TO COME TO THE court. Jefferson knew that, but all the same, he had hoped. He gave a tiny shake of his head, refocusing. *Think about Blaise later. Better still, be* with him *later.* Yes, that was the goal. Focus on this. Win.

"Doyen Wells, do you have representation?" Magistrate Hooper asked.

Hooper. Jefferson knew this judge. He had an uphill battle ahead of him, and Seledora was nowhere in sight. Vixen caught his eye, and she held up a package—no, a folder. Jefferson smiled, hoping that the contents were what he thought they might be. "I'll be representing myself in this matter." He inclined his head to the gallery. "I'd like to request that my team join me."

Rhys scowled at him. *Well, I suppose he's not Team Jefferson.* Maybe it was best not to have a known Tracker at his side for the moment.

Magistrate Hooper's gaze roved to Vixen, but he nodded. "Proceed."

The Persuader slipped over to him, sliding the folder onto the table in front of Jefferson. "Seledora had Blaise gather some documents for you."

"Outstanding," Jefferson murmured. He looked up at the magistrate. "Would you be so kind as to allow a brief recess?"

"Denied," Hooper barked. "Doyen Wells, you stand accused of identity fraud. How do you plead?"

Jefferson pursed his lips. Correcting Hooper on the name would get him nowhere. Possibly contempt of court, which wasn't what he needed right now. "Not guilty."

The magistrate stared at him as if he'd turned into a tap-dancing cockatrice. "Doyen Wells, are you aware that in this court, you're compelled to convince *me* otherwise?"

"How in Perdition are you going to manage that?" Vixen whispered.

Jefferson met his gaze. "Magistrate Hooper, as I understand it, I'm charged with fraud because there is reason to believe that Jefferson Cole is not my identity. However, I believe—"

"I don't have all day, Doyen Wells. Present your evidence."

Jefferson's jaw snapped closed. He did, in fact, have all day if needed. That was the way court worked in Phinora. But that didn't mean Hooper abided by the rules. Most likely, Hooper already planned to strike down any evidence Jefferson provided. He hoped that whatever Seledora had sent along was ironclad.

Swallowing, he opened the folder and thumbed through the pages. A sense of calm settled over him. Yes, he knew these forms. *I could just kiss that mare.* The only thing better would be if she could also guide him, but the salt-iron shackles on his wrists prevented it. Jefferson pulled out a handful of papers. "As I was saying, I've been charged with identity fraud. The burden is upon me to prove that I am, in fact, Jefferson Cole."

Hooper looked bored already. He leaned on an elbow. "Then do so."

And I will. Jefferson smiled. "Exhibit A: this notarized form from Rainbow Flat, where Malcolm Wells established Doing Business As paperwork for Jefferson Cole." That form was a closely guarded secret, which was why it had been filed originally in Rainbow Flat, a town indebted to him. Afterward, to guard his dual personas, he had stored the paperwork in a safe in the library at Hawthorne House. Seledora knew of it and must have urged Blaise to retrieve it.

The magistrate shrugged. "Jefferson Cole is a business, not a person."

He knows exactly how to annoy me. Jefferson huffed out a breath, pulling out another paper. "Exhibit B: this contract between two parties. One, Blaise Hawthorne, and the other, Jefferson Cole, for the joint establishment of a bakery in Nera." *Blast, and I told myself I wasn't going to think about Blaise.*

"Phinora doesn't recognize contracts made with mages." Hooper smirked.

Jefferson almost crumpled the contract in his fist. "May I remind the court that Breaker Blaise Hawthorne is currently the only land-owning mage in the Confederation? Thus, the contract is valid."

"And I will continue not to recognize it," Hooper shot back.

Jefferson straightened. It was time to call the judge on his dragonshit. The other defendants couldn't do it, but maybe he could. "Magistrate Hooper, you've set me the impossible task of changing your mind when it's clear that you intend to refute every piece of evidence I set forward. How is any mage expected to have a fair trial under these conditions?"

Hooper's eyes glittered. "You have yet to provide irrefutable evidence that you didn't commit fraud by taking the identity of Jefferson Cole."

"You can't win," Vixen whispered. "He won't let you."

Jefferson swallowed. She was right. He couldn't. Every scrap of evidence Seledora and Blaise had gathered wouldn't be enough for this man. "Leave me, Vixen." He hated to say it—he would lose the case. Phillip Dillon was making certain Jefferson didn't go free. Hooper would sentence him to time in the Cit. Possibly indenture. No, it wouldn't come to that. Blaise would come. He would tear the Golden Citadel apart.

"Not going to happen." Vixen tucked a lock of brilliant hair behind one ear. Jefferson glanced down to see her work the ring from her finger. Before he could caution her against it, she had it caged in her fist as she stepped around the table, smiling at Hooper.

Jefferson couldn't hear what she said, but it didn't matter because he knew her words weren't for him. He saw Hooper's full attention fall on Vixen, snared by her power.

"No magic!" a voice bellowed.

Jefferson blinked in surprise. It took him a moment to realize it was Rhys. He turned and saw the young Tracker standing at the front of the gallery, fists clenched, as he glared at Vixen. The Persuader whirled, jamming the ring back on her finger.

Hooper shook his head like a dog shedding water. "What?

Magic?" His glare fell on Jefferson first, then snapped to Vixen. "Tracker Kildare, I didn't recognize you out of uniform. Thank you for your intervention. Bailiff! Remove these mages from my court!"

Vixen stared at her brother, her expression desolate. She didn't put up a fight as a bailiff hooked a hand around her arm and led her to the exit. Jefferson balked when another bailiff came for him.

"I will not allow my documents to remain here," he told the woman, which he felt was very reasonable. She crossed her arms but allowed him to gather them up. Jefferson looked at Rhys. "Could you at least get these back to the house for me?"

The Tracker's mouth was set in a grim line, but he nodded. Jefferson suspected he felt guilty for ruining Vixen's gambit.

A moment later, he was loaded back into his least favorite form of transportation, the salt-iron reinforced jail wagon. Though, unlike his first trip, he was no longer alone. Vixen sat beside him.

"Sorry, but I had to try," she said.

"I know," Jefferson murmured. He rubbed the back of his neck, uncomfortable from the metal enclosing them. "It was never a trial I could win, not even with everything Seledora brought. And now I don't know how we're going to get out of this mess."

Vixen sighed. "I do."

"It's not Blaise taking apart the Citadel brick by brick, is it?" There wasn't a hint of humor in Jefferson's question. They both knew it wasn't an exaggeration.

The Persuader shook her head. "No. But I'd almost prefer that."

CHAPTER TWENTY-ONE

An Army of Gladiatorial Poultry

Blaise

He had to get out of the house. Guilt at abandoning Jefferson to his fate with the magistrate ate at Blaise —even though he knew he'd made the right choice to stay behind. With Vixen gone, the house was far too empty, and even the kitchen reminded Blaise of the jailed Dreamer. He needed a change of scenery, and he needed it now.

He almost jogged from the house to the barn. Rhys's silvery blue unicorn stallion grazed in the nearest paddock and lifted his head, nostrils flaring as the light breeze carried the scent of Breaker magic to him. But Darby did little more than read the scent before settling back to grazing. Blaise strode into the barn, heading for the tack room.

<What are we doing?> Emrys peered at Blaise curiously as the Breaker hauled saddle blanket, saddle, and hackamore out.

"I need..." Blaise hesitated as he balanced the saddle on the aisle floor, horn and pommel down. "It's hard to stay here doing nothing."

<We're going for an outing?> Emrys brightened. <Or must we stay on the estate?>

Blaise had the distinct impression that Emrys, too, was eager to leave the confines of Hawthorne House. "There's a market nearby, according to Tristan. I was thinking we could go there. See what they have." He opened the stall door, and the pegasus ambled out, standing square in preparation for being saddled.

<Oh, markets are good,> Emrys agreed, trying to sound nonchalant but failing. His interest in the potential for future treats was too strong.

As if summoned by the mention of his name, Tristan strode into the stables, whistling. "Mr. Hawthorne, I was thinking...since you're new around here, maybe I should show you how to get to the market."

Blaise hadn't even thought of that. He nodded. "Sure. I'd appreciate that."

Tristan grinned, hurrying to grab a saddle and bridle for a draft horse.

It wasn't long before both the pegasus and the draft horse were tacked up and ready. Blaise gave Emrys's girth a last tug before swinging into the saddle. The stallion ambled out of the stable, wings shimmering out of existence as he took on the guise of a normal horse. Tristan made a soft sound of astonishment at the trick.

Tristan tapped his heels against his mount's rounded barrel, the big beast lumbering ahead of Emrys. "Let's go. Follow me!"

Blaise took a deep, refreshing breath as Emrys's hooves rang on the gravel of the road, easily keeping up with the drafter. Maybe for a bit, he could relax and just...be. He could master his slumbering fear of Phinora, of the Golden Citadel. Of everything he'd endured on his last trip to the city. Blaise listened to the cheerful birdsong in the trees lining the road; watched the play of shadows across Emrys's dark neck. A hint of a smile tugged the corners of his lips.

Emrys glanced back at him. <We should have done this sooner if it makes you happy.>

Blaise agreed. He forgot how liberating it was to ride Emrys without having to worry about anything. All he had to do for the moment was stay astride as Emrys kept pace with Tristan's mount.

They followed the twists of the road, Blaise enjoying the simple peace of being with Emrys out in the world. He held the reins loose in his hands—there was no need to guide the stallion. But he still had to uphold the farce that they were a normal horse and rider.

"Not far now!" Tristan crowed, turning to flash a grin back at Blaise.

And he was right. Emrys's ears pricked forward, catching the buzz of sounds from the market. They followed a bend in the road, and then it spread before them: an assortment of tents and cobbled-together stalls that looked like a scene more at home in the Untamed Territory than the outskirts of Izhadell.

The marketplace reminded Blaise of home. Not Fortitude— but Bristle, his original home in Desina. Stalls lined pathways, makeshift tables set up to allow men and women to hawk their wares. It was a veritable feast for the eyes. Brightly dyed bolts of fabric vied for attention with artfully designed canisters of spices, fresh vegetables, hand-tooled leather goods, furs, and more that Blaise couldn't take in.

<Busy place,> Emrys commented, though he didn't sound pleased. The tight quarters meant he wouldn't be able to stay near his rider.

"Yeah," Blaise agreed, though for once, when he encountered a mob of people, he didn't feel fear—he felt a frisson of anticipation. No one turned to look at him as if he were unusual. No one knew him at all. There was a strange sense of freedom in that.

"There's a place for the...er, horses...over this way," Tristan said, guiding his mount to the right and aiming an apologetic look at Emrys. Blaise was glad the boy had erred on the side of caution.

Blaise found a hitching post where he made a show of tying Emrys, though he used a knot Jack had shown him—one Emrys could easily pull loose with his dexterous lips if needed. The stallion sighed heavily as Blaise put the finishing touch on it. Blaise scratched Emrys beneath his forelock. "I'll pick up a treat for you."

The pegasus perked up. <I would like that.> He blew out a contented breath.

"I have to run an errand while we're here," Tristan declared, though he shifted his weight as if nervous. "Is that okay?"

Blaise nodded. "Sure. I'm going to wander and take in the sights before I decide what I'd like to buy."

With that decided, Blaise parted from Tristan and wound slowly through the organized chaos. He kept one hand near the pouch at his belt, on guard against pickpockets. This was the first time he'd shopped anywhere outside of Fortitude in ages.

Blaise meandered through the market, smiling as merchants tried to draw his attention to their wares. He made a mental note of the locations of the spices and fresh fruits—those would be worth another visit before he left. There was a confectioner with tempting candies, too.

It took an hour, but he finally made a full circuit of the place. The market was lively and charming. Blaise liked it and hoped he could return to visit again. He stopped by the spice merchant and treated himself to canisters of allspice and cinnamon, even chatting with the young woman when she asked how he planned to use them. She was interested to hear of his baking and asked if he was thinking of opening a stall at the market in the future.

The suggestion was a shock—and a thrill. Blaise loved his bakery in Fortitude and missed it. It was tempting to consider renting a stall, even for a short time. He knew Jefferson would tell him to do it. Blaise told her he'd think about it, and she gave him the contact information for the man who ran the market in case he wanted to pursue the idea.

As he rounded a corner, a vendor he had overlooked captured Blaise's attention. The jeweler's setup wasn't as flashy as others. But there were artfully crafted loops of gleaming rings with intricate etchings, delicate chain bracelets, and metal necklaces hammered into different shapes.

The artisan was busy with another customer. Blaise leaned over to inspect a row of rings nestled on a layer of velvet. They were simple pieces, a far cry from the gaudy grandeur of Jefferson's cabochon ring. Blaise smiled at the thought, pulse racing as a realization occurred to him.

Gingerly, he picked up one ring. *He makes me happy. Wouldn't this be the next step?* Blaise swallowed. The next step, perhaps, but a big step. One that was a little scary. But was it more frightening than the thought of life without the Dreamer? That was a straightforward answer. *No.*

"See something you like?"

Blaise almost dropped the ring. He'd been so deep in thought he hadn't noticed the crafter shift over to his side. He settled the ring back in place, his face warming. "Um, your work is nice." It was the weakest compliment possible, and Blaise knew it. *Ugh.*

The vendor, an older man with a great bristle of silver brows, peered at him as if he were a curiosity. "Thank you. If you like that ring, it's yours."

What? Blaise took a step backward, shaking his head. "No, I couldn't possibly."

The artisan smiled. "Did you see what I etched on the sides?" He winked.

If he was so proud of it, then why would he want to give it away? Blaise frowned. A part of him wanted to flee, but a larger part found this man disarming and curious. Blaise licked his lips, picking up the ring again to study the delicate engraving. At first, he thought it was a pattern of galloping horses, but then he noticed the fanciful wings. Pegasi. This man, so deep in Confederation land, had etched a ring with pegasi. Blaise knew enough to understand that was unusual.

"Are you a mage?" Blaise asked.

The man picked up a polishing cloth and a nearby bangle. "There are those who say what I do must be magic. But it's all good, old-fashioned know-how." He set the cloth aside, shifting the bangle so it caught the light. A moment ago, its surface had been as smooth as butter. Now it boasted a similar etching to the ring.

A maverick. This man was a mage. "I should go."

The artisan mage put the bangle down beside the cloth. "Wait. Please take the ring you were admiring, with my thanks. It would honor me."

He knows who I am. Of that, Blaise was certain. But what could he do? If Blaise denied it, he might only draw more attention. Relenting, he stepped closer to the booth. "Thank you." He plucked the ring from the velvet, hardly believing this maverick was gifting it.

The vendor pulled out a small cloth carry-sack, holding it out. "So you don't lose it." When Blaise moved to accept it, the man continued to speak. "I was advised to watch for you." The jeweler glanced past Blaise's shoulder. "You should know there are others watching you, too. Those who work against you."

A chill threaded down Blaise's spine. "What?"

"You heard, Breaker. But there are also those who will back you. You're not alone." The mage thumped a fist to his chest.

Swallowing, Blaise pulled back. He shoved the bag with the pegasus ring deep into a pocket. "I need to go." He almost missed the artisan's grave nod as he pivoted to head back down the aisle.

He was six rows from Emrys when two men stepped into his path. If they had been in the crowded section of the market, Blaise would have thought they'd had no choice but to be jostled into the way. But this aisle was empty, the stalls vacant. Their looming appearance drew him up short, clutching his purchases.

"You made a big mistake," one of the men rumbled.

Don't panic. Blaise sucked in a deep breath, struggling to master himself. He frowned, doing his best to stay calm despite the way his heart had broken into a gallop. His brain scrambled to make some sort of response, and he blurted the only thing that came to mind. "Did I insult a local baker?"

His question confused the men momentarily. They paused, trading befuddled looks. But they weren't alone. Another man stepped up behind Blaise. "We know who you are, *Breaker*. And you're coming with us."

No. Panic surged, and for a brief, terrible moment, he was back in the Golden Citadel, tied to a chair, completely at the mercy of his captors. He froze—right until one of the men reached out, grabbing his arm.

The sensation of rough fingers biting into his flesh snapped him back to reality. *No. Never again.* Still clutching his spices in the crook of his right elbow, he reached up with his left hand, wrapping his fingers around his assailant's wrist.

"*Let go.*" Blaise almost didn't recognize the snarl as his own voice. It sounded too deep, too rough. Downright feral. But the man didn't let go, instead digging his fingers in to tighten his hold. Blaise sent a jolt of Breaker magic out, intending only to cause discomfort and make his point.

The man screamed as a sick crackling, snapping sound filled the air. He jerked away from Blaise, his wrist and hand flopping uselessly, the bones shattered by the force of Blaise's magic. Pulse thundering, Blaise shrunk back as the injured man shrieked, falling to his knees as he hugged his broken arm against his chest. Gods, he hadn't meant to do that. He'd only wanted the man to release him.

An old memory reared up. Heathcliff, a guard at the Golden Citadel. Heathcliff grabbing Blaise's arm to force him into the room where Gregor Gaitwood tortured him and tried to bind him with the geasa. Blaise's panic overcoming him. Heathcliff's scream as Breaker magic shattered his wrist.

<Blaise? Blaise!>

Emrys's mental voice roused Blaise from the suffocating memory. He shook his head. He hadn't succumbed to the panic for long—the remaining pair hadn't closed the distance to him yet. But one of them had drawn a revolver, and now the weapon was trained on Blaise.

"No more tricks. You're coming with us," the armed man said, voice low.

"No, he's not!" Both men whirled at the voice, and it took Blaise a second to realize it was Tristan. The boy threw something at the man with the revolver. It was a baked apple or perhaps a rotten one. Whatever it was, the teen's aim was true. The fruit hit the man in the face and splattered into a blinding, saucy mess. "Mr. Hawthorne, go!"

Even with Tristan's appearance, the men were undaunted. The one with the revolver cursed, wiping fruit from his face and lifting his weapon to aim at the teen. Blaise dodged his other assailant, tripping the man, though it was mostly unintentional. He dove at the man holding the gun, ripping the weapon from his hand with a growl.

Tristan pelted the downed man with more fruit. The disarmed attacker spun toward Blaise, hands reaching out like claws, seeking the weapon. "Give that back!"

The rhythmic thunder of Emrys's hooves heralded the stallion's arrival. Blaise took a few steps back, glad that the man couldn't see clearly with the apple grit in his eyes. He glanced down at the revolver, pulse pounding as he realized the only way out of this. "You want it back? Catch."

Blaise sent a tendril of magic into the weapon, this time mindful of what he did. Not panicked, as he had been when the first man grabbed him, but this time as deliberate as baking a cake. A precise expenditure of magic.

Emrys skidded up, dust swirling behind him like a miniature tornado. Blaise shoved a foot into the stirrup, looking at Tristan. "Get out of here!" By the time he spoke the last syllable, his bottom thudded against the saddle, the ebony stallion whirling to dash away from the market.

Ten seconds later, a sharp *boom* reverberated behind them. Emrys shied to the right at the unexpected sound, ears flattened. <What was that?>

"A warning," Blaise said, voice grim. He wasn't proud of anything he'd done back there. His stomach churned at the memory of snapping bone. Blaise tried to tell himself it had been necessary, even if it was an accident. That those men would have done far worse to him. He hoped Tristan had gotten to safety.

And it wasn't over. Not yet. Riders broke out of the cover from the side of the road, their horses surging to cut Emrys off, blocking the stallion. Emrys's hooves tore into the ground as he slid to a stop, abruptly shifting backward.

<I'm going to fly,> Emrys warned. Blaise was fine with that. Whatever got them out of this mess.

There wasn't enough room ahead for Emrys to take off, so with the riders closing in, he pivoted and galloped back in the direction they had come. His huge hooves rang out like thunder as his speed increased, wings rippling into existence.

Magic sizzled as something shot out of the ground a half-dozen strides ahead of them. Emrys was going too fast and could do little more than dodge to the left to avoid the construct. Blaise didn't see what it was—but he certainly felt it when something clamped around his right leg, jerking his foot from the stirrup.

For a gut-wrenching second, Blaise thought his boot would tangle with the stirrup and he would be dragged alongside Emrys. But that *something* had a tight grip on his leg, tearing him free of the saddle, the pegasus squealing in rage as he lost his rider.

The world spun around Blaise in a confusing jumble. Breath

whooshed from his lungs as he struck the too-hard ground. He
rolled before coming to a stop. Everything hurt, and his lungs
desperately tried to suck in fresh air. Blaise was distantly aware of
Emrys's frantic mental pleas, but his brain was too dazed to
understand.

There was a peal of thunder, and Blaise thought maybe there
was a storm—but no, it was hooves as a dozen riders moved to
ring him. No, not a dozen. When he blinked, there were fewer.
Maybe six.

A muddle of voices added to his confusion. Emrys's shadowy
form was a blur in the corner of his vision as the stallion swung
around, pawing at the ground as he prepared to charge at their
foes. Blaise shook his head, the world slowly returning to focus.

A pulsating black chain wrapped around his right leg,
anchoring him to the ground. It didn't hurt, not like Lamar Gaitwood's wicked cage had, but Blaise knew this had to be the work
of another Trapper. Wincing, banged-up parts of his body
complaining about the motion, he sat up. He'd torn one of his
sleeves, and the sticky warmth of blood oozed from a gash on his
elbow. He dismissed that as unimportant for now.

Blaise focused on the manacle. Magic pooled in his hands, and
it only took the barest of touches to shatter the arcane chain.

Emrys had moved in front of him, blocking their pursuers, but
the Trapper hadn't left the stallion unhindered. A pulsating fetter
wrapped around the stallion's right hind leg, tethering him in
place.

Blaise swallowed, assessing their situation. Five men slowly
circled them, and a sixth, who was surely the Trapper, stood
stationary as he focused on his targets. Another chain snapped out
of the dirt, seizing Blaise's left leg. It was more an annoyance than
anything else, and with a flick of his wrist, he shattered the magic.

<Free me, and let's get out of here!> Emrys's eyes were ringed
with white as he tossed his head.

Blaise nodded, expression grim as he studied their enemies.

They outnumbered him and Emrys, and Blaise knew he would have to leverage everything he had to win. He drew on his observations of Jack, channeling the Effigest's ruthless swagger. "Leave while you still can."

<Oh, that was good. Very intimidating. Let me try.> Emrys pinned his ears, snaking his head and snapping his teeth in warning. The stallion squealed, the sound echoing with fury.

At Blaise's words, the men paused, then guffawed. Their laughter was cruel, reminiscent of the bullies Blaise had encountered all his life. "You talk big, but you're only one man, Breaker," a burly man to Blaise's left said.

"That's what your friends back at the market thought, too." Blaise tasted the salty tang of blood in his mouth, and he spat it out. His tongue hurt. He must have bitten it during the fall.

His bold words didn't have quite the effect he'd hoped for. Or maybe they were too effective. The Trapper summoned more chains in quick succession. They lashed up from the ground with blinding speed, wrapping around Blaise's forearms before he could react. The chains pulled taut, forcing him down to the dirt. Gravel bit into his palms. He heard the telltale rattle and felt more wrap around his legs, waist, and then his neck, pinning him down.

<Blaise!> With his face pressed against the dirt, facing away from the pegasus, Blaise could only hear Emrys's mental cries and the sound of his hooves grinding against the gravel.

"You're coming with us, Breaker," another of the men said.

Dirt had gotten into his mouth, and Blaise spat it out. He couldn't let it end like this, for him or for Emrys. Maybe he couldn't get a grip on the arcane chains, but he wasn't ready to give in. His fingers clawed into the ground as he channeled his power.

"Let him go!" It was a voice Blaise had heard before, but he couldn't place where he knew it from. Female. He was too frazzled to think beyond that. Too busy trying to force his magic to undermine the chains anchored to the ground. Shouts and curses burst around him, followed by what had to be a skirmish.

His magic broke a great furrow into the road beneath him. The chain holding his right arm flew loose for an instant. It flailed like the tentacle of some great kraken, then dove downward as if it sought to root itself again. But Blaise's hand was free, and that was all he needed. When he moved, everything hurt, but he grasped the fetter on his left wrist and used his magic to snap it. Then he repeated the same for the opposite hand before the right chain found purchase again.

"No!"

Blaise was fairly certain that outraged howl came from the Trapper, who then yelled something he couldn't quite make out. Blaise staggered to his feet, his abused muscles complaining, accompanied by the damp sensation of blood trickling down his right leg. A downward glance revealed that he'd shredded the fabric at his knee in his fall, and the flesh beneath wasn't much better.

His attackers squared off against a trio of newcomers. Blaise had seen them before...on the train. He swallowed as he realized the woman was the same one from the dining car.

Blaise limped over to Emrys, crouching to free the stallion from his fetters. His power crackled against them, and they dissipated into a fine, dark mist.

<Thanks. You don't look good. Do you think you can mount?> Emrys bumped his soft nose against Blaise's shoulder, blowing out a worried breath. The stallion's ears flicked back and forth as he followed the sounds of fighting.

"No," Blaise whispered. Not without Emrys kneeling, at any rate. And he couldn't leave his mysterious rescuers to fight his battles. Even if he really, really wanted to run away.

The stallion seemed to follow his thoughts. <They're here to stop your capture. If you stick around and end up caught, it's going to make all this for nothing.>

A good point, but Blaise didn't want the assailants to see him as a coward. As easy pickings. Better to dissuade them from coming after him again. He sucked in a breath, then took a shaky step forward.

Blaise didn't get very far, though. And he didn't end up rejoining the fight at all. Blaise saw the woman—Holly, that was her name—dance out of the fray as a huge rooster strutted onto the scene. She reached down to pick him up, her lips moving as if she were crooning to the fowl. In her arms, the rooster's bulk almost hid the woman from view. The rooster's head reared back, and he crowed, the sound slicing through the grunts and dull thuds of fighting.

<Um, are you seeing what I'm seeing?> Emrys snorted in alarm.

Maybe Blaise had hit his head. Surely he wasn't seeing a veritable flood of chickens running toward them. Their taloned feet rasped as they found purchase on the gravel, heads swiveling this way and that as they clucked and grumbled. Blaise was used to chickens, having raised his share of them in the past, but he'd never seen so many moving as one, like an army of gladiatorial poultry.

The rooster crowed again, and the chickens joined the fray.

The former attackers shouted as birds shot toward them, pecking with their sharp beaks and harrying with talons, wings flapping. A man lashed out savagely, and a hen fell away with a broken squawk, feathers blowing loose in the wind. More of the birds fell, but it didn't matter. Three more arose for every one that shrieked as a killing blow landed.

With shouts, the attackers scrambled for their horses. Hens launched onto their backs, beaks latching onto ears as they beat at the humans with their wings. The assailants rode off in disarray, leaving behind a sea of milling birds.

The rooster crowed again, and just as quickly as they had arrived, the chickens retreated, hurrying away to their...well,

Blaise assumed they must have come from nearby farms. There was no other explanation he could come up with.

Emrys shook his head and neck, mane flying with the movement. The stallion positioned himself between Blaise and the unfamiliar mages, snorting a warning.

"We're on your side," the woman hoisting the rooster called around the bird's feathery bulk.

Blaise swallowed, placing a hand on Emrys's side. That was a mistake—his ravaged skin complained at the touch. "Thanks." He probably should have said more than that, but he wasn't sure what. He might not have walked away from that fight without their help, and he didn't like that thought.

The pair of male mages accompanying Holly moved to either side of the woman. "Blaise Hawthorne?" one of the men asked. He had sandy hair and a shadow of stubble on his jaw. The other man was bald and had a silver earring. Blaise had definitely seen him on the train.

Blaise nodded, but the approach of new hooves interrupted them. Emrys blew out a worried breath, but relaxed at the sight of the grey drafter rounding the bend. Tristan was perched on the gelding's back.

"Tristan!" Holly called as the teen reined the horse to a halt, dropping from the saddle. As soon as he hit the ground, she jostled the rooster in her arms to make room for the boy, pulling him into a hug.

Blaise raised his brows at that. "Tristan, is there something you want to tell me?"

The teen grinned, shrugging out of the woman's embrace to hike a thumb in her direction. "Yeah. She's my mom."

CHAPTER TWENTY-TWO
Maverick Underground

Blaise

"We're called the Maverick Underground," said the sandy-haired man, who had introduced himself as Ryan. He was a sort of mage Blaise had never heard of before, specializing in cleaning. As they'd left the scene of the attack, he'd joked that he would have been more of an asset in the battle if he'd had a mop and broom handy.

They sat in the kitchen at Hawthorne House. Blaise had decided that whatever was afoot needed to be explained somewhere private, and the house seemed the best bet. It had provided a chance for him to clean and bandage the worst of his wounds before bringing out leftover cookies and tarts. He wanted to use the healing potion his mother had sent along, but decided to wait until he was alone.

The trio of mavericks made their formal introductions. Holly Lewis, the self-styled Chicken Mage and Tristan's mother, was really a form of Beastcaller. The balding man's name was Daniel, and he was a Greenmage specializing in roots. Blaise's stomach had clenched when he'd learned the man's name. His mind had wandered to his deceased father, who shared the name, but Ryan's words brought him back to the conversation.

"What's the Maverick Underground?" Blaise asked. "I know what a maverick is, but I haven't heard the rest of it."

Holly smiled. "Good. If people knew about us, that would be a problem. We're mages who are tired of our treatment by the Confederation."

Daniel leaned forward in his chair, pinning Blaise with an intense gaze. "My brother was in the Cit when you were there." Blaise's pulse sped at the mention of the Golden Citadel, and he took a breath to calm himself so he could focus. "After the Breaker Inquiry, they freed him along with the rest of the mages who had been abused."

"Oh." Blaise had given little thought to the other mages who had been in the Cit, mostly because he did his best to forget everything about it. He licked his lips to settle his rising nerves. *This isn't about me.*

The Greenmage's gaze dropped to the table, where a half-eaten tart rested on a plate before him. "I thought with his release that everything would be okay. I knew he'd been hurt—he had the scars to prove it. But he wasn't the same after..." He shook his head, pushing his plate away.

Blaise's stomach twisted. He understood that far better than he wanted to admit. "What happened to him?"

Everyone else in the kitchen was silent, even Tristan, who had been munching on a piece of crunchy toast. Daniel's voice shook when he spoke. "My brother was an Animancer...sort of a mix between a Healer and a Greenmage. Not as rare or powerful as a Breaker, but unusual enough to be interesting." He took a ragged breath. "Shawn knew that his freedom would be fleeting, and he begged me to help him leave the Confederation. So I did what any brother would do. Together we set out, traveling overland because it's the only safe path for a maverick."

Blaise swallowed. He didn't know if he wanted to hear any

more of this story. He already knew it couldn't end well. But everything about this sounded important. Blaise nodded in encouragement.

"We were almost to the Godspines when a Tracker and unicorn caught our trail. I told Shawn I'd distract them and he should go ahead, find a place to hide. Greenmages like me are a copper a dozen. And I thought...I thought we were going to be okay." Daniel swiped a tear from one cheek. "I did distract the unicorn and Tracker. But by the time I found Shawn..." The Greenmage's shoulders quaked. "He was so afraid of being caught. Shawn swore he'd never go back. I guess...I guess that's why he took his own life."

Blaise's breath caught. Daniel stared at his hands, as if expecting Blaise to ask why his brother had done that. He didn't have to ask. No, he knew those dark thoughts. The desperate idea that death offered the only freedom and safety. He'd never entertained those thoughts for long, but he understood.

"I'm sorry," Blaise whispered. Tears stung his eyes.

Daniel sighed. "I didn't tell you this for your sympathy. I told you because you know the torment he went through. Not only that, you didn't let it destroy you."

This mage had no idea how wrong he was. The Cit had damaged Blaise in ways few understood. But there was no use trying to explain that now.

"*You* are why we formed the Maverick Underground," Holly said, picking up where Daniel left off. "Because you gave us hope that if only we can get our fellow mages and mavericks to a safe place, they can heal."

Jefferson's long-ago words came back to Blaise: *you're not the only one hurt by the Cit. Be the voice for the voiceless.* And now it seemed he was the hope for the hopeless. It should have been flattering, but Blaise had never felt as if he were someone people should look up to.

"So, what does that have to do with all of this?" He gestured around them, though he meant more than just the kitchen. "You were on the train. And Tristan was somehow the only person left working here."

Ryan nodded at that. "The Maverick Underground is more than just the three of us. We're a network of mages throughout the Confederation. This allows us to ferry mages out safely, with the added benefit of netting information."

"As soon as we intercepted the letter saying you were coming to Izhadell, we set to work. We'd been watching this house and knew that all the help had been hired away." Holly nodded to her son. "I made sure Tristan was employed here while we ferreted out how you were traveling to Izhadell."

Blaise had mixed feelings about this. The group's network was impressive—and Jack would be most interested in the informational aspect—but Tristan was, in essence, a spy. What if he had been working for the Quiet Ones instead of the Maverick Underground? "That was how you ended up on the same train," Blaise guessed.

Holly nodded. "Yes. We wanted to be certain you made it here without incident."

That brought Blaise back to the earlier battle. "How did you know to come help me?"

Tristan was the one with the answer to that. He had a guilty look on his face as he explained. "I've been keeping the MU updated on you. When we got to the market, I sent a message by chicken that you were there, and they were the closest to come keep an eye on things."

Blaise frowned, crossing his arms. He quickly regretted that—the skin on his arms was scraped up from his earlier fall. "I don't like being spied on."

The three mages exchanged regretful looks. "I'm sorry we couldn't tell you sooner. But if the Confederation knew that mages were working together like this..." Holly trailed off.

She had a point. The Maverick Underground would be

squelched if they were known. "I can imagine." Blaise worried at his lower lip. "But why so much interest in me? It sounds like you have a lot on your plate."

They gave him incredulous looks. "Because you're the *Breaker*," Ryan said, as if it were that simple.

"As brave as you are, you wouldn't come to Izhadell without reason." Daniel studied him, as if searching for the ghost of his lost brother in Blaise's visage. "You've done so much. And we're here to help you in any way that we can."

Blaise had been ready to refute the first point—he was anything but brave. But Daniel's last sentence brought him up short. "Wait, what?"

"The Maverick Underground is at your service."

AFTER THE DAY HE'D HAD, BLAISE WASN'T ALL THAT SURPRISED WHEN Seledora and Alekon returned to the estate, minus their riders. Judging by Seledora's perpetually pinned ears, Blaise figured the pegasi hadn't had the best day, either. The equine attorney's pride had been stung in more ways than one.

<You're taking this news well,> Emrys noted as Alekon and Seledora completed their tale. The black stallion had stayed close, attentive.

Blaise scratched the whorl of hair in the middle of Emrys's forehead. He was still bruised and banged up, but he'd used a potion his mother had labelled USE THIS ONE BLAISE to speed the healing on the worst of his wounds. But as with every potion, it had a cost. It sapped his strength to accelerate the healing, and before long, he'd have no choice but to sleep.

He was about to respond when Seledora slammed a forehoof into the ground. <I hear that thrice-damned unicorn coming. I'm going to give that Tracker a piece of my mind.> She bared her teeth, proving that it might not only be her sharp mind that attacked Rhys.

Blaise hurried out of the stables, though he had to take it easy since his muscles were still complaining. He hadn't noticed that Darby had even left the estate, but he must have gone during the market misadventure. Maybe to avoid the incoming mavericks. Whatever the case, he'd found his rider.

Rhys had dismounted and held his hands up in a placating manner as Seledora shook her head at him, unleashing a barrage of telepathic frustration. She lifted one of her hind hooves, as if she wanted to kick something. Or someone. The Tracker stood still as he weathered the onslaught, though the mare kept it private, so Blaise didn't know what she said.

When at last she finished, Rhys nodded. "I deserved that." His grey eyes settled on Blaise. "I came to apologize and tell you I'm going to make things right. I also brought back Jefferson's papers. They're in my saddlebag." Then he paused, noticing the bandage on Blaise's hand. "What happened to you?"

Blaise didn't feel like recounting his afternoon. He waved away the question, focusing on the more pressing problem. "You betrayed your sister."

<That's one of the many, many things I said.> Seledora snorted.

Rhys winced. "I'll understand if you don't believe me, but I couldn't help it." He waited a beat, as if expecting Blaise to argue. When he didn't, Rhys sighed. "Look, I don't know how much you know about Trackers…"

"I know enough to consider you bad news." Blaise couldn't keep the layer of frost from his words. He'd had a rough day, so he figured it was warranted.

"Ouch," Rhys murmured, but he nodded. "That's fair. I know you have good reason to think that." The Tracker blew out a breath. "This will sound like a sorry excuse, but I can't help reacting when I feel magic being used around me. It's like hearing wood scrape against stone."

The notion of wood scraping stone gave Blaise a sympathetic chill. He wondered if this was unique to Rhys or if all Trackers felt the same. But that didn't matter at the moment. Vixen and Jefferson did.

"Valoria—I mean, Vixen—told me about you. That you're one of the best people she knows, and you'd do anything for your friends," Rhys continued. The words came as a surprise to Blaise, and it took him a moment to absorb them. "I didn't want you to do something rash because of my mistake."

So, the Tracker thought Blaise might make a bid to free Jefferson and Vixen himself. He wasn't up to it tonight, but if they remained in the Cit, all bets were off. Eventually, the drive to help them would be too much, and he'd have to do something. "What are you going to do to fix this?"

"I'll get them out, I promise. It might take a little time. But I wanted you to know before you do anything you might regret."

Blaise studied the Tracker. Rhys seemed earnest and guilty about what he'd done. Could Blaise believe him after this? Trust him? He idly rubbed the bandage on his hand. "Vixen is right. I love my friends, and I'd do almost anything for them." He'd come to Izhadell, a place crawling with terrifying memories, for Jefferson's sake. "You know what I am. And you know what I can do." Blaise felt a little too much like Jack in that moment, veiling his words with threats.

<Maybe you aren't taking this news as well as I thought,> Emrys amended. Then, worried, he added, <I don't want you going near the Cit.> Blaise lifted his unbandaged hand to absently stroke the stallion's nose.

Rhys stiffened. "I'm well aware of what happened at Fort Courage and have heard reports from Thorn. That's what I'm trying to avoid."

"Then we understand one another," Blaise said. Yeah, he

sounded a lot like Jack. He didn't really like it but had to admit it was useful. Exhaustion pulled at him, a reminder of the healing potion's price. He stifled a yawn.

"I'll be on my way." Rhys inclined his head in a show of respect. "Have a good evening, Breaker Hawthorne."

"I will once my friends are out of the Cit, Tracker Kildare," Blaise said. Two could play the formal titles game.

Rhys swung back into the saddle, and moments later, the silvery unicorn trotted out of view. Blaise rubbed his forehead, sighing.

<You sounded very tough.> Emrys nudged him with his soft muzzle. <I know that was hard for you.>

"Yeah," Blaise mumbled. He rubbed at his eyes. "I need to get to bed. It's been a day."

He headed for the house but paused when he heard the sleepy cluck of a chicken. Blaise frowned. The estate didn't have chickens. Climbing onto the porch, he discovered the hen nestled beneath a rocking chair. It wasn't the safest place for a lone hen— too easy for her to be snapped up by a fox or feral cat.

"Come here," Blaise said with a yawn, gathering her up. The hen gave a mild protest before settling in his arms. Blaise trudged out to the stable, nestling the hen in a manger in the empty stall next to Emrys's.

<What is that?> the stallion asked, peering over.

"I'm pretty sure this means the Maverick Underground is watching me."

And since Blaise was alone on the big estate with only the pegasi and Tristan, that made him feel a little safer.

CHAPTER TWENTY-THREE

Family Reunion

Vixen

Vixen had never set foot in the Golden Citadel before. As with everyone raised in Izhadell, she'd seen it, though usually from a distance. It was the glittering, golden facade that reminded the masses that maverick mages went in and loyal theurgists came out.

If they came out at all.

Probably because of her association with Jefferson, she'd ended up in a cell that resembled a shabby boarding house room. Blaise never spoke of it, but Vixen knew in her gut that he hadn't been held in anything like this. Though maybe after what Jefferson and Blaise had done, mages were no longer treated like livestock at the Cit. For her sake, she hoped so.

She had a sleepless night and spent most of it replaying her own foolishness of the afternoon. *I shouldn't have risked that. Should have known better.* But what else could she have done? The magistrate wasn't going to let Jefferson go free any other way. He'd been doomed from the start.

The salt-iron embedded in the walls didn't help her situation.

When the guards had brought her in, they'd made her remove the ring, though Vixen had seen Rhys pocket it. That was good, at least—no telling if she'd recover it if the guards took it. But without the ring, she was susceptible to the relentless power drain of the metal, and it left her with a headache.

One day passed, and then a second. Vixen was having her doubts that she would be released soon. Wouldn't Rhys have gone to their mother? Maybe Blaise had been right to be nervous around him. He was a Tracker, and she was a mage. Two opposing forces, like fire and ice. And they had been apart for so many years. Maybe blood didn't matter when your twin was a mage.

She was mulling through those dark thoughts when the door to her cell creaked open. Light flooded in, accompanied by the sound of raised voices. One voice telling someone not to go in. Another voice, familiar through the haze of years, responding that she answered to a higher power and would do as she saw fit.

Vixen had been lying on the thin mattress of the bed and jerked upright, heart pounding. The woman framed by the light was achingly familiar. Emotions warred within Vixen. She wanted to get up, to run to her. But part of her stayed rooted, horrified and afraid that her mother would reject her.

"You have a visitor." Rhys entered first, coming over and taking Vixen's hand. He turned it over, pressing something cool into her palm. The ring. "Put it on. Quick." His voice was so soft she almost missed the words, but she did as he said. Rhys wasn't in his Tracker uniform, instead dressed in muted greys and browns that would hide him in shadows and make him look unremarkable.

The Luminary strode into the cell, statuesque as ever. Vixen's mother had always commanded a room with her presence—she assumed it was some facet of being the avatar of Garus. And, in that moment, this woman wasn't her mother. No, she was the Luminary through and through.

The Luminary studied Vixen with keen grey eyes. She wasn't

clad in her usual gold and white regalia, marking her as the avatar. No, like Rhys she wore drab grey clothing, a robe that reminded Vixen very much of the sort worn by the clergy. It was a similar design, though the Garusian priests wore either all white or all gold, depending on their rank. But even in the dull robe, she looked regal and otherworldly. The Luminary stood there, as if drinking in Vixen's essence with her eyes.

The woman chewed at her lower lip, and in that gesture, Juliette Kildare replaced the Luminary. "It's really you, isn't it?" Her voice was husky with emotion.

Vixen peered up at her, feeling like a lost little girl. She hadn't realized how much she had missed her mother. Now the dull ache of their time apart roared up, as wide as the canyons that made up the Gutter. "Yes."

Juliette took a shuddering breath, then closed the distance to envelop her daughter in a hug. Vixen froze for a second out of instinct. She had never imagined she'd see her mother again in this life, much less hug her. But she couldn't hold back. Vixen returned the hug, drinking in the scents she associated with her mother—honey and whatever incense had most recently wafted through the Asaphenia.

After a moment, her mother pulled back. "I thought you were dead."

"I know." Vixen had wanted her to think that. She had wanted no one to come after her, to discover what she was. At the time, it had been unthinkable.

Juliette swallowed. "When Garus refused to choose another Spark, I hoped..." Her intense gaze flicked over Vixen. "In my heart, I had hoped the reports of your death were wrong, since we never found a body."

Of course, the god of wisdom wouldn't select a new Spark. The Luminary might not have known Vixen was alive, but Garus knew. But he knew she was a mage, too. He couldn't possibly want her.

Could he?

Vixen would have to ponder that later. She needed to focus on getting herself and Jefferson out of there. She heaved a breath. Well, Vixen had planned to reconnect with her mother. Perhaps not quite in this way, but…she'd have to play the hand the circumstances dealt her.

She gave a wan smile. "I'm back. And I need a favor."

CHAPTER TWENTY-FOUR
Unexpected Guests

Jack

Kittie frowned at the glass of rose-colored liquid. "So I drink this, and it will give me the power boost I'll need for the spell?"

Jack stood beside his wife on the back porch of their home, which blocked them from the view of most curious citizens. Zepheus stood nearby, saddled and ready to go. Emmaline perched atop the railing, legs dangling as she lazily swung them. Jack had included her so that she could help her mother into the house once the portal was cast.

"Yeah. It tastes like brine and old boots, and you're gonna feel like you got trampled by a horse when you're done," Emmaline piped up.

The Pyromancer glanced from the potion to her husband. "You're going to owe me for this."

He grinned, closing the distance between them. "Sure. Anything you want. Name it."

Kittie met his eyes, hers steely with determination "Take me with you."

Gods damn it. He couldn't believe she was trying again. Jack's mouth went dry, and he shook his head. "We've been through this. I told you why you can't go." But he saw the flicker of doubt in her eyes. She didn't believe any of his reasons were worth a damn.

Her mouth tightened. For a moment, he thought for sure she would argue. But Kittie simply lifted her chin, eyes narrowing with disapproval. Yeah, she was pissed at him. But he could live with that if it meant he had a wife to come back to.

"Hand over the spell, you selfish piss-goblin," Kittie growled. Emmaline blew out a breath, mouthing the words, "You are so dead," to Jack.

He stuck his hand into the pocket where he kept the portal spell but didn't remove it. "This ain't gonna work if you cast while you're mad."

"You should have thought of that sooner." She glared at him.

Jack sighed. He put a hand on Kittie's shoulder, expecting her to jerk away. She didn't. He met the burning anger in her eyes. "I know you think I'm a jackass for wanting you to stay behind. But there ain't a lot in this world that scares me shitless. The thought of losing you again is one of 'em, though." Jack swallowed, hoping that she'd understand.

She shook her head, brushing the hair back from her face with one hand. "And don't you think I feel the same about you?"

The outlaw's lips drew into a thin line. It was the same old song and dance. "Nah, I know you do." He took her hand in his, lifting it to his lips. Jack kissed her knuckles, savoring the ever-present scent of smoke that clung to her. Not an unpleasant sort of smell, but the scent he associated with cheerful bonfires and good times. "There ain't many people I'll beg, but I'm begging you to stay here."

She sighed. "Let's see the spell."

Kittie hadn't agreed, but he figured she was stewing about it, and this might be the closest he'd get. He pulled the spell out, unfolding it before handing it to her. "You get to do the set-up."

She took the paper, frowning as her gaze flicked over it. Then she stepped back to look at the framing of the porch, which they were going to use as the basis for their portal. "This is outside of my magical expertise."

Jack smiled, moving in again and wrapping an arm around her waist. "Nah, you're just not accustomed to thinking about your magic like this. That's all. The idea behind this is magic is magic, no matter the source."

"Doesn't matter if it comes from fire or ritual?" Kittie asked.

"Doesn't matter," Jack agreed. At least, he hoped that was the case. It was what they were betting on, at any rate. Marian Hawthorne said Blaise could work a spell such as this, and his magic was pure chaos. Jack wondered if, at its root, all magic started the same, and it was the strengths of the practitioner that defined it.

Kittie nodded. "All right. I'll try it." She uncorked the potion bottle, taking a swig. The Pyromancer made a face at the taste, then drank the rest of it down. She wiped her mouth with the back of her hand. "Em, I'll take some tea later. When I'm up to it."

Emmaline grinned. "Got it."

Then Kittie limbered her fingers, focusing on the spell. Jack held it where she could read it. The casting called for turquoise, and Jack had already placed the stones. "Here we go."

He felt the pressure of her summoned power. It was like the rumble of distant thunder, something palpable in the air. A vibration magnified by the alchemical potion. Kittie made a soft exclamation. She snapped her fingers, and tongues of flame roared to life on her palms. Jack stepped aside, cautious around the might of her fire. He had a healthy respect for the destructive force, and though she wouldn't intentionally harm him, there was no telling what might happen under the potion's sway.

The flames leaped from her hand to the columns that supported the porch. Emmaline yelped, jumping down and skittering back a safe distance. The fire crackled, the white paint on the wood blistering. But the wood itself didn't catch fire. The flames simply skimmed along it like an insect skating atop a still pond. Kittie's hair blew back in a rush of magical wind, her eyes glowing with power.

Jack swallowed. "Kittie?"

She didn't look at him. "Almost done."

The flames danced along the wood until they framed the entire rectangle, creating a blazing doorway. Jack studied it, nodding. He supposed it made sense that a Pyromancer would make a portal of fire. "Ready for me?"

"Yes." Kittie's voice resonated with something almost other-worldly.

Jack handed the spell to Kittie, watching as she folded it and tucked it away for safekeeping. Then he took her hand, his breath catching at the intense heat of her skin. He shouldn't have been surprised—she'd been holding fire in her palms, after all. It was like touching a cooling stove. Still hot and uncomfortable, but possible.

He clutched a poppet in his left hand, using it as a focus for his contribution to the working. Like Kittie, this was something he'd never done before. But Emmaline had done it—and she was right. It shared some basic pillars in common with a spell like Rising Dread, or the lightning rod spell they had cast together. It was just a matter of twisting magic in a new way.

Jack felt the poppet in his grip activate. He formed a vision of his destination in his mind's eye. The peacock's home, though now it belonged to Blaise. The stables, he decided, would be the safest place. Close to the house, but hopefully clear of anyone who shouldn't see his arrival.

Amid the door of flames, the scenery wavered from the other side of the porch to the aisle of a faraway stable. He heard Kittie's soft intake of breath. Jack grinned. "We did it."

Beside him, his wife wove on her feet. "I don't know how long I can hold this."

Jack nodded. He leaned over to plant a quick kiss on her lips. "Thanks, darlin'. Come on, Zeph." The Effigest leaped through the portal of flames, feeling the momentary disorientation and discomfort of traveling so far in a short time.

The clatter of hooves proved Zepheus had made it through. Jack rubbed his temples as he recovered from the portal, squinting. Flames licked along his vision, evidence the magical gate was still open. Why? Kittie should have closed it.

Footsteps and a soft, pained groan. Jack shook his head, fighting off the effects. He knew that voice. When his vision fully cleared, he found Kittie clinging to Zepheus's mane, her eyelids fluttering. Her fingers loosened their grip, and she reeled. Jack lunged to catch her as the drain of the spell fully caught up to her. He cursed, gently easing her down, though he adjusted to cushion her head with his lap.

"Why did you *do* that?" the outlaw asked, unable to mask the tremor of confusion and fear in his voice.

<She did not wish to be left behind,> Zepheus said, lowering his head to nudge his rider. <You treat her like the porcelain doll that is her poppet.>

Jack didn't feel well enough to deal with this. A distant part of him knew Zepheus was right—that Kittie was right. She was a capable woman, and he should trust that she could handle herself. But the void of the years she had been missing from his life was still a gaping wound in his heart, and his fear of that happening again was too strong. Jack knew he wouldn't survive a second occurrence. Frustration burned his stomach. What had he done to be saddled with such a glorious, strong woman? He'd done nothing to deserve this sort of love.

He shook his head, wishing with his entire being that he had the power to send her back to the Gutter. To safety. But was the Gutter safe at this point?

A pair of pegasi had their heads over stall doors, ears pricked as they watched the scene with interest. Jack recognized Emrys and Alekon, which meant he was in the right place. He smoothed a lock of loose hair back behind Kittie's ear, then looked up at the pegasi. "Can you tell Blaise we're here?"

<Already have,> Emrys replied.

The Effigest breathed a sigh of relief. He still wasn't on the best of terms with the black stud, so he appreciated Emrys doing that much. Jack cupped his wife's cheek in one hand, mind whirling as he waited for the Breaker. He hoped Emmaline would be okay. Kittie wasn't the impulsive type—which meant she'd likely warned their daughter about this. Damned women, conspiring against him. But that conclusion made him feel a little better. Emmaline would stay with Clover, as she had in the past.

He adjusted his position, still cradling her head. "Damned persistent woman." But he smiled. He wouldn't trade her for anything in the world.

Blaise

WHEN THE STRANGE SENSATION OF MAGICAL PRESSURE RIPPLED through the house, Blaise knew exactly what it was. He'd felt it before in Ganland. It was the pulse of a portal opening. But who would use that to travel here? He had a few suspicions, but he knew better than to fall prey to them.

"I can't catch a break this week," he grumbled. With Jefferson and Vixen still jailed, he wasn't in the best mood. He had several tins of cookies and pans of pies to show for his efforts to distract himself. Blaise had made plans to have a pity party with the pegasi that evening. The equines were looking forward to gorging themselves on the treats.

<We have company in the barn,> Emrys informed him. The stallion didn't seem bothered, which was a good sign.

Blaise closed up the bag of sugar he'd been about to use and put away the butter. He had a cake in the oven, but he had about twenty more minutes before taking it out. Time enough to see what was going on, or so he hoped.

He stalked onto the porch and down the stairs. The resident hen pecked at the grass nearby, her head snapping up as he passed. She trailed after him as he hurried to the stables.

Tristan must have arrived only seconds before him. The lad was nearly boiling with fury, fists clenched. "Unhand her!"

Unhand who? Blaise came around the corner in time to find Jack holding a sixgun, the muzzle trained on the boy. Zepheus stood behind him, watching everything with his usual calm demeanor. Blaise pulled up short when he noticed the woman prone on the ground. He blinked, recognizing Kittie.

"Whoa, whoa, whoa." Blaise held up his hands. Tristan didn't turn, still staring at the outlaw with more courage than sense. Jack's cool gaze flicked to Blaise for a heartbeat, then back to Tristan.

"I found an intruder, and he's harmed this woman!" Tristan announced, reminding Blaise of a terrier facing down a bulldog.

Jack's chin jerked up at the accusation, his eyes narrowing as an atmosphere of impending danger bloomed. Blaise stepped in front of Tristan. He was pretty sure Jack wouldn't shoot him. Probably. To be on the safe side, he had his magic at the ready. "Tristan, it's not what you think. These are friends of mine." Blaise angled so that he could see the boy in his periphery. "Howdy, Jack. Wasn't expecting you."

The outlaw was kitted out as if he'd come prepared for a fight, a bandolier bristling with cartridges across his chest and a reagent pouch attached to his belt. "Yeah, didn't exactly have time to send a message." Jack's hand swept across Kittie's brow. A mixture of worry and defensiveness shadowed his face.

Blaise suspected Kittie must have been the one to cast the portal spell. Had his mother made a potion to give the Pyromancer the extra jolt of power necessary? He'd have to ask later. He looked at Tristan. "Can you prepare a guest room? Please?"

Tristan frowned but nodded, scurrying off.

Jack's shoulders relaxed. "Thanks. That's exactly what she needs."

Blaise smiled. "Do you need help to get her to the house?"

The Effigest shook his head. He shifted, holstering his sixgun and retrieving a poppet. "Nah. I'll give myself a little extra strength. Should do the trick."

Blaise chewed on his lower lip, though he let the outlaw do as he wished. He stayed nearby, just in case the other man ended up needing a hand. Jack was so intent on doing things on his own sometimes. And he was clearly worried about his wife. Blaise busied himself by settling Zepheus in a stall beside Alekon, filling a bucket with fresh water mixed with sugar and another with sweet feed.

A short time later (after Blaise had removed his cake from the oven), they had Kittie settled on a bed. She had roused as Jack carried her up the stairs, though her skin was as pale as porcelain, as if the magic had drained all the color from her body.

"Can I bring you something?" Blaise asked.

Kittie's eyes were slits, as if she were struggling to stay awake. Blaise remembered the exhaustion that came with expending too much power too quickly and had an idea of how she felt. She sighed, her breath barely a whisper. "Later. Sleep now." Jack sat at the foot of the bed. Kittie opened one eye wider. "Go away."

The outlaw scowled. "No."

"I'm not why you're here," she murmured.

Jack's face hardened, every line on his face taut with displeasure. The conflict he felt was clear. Kittie made a good point—she *wasn't* why he had traveled so far. Blaise saw the stubborn twist of the Effigest's lips and knew he was going to ignore his wife's wishes unless he had some other distraction.

"Why *did* you come?" Blaise asked, deciding that was as good an opening as any.

The distraction worked. Jack's gaze pounced on Blaise. "You seen Raven Dawson?"

Raven? Why would Jack ask about the other Ringleader? Blaise frowned. "No?" Then he coughed, hating that he made it sound like a question. "No."

The Effigest's lips thinned. "Not surprising. Where's Vixen?"

"Um, it's complicated."

"And the peacock?"

"Same complication."

The Effigest made a frustrated sound. "You gonna explain, or do I gotta torture it out of you?"

Blaise scowled. The odds were good that Jack was only venting, but Blaise didn't appreciate his tone. The outlaw was obviously upset, though he was unlikely to admit it. Blaise gave him a pass. "We ran into trouble as soon as we arrived in Izhadell. Jefferson was arrested." He blew out a breath, distancing himself from the distressing thought of the man he loved imprisoned. Even though he'd twisted his magic to visit Jefferson last night, it was a poor substitute for the Dreamer's freedom. "According to Seledora and Alekon, Vixen's bid to free Jefferson went sour. She ended up arrested, too."

Jack stared at him, as if he couldn't believe that things had turned to disaster for them so quickly. Blaise had to agree. It was impressive. "So, why are you sitting around here? You got the magic to break them out."

Blaise huffed. "I think you know exactly why I can't do that."

Jack winced, then nodded. "Yeah, yeah, I suppose I do. You'd be shot full of holes like Ravanchen cheese." He rubbed his cheek, gaze flicking to Kittie before settling on Blaise again. "You okay?"

Blaise moved over to the window, resting a hand on the sill. It was a good sign that Jack had calmed enough to think of someone else. The Effigest wasn't the most empathetic. "Yeah. I've been able to talk to Jefferson, even through the salt-iron. He's okay. I just..." He gazed into the distance, studying the outstretched canopy of trees. "It's the Golden Citadel."

The outlaw made a sound of agreement. Blaise knew he didn't need to say more than that. Jack understood Blaise's feelings about the place. Jack had his own history with it as well.

"That's not what I meant, though." The Effigest gestured to Blaise as if that explained it. Jack must have realized it didn't. "You're banged up. You got a bandage on your hand."

"Oh." Blaise rubbed the back of his neck. "I'm okay now, but I almost wasn't." He licked his lips, self-conscious, before Jack's intent gaze. "I was attacked when I went to the market."

"Why in Perdition would you go to a market in Phinora?" Jack asked, his tone somewhere between incredulous and condescending.

"Because I wanted to be normal for five minutes!" Blaise hadn't realized he snapped until he caught the way Jack cocked his head, looking at him as if he had turned into something dangerous. He sighed. "But you're right. It was a stupid thing to do."

"Nah," the outlaw said, to Blaise's surprise. "I get it. Maybe I was too hasty in what I said." That was the closest he'd come to an apology. Jack's eyes narrowed. "What happened?"

Blaise pursed his lips. The chicken had wandered into the yard below the window, pecking at the grass as she hunted for insects. "People knew who I was. There were mages there—mavericks. One of them warned me I was being watched, so I tried to leave, but then another group attacked me." He recounted the rest of the encounter, including the appearance of the Maverick Underground.

Jack's eyes flicked to Kittie. "Maverick Underground. Never thought I'd see the day."

"There's more. They knew I was coming—that we were coming. They intercepted the letters."

The outlaw cursed. "Damned Walkers. If you can't trust them with the post, what in Perdition can you trust them with?"

Blaise decided not to point out that he knew Jack made a habit of checking the correspondences that came through Fortitude. But the mention of Walkers reminded Blaise of Jack's earlier question. "Why were you asking about Raven?"

"Damn, I'm as distractible as a mewling jackalope." Jack shook his head. "He skipped town. Even ditched his pegasus."

"He abandoned Naureus?" Shock threaded through Blaise. He couldn't imagine doing the same to Emrys.

The Effigest grunted. "That, and more." Jack studied his wife, as if to reassure himself she was okay. Then he told Blaise what Naureus had said and about the stash of correspondence in the outhouse.

Blaise stared at him. "He *literally* told you not to come to Phinora. Why are you here?"

Jack cocked his head, lips pressed together. "'Cause he doesn't want me stopping whatever he's up to."

Jack and Jefferson are more alike than either care to admit. Both were determined to be stubbornly defiant. "You could have sent a letter."

"Too slow."

It wasn't worth arguing about—Jack was here, and that was that. Blaise abandoned that track. "So Raven is around doing who knows what. Jefferson and Vixen are jailed, and I get attacked." He sighed as he finished the summary, uncertain about what to do for any of it.

"Stinks of a plot," Jack commented.

Blaise frowned, rubbing at his bandaged hand. "You think it's all connected?" It wasn't something he wanted to consider. Each incident by itself was bad enough.

Jack nodded. "Someone's going too hard for it to be a coincidence. At this rate, you're lucky something didn't happen on the train."

The train car belonged to a Quiet One. Blaise swallowed, new worries mounting. "I don't know what to do about it—besides stay here and hope Jefferson and Vixen get free soon." And then what? Well, he supposed he would figure that out later.

Jack rose from the bed, pacing the short distance across the room. "You got any leads on the assholes that went after you?"

Blaise gave a hesitant nod. "The Maverick Underground might know something. I could go ask the chicken."

Jack stared at him. "Ask the chicken?"

"Yeah. Let me go do that." Blaise didn't feel like explaining that it would take Tristan longer to get the message to the Maverick Underground than it would to have a conversation with the hen, who would report back to her Beastcaller mistress. Blaise glanced over his shoulder to find that Jack had taken his boots off and had moved onto the bed beside Kittie, taking her hand in his.

CHAPTER TWENTY-FIVE
Last Gasp of Freedom

Vixen

The Luminary had the power to pardon whoever she liked—a power that was seldom used. Only a handful of staff at the Golden Citadel seemed aware that the Luminary was in their midst, garbed as she was in a drab robe. It meant that no one gave Vixen a second look as she accompanied her mother and brother out of the infamous building.

Vixen's mother didn't even have to give a reason for the pardons, which meant Vixen could leave the facility with no one any the wiser to her true identity. No doubt that would change soon, but at least she had a brief reprieve. Jefferson was another matter—everyone knew him, which meant that when he accompanied them out, the former Doyen was met with a host of hostile glares. Vixen imagined the gossip to come from his release would be astounding.

Jefferson had been respectfully quiet once they'd collected him. Vixen saw the questions brimming in his expression, but he was too cunning to spring them early. Their unusual group slipped out to a coach with the fox-head symbol of Garus emblazoned on the side in gold filigree.

Jefferson's brows raised when he saw the emblem, his gaze sliding to Vixen. He made a soft exhalation as he realized exactly where she'd gotten her outlaw name from. She bit her lip. Yeah, she hadn't been all that creative years ago. But she'd been scared and hard-pressed to think of something. It had been the first thing to come to mind.

As soon as they were ensconced in the coach, Juliette's shoulders relaxed as she shed the veneer of the Luminary. "I have many questions about why the Spark is in the company of a trait—of you, Jefferson Cole." Her lips pinched as if she had eaten something sour. Vixen didn't know if it was because of Jefferson's duplicitous past or because he was a mage. Maybe both.

"He's here because of me," Vixen said before Jefferson could speak. She took a breath before plunging onward. "I needed someone who..." No, she couldn't explain that Jefferson understood the awful position she was in. "I thought someone with political savvy would be good to have along."

"Fat lot of good I've done so far," Jefferson murmured.

Vixen gave her head a small shake. It wasn't his fault their enemies were doubling down on their attacks against them. In fact, she couldn't imagine coming here without Jefferson and Blaise.

Juliette remained tight-lipped, her expression pensive. "I'm curious about why you'd need his skills, but that's a discussion for another time." She glanced out the coach window at the city scenes flashing by. "But my more pressing concern is *you*, Valoria. When Rhys told me you were here...that you were in the Cit, I didn't believe him. I thought you were dead. Where have you been all this time?" Her gaze cut to Jefferson. "Did the mages kidnap you?"

"*No*," Vixen shot back immediately. "No, what happened to me is complicated and..." She faltered, struggling with what to say next. *Some Persuader I am.* But she didn't want to reveal her magic to her mother, not yet. The old fear returned. What if her mother rejected her because of it? "I'll explain later. But I'm back thanks to Jefferson Cole and Blaise Hawthorne." When questions flared in her mother's eyes, Vixen added, "The Breaker."

Juliette frowned, looking at Jefferson. "I'd heard rumors he was back in Phinora. I suppose you're behind that?"

"Blaise is here as my *friend*," Vixen cut in before Jefferson could respond. She hoped her mother would think of the Breaker favorably if she associated him with Vixen.

"Hmm." Juliette leaned against the wall of the coach. "Curious. And Rhys tells me he was assigned as your escort by an unknown superior." Her gaze slid back to Jefferson. "You have connections. Was that you?"

The Ambassador's brows raised. "I didn't know of Rhys Kildare until quite recently, so this is none of *my* doing."

Juliette's eyes narrowed, shrewd. "I see. This is too convenient to be coincidence. Someone knew you were coming back to me, Valoria. Even before *I* knew." Claws of concealed anger prickled in her words.

"We have enemies," Jefferson said.

Juliette scoffed. "As if I don't?" Then she released a long sigh. "For more than a decade, there's been no Spark. Garus ignored me every time I asked him to choose another. No heir in the event something happened to me." She stared out the window again. "There are those among the elite who would be happy to have Garus select the next Luminary from their family line."

Vixen frowned at the thought. Was that truly possible? She could imagine some greedy elite coming up with creative deceptions to rig the selection process.

"But that doesn't matter. You're here. You're *back*." Juliette's tone lightened. "We'll have to have a ceremony to reclaim you as the Spark." Her fingers drummed against the wood of the coach's side panel. "A gala to formally announce it and then the ceremony, most likely. I'll have one of my priests arrange it."

"Ooh, a gala," Jefferson said, unable to hide his glee.

"We'll invite my friends, of course," Vixen said quickly. She needed them by her side as much as possible. Though, she feared that her opportunities to be with them were about to be greatly reduced. Unless... "And maybe we should keep my presence here a secret until the formal announcement. There's a place I can stay with my friends."

Juliette stared at her. "You won't stay at Dawnlight? You still have a room there."

I want just a last gasp of freedom before I give it up. Vixen twisted the ring on her finger, longing to remove it. "I will—after the announcement."

"I'll vouch for the mages." Rhys's voice was soft. "I think I'd trust them more with Valoria than I would some of my fellow Trackers."

Vixen scowled at him, wondering how much of that was because they would sniff her out for the mage she was. In response, he gave her a one-shouldered shrug.

Juliette rubbed her forehead. "Very well. I can't believe I'm saying this less than an hour after getting my long-lost daughter back, but...I'll allow it. Temporarily."

A thrill of victory zinged through Vixen. *A final hurrah of freedom.*

CHAPTER TWENTY-SIX
A Thug and a Cheat

Jack

J ack had thought maybe Blaise had finally been through too much and had cracked like a dropped ceramic dish, but the Breaker had, in fact, spoken to a chicken. That had been strange, but a half-hour later, a woman ambled through the cypress trees that stood vigil on the north side of the estate. Blaise seemed to expect her, which led Jack to believe maybe there was something to this chicken business.

It had surprised him to discover she was a maverick. The woman—Holly—was mistrustful of Jack at first, apparently having heard of the Scourge of the Untamed Territory. But Blaise's opinion won her over, and before long, she spilled what she knew.

"We recognized the Trapper mage," she began. The words *Trapper mage* made Jack twitch, thinking back to Lamar. But Lamar was dead. Jack had made certain of that. "Name's Jeremiah Jones. He and some of the others are locals. Jones keeps his magic off the books by doing shady jobs for the elite." Jack grunted, familiar with that sort of arrangement from his days as a theur-gist. "He works at the slaughterhouse."

Jack scowled, glancing at Blaise. "Slaughterhouse, eh?" What had the attackers planned for the Breaker? And were they tangled up with the Quiet Ones, or was this some other group after Blaise for his unusual magic? Or, since they were in Phinora, it might just be a group of mage-hating assholes. Jack knew there were many who resented Blaise after the Inquiry.

Thankfully, Blaise must not have reached that conclusion. Jack wasn't about to enlighten him. The kid had enough on his mind.

"Yes," Holly said with a nod. She put a finger to her lips, thoughtful. The huge rooster that shadowed her made a rumbling sound. "Jones and the ones he runs with aren't easy marks. We only ran them off because we got the jump on them."

"The hundred or so chickens didn't hurt, either," Blaise said.

Jack shook his head, still not quite believing that chickens could turn the tide of any fight. "Yeah, well, I intend to get the drop on 'em, too."

As soon as he said it, Blaise groaned. "Jack, no. Can't you even cool your heels for five minutes before running off?"

"Best to go after the trail while it's still warm." Jack crossed his arms, turning to the Beastcaller. "Got a few more questions for you, if you don't mind."

He picked her brain for a few moments longer, trying to get a description of his quarry. When he was done, she and the rooster vanished back the way they had come.

"What?" Jack asked when he saw the frown on Blaise's face.

"You're going to hunt this Trapper down and just...leave Kittie here?"

Jack didn't like the way Blaise made it sound, as if he were abandoning her. That was the furthest thing from the truth. "I'm entrusting her to *you*."

The Breaker hissed out a long breath. "And what exactly do I tell her when she wakes up mad?"

"That her husband is an asshole who went and followed a lead without her."

"Well, at least it's the truth," Blaise grumbled. He shook his head. "I know you won't listen to me, but...just be careful, okay?"

"You're as bad as a broody hen." Though, Jack couldn't blame him. The Breaker had been through the wringer. "Look, all I plan to do is find this Jones and squeeze him for information. Simple."

Before long, he had Zepheus tacked up and ready. The stallion's banded wings stayed hidden as they trotted down the drive, leaving Hawthorne House. The name made Jack snort. *Hawthorne House.* It sounded so damn uppity and nothing like a place Blaise would willingly own. Yet here he was.

Back in the day, Jack had known all the ins and outs of Izhadell and the surrounding area. But he had been gone a very long time, and things had changed. When he reached the market Blaise had visited, he stopped to ask for directions to the slaughterhouse.

It wasn't hard to find. He and Zepheus simply had to follow their noses. They were downwind of the building, and the reek of death, shit, and smoke carried to them on a stiff breeze.

Zepheus shook his head, exhaling a mighty breath. <I don't like this.> His ears flicked backward, and he stomped a hind hoof in agitation.

"You don't like it because it stinks," Jack pointed out.

<That is only part of it.> Zepheus sidestepped as they drew closer.

The slaughterhouse complex was huge. Pens of animals surrounded the abattoir, filled with beasts aware of their fate. Cows lowed and shifted nervously, some of them pressing against the fences. Pigs squealed and shoved one another. A pair of old horses, their backs swayed with years, huddled together, their heads drooping so low their muzzles brushed the ground. Watching them, Jack understood why Zepheus didn't like it. The telepath faced a wall of fear and despair.

"Hang in there," Jack murmured, patting his pegasus's neck to offer some small comfort.

He found a secluded copse of trees near the slaughterhouse to stow Zepheus. It was clear of the worst smells but still close enough for the stallion to keep tabs on his rider. Though that would be difficult, the further away Jack got.

<How are you going to do this?> Zepheus bumped Jack's shoulder with his muzzle.

"Sneakiest way I can," Jack murmured, pulling out his poppet.

<Obfuscation?>

"Yep."

The stallion pawed at the ground, restless. <Don't do anything stupid.>

"Too late. I already came to Phinora." Jack grinned, starting his cast. The spell settled over him, hiding him in plain sight. As long as he didn't bump into anyone, he would have the advantage.

The outlaw headed for the building, smirking at the sight of one of the side doors gaping open as men loaded meat onto a wagon bound for market. Jack crept up to the group to eavesdrop and find out if any of them were his mark. Once he'd discovered they weren't, he made his way inside.

Jack wandered the building for longer than he liked. At this rate, he was going to have to accost one of the workers and bully them into telling him Jones's whereabouts. He toyed with the idea of trying this tactic on one of the men slaughtering the animals. The brute handling the lambs enjoyed his job entirely too much, torturing the innocent creatures before they died. Jack had a cruel streak, and he'd happily eat meat, but he wouldn't draw out the suffering of an animal the way that man was.

But that wasn't why he was here. He had to keep his focus. Jack trudged invisibly across the slaughterhouse floor, though he didn't notice until he walked onto a clean section that his boots were covered in blood, and he'd left a spattered trail of red footprints.

Shit. Jack stepped back onto one of the dirty sections of the floor. *Shouldn't have let the asshole distract me.* Jack shook his head. What were the odds someone would notice a new pair of bloody bootprints? The workers weren't paid for their attention to the finer details.

Besides, Jack didn't have much choice. He had to get a move on.

"—don't think we'll be able to do that, Jer." A voice echoed down a nearby corridor. Jer? The odds were good it was short for Jeremiah. Jack stayed where he was, cocking his head to listen.

"I don't want to hear it. No one's going to know we're selling meat from glandered horses. We do the job, we get our money," another voice answered.

Well, not only is my pal Jeremiah a thug, he's a cheat. Jack gritted his teeth. Glanders, that was a gods-awful disease. It would kill the horses slowly and painfully, and it could spread to other livestock or humans. Even pegasi. In the Gutter, if any of the outlying farms that provided meat tried to pull such a stunt, they'd suffer swift consequences. Not so in a bloated city like Izhadell.

Not a thing Jack could do about that except make Jeremiah Jones extremely uncomfortable. He crept forward again, following the voices. The complainant stormed off, leaving Jones alone.

Jack stalked closer, finally rounding the corner. He found the man inside a broad room filled with rows of carcasses hanging from hooks. Most of them appeared to be cattle. There were a few on the far side that might have been from the mystic races. One had the unmistakable look of a griffin, though it had been skinned. Jack's lips curled. *This place is evil.*

Silent as a cat on the prowl, he slipped into the room, sneaking behind Jones. Jack clutched his poppet in his left hand, willing a speed spell into it as he pulled his sixgun, dropping his Obfuscation at the same time that he leveled the muzzle at Jones's head.

"Howdy," Jack whispered. Jones tensed, muscles bunching. The

Effigest nudged him with the sixgun. "I've got questions, and you're gonna answer them, real quiet-like. If you get loud…well, this sixgun is pretty loud, too."

Jones swallowed. "Who in Perdition are you?"

"Nope, I'm the one with the questions," Jack said. "You went after the Breaker. Who are you working for?"

The man shifted to glance back at Jack. "I don't know what you're talking about."

"You need a refresher?" Jack murmured.

Jeremiah's head reared back at the question, nearly slamming into Jack's nose. The outlaw still had his speed working up, though, and narrowly avoided the painful move. He cursed and lifted his sixgun again to aim—

A black chain shot out of the floor, snapping around Jack's wrist and jerking his arm down. The sixgun flew from his grip, skittering across the cold floor with a metallic clatter. Growling, Jack banished his speed spell and cast strength. He felt the immediate drain of the working as he tugged against the chain, the arcane metal snapping beneath his might. But as quickly as he broke it, another chain flew up around his left wrist, leashing him again. *Gods-damned Trappers!*

In quick succession, more chains rose. In seconds, Jack was tethered in place. With a snarl, he flexed his right arm to snap the new chain.

A knife whispered beneath Jack's chin. The outlaw froze, painfully aware that so much as twitching the wrong way could end with his throat slashed. He knew the glint of the nine inches of steel, knew that the wielder was better with a blade than with a sixgun by necessity.

"Couldn't stay home, could you?" a familiar voice whispered.

"Howdy, Raven," Jack murmured, the words pressing his tender skin perilously close to the knife's edge.

He heard Raven's soft exhalation. Every muscle in Jack's body tensed against the threat. Jack wanted nothing more than to put a comfortable distance between himself and the rogue Ringleader, the room to work magic or snatch up the fallen sixgun. This was about the last place he'd expected to find Raven. The Effigest had a flurry of questions, and he was certain that even if the other mage gave him a chance to ask, he would receive no answers.

"This the one you were talking about?" Jones asked the Ringleader, keeping his chains in place.

"Unfortunately," Raven confirmed. "You can go, Jones. I'll handle him from here."

"You sure? He's a right bastard."

You got that right. Jack glared at him for good measure.

"I'll be fine," Raven answered. Yeah, not if Jack had a say in it. "I guess this means you found my stash. You should have paid attention to my warning," Raven said after a moment, regret shading his voice. "But sometimes you really *are* predictable, no matter what you may think."

Jack gritted his teeth. "You *baited* me." He wanted to say more but didn't dare risk it. Jack had seen what that blade could do in a fight, and he couldn't defend against that. Not like this. "Whose side are you on?"

"You're not going to delay me with questions," Raven said, annoyingly pragmatic. "And know this is nothing personal."

Before Jack could react, the knife slipped away from his neck. But Raven wasn't removing it, wasn't giving him any sort of quarter. Instead, it slashed against the top of the outlaw's upper arm, slicing through his duster and shirt like butter. Jack hissed as the steel bit into flesh. As quick as the knife was in, it was out again, a fine spray of blood salting the air as Raven stepped away. It joined Jack's bloody footprints on the ground.

Out of reflex, Jack clapped his hand to the wound, as if he might soothe the hot corona of pain. His fingers came away sticky. And more than that. A sickening realization struck him as fire raced through his veins.

"Go lick salt-iron," Jack growled as he went down to his knees, unable to stand against the wave of agony that surged through him. Raven hadn't only cut him. The blade's edge had been coated with poison. Jack had been cut before. None of those instances had ever felt like *this*.

Raven looked down at him, the younger man's eyes the coldest Jack had ever seen them. The Shadowstepper didn't move, just watched as Jack's breath rasped while he struggled to shrug off the poison.

The Effigest's fingers twitched. If he could get to his poppet, he might stand a chance. He knew workings that could dull pain or temporarily staunch wounds. The odds were slim they would work against poison, but Jack was willing to try. But his hand behaved as if it were no longer his to command, fingers flexing into a pained fist.

"Raven." Jack tried to load the single world with the certain promise of retribution, but his tongue was thick and spongy in his mouth. Panic seized him. He tried to thrash, tried to fight, but nothing worked. After a moment, it was all he could do to collapse onto his side, panting for breath.

The Effigest closed his eyes, trying in vain to gather his thoughts, to figure out some way around this. He was going to be pissed if this gods-damned traitor was the one who ended him. Poison was a coward's tool. That thought gave Jack pause. Raven could have killed him easily, could have slit his throat and been done with it. But he hadn't, instead nicking Jack's shoulder with a poisoned blade. Why?

The obvious answer was that he didn't want Jack dead. At least, not yet. Which meant that while the poison was damned inconvenient and bloody frustrating, it likely wouldn't kill him.

Whatever Raven was up to wasn't good, but Jack knew that as long as he lived, he had a chance. And that was all he needed. Now all he had to do was endure the gods-damned Perdition this poison was putting him through.

CHAPTER TWENTY-SEVEN

We're Being Serious Right Now

Blaise

Kittie showed no signs of waking. Blaise alternated between checking on her and puttering around in the kitchen. He had thought about staying with Kittie until she woke, but it wasn't long before that was downright awkward, and he'd retreated to the kitchen to busy his hands and his mind.

Jack had been gone for several hours. Blaise wasn't sure if he should be worried or not. But Emrys advised him not to concern himself too much, since Zepheus was with him. Of the all the pegasi, Zepheus was the most level-headed.

Blaise had just slid a pot pie into the oven when Emrys called to him. <There is a coach approaching. Alekon and Seledora say that Vixen and Jefferson are aboard!>

Jefferson? Blaise's pulse raced at the mention of his beau, almost weak with the relief that he was no longer imprisoned. He hurried outside, a wave of uncertainty rolling over him at the sight of the unfamiliar coach. Blaise stayed on the porch, worried it was some sort of trap.

The trio of pegasi stood at the fence nearest the coach, their wings hidden. Emrys must have picked up Blaise's nervousness. <If there is any threat, we are here.>

Blaise didn't need to worry, though. As soon as the coach drew to a halt, Jefferson didn't wait for the footman to set out the block of stairs. No, the door flew open, and the Dreamer leaped down, followed by Vixen. Jefferson's green eyes settled on Blaise, assessing him with every stride as he drew near. Blaise kept his still-bandaged hand behind his back, self-conscious.

Blaise trotted down the porch steps to meet him. As soon as Jefferson was within arm's length, he reached out and pulled his beau into a desperate embrace. The Dreamer opened his mouth to say something, but Blaise didn't give him the chance. He crushed his lips to Jefferson's. Blaise savored the assurance that the man he loved was here. Jefferson was okay. He was free.

Jefferson seemed surprised by the move for a beat, but he wasn't one to shy away from affection. He looped an arm around Blaise, his hand resting against the nape of the Breaker's neck. Comfortable and *right*.

"Y'all act like you were apart for a year," Vixen observed from somewhere nearby.

Blaise pulled away, glancing at her with feigned annoyance. He was glad to see her, though. "It was long enough." Then his gaze snapped back to Jefferson. "Howdy."

"I do so enjoy your greetings," Jefferson murmured, lips twisting with pleasure. Then, his voice even softer, he added, "I'm okay. I'm here, and I'm okay."

It was no surprise that Jefferson knew the heart of Blaise's response to his return. The old fear that even though things were different now, he might have been mistreated, as Blaise had been. Blaise nodded, heaving out a breath.

Mischief gleamed in Jefferson's eyes. "Though if you wish to give me a *thorough* examination later, I wouldn't refuse."

The corners of Blaise's mouth twitched. He should have

known the Dreamer would say something like that. "We're being serious right now."

"You think I'm not serious?" Jefferson asked with a wink, though he released his grip on Blaise and took a step back. His flirtatious humor meant that he really *was* okay, which did much to put Blaise at ease. Then Jefferson cleared his throat, making a show of straightening his clothing, which honestly hadn't been mussed at all by their embrace. "I suppose we have some catching up to do."

That was an understatement. Blaise paused, wondering if Kittie was awake yet. Gods, they didn't even know about Jack and Kittie's arrival. He rubbed the back of his neck.

Vixen cocked her head. "What are you not telling us?"

"Um, Jack and Kittie are here. Well, Jack's not *here* here, but..." Blaise waved a hand. "It's complicated."

Jefferson and Vixen stared at him, baffled. Clearly, neither had expected that bit of news. Jefferson heaved a dramatic sigh. "Sounds as if my examination will be delayed. More's the pity."

Vixen stifled a laugh, shaking her head as she headed for the house. "It's a miracle Blaise puts up with you."

"It actually is. I'm quite thankful for it, though," Jefferson agreed, moving to follow the Persuader, though he glanced back at Blaise, grinning. He was acting the part of a rake, but Blaise couldn't even pretend to be annoyed because he knew it meant Jefferson *cared*. About *him*. Blaise couldn't express how precious that was.

The savory scent of baking pot pies greeted them as they entered, which served as Blaise's much-needed reminder to check on them. He hurried to the kitchen and pulled them out of the oven, pleased to discover they hadn't burned.

"I thought I heard voices."

Blaise looked up and saw Kittie at the base of the stairs, though she leaned heavily on the railing. She was still exceedingly pale, her dark hair stark contrast to her complexion. She reminded

Blaise of the porcelain doll Jack used as her poppet. "Should you be up?"

"I'm up," the Pyromancer said, voice as fiery as her magic. Blaise wasn't at all surprised that Kittie was as stubborn as her husband. "And I'm hungry."

Jefferson, ever the gentleman, hurried over and offered her his arm. "Good afternoon, Kittie. I certainly wasn't expecting to see you here." His voice was warm and full of welcome as she took his arm, leaning against him for support. "I suppose your trip here was *taxing*."

"You could say that," Kittie agreed as she sat at the table.

Vixen claimed a seat beside the Pyromancer as Blaise dished out the piping hot pot pies. She flashed him a look of thanks before focusing on Kittie. "Blaise said you and Jack came here together?"

Mention of the Effigest prodded the Firebrand to glance around. "Where *is* my meddlesome husband, by the way?"

"Um." Blaise set the empty bakeware aside, then turned back to their inquiring gazes. "That's a long story, but the quick version is someone attacked me, and now Jack is hunting down one of the men who did it."

Jefferson went still, staring at Blaise's injured hand. A thousand questions crossed his expression, but he left them unspoken. Instead, he nearly growled as he said, "Someone *attacked* you?"

Blaise nibbled his lower lip, nodding. Now everyone's attention was on him, as intent as cats waiting to pounce. Their focus was so overwhelming, he turned to face the counter. "I'm okay." Blaise didn't realize Jefferson had risen, moving close to him until he felt the light touch of a hand on his shoulder.

"Jack went off without me?" There was a distinct twang of disapproval in Kittie's tone.

"Honestly, not all that surprising," Vixen drawled. "It's a very Jack thing to do."

"And I'm still mad at him for it," Kittie retorted. "That *man*."

Blaise was fairly certain she'd considered adding some colorful language but had held her tongue. Now that the focus had shifted from him, he turned back, though he shot a grateful glance at Jefferson before moving to claim a seat at the table. "Kittie, can you tell them about Raven?"

Vixen went on alert at her former beau's name. "What about Raven?"

The Pyromancer gave her a sympathetic look, then explained what had spurred her and Jack to portal such a great distance. Kittie spoke slowly, her words deliberate—Blaise saw the exhaustion in her every move. She really should have stayed in bed, but he wouldn't risk the suggestion. Not now.

When she finished, Vixen looked utterly baffled. "He can't…he wouldn't…" But she frowned, as if realizing that he could and he would if he had reason.

"Do you have any idea why he's behaving in this way?" Jefferson asked, tone neutral as he sank his fork into the flaky crust in front of him.

Vixen shredded her own pot pie until it was more crumbs than anything else. "We didn't part on the best of terms."

"Do you think he's come to spite you?" Kittie asked.

Vixen shook her head. "No. Raven's many things, but he's not spiteful. If anything, he's doing it because he thinks it's a way to win me back. Or protect me." She made a face at that.

"Would he jeopardize the Gutter for you?" This from Jefferson, whose green eyes had turned serious and contemplative, all of his earlier flirtations brushed away.

Vixen hesitated, licking her lips. "I want to say no, but…if it came down to the Gutter or Blaise, what would you pick?"

"I already made that choice once before, but it wasn't the Gutter that was involved," Jefferson replied, his words crisp. The matter-of-fact statement made Blaise's heart squeeze. *Jefferson chose me above everything else.* "Regardless, when it comes to someone you love, you'll go to great lengths for them."

"Without fail," Kittie murmured.

Vixen visibly bristled. "However he feels for me, it's not mutual. Gods-damned idiot man." She tapped her nails against the table in irritation.

Blaise decided it might be time for a change of subject. And besides, he was curious... "How did the two of you get released?"

Vixen's silver eyes darted to Kittie, uncertain. The Firebrand smiled. "Jack may try to run off without me, but he doesn't keep secrets from me."

The Persuader nodded at that. Kittie knew who and what she was. "The Luminary pardoned us." Her tone was neutral, though Blaise suspected there was a wealth of emotion behind that simple statement.

"Did something happen? Why are you back here?" Blaise asked Vixen. He had assumed that the Persuader wouldn't have been allowed to leave once her mother realized she was back.

"Since only mother knows, she let me leave." Vixen pursed her lips, looking very much as if she'd bit into a lemon instead of a savory pot pie. "But there will be a gala tomorrow night to announce my return."

"We're invited," Jefferson added cheerfully.

"Wait, what?" A gala was about the last thing Blaise had expected to pop up in this conversation.

"The Luminary is hosting a gala to announce the return of the Spark. Vixen made sure we'll be on the invite list." Jefferson's eyes gleamed at the prospect.

Now it was Blaise's turn to look as if he'd eaten a lemon. "But I'm a *mage*." *And I don't want to go. There will be people there.*

"You're not just a mage," Jefferson reminded him, voice gentle. "You're the Breaker, the mage who had an Inquiry end in his favor. You're a land-owner, which is remarkable for a mage in the Confederation. And you're one of the mages who returned the Luminary's daughter."

Blaise glowered at the logic. "No one told me when I came that I'd have to be *social*."

Jefferson's green eyes danced with mirth. "You're welcome to attend and be mysterious and taciturn. That will only make you more interesting to everyone."

Blaise huffed an annoyed breath. "Can I just bring a plate of cookies, throw them on a table, and call it a day? You can go without me, right?"

Kittie rapped lightly on the table with her knuckles, drawing Blaise's attention. "You have the option to be left behind. Ask yourself if you want to be."

He swallowed at her words. She was right—Blaise didn't want to be left behind, not where Jefferson was concerned. He turned, meeting Jefferson's rich green eyes. "I've never been to anything like that before." He knew it was ridiculous to be scared to go for that simple reason. Blaise had done harder things—but sometimes the fact that he'd survived harder things made the small ones seem just as daunting.

"You won't be alone," Jefferson reminded him, smiling.

Blaise nodded. "Looks like I'll be coming to your party, Vixen."

"*Gala*," Jefferson whispered. "It's a *gala*."

CHAPTER TWENTY-EIGHT
The Elite Event of the Season

Jack

His shoulder burned. With a grunt, Jack's eyes flew open. He tried to roll his shoulders to relieve the throbbing pain, only to discover his hands were bound behind his back. Not only that, but someone had tied his legs and torso to a chair. Jack had a moment of disorientation, his memories of how he'd gotten into this situation murky.

Someone had stripped off his duster. Crusts of drying blood stained his shirt. *Raven.* That traitorous bastard had worked with the Trapper. Which meant the shadow-stepping asshole really was associated with the attempt to snag Blaise. And what else?

"Oh good, you're awake."

He didn't know the speaker, but the outlaw recognized the polished, *I'm-better-than-you-so-I'll-rub-it-in-your-face* speech of one of the Confederation elite. A woman circled around him, hands clasped at her waist as she peered at her quarry. She was dressed in fine clothing that probably would have made her the talk of the elite social circles, but Jack didn't give a shit where this woman bought her glossy boots. She was an enemy, and that was all that mattered.

"So, you're the fearsome Wildfire Jack," the woman said, tone bright. "The so-called Scourge of the Untamed Territory."

Jack glared up at her. Something about this woman was vaguely familiar. "You know me, but you must not be worth a unicorn's rainbow shit 'cause I sure as Perdition don't know you."

She clucked her tongue, as if she were disappointed. "*Manners*. You were a theurgist; I know you had manners once upon a time."

Theurgist. The word turned Jack's blood afire. "I'm a far cry from a lapdog now."

"I suppose you are," she agreed, her chin tipped to a jaunty angle. "Well, you may not have manners, but I do. I'm Tara Woodrow. Pleased to make your acquaintance." Somehow, she managed to make her words both welcoming and sardonic.

Tara Woodrow. That name tickled the recesses of Jack's mind. How did he…? Oh, yes. Woodrow was one of the Quiet Ones. Jack had likely seen her in Nera when the peacock had made his grand announcement refuting his old name and declaring himself an outlaw mage.

Now, how could Jack use that nugget? He didn't see any use for it, not yet. "Yeah? Well, it ain't mutual."

Tara's lips twisted into a pout. "A pity. At the very least you should have a bit more respect for your situation. I hope you enjoyed the poison that immobilized you. Alchemy really is a modern marvel, isn't it?"

Alchemy. That explained the coating on Raven's blade. "Can't say I agree."

She shrugged. "Agree to disagree. But we should get to business." Tara's calculating look slid over him. "When you threatened Phillip Dillon, you threatened *all* of us."

Jack allowed himself a lazy shrug, though the gesture was difficult with his hands bound behind the chair. The movement made the fire in his injured shoulder burn brighter, a blaze of pain in his skull. "Glad to hear he understood it for the threat it was. Sometimes y'all ain't that smart." He backed up the words with a feral grin that promised bravado he currently didn't have.

A muscle ticked in Tara's jaw. Yeah, Jack was definitely getting to her. Good. Maybe she'd get sloppy, and he'd figure out some way to take advantage of the situation. There was no sign of his sixgun, poppet, or reagent pouch, but Jack wasn't going to let those inconveniences stop him. Not if he had half a chance.

Woodrow took a step back. "You may talk big, but you're at our mercy now. Phillip will be pleased to hear of your capture." She angled a coy look at the outlaw. "I'm sure he'll want to attend to you *personally* before your hanging."

The blood in Jack's veins froze. He'd faced the threat of the noose countless times before but had always dodged it. A small part of him knew at some point his luck would run out. And it might be now.

No. He couldn't let those thoughts, the potential for despair, weigh him down. That was what this woman wanted. Jack tamped down his fear, summoning up his swagger. He wasn't dead yet, and as long as he drew breath, he had a chance. It wasn't as if he was in Phinora alone. Blaise, Vixen, and the blasted peacock were here. Zepheus, too. And so was Kittie, though fresh fear rooted in him at the thought of her swinging beside him.

"All that fuss for me?" Jack asked. "Nice to know my death will be the elite event of the season."

She met his snark with her own, beaming. "Yes, I plan to wear my finest gown. It'll be quite the occasion. And your death will serve as a warning to other outlaws."

Jack met Tara's gaze with his own frigid glare. "That so? I don't think you know outlaws all that well. Your *warning* will be your end."

The Quiet One frowned, as if Jack's words made her uncomfortable. Good. Tara turned, snapping his fingers. "Raven, darling!"

Raven slipped into the parlor, his jaw clenched. The Shadow-stepper refused to look at Jack, nodding to the Quiet One as if he were subservient.

Traitor. Jack's gaze burned into the other Ringleader, a man he had once considered a friend, as he thought of all the things he'd do to Raven if given a chance.

"I'm bored with him. Take him away," Tara commanded, gesturing to Jack. "Somewhere that his friends won't be able to get him."

Jack frowned. What did they intend, the Golden Citadel? A hidden dungeon? Raven didn't know Kittie was here. And Jack figured Blaise wouldn't let this stand. Yeah, if they thought Jack was powerless, with no one to help him, they had another thing coming.

Raven nodded to the Quiet One, moving over to Jack. Almost too fast for Jack's gaze to follow, the Shadowstepper pulled a knife and slashed the ropes binding Jack to the chair. He clamped a hand onto the outlaw's shoulder, right over the inflamed wound. Jack snarled at the pain, rocking beneath the other mage.

"Don't fight me," Raven cautioned, his tone flat.

Jack didn't fully understand what happened next. He felt the pull of magic and the parlor seemed to twist around them, warp-ing. There was a sensation of motion, vertigo clawing at him. His stomach lurched, and for a few seconds, he was in danger of retching up the contents. He squeezed his eyes closed, inhaling through his nose to gain control over his body. Jack's stomach settled after a moment, and his eyes flashed open.

Where was he?

It was like a room but also nothing like a room. His chair had vanished, and it was only Raven's grip that kept Jack from a tail-bone-jarring fall, hands still bound behind his back. Jack sank to the ground as he tried to make sense of where he was. It was all darkness except for a puddle of dim light. Jack couldn't figure out where the light came from. There was no sun. No mage-lights. No lanterns. Pitch black fringed the area for as far as he could see, which wasn't far. The air was still but not stale, the climate temperate.

"Did you bring me to Perdition?" Jack asked drily, though it wasn't fully sarcasm.

"You and the Breaker aren't the only ones learning new tricks with your magic," Raven said, though he sounded distracted. He shifted uneasily, as if grappling with the enormity of what he'd done. Good. Jack hoped the betrayal tormented him. Raven pulled a knife from a sheath at his belt, the blade making a soft *skree* as it came free. Not one of his standard knives—Jack could tell by the hilt. The Shadowstepper sank it blade-first into the strange, spongy ground. "I don't know what to call where we are. This is the in-between, the realm between shadows. One of the few places I suspect our friends won't be able to reach you."

Our friends. Interesting choice of words. Raven still counted himself as an outlaw mage, despite whatever he had done. "Why are you working with the Quiet Ones?"

Raven clenched his jaw. "You wouldn't understand. I know you, Jack. By now, you only see me as one thing: a traitor."

The other Ringleader knew him well, which was unfortunate. "Then convince me you're *not*."

For a moment, Jack was sure Raven would give in, would unpack whatever had led him down this road. Instead, the Shadowstepper shook his head. "What does it matter? You're not the one I have to convince."

"Did they bind you?" Jack asked. He couldn't help it. He had to know. "You got a geasa tattoo? Did they make you a theurgist?"

Raven's lips thinned. "There are more ways to bind someone than the geasa." Suddenly, the other man looked older than his years. Jack didn't know Raven's exact age, but he figured he was about as old as the peacock. But now, he looked as if the worries of the world had added years to him. "I'll be back to check on you. They'd be unhappy if you died in the shadows before they had the chance to make a spectacle of you." He winced, as if the words were as sour on his tongue as they were to speak.

Raven pursed his lips, then pulled something from his back pocket that was rounded and no longer than his index finger, setting it on the ground. Jack frowned, realizing it looked like one of the smallest mage-lights he'd ever seen, though it wasn't illuminated. "Don't think to attack me here. This is *my* realm."

Without another word, Raven melted into the shadows and vanished. Jack glared at where the other mage had stood, then sighed. His shoulders and arms hurt from being tied. He licked his dry lips, assessing the surrounding area.

Raven had left the knife. Jack's eyes widened as he realized what that meant. It was an outlaw custom from the times they robbed a stagecoach or pack train. They often tied up their victims—at least the ones who hadn't chosen death by fighting—but made a point of leaving a knife where the victims could retrieve it once the outlaws left the scene.

"Hmm." Jack thought about that. Raven had said the Quiet Ones didn't want him dead yet. But there were ways to keep a man alive and captive. The Shadowstepper had made a very deliberate choice in leaving the knife. And his warning not to attack.

Somehow, Jack had the idea Tara Woodrow wouldn't want him to be untied, to have any sort of freedom in this shadow prison. Raven was dissenting in a small way the elite would likely never know about.

The outlaw heaved in a deep breath. Time to see about getting to that knife.

Zepheus

AT FIRST, ZEPHEUS THOUGHT JACK HAD SIMPLY SLIPPED PAST THE range of his telepathy. As one of the oldest pegasi living in the

Gutter, over the years, he'd honed his ability to a hoof knife's edge, able to keep tabs on his rider as long as he was in the vicinity. The number of other minds in the area affected Zepheus's accuracy, too. It didn't help that he was so close to hundreds of minds ripe with terror and despair inspired by the slaughterhouse. Zepheus was careful as he sifted through the different thoughts, seeking Jack. He shuddered as he brushed the mind of a heifer in line for slaughter.

Where was Jack? The pegasus snorted, shaking his head as he swept past the auras of the dying. He hated it, but there was nothing he could do except focus on his rider.

There. He found the bright spark of his outlaw, the warmth he associated with Jack. Zepheus sensed his mage was stalking someone. He must have found his prey.

Alarm flared in his mind like lightning. Something was wrong. He felt a jolt of momentary chaos and calculation as Jack struggled against someone. Zepheus pushed his telepathic power harder, burrowing deeper to get a better idea of what was going on. Sometimes, if he strained, he could almost see through his rider's eyes, hear through his ears. The stallion poured all he had into the connection, but he failed when instead, he was struck by the white-hot sensation of agony in his shoulder.

Something had happened to Jack. Zepheus weighed his options. He could go back to Hawthorne House for help, but he might be too late. The stallion pawed a furrow in the grass beneath him. He'd gone after Jack before and gotten him out of hairy situations—even in Confederation lands. Not that he was eager for such a thing. But he would not leave Jack behind, not if he could help it.

Dusk was falling, and he observed the workers leaving the slaughterhouse and new ones arriving. Zepheus understood that meant they worked in shifts, thus the abattoir was always serving its brutal purpose. The slaughterhouse was a dangerous place for an outlaw or pegasus—Zepheus knew it would be a simple thing for him and Jack to end up in a sausage, and no one else the wiser.

He shoved that grim thought aside. Zepheus was certain he would know if they had killed Jack. He had sensed Jack's near-fatal injury when he'd been shot by Lamar Gaitwood, despite the salt-iron ropes that had dampened his flight and telepathy. Jack was not dead. He couldn't be. Zepheus refused to believe in such nonsense.

The stallion picked his way out of the cover that had concealed him. It wouldn't be long before someone spied the loose *horse* and tried to catch him. He was going to have to work quickly—and probably reveal his true nature. It was a sacrifice he was willing to make.

He broke into a trot, approaching a gaping open door to one side of the slaughterhouse. The closer he got, the more pungent the reek of death and fear. Zepheus flattened his ears, snorting out great, huffing breaths. He got farther than he'd expected before someone realized he was unaccompanied by a human.

"Get that horse!" a cry rang out, followed by the slap of booted feet breaking off from other tasks.

Zepheus blew out a breath, shaking his head against the stench. The carcass of a steer hung nearby, blood dripping into a massive metal bucket beneath the corpse. Men circled around him, but Zepheus ignored them, scanning the area for any sign of Jack.

He wasn't there. It was as if he'd just...vanished.

A man held up his hands, whistling softly at the sight of the golden stallion. "Easy there, boy. Did you throw your rider? You look like you're worth a load of coin." The man took a tentative step closer, though his fingers curled in anticipation of snagging the hackamore reins.

Three more men flanked him. Zepheus spun, bugling a challenge. He lashed out with his hind hooves at the man who'd tried for his reins, catching him on the shoulder and sending him flying backward with a grunt.

"Get him!" one of the other men urged his counterparts as they inched closer.

Zepheus snapped his teeth at them, unfurling his wings as he did so. The trio gaped, then had no choice but to dive away as he stampeded toward them. He extended his wings, sweeping the slowest of the men away with a flick of his long primaries.

Then he was out in the darkening evening. More shouts rang out behind him, but he didn't care. He was fast and had the advantage of flight. All he had to watch out for was griffin riders. Zepheus bolted into the sky.

He was a little disoriented, but as he flew low over the land, he sought familiar minds—his fellow pegasi. Blaise. Kittie. *Mother of Mares, what will Jack's mate think?* He wasn't looking forward to that conversation.

It wasn't long before he found the fire-bright mind of the Firebrand. Zepheus adjusted his course and moments later alighted in the driveway of Hawthorne House. Emrys, Seledora, and Alekon immediately peppered him with questions, but he ignored them. The palomino stood stock still in front of the house and whinnied, pushing out a commanding mental call. <Kittie! Blaise!>

Kittie was the first to come out, though she was quickly followed by the Breaker and—Jefferson and Vixen had arrived while he was away. Zepheus noted that but focused on his current need. He hurried over to Kittie, shoving his head against her chest. Zepheus sensed she was still weak from the magic drain, but she was up, and that was what mattered.

"Zeph?" Kittie asked, rubbing his glossy neck right behind his ears. "Where's Jack?"

He huffed out a distressed breath. <I don't know. He was there one moment, then gone the next.>

The Pyromancer went still, and Zepheus felt a wave of fear and anger wash over her, focused at Jack for leaving her behind once more. But just as quickly, she set it aside. "Where did you last detect him?"

<Deep inside the slaughterhouse.> He pulled away from Kittie, looking at the other outlaws.

Vixen frowned. "That doesn't sound like a good place to go missing."

<I went inside. He was not in there.> Zepheus didn't mention that scenting the man would have been impossible. So much death. So much pain and terror.

The Persuader heaved a sigh. "We'll figure something out. I know we will."

Yes, Zepheus knew they would. They had to. He turned to look at Jefferson. It was fortunate the man was here. Zepheus kept his next request to only Kittie, Blaise, and Jefferson. Vixen didn't know of the Dreamer's power. <You will search for him tonight?>

Surprise crossed Jefferson's face at being addressed, but he gave the tiniest of nods. Zepheus relaxed. They would find his rider. They would.

They had to.

CHAPTER TWENTY-NINE
Night Terror

Jefferson

"I'm happy to announce I've completed my examination, and you seem to be fine," Blaise said, leaning his head against Jefferson's bare shoulder.

Jefferson savored the gesture, though Blaise's beard tickled his skin. "Are you sure? I might need another going-over." He most definitely wouldn't mind more of Blaise's attention.

The Breaker snorted at the suggestion. "It's getting late." Though he delivered another spate of kisses up Jefferson's neck, every single one bringing the Dreamer closer to melting.

Jefferson hissed out a breath. He treasured every private moment with Blaise, but it wasn't enough. It would never be enough. And then Blaise went and did something like...well, like he was currently doing.

"I fail to see how you think I'll sleep after you cover me in kisses," Jefferson murmured.

Blaise pulled back, though he regarded Jefferson with a smile. "Because we have work to do. You promised Zepheus." He flopped onto the goose-down mattress.

"So I did," Jefferson agreed, sobering. With a soft sigh, he reclined beside his beau.

Blaise rolled onto his back, yawning. "It's the middle of the night. If Jack's asleep, this is the best time to find him. And it's better if we're not exhausted in the morning."

"But we don't have to wake before dawn. You're not running a bakery right now." Jefferson propped his head up, gaze lingering on his beau's shadowed profile.

The Breaker placed an index finger against Jefferson's lips. "You're just being contrary to stall."

Jefferson was rather pleased that Blaise knew him well enough to notice that. He kissed the finger, chuckling when his love pulled it away with an annoyed huff. "Can you blame me?"

Blaise's enchanting blue eyes softened. He knew that Blaise didn't fully understand why Jefferson was so captivated by him. Sometimes Jefferson didn't, either. All he knew was that Blaise made him happy, made him feel complete and grounded like no one ever had before. Jefferson was determined never to take that gift for granted.

"No." Blaise's voice was whisper-quiet. "But we still need to find Jack."

"We do," Jefferson relented, turning onto his side. He shifted, adjusting his position until his back was flush against Blaise's chest, as close as a pair of the Breaker's favorite measuring spoons.

Blaise tensed. "*Jefferson.*" His voice was husky.

"What? I'm not being improper. Not at the moment, anyway." He glanced over his shoulder. Jefferson couldn't help that he wanted Blaise so close. However, he knew Blaise may not feel the same. Sometimes his beau needed space. "But I can move away if you prefer."

Blaise slung an arm over Jefferson's side, splaying his hand against the Dreamer's stomach. "I'm not saying *that.*"

Jefferson grinned, content. Blaise never admitted it, but he was a cuddler—at least, with Jefferson. He awoke some mornings to discover Blaise snuggled against him, as if they were a pair of kittens. It was another heartwarming sign that the shy younger man was comfortable with him, a detail that made Jefferson ridiculously happy.

"Mmm, good. Now, let's get some sleep and track down a surly outlaw." Jefferson savored Blaise's warmth behind him as he summoned his magic to send them to the dreamscape.

Moving into the strange realm of dreams had become second nature to Jefferson, along with drawing Blaise into it. The Breaker never fought it, too aware that without Jefferson, he was likely to succumb to the nightmares that plagued him.

The bakery took shape around them, one of the easiest locations for Jefferson to create. It was the place he knew Blaise would always feel most comfortable. The dream town of Fortitude was empty of its citizens and structures, aside from the yellow-and-white building surrounding them. Jefferson wouldn't bother with those details tonight. They had work to do.

Blaise pulled out a chair at the small table in the corner. "Do you need me to help find Jack?" He sat.

Jefferson pursed his lips. "Possibly. If he's not nearby, I might have difficulty finding him, since we're usually not on the best terms."

"I doubt he's nearby," Blaise said. And that stood to reason. If he was, Zepheus would have certainly found him.

Jefferson nodded, accepting his beau's offer. It was hard to explain how Blaise melded his magic with Jefferson's. It might have been some component of the unusual Breaker power, a side effect of their dead geasa bond or their relationship. Jefferson secretly hoped it was the latter.

With their magic combined, they searched for the Effigest. Often, when Jefferson was left to his own devices, it felt like looking for a specific book in a library that had no organization to it. Blaise usually had more luck, for some reason. But this time, the Breaker came up short, unable to find the outlaw.

"That's strange," Blaise murmured, shaking his head. "Even if he's not asleep, I would think we'd feel some hint of him."

Unless he's dead. Jefferson didn't want to suggest it, though he thought Jack was too stubborn to die. He would probably fight off the demons that hoped to drag him to Perdition. "Hmm. Maybe I should see if Kittie can help us locate him."

Blaise cocked his head, thoughtful. "Would it worry her more that we can't find him?"

"We'll have to tell her regardless," Jefferson reasoned.

"Then we may as well bring her in," Blaise said.

With the Breaker's agreement, Jefferson sent out his dream tendrils, roving through the house for Kittie. She was nearby, easy to find. Simple to draw into the dreamscape. In her dreams, the Pyromancer ran from something with many legs and gnashing teeth. Parts of it were mechanical, metal and gears clanking and rasping. As Kittie ran, the footprints left in her wake glowed with red-hot embers.

Jefferson dissolved the bakery around them, though he left Blaise's chair. The Dreamer lifted a hand, curling it into a fist. He gritted his teeth as he seized the nightmare creature with his power. The horror roared and struggled against his magic, thrashing as it tried to go after the Pyromancer.

Blaise rose, moving to stand beside Jefferson. "Do I need to do something?"

"No, I've got it. Wasn't expecting a nightmare." Sweat beaded Jefferson's forehead. Whatever Kittie feared, it was powerful. Sometimes the things that haunted dreams made no sense, except to the sleeper. He was used to handling Blaise's nightmares and was prepared for those. Jefferson focused on the terror, raising his other hand, making another fist.

Kittie had stumbled and lay nearby, panting. She stared up at them, her eyes wide. "Jefferson? Blaise?"

"Might need your help with this, Kittie." Jefferson strained as the night terror nearly snapped through his restraints.

Kittie swallowed. "What do I do?"

"Kill it with fire."

Jefferson had expected that she might incinerate it. But Kittie didn't do that, not exactly. She lifted her right hand, and a long spear flickered into existence. A spear made entirely of fire, flames licking up the shaft and ending in a point made of molten metal that gleamed as fiercely as a tiny sun. Kittie hefted it as if the spear was her weapon of choice. Perhaps she understood that in the dreamscape, if she wished to be a mistress of spears, she could be.

The Pyromancer drew her arm back and then sent the fiery spear hurtling through the air. It struck the night terror square in the...well, Jefferson wasn't sure if it even had a chest. The spear caught it in its midsection, causing the nightmare creature to wail as tongues of fire consumed it from the inside. It shrieked, writhing free of Jefferson's magic. But it didn't matter. Kittie's spear worked, reducing the terror to ash that drifted away on a phantom wind.

"Huh," Blaise said, eyebrows brushing against a curl of his copper hair.

Kittie shook her head as if clearing her mind, then turned to them. "Are you real?"

Jefferson waggled his fingers, wondering why every new person he brought into the dreamscape asked the same question. He was never certain how to answer. "We're...ah, something. This is the dreamscape."

At that, the Pyromancer nodded, as if it made some level of sense. "Thanks. I was worried about Jack. Wasn't sleeping well."

"You're welcome." It was something to think about later, but Jefferson wondered if there was a way he could help her sleep, too. With his magic, he didn't *like* when people he knew suffered in their dreams. Well, unless they were an enemy. Then they were fair game. "I'm happy that I could help you banish the night terror, if only for now." Jefferson cleared his throat. "Ah, we brought you here for a reason, though. We can't find Jack."

Kittie pursed her lips. Something flickering in the depths of her eyes. "You can't? Is he awake?"

"We'd be able to detect him," Jefferson explained. "You know I can pull people into the dreamscape if needed." Kittie had witnessed it before, when she had first learned of his magic.

She huffed out a breath. "What are the other options? Dead? Unconscious?"

Jefferson nodded. "Those are unfortunate possibilities."

"Wards could block it," Blaise mentioned, drawing their attention. "Or salt-iron."

"Ah, that is true." While they weren't ideal, Jefferson appreciated that there were options beyond death and loss of consciousness. "But in the event it's something else, I thought your connection to Jack might help our search."

Kittie tilted her head. "What do I do?"

Jefferson blinked, then glanced at Blaise. This was where it became difficult to explain out loud something that came naturally. It was like explaining how to walk. There was so much more to it than putting one foot in front of the other, but Jefferson wasn't certain if it would make sense to someone else.

"Just think of him. You have a stronger connection to him than either of us," Blaise said. Jefferson breathed a sigh of relief, shooting him a look of gratitude.

Kittie's brow furrowed with determination, and with a start, Jefferson realized Blaise was correct. He could feel her thoughts influencing the surrounding dreamscape with her own perspective of the outlaw. Jefferson wrapped his magic around the Pyromancer's thoughts.

It was no longer like searching inside a disorganized library. Now, his magic was like a pack of hounds on the trail of a rabbit, seeking the Effigest. His power roved over miles and miles, almost

as if they found traces of Jack but not the man himself. The last
hint of the outlaw felt like it was in a home.

"I don't understand. He's there, but not there," Jefferson
murmured.

"This place. Is there a way we can figure out where this is?"
Kittie asked, gesturing to the indistinct landscape around them. It
was ever-shifting, taking on the aspects of various houses, none of
them the same.

"Not that I know of. I don't know how much the dreamscape
overlaps with the physical world. If it does at all." Jefferson felt as
if they had traveled miles to search for Jack, but he wasn't confident they actually had.

"Are there slumbering minds here?" Blaise asked.

Now, that was a good question. If nothing else, perhaps
Jefferson could glean something from another sleeper. But that
would require more power, and after fighting Kittie's night terror
and searching for Jack, he was nearly spent.

"Yes, but I don't think I can sustain this much longer."

Blaise caught his eye. "Do you want my help?"

Always. Jefferson smiled. "Whatever you wish to give."

The Breaker didn't move, did nothing at all, but Jefferson felt
the power siphon from Blaise and into him. The magic seeped
into his being, and he felt like a ship catching a stiff wind after
days in the doldrums. Jefferson hissed out a breath in relief.

"Thank you. That will do," Jefferson said. "Let me take a peek
into the slumberers."

It was definitely an estate of some sort. Jefferson touched the
minds of some of the staff, finding a cook who was nearly awake
to start her day. He skimmed her thoughts, trying to find out
more about where this was, but she was distracted with thoughts
of all she had to prepare. Jefferson left her alone, though she
reminded him of Blaise, and he very much liked that.

He latched onto another sleeper, and this time he knew he had
struck gold. It took some effort to sift through the layers of

dreams wrapped around the man. They were filled with darkness, despair, and something like self-loathing. Jefferson dug a little deeper, his breath hitching.

"What is it?" Blaise asked.

"Raven. I found Raven."

Blaise

"WAKE UP." BLAISE NUDGED JEFFERSON'S SHOULDER. THE DREAMER groaned softly, rolling over and showing no outward signs of waking. Blaise sighed. "Jefferson, wake up."

In response, Jefferson buried his head under his pillow and muttered something indecipherable. Blaise retaliated by pulling the sheets away.

"Mrmph!" The lower half of Jefferson's face appeared from beneath the pillow. "What was that for?"

"It's time to get up."

"I disagree." One of the Dreamer's hands groped for the missing covers.

"Told you we needed more sleep last night." Blaise shoved the covers as far from his beau's reach as possible. Under other circumstances, he would have let Jefferson sleep. He'd expended a lot of power through the night, and Blaise knew that true slumber would help Jefferson recover. But they didn't have that luxury at the moment. "We have problems."

The Dreamer yawned, but at Blaise's statement, he shoved the pillow off his head. He rubbed his eyes, and Blaise realized Jefferson had never looked so rough. Under normal circumstances, his beau seemed immune to anything that made him look less than dashing. Red-rimmed his eyes and his golden hair tangled. It was enough to convince Blaise to send him back to sleep—almost.

"I'm just so tired." Jefferson rose into a sitting position. "Last night was more difficult than what I usually do."

Sometimes it was easy to forget that magic was new to Jefferson. The man was so self-assured in all he did, it was almost as if he'd been born a mage. But he hadn't, and in many ways, he was less experienced than Blaise. The Breaker scooted closer to him. "I know. You did good, though." Blaise swept an arm around Jefferson.

A sleepy smile drifted across the Dreamer's lips. He yawned again, then shook his head. "You're right. I'm going to need a nap before the Luminary's gala, though."

The gala. It had slipped Blaise's mind with everything else they had discovered through the night. Ugh, he still wasn't enthused with the idea of going, but it seemed he would have to tolerate it. But that was a concern for later.

"I think we need to tell Vixen what we discovered. But the problem with that is we have to tell her about your magic," Blaise said.

Jefferson said nothing, and for a moment, Blaise thought he might have drifted back to sleep. Then the Dreamer sighed. "Yes, we can tell her. I believe she'll keep it in her confidence."

But would she keep it a secret from the Luminary? That was Blaise's concern. Vixen might be an outlaw, but she also had deep, deep ties to Phinora and the Confederation. The same Confederation that would be extremely interested in Jefferson if they caught wind of his magic. A Dreamer, a completely unknown magic type, would be lucrative.

"What?" Jefferson asked.

"Just thinking," Blaise said.

"About your lack of clothing?" Jefferson cast a flirtatious side-long glance at Blaise.

Blaise snorted. "And suddenly, you're much more awake." Besides, he had pulled the covers over himself. He was nowhere near as naked as Jefferson. Though, it was likely Jefferson intended to point that out in a sneaky, roundabout way.

"Mmm, yes." Jefferson stretched, then combed his fingers through the mats in his hair. "I stand by my nap idea, though. I really am quite bushed."

"I know." Blaise leaned over, brushing a kiss against Jefferson's brow. "We'll make sure you get one. I can plan our outfits for the gala while you rest."

"You most certainly *will not*." Jefferson's eyes widened, then he frowned. "If you're trying to get a rise out of me, there are other ways I prefer you go about it."

Blaise rose from the bed, moving to the dresser and pulling out clothing. He put little thought into matching any of the items, too busy focusing on other things. Like Jefferson and his rakish ways. "Maybe. But now you're motivated to get out of bed and dressed."

"Quite unfair." But Jefferson joined him in donning clothing. The Dreamer gave a pained sigh at Blaise's mismatched attire. "You are adorably *frustrating*."

Blaise smirked. "I know. Now come on, breakfast isn't going to make itself."

They padded down to the kitchen to discover that Tristan had scrambled a skillet of eggs, though he somehow made them both runny and burned. Vixen was there, too, looking like she'd just awoken. She gave them a half-hearted wave and rubbed her face, staring at the empty pot. "I'll make coffee." Vixen gave her red locks a shake as she groped for the bag of grounds.

"I know exactly what I'll make," Jefferson said, puttering over to a counter and opening the breadbox.

Blaise eyed him. "You're not going to mistreat my bread, are you?"

"Wouldn't dream of it." Jefferson still sounded tired, but at least moving around seemed to have roused him. Blaise decided not to begrudge him the bread. He edged over to the stove to see if he could help salvage the eggs.

They worked in companionable, sleepy silence as they assembled the makings of breakfast. Kittie appeared midway through and lent her talents. Her hair was bedraggled, and she had dark circles under her eyes, as if whatever terror she had defeated with Jefferson had come back for another round. Before long, they plated their food and sat to eat.

Blaise's brows rose as Jefferson brought his contribution to the table. The Dreamer shot him a smug look. "I present to you medium-rare bread with a buttered glaze."

The Breaker made a strangled sound. "Toast. This is toast."

"It's so simple, yet so elegant." Jefferson offered a piece to Blaise, barely hiding his smirk. Yes, he was definitely more awake now and trying to lighten the mood. Kittie and Vixen were amused by his antics, so maybe it was worthwhile.

Blaise accepted the toast, biting off a corner. When he finished it, he nodded. "Careful, or I'll have you help in the kitchen more."

"Don't threaten me with a good time." Jefferson winked at him. The simple statement made Blaise feel fluttery inside. He really *did* like it when Jefferson baked with him. His preferred activity, in fact.

Once Tristan finished his plate and skulked out, Kittie's gaze sharpened, flicking between Blaise and Jefferson. There was a question in her eyes, one she wasn't willing to voice because she, too, knew that Jefferson's magic was a private affair.

"Vixen, there's something I have to tell you," Jefferson said without preamble, pushing aside his half-eaten plate of scrambled eggs. Sadly, Blaise hadn't been able to salvage them as much as he'd have liked. The flame-haired outlaw's eyebrows rose, an invitation for Jefferson to continue. "I've kept this quiet to protect myself, but we're at the point where you should know about my magic."

That piqued her curiosity. "I know what it means for another mage to share that information with me," Vixen said, her tone soft.

Jefferson smiled, then explained his Dreamer magic as best he could. The Persuader listened, asking a few questions for clarity. When she nodded with understanding, Jefferson moved to the next component. "Last night, I used my magic to look for Jack. I wasn't able to find him. But I did find Raven."

CHAPTER THIRTY
What Could Possibly Go Wrong?

Vixen

*R*aven. Even now, his name brought a rush of confusing emotions. If Vixen had known parting ways with him would be so hard, she'd have never given their relationship a chance to begin with. But that wasn't fair. She'd deserved a chance to try. She blew out a frustrated breath. But had her dalliance jeopardized their bid to protect the people and the land she cared about? Vixen wouldn't allow that—not if she could help it.

She heaved a sigh. "Where is he? Who is he working with?"

Jefferson shook his head. "Those are things I couldn't quite pinpoint with my magic. Not to mention that by the time I found him, I was wrung out."

Vixen nodded. The ambassador had shadows under his eyes, which was unusual for him. "I'm not sure how we can use this information. Especially since you didn't actually find Jack."

Kittie pursed her lips. "We may not have found Jack last night, but I'll see what I can do about that today."

Blaise looked at the Pyromancer in alarm. "Is that a good idea?"

Kittie regarded the Breaker with a cool look, and when she spoke, her tone was gentle. Proof that she understood Blaise's nerves. "He's my *husband*. What would you do if Jefferson vanished without a trace?"

There was a time when Vixen knew it wouldn't have occurred to Blaise to go after the other man. But that time had come and gone. The Breaker didn't hesitate. "I'd search for him from one sea to the other."

"So, you understand," Kittie said, to which Blaise nodded, though he still didn't look happy about it. She turned to Vixen. "If I can find Jack, I suspect he'll have ideas about Raven. He might have even learned something."

Vixen didn't doubt that. The problem was she feared the Firebrand might not find Jack. They couldn't rely on the missing Effigest to be of help in any of this. But she also recognized it was a fool's errand to dissuade Kittie.

"Right. Kittie will search for Jack." Vixen blew out a breath. "And we'll attend the gala tonight."

She didn't enjoy thinking about the gala. Vixen stood on the precipice between her old life and her outlaw life. She touched a hand to the pocket that held the enchanted ring. After tonight, she wouldn't stay at Hawthorne House with her friends. And she didn't know what she would do about Alekon. Vixen couldn't bear to part with him, but he was a pegasus. He was in danger if he stayed in Phinora long term. A pegasus would be a tempting addition to an elite menagerie.

"Vixen?"

She blinked. Kittie had risen from the table to head off on her quest to find her husband. Jefferson and Blaise had been speaking and must have asked her something. "Sorry. I was distracted. What?"

"I asked if you knew who's invited tonight. I would assume all the Phinoran elite, but since this is secular..." Jefferson drifted off, waving a hand.

Right, even though Jefferson hailed from the Confederation, he wouldn't know all the ins and outs of the Luminary's traditions. "Yes, this will be celebratory, so most of the guests will be elite or dignitaries." Gods, Vixen didn't like the thought of being around the elite. If they knew about her magic... She wet her lips, setting that worry aside. "The Reclamation Ceremony will be held in the Asaphenia, and everyone is invited to that, regardless of station." Entry to the ceremony would be a frenzy, but that wasn't something she had to worry about.

She'd have a front-row seat.

"Do we have to go to that?" Blaise asked, his voice almost a whine.

The Breaker wouldn't like the Reclamation Ceremony. If they kept to tradition, it would involve the spilling of blood. She saw Jefferson was about to speak, but she shot him a look to quell his tongue. "You don't have to go to the Reclamation Ceremony if you don't want to."

Blaise rubbed his arm, the one with the dead geasa tattoo and the long, pale scar. "I feel like an awful friend, not wanting to be there for you."

Vixen shook her head. "You came here all the way from the Gutter, and you didn't have to. You're a damn good friend."

He gave her a wan smile. She didn't miss the way his gaze flicked to Jefferson. Vixen knew Jefferson was the real reason Blaise had come, and she didn't begrudge either of them. She stood by her words. Blaise *was* a damn good friend.

"But we *will* be at the gala," Jefferson said. "And this may be one of our best opportunities to learn about any ongoing plots."

"How are we going to find out anything?" Blaise asked.

Jefferson grinned. "You forget, I can be quite charming."

"And you attract trouble," Blaise added.

The Dreamer slung an arm around Blaise's shoulders. "It's a gala. What could possibly go wrong?"

CHAPTER THIRTY-ONE
Slaughterhouse Tour

Kittie

Kittie's strides were resolute as she headed to the stables. She still wasn't at her best, but there was no way in Perdition she was going to sit around like a fragile flower with her husband missing. Especially after that same husband had left her in the dust. *Jackass.*

All four pegasi were out in the paddocks, grazing together. Their heads lifted at her approach, swishing their tails. <Jefferson did not find your mate,> Zepheus said, voice mournful. Kittie supposed Emrys or Seledora had already shared the news.

"No, he didn't," Kittie agreed, the old pain of loss searing deep inside. A reminder of the time she had thought she'd lost her family forever. A time when losing herself to the oblivion of alcohol had been the answer. And damn, that was tempting at the moment. Oh, what she wouldn't do for a cup of caladrius root tea right now. She shook her head, refocusing. "But I'm going to go after him."

The palomino's ears swung toward her with interest, though indecision warred in his rich brown eyes. He wanted to go with her, but his instinctive fear of fire won out. Kittie understood, though her heart twinged once more at the pegasus's fear of her.

<I'm sorry.> Zepheus lowered his head. Kittie noticed a sheen of sweat on his neck. He was agitated, and going with her wouldn't help, even though he wanted Jack returned as badly as she did.

"I won't be alone." She patted her pocket, then pulled out an earthen fire pot. "I have Najaria."

At that, the pegasi shifted nervously. They had a healthy respect for the aethon's potential inferno. <An elemental in Phinora may be a risk,> Zepheus said after a moment.

Oh, she knew. But Kittie also had a lot of faith in her unusual equine. "She'll keep to her harmless state, I'm certain." Unless they needed fire. "As far as anyone who sees us will know, she's only a chestnut mare. And I need her to help me find Jack." Kittie's mind drifted back to Fortitude, where the aethon had led them to the fire pit with the burned papers. Najaria knew something.

Kittie picked up additional information from Zepheus about the slaughterhouse. Unfortunately, Jefferson hadn't been able to figure out where the estate house was, so the slaughterhouse was the best place to start. Once she had gleaned everything from the palomino that she could, Kittie opened the fire pot to release the mare.

A plume of smoke curled over the lip, billowing into the form of a pawing chestnut mare. Najaria regarded Kittie with bright eyes, twisting her head around to snap her teeth at the pegasi.

"Behave," Kittie murmured, stroking the elemental's sleek neck. "You'll have to wear a saddle and bridle." The mare snorted in annoyance.

<I believe there are spares in the tack room,> Seledora said. Of the pegasi, she was the least nervous around Najaria. Perhaps because they were both mares.

The Pyromancer headed for the tack room, Najaria clopping alongside. Seledora was right. There were saddles and bridles there, though they were not at all the sort outlaws used. Jack called them pancakes, as they were flatter and more rounded than the outlaw saddles, and they lacked the horn. Fortunately, Kittie was quite familiar with the Confederation saddle, so it made little difference to her.

The elemental hated being saddled. The entire time Kittie tacked her up, the mare's ears lay flat against her skull, and she stomped a rear hoof to display her agitation. Kittie knew Najaria would settle once the task was complete. She found a bitless bridle, and a short time later, Kittie and her aethon set out on their hunt.

Kittie wished Emmaline had come with them. The young Effigest had a talent for finding people, and Kittie felt certain her daughter would have been able to narrow down Jack's location. But as it was, Kittie would have to go about things the old-fashioned way: making inquiries and using every trick she could think of to get results.

While they didn't know where Jack was, Blaise had given her a name to work with: Jeremiah Jones. Kittie repeated his name over and over in her head like a mantra. Maybe if she thought about him enough, he'd be easier to locate.

A mundane horse might have grown nervous approaching the slaughterhouse, but not Najaria. The reek of death clung to the area like a fog. Livestock milled in the pens, their anxious sounds filling the air. There wasn't a pig, sheep, or cow on the premises unaware of their fate. Kittie swallowed as she rode past a bleating sheep, keeping her eyes focused ahead.

The slaughterhouse was so much larger than she had expected. It was a massive building with stockyards butting up to it. The building had a lovely stone facade topped with dainty cupolas, as if the architect had tried to make the building of death into something classy and modern. They had tried but ultimately failed.

A man came out of the slaughterhouse gates. He squinted at her. "It's not time for tours, miss."

Tours? Kittie flicked a glance at the slaughterhouse. Who in their right mind would seek to tour a slaughterhouse? But she answered her own question—she knew. There were many in the Confederation who would see nothing wrong with witnessing the spectacle of slaughter. While Kittie had no issues with eating meat, she disliked the idea of the process turned into some sort of deranged entertainment.

Burn. Najaria pawed at the ground. The aethon couldn't communicate like the pegasi, but she had a way of getting across her ideas. And right now, the mare was very interested in the idea of burning the slaughterhouse to the ground. A picture flashed in Kittie's mind of the aethon fully engulfed as she raced through the structure, setting it ablaze.

As tempting as that was, it wasn't their purpose. Kittie cleared her throat, drawing on all the bravado her younger self had possessed. "I'm not here for a tour. I'm here to see Jeremiah Jones."

The man frowned. He scratched his forehead and inadvertently left a line of dirt on his brow. "Huh. Didn't know he had any business today. You can come in."

"No, I won't be leaving my mount," Kittie said quickly. Then she cleared her throat, realizing she had spoken too forcefully. "The stink of death makes her nervous."

Najaria snorted, annoyed by the lie. The man appeared not to notice and nodded. "Right. I'll see if he'll come out."

A few minutes later, a man strode out to meet them. Kittie licked her lips, keeping her inner fire under wraps. She had dismounted while she waited, and now she pasted a pleasant smile on her face. Let him think her soft and weak. "Mr. Jones. Thank you so much for meeting with me."

He regarded her with curiosity. "You're welcome. I wasn't expecting anyone today. Are you here for a contract?" Jones nodded toward the slaughterhouse.

"I'm here to make a deal, yes," Kittie agreed. She glanced away. "Could we walk a bit? I need to stretch after being in the saddle."

"Of course, Miss...?"

"Larue," Kittie supplied, using her birth name. "Kittie Larue."

So far, so good. Kittie started at a sedate walk, Najaria trailing along as if she were a stolid pony. When they were a healthy distance from the abattoir's entrance, Kittie started. "I'm here to speak with you because I have it on good authority you can provide the information I need."

Jones hesitated. "I'm not sure what you're after. I run the slaughterhouse."

"Mmm, you do." Kittie turned, looking at the modern facade in the distance. "And yet, I suspect there's more here than meets the eye."

He scowled. "Are you a reporter with the *Izhadell Tribune*? I've already told you people, I have nothing to say about my business. Especially after the last reporter *disappeared*."

A chill threaded down her spine. There were so many horrifying ways a slaughterhouse worker could make someone disappear. That only solidified her suspicion that this man was up to no good, especially if he didn't want a journalist looking into his work.

Kittie shook her head as she started walking again. They passed a pen of milling cattle. "No. I'm looking for someone who's missing, and you're one of the last people he saw." It was a guess, but she figured it was a worthwhile bluff.

The slaughterhouse worker laughed, turning to lean against the stockyard fence. "That so? This wouldn't be the first time someone has accused me of running a troublemaker through the works."

Her rage wanted to roar up like an inferno, but Kittie kept it corralled like a cheerful hearth fire. If Jack had met his end inside this slaughterhouse... No, she couldn't think that. He wasn't dead. Couldn't be dead, not to a man like this. Jones was trying to prod her into making a mistake, and she couldn't allow that.

"I'm looking for a man with blonde hair. Mid-forties. Dresses like an outlaw and has an attitude to match."

Jones's bravado wavered for a beat, a clear tell that he knew who she meant. Then he shrugged. "Can't say I've seen anyone who looks like that."

"I think you have," she challenged.

He moved fast, closing the distance between them and grabbing Kittie's wrists. A dark chain shot up from the ground, wrapping around her right leg. His face twisted into a snarl as Najaria flung up her head, nostrils flaring in alarm, issuing a warning whinny. Jones ignored the mare, focusing on the person he hoped to intimidate. "Listen, woman—"

Kittie bared her teeth at him. "No, *you* listen. You don't know who you're dealing with." His dirt-encrusted nails gouged her skin, but she didn't break his grip. Not yet. She glanced over his shoulder, catching sight of a steer that stood nearby, tail swishing away the cloud of flies that harried it. The Firebrand's brow furrowed as she focused on the tiny insects.

The steer bellowed in terror as the swarm of flies turned into a mass of burning embers. The nearby cows heard the cry and caught the scent of smoke. They rushed to clump on the far side of the pen, pressing against the boards of the fence, the lumber groaning under the pressure. Jones twisted to look over his shoulder, eyes widening when he saw the smoldering flecks that had once been horseflies.

"What?" he gasped, voice almost a squeak.

"Tell me what you know about the outlaw, or I'll burn you from the inside out," Kittie growled, her eyes sparking with anger. She snapped her fingers, almost an afterthought, and sent a gout of flame into the arcane cuff Jones had used to bind her. The metal fell away like slag.

He released her, stumbling away. Jones trembled, and for a moment, he looked like he might consider fleeing. But Najaria stood nearby, pawing the ground, eager for a chase. No living man could escape the aethon's flashfire, and Kittie had a decent range on her fire. He would be ashes before he made it to the safety of the slaughterhouse.

"The outlaw...he was here. The other mage nabbed him, though." Jones swallowed, his eyes wide with terror.

Good. He had a respect for fire. "What other mage?"

Jones shook his head. "I don't know. Black hair. Didn't say much, but he's working for the same woman I am." Then the slaughterhouse worker realized he'd said too much, biting down on his lower lip.

"Who do you work for?" Kittie demanded.

"I don't know the name. I just know she has money. One of the elite. Rents a house nearby. The boys took the outlaw there."

Kittie's pulse raced. That was just the sort of lead she'd been hoping for. "Take me there."

Jones shook his head. "No. I can't."

Kittie pulled on her magic, lifting her right hand. Flames danced in her palm. She curled her fingers around them, then smiled as they lazily licked up the length of her arm like a fiery snake. The flames settled around her shoulders like a brightly burning shawl. Kittie said nothing, just watched him while the fire crackled cheerfully.

"I...I can tell you how to get there," Jones hazarded.

She canted her head, considering. Kittie glanced at Najaria. The mare bobbed her head. Maybe she was right. Traveling with this man might be more trouble than it was worth. "Do that."

Moments later, Kittie had directions. She met Jones's eyes before she dismissed him. "If these directions are wrong, if you have betrayed me, I'll burn this slaughterhouse to the ground with you inside of it, hanging from a meat hook. Do you understand?"

He stared at her in disbelief, then anger clouded his face. No doubt hazing his healthy fear of her. "You bitch—"

Najaria pinned her ears, her mane and tail igniting. Fire caressed the edges of her hooves, dangerous sparks lighting her eyes. Her head snaked toward the man, teeth bared as she bit his shoulder, lifting him up and shaking him like a terrier with a rat. Jones screeched in agony and fear, collapsing in a whining heap when the aethon released him.

Kittie stood over the fallen man. "Consider yourself lucky she only bit you. We both could have done much worse. This is a warning." She turned to mount as Najaria's mane and tail returned to thick horsehair, and once she was in the saddle, she glanced back at the man who was staggering to his feet. One arm was clapped to his wounded shoulder. "Thank you for the information and directions, by the way."

Najaria was already on her way when he shouted a litany of curses in their wake. Kittie smiled, satisfied. She knew well that the man's pride was battered, in addition to his flesh.

An hour and two wrong turns later, they found the residence Jones had described. Najaria ambled down the road outside it while Kittie considered what to do. She couldn't get inside. But the aethon was another matter.

Kittie asked Najaria to move off the road, into a copse of trees. She had an idea. "You are fire. Can you become part of the fire that's in the house, possibly eavesdrop?"

The mare tilted her head, ears flicking with uncertainty, telegraphing that she didn't understand the question.

Right, fire elementals had little knowledge of something like this—especially one like Najaria, who had been imprisoned for so long. "That means you would go in there and listen. Or look, if you can. I don't know what it's like for you when you're pure fire. Can you see?" Najaria bobbed her head to say that she could. "Good. Perhaps if they use any lanterns instead of mage-lights, you can keep an eye out for Raven? Or whoever the elite is that he's working with?" Though how Najaria would communicate that, she didn't know.

The mare blew out a soft breath, then turned to nudge the leather of the saddle. Oh, good plan. Wouldn't do to burn up the tack when she went full flame. Kittie hurriedly removed the saddle and bridle, stowing them nearby.

"I'll wait here."

Najaria nuzzled her affectionately, then stepped away, arching her neck. The mare reared, her body dissipating into a puff of smoke. The smoke wafted away on the light breeze, though it didn't follow the course of the wind. It undulated toward the fence surrounding the house and then flitted up to the chimney.

CHAPTER THIRTY-TWO
Passive Aggression

Vixen

Once they finished making plans, Jefferson drifted back to bed, his handsome face lined with exhaustion. Blaise transitioned to a flurry of nervous baking, which Vixen didn't complain about because everything he made was mouth-wateringly delicious and filled the house with sweet, yeasty scents. Nibbling on an assortment of cookies, muffins, and tarts was a pleasant distraction from what was coming.

Mid-afternoon, Blaise headed upstairs to rouse Jefferson so that they could dress for the gala. Vixen went to her own guest room, sighing as she regarded the lovely dress that had been delivered late that morning. It was a striking emerald green, a color that would bring out the vibrant red of her hair. But the fact remained that it was a dress, and Vixen didn't much care for them. Trousers were much more comfortable.

She chewed on her bottom lip, reconsidering. While she might have to return to her former life, Vixen had changed—and wouldn't it be fitting for some of those changes to come with her? With a nod, she decided she liked the idea. Her reintroduction was going to cause a ruckus, so she may as well run with it in her own way.

And in that case, she had just the thing. Vixen grinned as she popped open her travel trunk. In all the chaos of their arrival, she hadn't even unpacked. She dug around and pulled out the outfit she'd finished back in Fortitude shortly before they'd left. The fabric of the corset had wrinkled, but that was something she could fix.

"Gods, this will be almost scandalous," Vixen murmured to herself, running a hand over the silky ruffles of the short skirt. But something about it felt right. As the Spark, she'd always been told to trust her gut. That Garus had given her the wisdom to find her way. There had been many times she'd doubted that after she'd discovered she was a mage. But now, in this moment, Vixen wanted to believe that the god she'd been born to represent approved.

She remedied the wrinkled fabric, then set about dressing. Vixen paired it with some flattering striped trousers she'd brought along. They clung to her shape in a manner that a proper Confederation woman would disdain. *I'm not a proper Confederation woman, though.* That thought made her smile.

To complete the outfit, Vixen pulled out her knee-high riding boots. They were dusty and scuffed from use. That wouldn't do— if she showed up with footwear in such a state, she'd lose any advantage this was giving her. She visited Blaise and Jefferson's room to inquire after boot polish. With her prize in hand, Vixen headed back to her room to clean and polish the leather until it gleamed.

Once the boots were on, she saw to her hair and rouged her lips. Then she studied her reflection in the floor-length mirror, swallowing. The creature staring back at her was a cross between the Valoria of old and the Vixen of now. She lifted her chin, deciding that she liked the woman staring back at her. A blend of Phinoran and outlaw.

She stepped out into the hallway and headed downstairs to where Blaise and Jefferson waited in the parlor. She heard them discussing the Breaker's ensemble—Blaise was apparently unhappy with the puff tie his beau had selected for him.

"But it completes the *look*." Jefferson gestured to encompass all of Blaise as she entered. He glanced over his shoulder at the sound of her boot heels on the hardwood floor. His eyebrows lifted with appreciation. "Well, *hello* there. That's quite a striking outfit."

Vixen grinned. "I decided that even if I'm returning to my old life, I'm a different person now, and I should remind everyone of that."

"It works," Jefferson said, his voice husky. Blaise jabbed him with an elbow. "What? You don't need to be jealous."

"I'm not *jealous*," Blaise grumbled, in exactly the manner of someone who was, in fact, a little jealous. Or maybe not jealous, Vixen decided. *Anxious*.

Jefferson heard it, too. His focus shifted to Blaise, stepping closer to take his hands. "Good, since you have absolutely no reason to be jealous. You look magnificent, puff tie and all."

"The word *puff* should only be used with pastries." Despite his observation, Blaise seemed mollified.

"Noted," Jefferson said, eyes twinkling.

Blaise tugged at the offending puff tie, though now his gaze had fallen on Vixen. "I guess he's right. You *do* look nice."

Vixen grinned. From Blaise, that was high praise. He didn't concern himself with how other people looked all that often, not like his beau. Now, if she'd been bearing a tray of cupcakes, then she'd have his complete attention as he dissected how they were made and what he thought about them.

"She'll be the talk of the town by the time the night is done," Jefferson said. Then he cocked his head. "Our coach will be here soon. Are you ready for what's coming?"

"No. Can I stay here?" Blaise asked.

Jefferson nudged Blaise's side. "You very well know I wasn't talking to you."

Vixen was going to miss their banter. She took a breath to steady herself, then nodded. "What other choice do I have?"

"You always have a choice." Blaise's voice was soft, almost a whisper. Jefferson had a contemplative look on his face, but he nodded in agreement. "If you don't want to do this, we can figure something else out."

Vixen shook her head. "It's too late for that now." She heaved a breath. "But I can do this. I have my friends beside me."

Her words influenced Blaise. She saw his spine straighten, a determined jut in his jaw. "You do."

<There is a coach coming up the drive,> Alekon informed her, his tone neutral. Vixen knew he wasn't happy about being unable to accompany her to the gala, though the pegasus was relieved the other mages would be with her. <Will you come see me before you go?>

His request was heartbreaking, as if the bay stallion expected to never see her again. Like she was abandoning him. Vixen swallowed a lump in her throat, knowing she would do everything in her power to prevent it, but it may not be enough.

"Our ride is here, but I need to stop by the stables for a moment," Vixen said.

"There's a tin of cookies on the kitchen counter," Blaise offered.

"Thank you. I'll be at the coach shortly." Vixen headed out, her boot heels ringing on the floor as she went to snag the cookies that were the only solace she could offer her best friend right now.

Blaise

"Now I know how the animals in a menagerie feel," Blaise murmured to Jefferson as yet another elite couple drifted away after a stilted conversation instigated purely so they could goggle at the Breaker.

"Not that it will make you feel any better, but at a gala like this, everyone is on display to some extent. Not just you," Jefferson said, voice soft. He pressed a reassuring hand against the small of Blaise's back.

"Do you have any good conversation stoppers?" Blaise asked, trying to hide a grimace as another couple strode toward them.

"Don't you mean starters?"

"No. Definitely stoppers." Then Blaise had no choice but to paste on a smile as the approaching woman cooed about meeting *the* Breaker. Maybe he should take another look at the Ravanchen grimoire. There had to be an invisibility spell, right? Or maybe he could figure out how Jack cast his Obfuscation spell.

When they had arrived for the gala at Dawnlight, the official residence of the Luminary, attendants had whisked Vixen off to meet with the Luminary. Guards in the gold and white uniforms of the Luminary's Lightguard escorted Blaise and Jefferson to the front entry, where Blaise discovered that this was an important enough affair to warrant an announcement of each guest's arrival. Or at least the guests who mattered, according to Jefferson. Apparently, *they* mattered. Blaise had hated every second of those eyes on him, and he had definitely entertained the idea of running away to live the rest of his days in the surrounding swamps. Swamp hermits didn't have to endure the predatory gazes of a hundred elite men and women.

Jefferson had been right about one thing: the other elite barely tolerated the Dreamer's presence there. Whenever they approached, they shot cutting looks at him. The worst part was that they were mostly civil to Jefferson, but there was a level of antagonism to their words and gestures that even Blaise—who knew he still sorely lacked in his understanding of social interactions—could detect.

"Why are they behaving like that to you?" Blaise asked.

"Like what? Oh." Jefferson linked an arm through his, starting on a casual stroll. "They're being passive-aggressive."

"I don't like it."

Jefferson chuckled. "Nor do I, but their words and pettiness can't harm me anymore. They're not—" He stopped walking. "Blast."

"What?" Blaise felt the sudden stiffness of Jefferson's biceps against his as the Dreamer's muscles tensed.

Jefferson stared across the vast room. "Tara Woodrow is over in the far corner speaking with Phillip Dillon."

The names were vaguely familiar to Blaise, but he hadn't seen either person before, so only knew of them from Jefferson. "Quiet Ones?"

"Yes." Jefferson pursed his lips.

Nothing set them apart from the other attendees at the gala. If Jefferson hadn't pointed them out, Blaise would have thought they were just another set of wealthy blowhards. He chewed his lip as he thought back to the things Jefferson had told him about the Gutter delegation's time in Nera. Woodrow was the woman who had dosed Kittie's drink in a bid to have the Firebrand blamed for a deadly fire. And Dillon? He was the one who had orchestrated the campaign that had drained Jefferson's fortunes, poking holes in his preferred identity. He was dangerous in a way Blaise didn't understand, wielding power, wealth, and influence.

"Should we leave?" Blaise asked. He disliked the idea of Jefferson being around people who had hurt him in a manner Blaise could do little to fight.

Jefferson shook his head. "No, we need to be here. They haven't even introduced Vixen yet. Besides, if we leave, they win."

Blaise considered this. He didn't enjoy backing down, but

sometimes it was the safest idea. But Jefferson had a better grasp of the undercurrents of the gala, so he trusted in him.

He didn't have long to ponder. Someone squealed nearby. "Blaise Hawthorne! I *thought* I heard them announce your name!"

When Blaise turned, he couldn't help but smile because he knew the woman hurrying over to them—and more than that, he *liked* her. Lizzie Jennings grinned at him, her eyes dancing. "Oh, howdy, Lizzie."

She gave him a friendly pat on the arm, which Blaise made himself tolerate, knowing she meant well. Although she was the woman behind the award-winning musical about his life, there were some things she didn't know—his dislike of being touched by most people, for one.

"It's so good to see you again." Then she turned her attention to Jefferson, crossing her arms. "And *you*. I have mixed feelings about you."

Jefferson spread his hands. "You and everyone else, it seems."

Blaise canted his head. "How's your writing going, Lizzie? Anything new in the works?"

The playwright—no, that was the wrong word; Jefferson said she was a *librettist*—sighed at the question. "It's not gone well. I've lacked inspiration since *Breaker* debuted. And now I'm afraid I don't have another in me. It's as if my creative well has dried up."

Blaise nodded, careful to keep his expression neutral. "That's too bad. Have you considered something about...oh, I don't know...a politician who secretly moonlights as an entrepreneur and mage?"

Jefferson made a choking cough at the suggestion. Blaise met his gaze and winked before refocusing on Lizzie.

She raised her eyebrows. "Are you...wait, you're suggesting the Malcolm Wells story?"

"Maybe."

A sideways glance at Jefferson proved he was a conflicted blend of flustered, appreciative, and embarrassed. It was an unusual combination on the Dreamer, and it made Blaise chuckle. The gala was getting better.

"Hmm." Lizzie's eyes flicked over Jefferson. "I hadn't thought about that, but...yes, that would be the natural successor, wouldn't it?"

"Does this mean I'm forgiven?" Jefferson asked, canting his head and offering an endearing smile.

Lizzie scoffed. "You were duplicitous to not *only* the entire Salt-Iron Council, which includes my darling husband, but also *me*. Just because I think you might make an interesting subject, doesn't mean you're *forgiven*."

She might be annoyed now, but Blaise didn't think she'd stay that way for long. Especially if she sat down and talked to Jefferson the same way she had Blaise and uncovered why the Dreamer had behaved as he did. Malcolm Wells might have been born among the elite, but nothing about his life had been pleasant.

"I forgave him," Blaise pointed out, his voice gentle.

Lizzie nodded. "I suppose you did. Well, what do you say, Mr. Cole? Shall I plan to speak to you some time for this production?"

"It would be an honor," Jefferson said, inclining his head graciously.

A few moments later, the librettist hurried off in search of her husband. Once she was a distance away, the Dreamer edged closer to Blaise.

"You can be quite the cunning schemer when you want to be." Jefferson's voice was husky, caught somewhere between deep gratitude and amazement.

"Consider it retribution," Blaise said, though they both knew it wasn't retaliatory in the least.

"Do you want to dance?" Jefferson had frozen again, staring over Blaise's shoulder.

The question caught Blaise off guard. He blinked, confused. "What?"

"Dance. I asked if you wanted to dance," Jefferson repeated.

His green eyes flicked back to Blaise, troubled. "Because Phillip Dillon is walking this way."

Of all the things to do, dancing wasn't high on Blaise's list, but he didn't want to allow Dillon a chance to corner and threaten Jefferson. "I'm going to step on your feet."

Relief washed over Jefferson's face. "No, you won't. And even if you do, I'll forgive you. Come on." He took Blaise's hand, tugging him to the dance floor full of swirling couples.

Blaise felt awkward, and a glance at the surrounding men and women who clearly knew how to move to the music did nothing to ease his anxiety. But Jefferson wrapped his right arm around Blaise, pulling him near. The Dreamer twined the fingers of his left hand with Blaise's right, the simple gesture doing much to ground Blaise. For a heartbeat, it was just the two of them, close and comfortable. Safe.

The music seemed to curl around them, and though Blaise didn't know how to do much more than sway with the beat, even he had to admit there was almost something magical about it.

"See? We don't have to do anything fancy," Jefferson murmured, leading Blaise to the left to avoid an oncoming couple. "Though if you'd like to learn to dance one day, I'd be happy to show you."

If anyone else had made the offer, Blaise would have immediately rejected it. But it was Jefferson, so he smiled. "I'll think about it."

"Ah, so that's a no." Jefferson's full attention was on Blaise, as if he hoped that in doing so, he could evade the notice of the Quiet Ones.

"That's not what I said, and you know it." Blaise leaned in to brush his lips against Jefferson's. The Dreamer's soft exhalation of welcome rewarded him.

Their kiss was short-lived. The music stopped, and somewhere a bell rang with a clarion chime, drawing everyone's attention. Blaise drew away from Jefferson, but only enough to see what was afoot. The man he thought was Phillip Dillon stood about ten feet away, speaking with someone, though his gaze flicked from Jefferson to the far side of the room.

"What's going on?" Blaise asked.

"That sound means an *entrance*," Jefferson explained. The way he stressed the last word made Blaise think this would be someone noteworthy.

He wasn't wrong. It took Blaise a moment to figure out where he should look, but then he saw people herded out of the way by the Lightguard. "Make way for the Light of our Land, the living avatar of Garus, our Luminary." The herald's words echoed across the room, followed by murmurs of anticipation.

The woman who strode in with an entourage didn't look like anyone special to Blaise, but then again, he was a poor judge of such things. She looked much like the other elite women in the room, her strawberry blonde hair twisted into an artful braid that was piled atop her head. The Luminary wore a dress made of rippling gold fabric with ivory embellishments. Blaise assumed it was probably very expensive—if he had to guess, the outfit was probably worth more than everything in the town of Fortitude.

He caught sight of Vixen trailing in the Luminary's wake, though she wore some sort of flowy frock coat that hid her attention-grabbing outfit. The Persuader kept her head down, as if willing the crowd to ignore her. With the flashy Luminary preceding her, no one gave Vixen a second look.

"So the games begin," Jefferson whispered.

"You're enjoying this," Blaise accused.

The Dreamer chuckled. "Guilty. Though having you in my arms is half the fun." With reluctance, he released Blaise. "Unfortunately, this means we'll be seated for the meal before any further dance opportunities."

Blaise's cheeks warmed with pleasure. While the gala wasn't the sort of entertainment he would choose to attend on his own, he enjoyed being with Jefferson. He cleared his throat. "Food isn't a bad idea."

The elite milled toward the tables arranged on one side of the room. Blaise thought for a moment that the seating was assigned, judging by the way the men and women examined the options before claiming a chair. But as they drew closer, he realized it must be subtle political and social posturing. Jefferson guided them to the table where Lizzie and her husband, Seward, sat, but a rush of elite claimed the free chairs first, forcing them to a nearby table where a middle-aged couple sat.

Oddly, as soon as Blaise and Jefferson selected their seats, the man and woman made hasty excuses to find another table. Blaise frowned. "Is this because of how they feel about you specifically? Or because they don't like mages in general?"

Jefferson studied the other elite as they slotted themselves into their seats. "Perhaps, but I suspect something else is going on."

A shadow loomed over the chair beside Blaise, confirming the Dreamer's suspicion. "Is this seat taken?"

It took every bit of self-control Blaise could muster to keep from reacting as he glanced over his shoulder at Phillip Dillon. The man had salt-and-pepper hair and a handsome face that was lined with stately wrinkles. He looked down at the pair of mages as if they were rabbits caught in a snare. Blaise knew a bully when he saw one. The palm of his left hand grew warm and fuzzy as his magic manifested. No, that wouldn't do. He took a breath and forced the power away.

"I can't say that it is," Jefferson answered, somehow keeping all the earlier tension from his voice. His hand moved to settle on Blaise's thigh—whether in warning or as a show of solidarity, Blaise didn't know.

Phillip Dillon pulled out a chair, offering it to the woman accompanying him. Once she sat, he moved to claim the chair beside Jefferson.

"Thank you, Phillip. You're too kind." She batted her eyelashes, though there was something hollow about the gesture and words. Then she turned her attention to Jefferson. "So good to see you again. You certainly made quite an exit the last time we saw you."

Blaise could have cut the tension with a butter knife. Jefferson's eyes had narrowed, his mind no doubt whirring through possibilities. Blaise didn't know what his love might say, but he couldn't sit here and let these elite spout their abuses. "Howdy. I don't believe we've met. I'm Breaker Blaise Hawthorne." He felt Jefferson's zing of surprise at the sally.

Phillip's mouth drew taut. "We're well aware that Jefferson brought his pet mage along."

The Quiet One aimed the words with the same devastating precision Jack used with his sixgun. The intent was clear: Blaise was as easy to dismiss as the carriage horses that had brought them to the event. Useful, but ultimately irrelevant. Jefferson's anger was almost a palpable thing, his hand tightening on Blaise's leg.

Tara, the woman, waved a hand as if hoping to clear the air. "Really, Phillip, there's no need for such savagery." The smile she flaunted belied her true sentiment. "We leave that to the *outlaws*." Her expression shifted into blissful innocence. "Honestly, we're surprised to see you at an event such as this. You've fallen so far out of favor, *Malcolm*—or, my apologies, you prefer Jefferson, now, do you not?"

"I do," Jefferson's voice was gravelly with warning. Blaise hated this. They were picking at Jefferson piece by piece, trying to crack his armor with their comments. Blaise had the sinking suspicion that this was going to be a very long, tense night.

CHAPTER THIRTY-THREE
Realm of Shadows

Jack

Damn Raven, but moments after the mage left, true darkness descended over Jack. Even worse, he realized that this realm, whatever it was, drifted—similar to the way shadows shifted as the sun changed position. The surrounding area was perfectly silent, and he only discovered the strange movement by the sensation of it veering beneath him, as if he were on a raft in the world's slowest river. If the world's slowest river was made entirely of shadow.

With effort, he eased in what he thought was the knife's direction, but after a short time, he realized that it, too, had shifted with the flow of shadows. Cursing Raven, the mage's parents, and all the generations that came before, Jack butt-scooted around the shadowy realm, hoping he would blunder into the knife without slashing himself in the process.

He was sweating by the time his thigh brushed against something. With a grunt of surprise, the Effigest angled his body until he could grope at the object with one hand. The whisper of cool, flat metal against his index finger revealed he had finally succeeded.

Cutting himself free proved to be a challenge. It was a difficult enough task with his hands tied behind his back, aching and sore, and the challenge only increased with the ever-present darkness and the way the shadows gradually drew the knife away from him when he fumbled and dropped it. Jack muttered a litany of curses. "Son of a five-legged chupacabra. Fizzlin' piece of dragonshit. Yellow-bellied Saltie-lovin' maggot..." It didn't help, but it made him feel better.

By the time his bonds frayed enough to release his hands, Jack was winded from the effort. He winced, flexing his shoulders as he massaged his wrists. His arms hurt, but he wasn't in a situation where he could sit around and wait to feel better.

He groped around in search of the mage-light. It had been further away, thus took longer to locate. But find it he did, and he breathed a sigh of relief as the soft blue glow illuminated the surrounding area.

Jack rubbed his chin, eyes narrowed as he surveyed the area. *What, exactly, is this place?* Was it something like the peacock's dreamscape? None of the magical theory he had been taught by his mentor or anyone in the Confederation covered something like this. Realms that existed within their own world. Was it an overlay of the real world, and he was in a shadowy version of that damned Quiet One's home? Or was it something else entirely? And did it even matter? Without sixgun, reagents, or anything to craft into a poppet, he was as helpless as an orphaned pegasus foal.

He had a knife, though. And his characteristic stubbornness. Raven had said not to try anything, but a large part of Jack wanted to bury a fist in the traitor's face the next time he saw him. But the odds were good that Raven was his only ticket out of here.

"Well, I ain't gonna figure out much of anything by staying

put," Jack reasoned aloud. Didn't care that he might sound crazy speaking to himself. Who was around to judge him?

He shoved the knife in his belt and picked up the mage-light. Raven would probably come back eventually, but then what? Jack was unwilling to leave his fate up to the traitorous Shadowstepper. No, as always, he was going to do things his own way.

Mage-light in hand, he set off into the strange world of shadows.

Kittie

NOT FOR THE FIRST TIME, KITTIE WONDERED IF ELEMENTALS grasped time in the same way humans did. She waited and waited, the sun setting in the distance and her stomach rumbling, a reminder that she hadn't eaten since her breakfast at Hawthorne House. Had something happened to Najaria, ensnaring her somehow?

She pulled the small fire pot out, cupping it in her hands. Remnants of ash shifted within the confines of the enchanted clay. Kittie wondered if she could use the ashes to call the aethon back.

"Come on, horse. I'm getting hungry." Like the pegasi, Najaria didn't appreciate being called a common horse. Kittie hoped maybe the jab would bring the aethon back, but there was no sudden reappearance of the mare. So much for that idea.

Well, Kittie had lived in Phinora long enough to know a little about the place. The light was waning, but that wasn't much of a problem since she could provide her own light. Kittie summoned a ball of flame in her left hand, then foraged for any edible berries or roots. She came across a bush of late-season sun-gold jester-berries. They were a little on the mushy side and not as sweet as she would have liked, but it was something to fill her belly while she waited.

Kittie was wiping her berry juice-stained hands on her trousers when she felt a sudden change of pressure behind her. "Najaria, it's about time—"

She turned and found herself face to face with Raven Dawson. He held a knife in his hand, perilously close to her throat. Kittie swallowed. She'd seen him practice with his knives in Fortitude, and even Jack respected his speed and skill. Kittie knew she had a good chance of immolating him, but probably not before he dealt what would be a fatal blow. And that wouldn't help her find Jack.

"Jack shouldn't have brought you along," Raven said, but there was no malice in his words. Only regret, and maybe sadness. "Quench your fire."

Kittie met his eyes, hoping that Najaria would choose this as her moment to reappear and tip the odds in her favor. "It was *my* choice." She didn't extinguish her ball of flame.

"Put it out," Raven repeated.

The Firebrand weighed her options. She didn't want her throat slit, but she wasn't about to drop all of her defenses. She wasn't helpless. Kittie trembled with adrenaline, closing her hand around the crackling orb. The fire caressed her skin, and though she felt the heat, it didn't burn her. She focused on the fire, willing for the smallest spark to free itself. *Just one spark.*

There. The spark pulled free, leaping from her hand onto Raven's shirt.

The Ringleader did what almost anyone would do when confronted with an unexpected run-in with fire: he reacted. With a yelp, he jerked away from Kittie, taking the knife with him and leaving her skin unmarred. The spark caught the flammable fabric—

There was a soft pop, and he was gone, leaving the spark behind. It drifted to the ground and died out. Swallowing, Kittie whirled, surveying the surrounding area. He must have used his magic to escape the threat. A wise tactic, but now she didn't know where he was, which was infuriating.

"Cursed aethon, get back here," Kittie muttered, wishing the mare would return. But she couldn't wait any longer. Raven knew where she was, which made her vulnerable. She didn't know who he was working with, and he might have gone to get reinforcements. It was time to admit defeat and make her way back to Hawthorne House—if she could figure out her way there at night on foot. Regardless, her priority was getting out of this area. She headed for the road—

A hand clamped down on her shoulder. Before Kittie could whirl to meet him, the world swam around her in a dizzying spiral. Her gut roiled, even worse than cramps during her monthlies. She wanted to curl up into a ball, anything to get away from that feeling, but she couldn't. Kittie was pulled through inky darkness, helpless to do a damn thing about it.

When, at last, the world around her stopped, she was in an unfamiliar place. Shadows stretched for as far as she could see—which wasn't far. It was like being out in the middle of nowhere on a starless night. The only dim light came from Raven, who stood over her.

With her gut finally settling, Kittie glared up at him. She wouldn't get mouthy, not like Jack would, but she wouldn't roll over and take it, either. "Where in Perdition am I?"

Raven gave her that kicked-puppy look again. "I wish I didn't have to do this, but I can't have you interfering."

That wasn't any sort of answer at all. "Did you take Jack?"

He made a point not to meet her eyes. Kittie knew Jack got under most people's skin, so she would have expected some level of glee at getting one over him. But Raven only gave a resigned nod. "Yes."

Kittie weighed her options. She didn't know where she was or how to get back, so if she attacked the other mage, the odds were good she'd be trapped for a while. Maybe forever. But she wasn't hurt, even though he could have stabbed her or worse. And he was talking—a little, anyway. Maybe she could lure more information out of him.

"Why did you take Jack?"

Raven made a frustrated sound. "Same reason I took you. Because he *found* me."

Something in his tone made Kittie think that wasn't the only reason. But Raven crossed his arms, and she suspected she wouldn't get much more from him on that subject. "Whatever's happened, whatever's driven you to do this, doesn't have to be this way. Let us help you."

Raven shook his head. "That's the thing. You can't help—you *or* Jack." He took a step backward. "You asked where you are. This is my realm. I'll be back to check on you. When I return, don't think to attack me. You won't like how it ends." And with that dire warning, he vanished.

His realm? That surprised her—this was the first she'd heard of such a thing. But it made sense. A realm of shadows. The faint light that had existed faded with Raven's departure. With a sigh, Kittie called up her flame again.

Her fire came, but not only that—Najaria. The aethon shimmered into being along with the orb of fire on Kittie's palm, though the light provided by the fiery mare did little to penetrate the ever-present dark.

Kittie sighed. "Najaria! Where have you been all this time?"

The mare tossed her head, pinning her ears back in a sign that whatever the reason, she was unhappy. Kittie didn't know if that meant something had interfered with her, or if the aethon was simply frustrated that she had come too late. Regardless, it didn't help the situation.

The Pyromancer carefully got to her feet, bracing against the elemental. Her gut wasn't completely happy yet, but it was better than it had been. Either the berries had been bad, or Raven's method of travel disagreed with her. She suspected the latter.

Kittie met the mare's obsidian eyes. "Well, at least I'm not alone."

CHAPTER THIRTY-FOUR
A Flame to Light the Ages

Vixen

The food spread before Vixen was some of the finest fare she'd seen since the last Feast of Flight, but she had little appetite for it. It was hard to focus on eating when she knew that her life was about to change.

She sat at the head table, though not beside her mother. The Luminary had thought it best to sit apart until they made the announcement revealing the Spark was alive and well. The people around her were under orders not to speak to her, and Vixen had been advised not to start any conversations. The Luminary wanted to control the narrative of her daughter's return, and she didn't want any attendees to figure it out in advance.

Rhys was there, too, though only in his capacity as a Tracker. Vixen wondered if he felt left out, alienated from this world that could have been his. *Should* have been his. She was too far away to discern anything from his face, though he leaned against a wall with arms crossed, scanning the assembled mass for any sign of trouble.

Vixen found Jefferson and Blaise in the throng, seated with

two others. Anyone else wouldn't have noticed anything amiss, but she knew Blaise. The Breaker fidgeted in his chair. Tension pooled in the shoulders of both men, and Vixen suspected it was because of their tablemates. She pursed her lips, wondering who they were. It was unfortunate she couldn't ask anyone around her.

After what felt like an eternity but was only an hour, the meal finished. Vixen had forgotten how interminable these events could be. Perhaps Blaise's disdain for them was warranted. If she had a lifetime of these ahead of her, it might be a better option to run back to the Gutter for good. She held back a sigh.

The Luminary arrowed a look in her direction, chin lifting in a manner that communicated the time had come. Vixen's mother rose from the table gracefully, gliding over to a dais. Her golden gown shimmered with each step, catching the light. Murmurs rose as the elite noticed she was on the move. As she mounted the dais, all eyes shifted to the theocrat. Conversations waned and then died, the attendees giving her their full attention.

The Luminary smiled across the throng. Juliette Kildare wasn't a tall woman, but she had a presence that commanded their focus. "Honored guests, Garus truly smiles down upon us this night." She lifted her hands as if offering thanks to the absent god. "I appreciate all who took the time to attend tonight. I know you had little notice, and your steadfastness heartens me."

Vixen fought the urge to roll her eyes. As if anyone here would make the mistake of not attending a gala put on by the Luminary herself. Vixen may have been absent from elite society for years, but she knew few would be so foolish. Besides, the elite were no doubt dying to know what warranted the usually-reclusive theocrat to hold such a celebration.

"The time of the Luminary Festival is nearly upon us, which makes my news auspicious." Juliette's gaze flicked back to Vixen before roving over the masses again. "Garus has blessed us. His wisdom has granted us a veritable miracle—the return of Spark Valoria Kildare, the soul we thought lost forever to Perdition."

Her words seemed to suck the air from the room. Silence fell over the crowd, not even broken by the tinkling of glass or the rasp of flatware. The staff had gone as still and quiet as the guests. Vixen swallowed, rising from her seat and sweeping the plain robe off to reveal her modified outfit. Her boot heels shattered the silence, rapping on the stone floor like the blasts of a sixgun. Vixen liked to think she was bold, but with all of those prying eyes on her, she felt anything but. She quivered as she joined her mother, reflexively touching the ring that veiled her magic.

Juliette took her daughter's hand and lifted it high. "The Spark has returned! May her wisdom grow into a flame to light the ages!"

"Her wisdom will light the way!" the crowd responded. Many rose to their feet, applauding. Several women burst into tears, clutching at their chests as if they couldn't imagine a more beautiful scene. Others went to their knees in supplication.

Surrounded by hundreds of people, Vixen had never felt more alone. Frozen in place on the dais, her eyes sought Blaise and Jefferson amid the throng. Jefferson's attention was on their seatmates, but the Breaker was watching her. He was just as helpless as she was, but his familiar face was like a watering hole in the Untamed Territory. An oasis for her survival. Vixen smiled at him, and her spirit soared when he tipped his chin, returning her smile with one of his own.

I'm not alone. I still have my friends. Thank Garus they had come with her. She couldn't have done this alone.

As quickly as it had come, the moment of reverie shattered. Questions boiled up from the elite, but none of them were loud enough to be anything more than murmurs. Vixen kept her head high, reminding herself why she was doing this. For the Gutter. For her friends. For the people she cared about. She lifted her chin, knowing that her flame-red hair made her stand out like a firefly in the night.

Juliette lifted her hands and the audience quieted. "Peace, my people. This is a time for celebration. Let us enjoy the night and all that Garus's wisdom had provided."

The Luminary returned to her seat with Vixen close behind. The others at the table shifted positions to allow Vixen a space beside her mother. Every bit of this felt like a half-remembered dream, the people around her familiar, but not. To her right sat Celestine Currington, a priestess on the Clergy Council. The older woman slanted a look at her, lips twisted into an expression that bespoke doubt.

"You should have let me speak," Vixen said to her mother, keeping her voice low.

"That would invite the rest of them to speak as well," Juliette pointed out, not even glancing at her daughter. "Besides, you'll have the opportunity to speak with them individually after the meal."

Wonderful. Vixen would rather face down a murder of half-starved chupacabras with her hands tied behind her back, but she would have to suffer through this. She fidgeted with the magic-concealing ring before going back to poking at the plate of food.

As the staff returned to take up empty plates, musicians returned to their instruments and the attendees drifted away from the tables. When the Luminary rose, Vixen took that has her cue to do likewise. Juliette nodded to her before stepping down to circulate among the faithful who crowded close to speak with her.

Vixen made her way down as well, and moments later found herself swarmed by the curious. They peppered her with questions, hands brushing against the fabric of her outfit. Their closeness and persistence made her want to scream for them to get away. Made her want to run, find Alekon, and never come back. She was remembering all the reasons she had left.

And a chance shifting of the crowd offered her a glance at Blaise, reminding her of all the reasons she had come back. *I can do this. It might not be what I* want *to do, but I can do it.*

So she smiled, answered their questions with all the patience she could muster, dancing around the circumstances of her disappearance, and carried on.

A sheen of nervous sweat had Vixen's clothing clinging to her by the time Blaise and Jefferson made it through the receiving line that had formed to meet her. It was late—or maybe early, since the clock had tipped past midnight. Jefferson leaned against Blaise, and for a moment, Vixen thought he was still tired. Until she realized he was tipsy.

"I don't think I've ever seen him drunk," Vixen commented to Blaise, suspecting that this wasn't a promising development.

"You look fabu..." Jefferson started, then paused as if he'd lost track of his words. "Fantas...amazing. Yes, *amazing*. That's the word." He aimed an index finger at Vixen, as if he wanted to be certain she knew who he meant.

Blaise made a frustrated noise. "We've got trouble."

Vixen pursed her lips, gaze shifting between the men. "What happened?"

"I can't use my magic right now," Jefferson declared loud enough to spur Blaise to slam a hand over his mouth.

"I really need you to be quiet right now," Blaise whispered to his beau, urgent.

"I'll be quiet if you kiss me." Jefferson puckered his lips and made a kissy sound.

"Why is he drunk?" Vixen hissed, deciding the Ambassador's inebriation must surely play a role in whatever new problem had arisen.

"It was the only way I could keep him from doing something we'd regret," Blaise explained, jerking a thumb toward Jefferson. Then he mouthed the single word: *magic*. "You saw who we sat with?" When Vixen nodded, he continued, "They're Quiet Ones. They were baiting us, and then once everyone had the chance to visit again, they've been planting rumors."

"Rumors?" Vixen glanced past Blaise to the remaining guests.

She didn't miss the cool looks aimed her way. "What kind of rumors?" If she knew, she could head them off at the pass.

A flush of anger clouded Blaise's face for a moment. "All sorts, and none of them good. They said that you're not really the Spark, that this is just an outlaw trick. That you seek to undermine the Confederation. And that if you really *are* the Spark, outlaws must have been the ones to kidnap you." He paused, swallowing. "That the timing is too convenient, that we've only brought the once-dead Spark back to life when the Gutter is under a threat."

"Also that you're a soiled dove," Jefferson added, in his too-helpful drunken way.

"Also that," Blaise agreed grimly.

"Gods damn it," Vixen cursed. A nearby elite woman heard her and gasped in horror, clutching a hand to her breast. *Great. Blasphemy. That's sure to help matters.* "What did Jefferson want to do about it?"

"Drop Dillon and Woodrow in the dreamscape and terrorize them." Jefferson suddenly sounded less drunk and more menacing. Vixen was glad no one was near enough to hear his suggestion.

"He can do that?" she asked Blaise. The Breaker gave a tiny nod, something unreadable flickering across his expression.

"I don't know what we can do against this without..." Blaise flexed the fingers of his left hand, a wash of silvery magic playing across it as quick as a blink. So quickly, anyone else would have not believed their eyes.

Vixen mopped at her forehead. "We'll figure something out. I'll be in touch soon."

CHAPTER THIRTY-FIVE
Pity Party

Vixen

"What did you tell them?"

Vixen's spine was ramrod straight as she stared at the opposite wall, counting the number of stripes that decorated the wallpaper to help keep her composure. "Nothing that spoke to any of those *rumors*."

Juliette Kildare paced before her like an irritated grasscat suffering from a case of weevils. "Then perhaps you should have. Now we're in a very tenuous position."

That was unfair. Vixen crossed her arms. "I didn't know until too late." And she foolishly hadn't anticipated the potential gossip. Gods, she'd been too long gone from this infernal place. Fortitude was a rumor mill, too, but nothing like this. "I didn't think—"

"That's exactly it," Juliette snapped. "This is not some feral outlaw town. Every small thing we do, every word we say or don't say matters. Garus grants us wisdom for moments like these. Use it."

Vixen uncrossed her arms, clenching her fists. "You don't think

Garus granted me the wisdom to survive *sixteen years* as an outlaw in the wilds?"

The Luminary sighed, her shoulders slumping. She shoved back a lock of golden-red hair, smoothing it behind her ear, and with that gesture, turned into Vixen's mother of old. "Sixteen years. More than half of your lifetime."

Good, her mother was grounded once more. "I'm an adult. Not the child you remember."

Juliette gave a small nod, then moved to sit beside her daughter. "And there's much for you to learn. You're still new to the intricacies that I'm balancing."

"Such as?" Vixen pressed.

It was her mother's turn to consider the wall interesting. "There are factions among the elite who no longer wish to answer to a Luminary." She paused, glancing down at her shoes. "Or, at the very least, not *this* Luminary."

Vixen frowned. This wasn't the first time in her life she'd heard of such a thing, though it sounded more serious now. "They support your cousin?" Vixen had never been clear about how her mother's cousin, Phoebe Millner, had ever been a contender for the position. From everything she understood, if something happened to the current Luminary and there was no Spark, Garus would select a new avatar. The elite just couldn't up and choose a new Luminary. Could they?

Juliette shook her head, her face stony. "No. Phoebe died five years ago."

"Murder?" Vixen swallowed, remembering her own father's death. While the official story was that her father had died of an illness, Vixen had always suspected that he'd been murdered.

"The undertaker claimed it was a natural death. But I suspect it wasn't. That perhaps some of the elite wanted her out of the way so they could make their own cases. In the event that anything happened to me." Juliette flicked a glance at Vixen.

A chill traced Vixen's spine. How hard would it be for the

more insidious among the elite to pull strings to create their own Luminary? It was possible Garus would truly work a miracle and select a new Luminary, but the gods and goddesses had been absent for so long...what if he didn't? Suddenly, Vixen realized she had stepped unawares into a potentially dangerous situation. The elite could be just as bloodthirsty as the fiercest creatures in the Untamed Territory—and twice as sadistic.

"I see," Vixen murmured. "So, they seek to take the power for themselves."

"Yes." Her mother sighed, sounding weary. She seemed nothing like the aggressive, mage-hating figurehead so many thought her to be. "And that's where the precariousness of our position lies. For you to be stolen away by mages and then returned by them...to let this go uncontested and forgiven puts me in a position of weakness."

Vixen gritted her teeth. She hadn't mentioned anyone stealing her away, much less mages. "I wasn't—" she started, then stopped, shaking her head in frustration. It would be so much easier if she could reveal her magic to her mother, to say that she was the one who had left of her own accord. But even if her mother could overlook her magic, if these troublesome elite found out, it would be their ruin. That begged the frightening thought: what if they already knew? Vixen Valerie hadn't exactly kept a low profile in the Gutter. But as long as they knew her as Valoria and not Vixen, it might work out.

"Yes?" her mother prodded.

Vixen blew out a frustrated breath, trying to figure out where to go from here. She thought about Blaise, who contained so much raw power, so much potential for destruction, yet practiced kindness whenever he could. "Garus teaches us to see that justice is done according to his scholarship. It's time to stop fearing mages and their magic—"

"I don't *fear* them," Juliette insisted, voice low. "Magic flies in the face of reason."

"And that's not a reason to keep them down, to blame them for everything." Vixen's pulse raced. "It should be seen as wisdom to forgive, to appreciate the gift of my return."

She knew by the way her head tilted that her mother was considering it. But Juliette shook her head after a moment. "Our memory is long, Valoria. And you forget, even though he was cleared in the Inquiry because of the Golden Citadel's cruel conditions, your Breaker friend killed many Confederation soldiers."

Fort Courage. The reminder fed the fire in Vixen's veins, and her cheeks warmed with anger. "You mean the same soldiers who killed dozens of innocent people in the Gutter? I saw what they did. I was *there!* They took me captive and—" No, she couldn't tell the Luminary they had stripped her magic. That was foolish. She wished her mother hadn't mentioned Fort Courage. There was no easy way around it.

Juliette stared at her, a mixture of horror and longing etched on her face. "*Wait.* I could have had you back at Fort Courage?"

Vixen nodded, kicking herself for her rash words. She was normally more composed, but she was too upset about the entire situation. "Yes."

Her mother cursed, a litany of colorful words Vixen couldn't remember ever hearing from her before. It was enough to make her sound almost like the surliest of outlaws. Then Juliette fisted her hands at her side. "Why didn't you tell them who you were?"

Vixen weighed the answer. From what she understood, most of the forces who'd taken her were dead. Jack had slain Commander Gaitwood himself. She settled on an answer that felt sensible and safe. "Do you think they would have believed me? Or, even if they had, that they wouldn't have used me to gain some advantage?"

Juliette frowned but accepted the response. "I suppose you're right." She rubbed her forehead. "It's late, and this gala was quite the disaster. Let's sleep on it, and tomorrow, we'll make plans for how to spin this to our benefit."

"Sleep on it?" Vixen muttered. "As if either of us will sleep after all that."

To her surprise, her mother laughed. "We should try. I only had a little wine at the gala, so I think I'll enjoy a full glass before I find my bed." She raised her brows. "Would you like to join me?"

Vixen grinned. "Got anything stronger than wine?"

Her mother flashed her a surprised look, then nodded. "We do. Perhaps that's not a bad idea."

"SURROUNDED BY A BUNCH OF OILY WEASELS, THAT'S WHAT I AM." Juliette hoisted the crystal goblet that was meant for fine wines, but currently sloshed with the golden amber of beer. They'd been discussing the various Phinoran elite who might plot against the Luminary, which seemed to be the majority of them.

Vixen discovered that alcohol loosened her mother's tongue, which perhaps explained why all of her distant memories of the woman included her only taking sips of wine and little more. It was also possible that Juliette Kildare had changed over the years they had been apart.

"They can go sit on a cactus," Vixen agreed. "The whole lot of them."

Juliette made an unladylike snort, setting her goblet down with a clank. A wave of beer sloshed over the side and onto the antique table, but she paid it no mind. "Pity that's about all we can do. Talk about them and wish they'd sit on a cactus, I mean." She sighed. "What was it like?"

Vixen blinked. She wasn't drunk, not quite, but she was in that pleasant, fuzzy place where it took her a moment to gather her wits. "What was what like?"

Her mother leaned forward, eyes glittering. She smacked the

table with one hand, her mouth twisting into a smile that could almost be described as wicked but not cruel. "The outlaws. Being with the outlaws. The Gutter. Everything."

The prompt gave Vixen pause. To buy herself time, she took another sip. Even in her current state, she remembered that her entire reason for being here was for the Gutter. For her friends. The words she spoke mattered. "It's very different from this, and in some ways, the same. Not a simple life. There's danger, plenty of danger." She barely suppressed a shiver as she recalled the day the airship had come to her town. The day she had lost friends and neighbors. Vixen swallowed. "And lots of good people."

"Hmm." Her mother was quiet for a moment. She reclined in her seat, and Vixen almost thought she had fallen asleep. Then Juliette adjusted her position in the sumptuous chair. "In some ways, it sounds better than Izhadell." There was a longing in her voice, and with a start, Vixen realized her mother had never had the chance to form friendships like she had in the Gutter.

There. That was the lead Vixen needed, and she pounced on it. "Parts of it are. No matter what the Confederation thinks about mages, we—" Vixen caught herself, clearing her throat to cover the fact that she had counted herself among the mages. "When you get down to the heart of the matter, mages are people the same as we are. They bleed, they love, they want to live their best lives."

Her mother pursed her lips. "But they're lesser. Magic makes them impure. Can't be trusted." She said it with the same conviction as a child declaring the sky was blue and water was wet. A fact. Something everyone knew.

Ah, there it was. Generations of lies served as truths, poisoning minds. Vixen rubbed the band of the ring. "None of that is true."

Juliette frowned, waving a hand in the air. "Even if that were the case, it does us no favors right now. The elite won't tolerate such nonsense. They're already up in arms with all the mages we've lost in the wake of the Breaker Inquiry."

The callous words helped to shake away more of Vixen's haze. She scowled. "Do you hear yourself? Speaking of mages as if we—as if they're livestock. Why don't you grow a spine and some wit? Stand up for what's right?"

"You are out of line." Her mother's words were frigid, all traces of her earlier ebullience faded. "Do you forget a mage stole you away? Mages have taken everything from me!"

Vixen fisted her hands. So, that was what her mother believed had happened. That had to change. "A mage didn't take me. I ran."

"*What?*" Juliette's eyes glinted with steel. "Why would you do that? Why, when you *knew* exactly what you are?"

Oh gods, I should have kept my damn mouth closed. Vixen stared at her knees. How could she possibly answer that question in a way that wouldn't make things worse? But she couldn't tolerate all the blame that had been laid on mages any longer. It was unjust. It had to change.

"Valoria? I expect an answer."

Vixen met her mother's eyes. "Why do you *think* I might have wanted to run away?" Even in her inebriated state, the Luminary was smart, and Vixen knew that if she thought about it for long enough, she'd make the logical leap. Garus was the god of wisdom, after all.

Juliette's brow creased in confusion. Vixen's mother rose, surprisingly steady. She paced across the room, stopping in front of the glass-paned doors that led to a veranda Vixen knew overlooked a garden, though it would be full of shadow-darkened flowers at this time of night. "I don't understand."

Vixen set her goblet down, pushing up from her seat. "I think, in your heart, you do. You just don't want to admit it."

Juliette's jaw set. "*Sorcerer.*" The word was pure vitriol on her lips. She had one hand on the doorknob, eyes on her daughter. "Maybe it would have been better if you really had died." She shoved the door open and strode onto the veranda.

Of all the things she could have said, those words gutted

Vixen. "You don't mean that!" She stalked toward the open door, trembling.

Outside, something stirred in the shadows. Vixen should have known what—or rather, whom—she was looking at, but she was distracted, trying to reconcile her mother's awful words. Raven stepped out of the shadows, knife in hand. He slipped around Juliette, blade at the woman's throat.

"Now, now. That's no way to speak to her." Raven's voice was edged with anger.

Gooseflesh trickled down Vixen's arms. Gods, Raven, here? It took her far too long to assess the situation, the danger her mother was in.

"You *will* release me," Juliette hissed with all the command of a woman accustomed to unquestioned obedience.

"Raven, *stop*," Vixen pleaded, hoping he would meet her eyes. If he did, she could—no, blast it all, she couldn't. Vixen furiously tried to wrest the ring from her finger, knowing she was losing precious time. Maybe she could stall him, buy time to use her magic on him. Yeah, and maybe pigs would fly. Raven wasn't an idiot and would know the danger she posed. He was clear-headed, not tipsy like she was. "Let her go. That's my *mother*."

He didn't meet her eyes. Raven wasn't taking any chances. "I know. I'm sorry, but this is the only way."

"The only way for what?" Vixen demanded.

But it was too late. Raven disappeared into the shadows, taking the Luminary with him.

Vixen cursed. How in Perdition had this situation just gone from bad to worse?

CHAPTER THIRTY-SIX

Lovesick Fool

Vixen

"Gods damn it!"

With some difficulty, Vixen wrestled the ring off her finger and threw it at the floor as hard as she could. The metal loop struck with a sharp *clink*, then skipped into the shadow of a chair. Her magic swirled to life within her, like a bullet in the chamber of a sixgun, ready to be loosed. Vixen blew out a frustrated breath. None of this was the ring's fault, and it wasn't fair that she blamed it. Besides, she was only borrowing it. With chagrin, she hurried over to retrieve it, though she jammed it into a pocket rather than putting it on.

She blamed herself. If she'd been faster, more alert, more aware, she could have stopped Raven. Or if she had said something different to her mother. But there was no use in wishing she had behaved differently—that pegasus had taken flight, and now she was forced to confront the reality of what had happened.

Raven had taken the Luminary of Phinora, one of the most powerful people in the Salt-Iron Confederation. And Vixen didn't know *why*. Did he have some misguided notion that this would help the Gutter's predicament somehow? But that made little sense—he was a Ringleader. None of this fit with Raven Dawson, Ringleader.

But it might align with Raven Dawson, lovesick fool. Scorned beau.

Vixen closed her eyes, thinking. She was tired and still a little tipsy, though the hard edges of danger were steadily wearing away at the lingering effects of inebriation. Whatever came of this was now up to her. What did Raven have planned for the Luminary? That would make a difference. If he were working alone, this might simply be a ploy for attention. Or revenge. But if he was beholden to someone else...there was no telling. It could be a kidnapping—or a murder.

She swallowed. With her mother gone, she was the next in line. Vixen opened her eyes, rubbing her forehead. The more she thought, the more she realized that her mother's sudden disappearance was going to cause almost insurmountable problems for her. The elite would link Vixen's return to the crime and accuse her.

And with Raven involved, would they be wrong? Whatever he was up to, it was because of *her*.

Vixen growled in frustration. She wished she wasn't alone, that she had an ally to speak with. Alekon. Jack. Or Jefferson. Kittie. Even Blaise, though he wouldn't be enthused by any of this. But...she had an ally, of a sort. Rhys.

Decision made, she left the parlor. The corridors were drenched in darkness, lit by the occasional lantern. Guards watched her progress with curiosity, though none challenged her. She wondered if any of them thought it odd she had arrived with her mother and then left without her. If they did, they declined to ask.

She knew she had to look ridiculous, marching out into the night dressed in the same finery she'd worn to the ill-fated gala.

But it marked who she was, the moonlight reflecting off the shimmering ruffles.

The unicorn stables were quiet—at least, until she walked in. As soon as the breeze blew her scent down the aisle, equine heads swung over the stall doors, nostrils cupped as they read her magic. One of them issued a throaty nicker but nothing more. The unicorns knew it was night, and they seldom worked in the darkness. She was merely interesting to them, a distraction from their routine.

Vixen strode down the aisle to Darby's stall. The stallion bumped her with his soft nose, a welcome that made her smile despite the terrible chain of events. She scratched his forehead, right at the base of his horn. He blew out a contented, hay-scented breath.

"Darby, I need Rhys, but I don't know where he lives. Can you take me to him?"

She knew unicorns were intelligent, though she was uncertain if they grasped language the same way as pegasi. But Darby arched his neck, then bobbed his head up and down as if in agreement. He nosed the latch on the stall door, attempting to open it with his lips but failing. Vixen saw with chagrin that someone had tinkered with it to prevent the stallion from letting himself out.

"You're an escape artist, hmm?" Vixen asked, working the modified latch. The door swung open, allowing the stallion to clop into the aisle. Was she going to get into trouble for rustling a unicorn? The punishment for that probably wasn't any worse than being an accessory to the Luminary's kidnapping.

Vixen was glad she'd selected her own gala outfit. With a great deal of effort, she pulled herself up onto the unicorn's back, grasping handfuls of silky mane. Darby set off at a trot, sure-footed in the darkness. His horn was lambent in the night.

If anyone who knew her true nature saw her, she'd make quite the sight: an outlaw mage riding a Salt-Iron Confederation Tracker's unicorn. Everything about that was a contradiction. Vixen shook her head at the idea.

"This is what it *should* be like, though," she whispered to Darby as his hooves splashed through a bog. "There shouldn't be any animosity between mages and the Confederation. Unicorns are one of the mystic races—you shouldn't be seen as an enemy." The unicorn blew out a loud breath, and Vixen hoped it was in agreement.

A few minutes later, they arrived at a small home. A modest garden stood to one side of the house, a henhouse nearby. Darby halted and whinnied.

Vixen almost thought Rhys wasn't there, or perhaps he was too deeply asleep, but moments later, he pushed the door open, rubbing sleep from his eyes. "Darby? How did—? Oh." He swallowed, stepping out onto the narrow porch. "Valoria, what are you doing here?"

She slid off Darby's sleek back. "Can I come in?" Vixen gestured to the house.

Rhys's eyes widened. "That's not appropriate. Not for the Spark."

She snorted at that. "You act as if I'm not also your *sister*. And an *outlaw mage*." Vixen ignored his choked sound at her bold declaration, marching up the porch steps and shoving the door open. She didn't have time for these delays. "I came because you're the only one around here I can trust."

Rhys followed her inside. "What makes you say that?"

Vixen glanced around at the dim interior. He had lit a lantern before coming out to greet her, which was odd. It meant he either couldn't afford or lacked the means to get a mage-light. As she had thought, the home was a single room with a bed, a table with a chair, and a wood stove for cooking. Everything about it was spare, not a hint of luxury. That was infuriating. Just like a mage, Rhys was *less* because he hadn't been born the right thing.

She pulled out the chair and sat. "You were at the gala. You saw how things went."

Rhys's expression shifted, and he looked as if he'd tasted something sour. "Saw and heard. The rumors…" He shook his head, lips taut. "Those elite made it a point to skirt around the truth about you, but I assume they know. So, how many of the other rumors are true?"

Vixen's mouth went dry. She had thought Rhys was an ally, but maybe she was wrong. As much as she needed to tell him about the Luminary's disappearance, she wouldn't tolerate this. "What do you think? That I really *am* a soiled dove? Or do you think I'm not your *sister?*" Too late, Vixen realized she'd allowed some of her power to ebb into the question.

Rhys winced as her magic clashed against his immunity. He groaned, shaking his head to ward away his irritation. His mouth tightened even more. "I know you're my sister because of the magic you command. But I don't know any of your life between the day you left with an outlaw and when I saw you at that train station."

She deflated. That was fair. Vixen sighed, rubbing her forehead. "Sorry. You're right. I'll make the time to tell you sometime." Dread suffused her next words. "But that's not why I came here. Things got worse."

Rhys's brows shot up. "Is that even possible?"

Vixen made a face. "I was talking with mother, and we had a disagreement." No need to tell him the source of the disagreement. Besides, he could probably guess. "And during that time, she was…taken by another mage."

Her twin's eyes widened, and he cursed softly. "You're telling me the Luminary was kidnapped right under our noses?"

She winced. "Yes."

He spun in a slow circle, rubbing his face. "Why did you come to me? Did you tell any of the guards?"

"No. I didn't know who else I could go to. After last night, they'll pin this on me. I'm too new. They'll see it as convenient."

Rhys nodded at her assessment. "Not just you, but your friends, too."

Jefferson and Blaise were undeserving of such blame. "I need to head off this disaster before it breaks." If she couldn't, this would only fan the flames of war against the Gutter.

He paced to the nearby window, peering out into the night. "I think the only way that's possible is if you can get her back before anyone realizes the Luminary is missing."

And that was unlikely. Vixen mentally kicked herself for her inaction. "I don't think we can. But I know the mage who took her. Can you and Darby search for him? Capture him, if possible?" It was a long shot. Raven knew a frightening amount about the Confederation, about how to avoid those who sought him.

Rhys frowned. "You know the mage? He's an outlaw?"

"It's complicated." Vixen rubbed her forehead. She was tired, needed to sleep. But that had to wait. "He's from the Gutter, but based on what he's doing, I don't think he's friendly anymore." And that was what hurt the most about the whole situation.

Rhys nodded. "We can try, but the odds are not in our favor."

"Anything you can do to help will be useful." Relief washed over her with the knowledge that he would help. "And do you think you can warn Jefferson and Blaise about this? I don't think I'll be able to."

"I'll pass the message to them in the morning." He pushed away from the window. "Well, it's already morning. Later, I mean." Rhys cast a longing look at his bed. "If I'm going to be any good for this, I need rest. And you look as if you do, too."

He wasn't wrong. Vixen rose from the chair, heading to the door. Then a thought came to her. "Rhys? Can my pegasus come to the unicorn stables?"

Rhys yawned. "I think that can be arranged. After sleep."

Vixen smiled her thanks, then clattered onto the porch, back to the waiting unicorn. If Alekon came, she would have one more ally, and that thought cheered her.

CHAPTER THIRTY-SEVEN

Secret Recipe

Jefferson

"That could not have possibly gone worse." Blaise sighed wearily as they climbed out of the coach.

Jefferson stumbled out behind him, lurching as he misjudged the distance between the last step and the ground. He caught Blaise's shoulder with one hand, earning another sigh from the Breaker. The world swirled around Jefferson for a harrowing moment, and he came perilously close to losing the contents of his stomach. They were lucky the coach had been there to return them to Hawthorne House, and not deliver them to the Golden Citadel. It had been a close thing.

Apparently, he must have said that out loud. Blaise froze beneath him. "Don't say that. I'm not going back there. And neither are you. *Ever.*" The Breaker's fear had returned, brought to the surface by the gala.

Blaise's panic opened a deep pit of sorrow in Jefferson. *Blaise shouldn't be sad. Shouldn't ever have to be afraid.* Jefferson tried to think of something to say to make his beau feel better, but his face felt numb, and everything around him seemed soft and fuzzy. "You have beautiful eyes, you know that?" Yes, his brain was utterly failing him at the moment, despite the truth that Blaise's blue eyes were lovely in the moonlight.

The Breaker paused, the sudden, unrelated statement distracting him. "What?"

"I said you have beautiful eyes."

"I know. That's not what I..." Those same wonderful eyes focused on Jefferson again, though they'd lost the sharp edge of terror that had defined them only moments ago. Beneath Jefferson's hand, Blaise's shoulders relaxed. "Thanks."

<Are you drunk again?> This from Seledora, who had awoken at their arrival. Jefferson felt the dull pressure of her disapproval like a tension headache.

To Jefferson's surprise, Blaise guided him toward the stables. "The pegasi should know." His voice was soft, which led Jefferson to believe Seledora had projected so that Blaise heard, too.

"Everything's botched," Jefferson announced as soon as they entered the dark breezeway. He thought it was helpful information, but Blaise's long-suffering sigh proved the Breaker didn't consider it such.

<You know he doesn't get drunk often, but he's a mess when he is,> Seledora pointed out, her silvery head thrust over her stall door. The other pegasi were awake, too, their bright eyes on the mages.

"I had reason!" Jefferson protested, then tried to remember that reason. It was a good reason, too. Or maybe a terrible reason, depending on how one looked at it.

"It was a wreck," Blaise said, putting an arm around Jefferson. That was nice. Jefferson enjoyed it when his beau did small things like that. He rested his head against Blaise's shoulder. *So comfortable.* "The Quiet Ones were at the gala. They started rumors to cast doubt over Vixen and implicate us." Blaise huffed out a frustrated breath. "And they tried *very* hard to rile up Jefferson. It was as if they wanted him to make a mistake and use his magic."

Oh, that was it. Jefferson gave an exaggerated nod. "I can't be the Dreamer when I'm the Drunk!" He laughed because it was literally the most clever thing he'd ever said in his life, he was certain.

<Where is Vixen?> Alekon asked, his ears flicking back and forth with uncertainty.

"Safe with the Luminary," Blaise said. Jefferson wasn't sure safe was the right word, but he didn't know what else to offer. The Breaker said something else, but Jefferson could no longer focus on the words. Everything around him blurred, like water dumped across wet paint.

Jefferson must have dozed. The next thing he knew, sunlight poured in through the window. Where was he? Plump pillows and silky-soft sheets ensconced him. Ah, yes, his favorite bed at Hawthorne House. Blaise was curled up beside him, which was unusual for this time of day. Jefferson didn't rightly know what time it was, but the Breaker was normally up before the sun to start his day of baking.

He laid there, more clear-headed than he'd been at the end of last night, though a dull corona of pain in his skull reminded him he'd assuredly had too much wine. His stomach felt like a hollow pit, though it threatened to eject any new food if he wasn't careful. Jefferson hissed out a soft breath and studied Blaise, wondering what they were going to do now.

Tara Woodrow and Phillip Dillon had been ruthless in the way they had eviscerated not only the outlaws with their rumors at the gala but the Luminary as well. Scandal could weaken the office and cast a pall over Vixen's claim as Spark.

Jefferson hated to admit the gossip was artful, each with enough potential grains of truth to be harmful. They were certain to discredit Vixen, their small delegation, and the Gutter. They were already coming in as underdogs.

Blaise stirred beside him, rubbing his eyes as he awoke with a groan. The Breaker rolled over. "Morning. How are you feeling?"

Jefferson shook his head. "Like this is all my fault."

The Breaker frowned. "What do you mean?" He shifted closer to Jefferson, warmth radiating from his skin.

"I should have agreed to stay out of it. To stay in the Cit. Everyone is suffering from my choice." Jefferson's gut twisted, and not just from the need for food that would agree with him.

Blaise snugged an arm around him. "None of this is your fault. They're bullies." His love was quiet for a moment. "Even if you had agreed, I wouldn't have let you stay there."

"No, I suppose you wouldn't," Jefferson whispered.

He closed his eyes. There was another option, too. One Jefferson dared not voice. He could have folded, could have agreed to obey the whims of the Quiet Ones. But he knew the Quiet Ones would want to use Blaise through him, and that was something he couldn't allow. To bow to the Quiet Ones would require him to end his relationship with Blaise, and Jefferson was ashamed to admit he was too selfish for that. He couldn't imagine life without the Breaker. And he feared that without Blaise, he would slowly devolve into his father's shadow. Only this time, he would have powerful magic, perfect for cruel intentions.

Blaise touched Jefferson's smooth chin. "Whatever else you're thinking, stop."

Jefferson leaned into the caress, shifting so Blaise's fingers traced his cheek. "How do you know I'm thinking anything else?"

His beau smiled, leaning over to kiss Jefferson's forehead. "Because you're not good at guarding your expressions when you're hungover." Blaise settled back down. "We had a visitor this morning."

Jefferson blinked rapidly. "Wait, already? What time is it?" He cast around for his pocket watch, but it was across the room. Farther than his recovering body felt well enough to travel, at any rate.

"It's almost noon." Blaise's expression softened. "I got up at my usual time and did a few things before coming back to bed. Rhys was here."

Jefferson didn't know how Blaise could function after arriving home in the middle of the night and then rising at his normal time. "Why did the Tracker come here?"

Blaise blew out a breath, edging over until he was companionably close to Jefferson. "Vixen sent him with a message. Raven took the Luminary last night." He paused, brow furrowing. "I mean, this morning. Early. You know what I mean."

A chill threaded through Jefferson. "Blast. That doesn't bode well for us." All things considered, Blaise was handling the latest news relatively well. Though, perhaps that was why he'd returned to their bed.

"She's requested Alekon, too. So there's that." Blaise's hand idly drifted along the muscles of Jefferson's arm. Then he shifted, levering upright. "I'm going to get us something to eat. Stay here."

"You don't want me to come down with you?" Jefferson asked.

Blaise's brows hiked up on his forehead. "You don't look ready for stairs yet. It won't take long for me to gather a few things and come back up."

True to his word, Blaise returned a few minutes later, bearing a tray. A familiar tray, in fact, laden with buttered toast and a banana and...Jefferson chuckled. "Ah, so you recalled how to treat my hangover." He levered upright, grunting with the effort.

Blaise handed him a plate. "Medium-rare bread with a buttered glaze."

Jefferson accepted the plate of toast. "My secret recipe."

The Breaker sipped from a cup of coffee he'd brought up for himself, then placed it on the bedside table. "Only the best for you." Then his expression shifted, turning contemplative. "You know, the last time you were drunk was here." He gestured to the master bedroom. Blaise paused, as if he were choosing his words. "That was a difficult time for us, too."

Jefferson raised his eyebrows, remembering. It had been the conclusion of the Inquiry, and he'd foolishly drunk too much at a celebration and then pressured Blaise over his wishy-washy feelings. Looking back, it was mortifying. He should never have said those things to Blaise. But it had led to a discussion about how they felt about one another and...well, *more*. He cleared his throat as those memories swelled. "But we got through it."

Blaise took a bite of his own toast, and didn't speak until he'd finished chewing. "That's my point. I was thinking about that when I gathered breakfast." He ran a hand through his unruly hair. "We've been through some pretty tough situations."

That was an understatement. And that was exactly why Jefferson didn't want Blaise to suffer ever again. But the Breaker was trying to make a point to him, and Jefferson wasn't thinking clearly enough to see it. "We're going to have to be quite creative to figure a way out of this disaster."

Blaise put a hand on his knee. "We're not in this alone. Vixen is here—well, not *here*, but you know what I mean. The pegasi. And Kittie and Jack are...somewhere." The Breaker frowned. "Okay, that doesn't sound great right now, but I stand by what I said."

Jefferson chuckled. "Speaking of Jack, has Kittie returned? Do we have any news?"

Blaise shook his head. "Emrys says Kittie never came back. And still no sign of Jack."

That seemed unusual for the Pyromancer. Jefferson chewed the crust of his toast as if it were to blame for everything. "I have a bad feeling about whatever's befallen the Dewitts."

Blaise's expression turned grim. "I agree. I thought about seeing if one of the pegasi could find Kittie, but..."

But he didn't want to risk losing a pegasus to whatever had snared Jack and Kittie. And he was right. It wasn't wise at this point. Jefferson took a sip of the tea Blaise had brought up. Caladrius root, Kittie's preferred blend. It worked wonders for a hangover, too. "As much as it pains me to say it, I think we can't worry about them until we know how to handle things with the Luminary and Quiet Ones. We—" He paused, hearing a sudden clatter downstairs.

Blaise rose, silver magic pulsing on his fingertips. He went to the door, but a moment later, they heard a high-pitched voice call out, "Hey, it's me! Hope you two are decent 'cause I'm coming in!"

And then, without so much as a knock, Flora threw open the door and ambled inside. She gave them both disappointed looks. Knowing the half-knocker, she had been hoping to find them in a state of undress—or a compromising position. "Hello, Flora," Jefferson greeted her.

"Toast?" Blaise held up an extra piece.

"Don't mind if I do." Flora snagged the slice and munched on it. The stony skin around her eyes seemed darker than usual, as if she were tired.

"I thought you were keeping tabs on Madame Boss Clayton?" Jefferson watched her demolish the toast in two bites.

Flora licked a glob of butter from her fingertips. "Yeah, well, that's the thing. I can't keep tabs on someone who's not there."

Jefferson stared at her, certain that he'd misheard. "Excuse me?"

The half-knocker sighed, then looked at Blaise. "You got anything else? A girl has to eat, you know."

The Breaker nodded, relaxed now that Flora was here. "Just a moment."

Jefferson crossed his arms, frowning at the pink-haired woman. "You were supposed to keep her safe!"

Flora flapped a hand at him. "Oh, hush. When Blaise gets back with my breakfast, I'll fill you both in. I can't work miracles, you know."

The thing was, Jefferson thought she *could* work miracles. He relied on her—he'd never known her to fail at any task he'd set her. Then he winced, realizing it had to sting her pride that this had happened.

Blaise returned with another tray, this one filled with day-old blueberry muffins, in addition to more slices of warm, buttery toast. Flora's eyes widened with delight, and she didn't speak until half of the assorted goodies were in her stomach.

"Thanks, I was feeling faint," Flora said, patting her belly. The half-knocker claimed a place on the bed between the two men, though she clucked her tongue and winked at Blaise for good measure. The Breaker was oblivious to her flirtatious ways. "So before you get all huffy and annoyed that I wasn't doing my job, let me tell you what happened." She paused dramatically, then glared at Jefferson. "Oh wait, you already got all huffy."

He sighed. "I'm sorry. We've had difficulties of our own here."

At that, she raised an eyebrow, then nodded. They would tell her their side of the events later. Flora flopped backward onto the bed, threading her hands over her full stomach. "Oh, forgot how comfy this bed was."

"Flora…" Jefferson rubbed his forehead.

"I'm getting to it," she grumbled. "Anyway, so I was keeping an eye on Rachel, just like you asked me to. I didn't get distracted or anything, I promise! So get this: one day, she was outside with her kids, and then *bam*, she just disappears."

Jefferson and Blaise traded looks. "Disappeared?" Blaise asked.

"Yeah." Flora blew a frustrated raspberry. "Boom, gone."

"How long ago?" Jefferson rubbed his chin.

"A week." Flora held up a hand to stave off any interruptions. "And before you ask why I didn't come tell you straight away, I was working with Captain Cerulean of the Bossguard to search for her. We couldn't figure out what happened. Her kids didn't see anything, so it's not like she was kidnapped."

Blaise canted his head. "Was she near a shadow?"

Flora lifted her head enough to give him an incredulous look.

"That's a weirdly specific question. It was the middle of the day, and the sun was out, so...yes?"

The Breaker glanced at Jefferson. "Are you thinking what I'm thinking?"

Jefferson nodded. "Raven Dawson."

CHAPTER THIRTY-EIGHT
Can't Say You're Memorable

Kittie

"I could really go for a cup of tea right now," Kittie murmured to Najaria. Or a stiff drink. Sadly, neither of them were available in this damned shadow realm. Maybe it was for the best, since she'd rather not backslide on the progress made with her drinking habit. But that blasted Shadowstepper was making it awfully tempting to take it up again.

The mare snorted, tossing her head so her mane flared around her. And it truly did flare—for the time being, she had allowed her mane and tail to ignite, providing them with a cheerful halo of light to pierce the darkness. Between the pair of them, they would never want for light. Not that it did much of anything in this place.

She and the elemental had decided it was best to explore their shadowy surroundings. Staying in one place wouldn't get them anywhere, and Kittie hoped she might find some way out. Nothing was immediately forthcoming, though. It was like being trapped in a never-ending cave, if the cave were formed from pure shadow. Sometimes, she caught glimpses of what she thought must be the real world beyond their prison, but they had yet to discover a way to win free.

Kittie paused, glancing over at the mare. It was possible Najaria might have experience she lacked. There was no telling with an elemental. "Do you know of any such place as this?"

Najaria drew to a halt, tilting her head as if considering. After a moment, she shook her head, the flames in her mane sparking with the motion. Then she blew out a warm breath on Kittie's arm, an apology.

Kittie smiled, rubbing the elemental between the eyes. "It's not your fault. And I'm glad I'm not alone here." The thought of being alone was almost unbearable. And to think Jack—*her* Jack—was likely trapped in the same shadows somewhere. And he was alone, no Zepheus at his side. As tough as he pretended to be, she knew this would be hard on him. He was only a man, alone in the darkness.

That thought strengthened her resolve. If she found him, they would make a way out together. There was nothing that could stop them when they put their minds to it. Kittie nodded. "Let's keep going."

She considered calling for Jack, but she didn't know who—or what—else might lurk in the shadows. Sometimes she had the sense that something was watching them, stalking them. But she reasoned that could be Raven, somehow using his magic to track his prisoners.

They walked for what felt like hours, stopping occasionally to rest. She didn't know if time passed here as it did in the normal world. Kittie discovered she didn't hunger or thirst as she would normally. Which was helpful, since she wasn't certain how to handle biological needs in this place.

"This makes me think *we're* somehow shadows," Kittie told Najaria, watching as the darkness undulated around the edges of the mare's light. "I wish I knew more about how Walker magic worked. Do they shift us into whatever their power commands?"

The elemental flicked her tail, offering no insight. Kittie doubted the mare knew, either.

The pair started onward again, following the sinuous trail of shadows. Kittie was lost in her thoughts when Najaria tensed beside her, ears pivoting forward as she flared her nostrils, suddenly on alert. She made a soft warning rumble, stirring Kittie to attention.

"What is it?" Kittie asked, straining her own ears to hear.

The chestnut mare remained frozen in place as if she were a molten statue for a handful of heartbeats. Then she lowered her head and ambled forward, glancing over her shoulder at Kittie, as if to say, "*Well, what are you waiting for? Let's go.*"

Puzzled, Kittie followed, surprised when Najaria picked up the pace, forcing her into a jog to keep up. The mare followed the twists of shadow. After a moment, Kittie heard what Najaria had: voices.

It wasn't Jack. Urgent female voices, muffled by the blanket of gloom. They pressed onward and came face-to-face with a pair of women who stared at Najaria as if she were a creature of nightmare.

"Back, beast from Perdition!" one woman declared, her hair a brilliant red in the firelight. For the barest of seconds, Kittie thought Vixen had somehow ended up in the shadow world, too. But this woman was older, closer to Kittie's age, with hair that was likely a much lighter shade of red. The redhead held a single hand up as if the force of her words could turn away a demon.

Najaria snorted, unimpressed by the threat. She was an elemental and thus of the land, not of Perdition. Kittie caught sight of someone beyond the redhead's shoulder—someone she recognized in the flickering light.

"Madame Boss Clayton?"

The Gannish leader peered around the other woman. Her eyes widened in surprise, and she stepped around the protective woman, who shot her an annoyed look. But Clayton wasn't one to be hindered by others. "Kittie? Is that truly you?"

Kittie edged around Najaria, moving closer to the women. The redhead lifted her chin, still in a defensive stance—though, Kittie didn't know how the woman thought she might defend herself against them. Maybe she was a mage. That would make sense. But for the moment, she kept her attention on the Madame Boss. "It is."

Rachel breathed a sigh of relief. "Oh, you're a sight for sore eyes."

"Who is this *mage*?" the imperious woman asked, an unmistakable inflection of deep mistrust on the last word.

The Madame Boss drew herself up, adopting a formal air. "Firebrand Kittie Dewitt, allow me to introduce you to Luminary Juliette Kildare."

Oh shit. Shit, shit, shit. The Luminary was here in the shadows. Raven Dawson had kidnapped the Luminary. The Shadowstepper might as well have punched Kittie in the gut for how much this surprised her—and how much worse it made every aspect of their situation. Kittie sucked in a breath, cobbling her thoughts together.

"*Firebrand*? This is the woman who was a part of the delegation you met in Nera?" the Luminary asked, her gaze flitting between them.

Kittie wondered if it was good or bad that the Luminary had heard of her. Twenty years ago, it would have been extremely dangerous and certain to end her freedom. But times had changed in some respects. This Luminary, though...she had never liked mages.

"The very same," Rachel agreed with a smile. She ran a hand through a tangle in her hair. The Madame Boss was dressed in a pair of linen trousers and a white button-down shirt, as if she'd been at leisure when Raven had taken her. At least, Kittie assumed Raven had taken the pair. She didn't know anyone else capable of accessing this place. "Am I allowed to be cautiously optimistic now that we've come across you? I've been stuck here for days. And the darkness keeps shifting me around like a rudderless boat, which is rather unnerving."

"I'm as much a prisoner here as the both of you," Kittie admitted, stroking Najaria's neck. The mare had quieted, though she listened to their exchange with rapt attention, her obsidian eyes glinting with intelligence. The Pyromancer wondered what the aethon picked up from them.

The Luminary crossed her arms. "Why would the shadow mage trap you?"

"I don't know exactly," Kittie admitted. Raven didn't want her interfering, that much she knew. "Can you both tell me exactly who brought you here?"

Both women described Raven, though the Luminary hadn't gotten the best view of him before he'd dumped her in the shadow realm. Based on the heated conversation with Vixen she described, however, Kittie was certain it was him. Why was the Shadowstepper sabotaging their attempts to make peace for the Gutter? Taking the Madame Boss, the leader the Gutter had signed the initial declaration with, was bad enough. The Luminary's disappearance might lead to a war that would obliterate the outlaw lands.

Emmaline is still there. The thought sent a chill of dread through Kittie. While her daughter would never truly be safe anywhere because of her magic, Raven had made things worse. Kittie clenched her jaw. She would be hard-pressed not to roast him the next time he crossed her path.

"How long have you been here?" Kittie asked, though she wasn't sure if they could even grasp the flow of time in the strange realm.

Rachel pulled out a silver pocket watch, a lovely piece decorated with engraved vines peppered with tiny flowers made of rubies that blazed in the firelight. "This is the only way I have any idea, though I'm afraid I'll lose my mind checking it. Unless something's amiss with my watch, I've been here for more than a week."

"Not long," the Luminary said of herself, her voice tight. "According to the Madame Boss's watch, about six hours."

Six hours. Not long, but an eternity when someone important was missing. And the Madame Boss...well, it would be a miracle if Ganland had anything to do with the outlaws after this. Kittie blew out a breath, wondering how long she had been here herself. No watch, thus no way to know.

"You haven't come across a man here, have you? I mean, a blond-haired man. Not the one who took us." It didn't hurt to ask.

"No. It's only thanks to Garus we fumbled through the dark and found each other." The Luminary crossed her arms, giving the aethon a grudging look of respect. "It's a relief to have light again."

"Tabris granted us his fortune," Rachel agreed with a wink, clearly not wanting to leave her nation's favored god out. Then she sobered. "Are you saying the shadow mage took someone else?"

Kittie swallowed a lump in her throat. "My husband."

"Oh, honey." Rachel's voice was soft, the expression that of a sympathetic friend, not a politician. She stepped closer, putting a hand on Kittie's arm. "I'm sorry."

Kittie nodded, wetting her lips. She couldn't dwell on that now. "But I found the both of you. Perhaps we'll come across him, too. If we do, our odds of getting out of here are better."

"Another mage?" the Luminary asked, hesitant.

The Scourge of the Untamed Territory. Kittie only dipped her chin in agreement. "He's one of the best. If anyone can help us figure out how to escape this, it's him." Kittie liked to think she could find a way out of this realm herself, but she wanted Jack for her own reasons. She loved that oftentimes-infuriating man, and the thought of him wandering the darkness for eternity without her was enough to gut her soul.

"Sounds like we need to find another outlaw then," Rachel said, sounding chipper though the lines around her eyes revealed her worry.

The Luminary watched the pair of them, thoughtful. *"Let the flame in the darkness guide you home."* Her words sounded as if she were quoting something, but Kittie didn't know what.

"What's that?" Rachel asked.

The redhead turned, her intense gaze on Kittie. For a heartbeat, it was as if someone greater peered out of those eyes. Someone infinitely more powerful than the woman standing before her. Then the Luminary's eyes cleared. "That's one of the Old Teachings of Wisdom. They're usually meant as metaphors." The Luminary heaved out a breath. "But sometimes...they're truths."

Jack

THE WORLD REELED AROUND JACK, SPINNING SO FAST THAT HIS stomach lurched. His guts roiled, and for an agonizing minute, he was certain that Raven's damned shadow magic was going to kill him. The Shadowstepper had come out of nowhere and nabbed him as he wandered the never-ending, labyrinthine darkness. But then the world resolved itself into order once more, revealing—

"Shit." Jack squinted against the too-bright light of a prissy-looking parlor. It was decorated in pastels and gold leaf, dark mahogany woods, and carpeted with rugs that somehow matched the eyesore design. He'd seen this place before, when Raven had first taken him.

He tried to move, but quickly discovered his hands had been bound behind him and his feet bound at the ankles. Took him another moment to realize he was on the floor, sitting in the middle of one of those gaudy rugs. At least it offered a decent cushion. But that was his only comfort. Where was Raven? Where had the traitor brought him?

"There you are." A dark shape shifted into Jack's field of vision, the smooth, precise tone denoting someone cultured. *Elite*. It took the outlaw a moment for his eyes to adjust, dismay surging through him when he recognized the man. It was the Quiet One he'd baited back in Nera, Phillip Dillon. The older man grinned down at him. "Remember me?"

"Nah, can't say you're memorable," Jack said, attempting a shrug. It was difficult, bound as he was. It made the muscles in his arms scream, and he bit down on the inside of his cheeks to mask the pain.

A cruel smile slid across Dillon's face. "Well, *outlaw*, let me remind you." The emphasis boded ill, and Jack had no time to prepare for what came next. Despite his age, the Quiet One moved like a diving hawk.

Air whooshed from Jack's lungs. The kick to his side sent him down onto the rug again, his bound arms and legs rendering him helpless to defend himself. Faintly, he realized Dillon had prepared for this, had planned for the coming torment. He wasn't wearing the soft shoes of an elite going to a gala or meeting. No, he wore a modified style of boot favored by some of the Salt-Iron soldiers when they went into battle. They had hard, pointed toes of reinforced steel, designed to inflict as much damage as possible with a simple kick.

Jack couldn't bring his hands around to protect himself, couldn't do a damned thing as his tormenter cocked his leg back time and time again, taunting him with each blow. The outlaw tried to curl into a ball, tried to crawl away. There wasn't an inch of his body that didn't scream from the abuse. His vision swam—no, that was blood in his eyes. Blood in his mouth, thick on his tongue. Pain spiraling through every limb. His world was throbbing agony, the pounding of his own heart, the flash of light against the blood in his eyes, the dull sound of boot meeting flesh and bone, again and again.

Then it stopped. Well, the pain didn't. That was going to be eternal. But the kicking did. A dark shape loomed overhead, a hot breath close to his ear. "Do you remember me now? Dragons don't fear other dragons—even when they should."

Jack whimpered, which was the closest he could come to the thorough string of curses he'd been attempting. His damned lips and tongue refused to obey.

Stars exploded in his eyes when Dillon scored a savage kick to Jack's gut. He gasped, whining as bile rose in his throat. Tears mingled with the blood in his eyes, and he panted for breath, trying desperately to distance himself from the pain. He'd done it in battle before, but in those instances, he hadn't been bound. Hadn't been utterly defenseless.

Come on. Can't let this asshole win. His mind raged, but his body couldn't match his spirit. This lone, petty man had damaged him too badly. Jack had to get out of this, *had to.* Had to for Kittie. For Emmaline. For Zepheus. For all the people he gave a damn about.

"What? No stubborn words from the infamous Scourge of the Untamed Territory?" Dillon asked, disappointment ripe in his voice. "Too bad. I thought you were *legendary.*"

No, I'm just a man. Flesh and blood. And that very flesh was failing him now. He panted out another breath, then summoned the will to spit blood onto Dillon's boots. Though it probably didn't matter much, since Jack's blood already spattered them.

"Disgusting filth. You have no manners," Dillon said with a sigh. He vanished from Jack's view for a moment, and he realized the man was using Jack's shirt to clean off his boots. The bastard. Then the Quiet One clicked his tongue. "Oh, what a mess you've made. I don't know how the housekeeper is going to get the blood stains out of this rug. That was really thoughtless of you."

"Go...sit...on...a...cactus," Jack rasped. Every word cost him, his tongue a strange and shapeless lump in his mouth. Like it didn't belong to him anymore.

Darkness again, but not the realm between shadows.

The Effigest must have blacked out, which was a mercy of a sort. When he came to, he was still on the floor, and he was grateful that he'd awoken. There wasn't a part of him that didn't throb, and he figured there might be something to Blaise's assertion that he was too damned stubborn to die. That, or maybe back in Fortitude, Emmaline was keeping him alive, her heart clouded with worry for her parents and friends.

Whatever the case, he was glad to be alive, even if surrendering to the pain was tempting. It was difficult to breathe, almost impossible to think. He lay in darkness—when had it become dark? Confusion clouded his mind for a moment, wondering if Raven had taken him back to the shadows. No, he felt the rug beneath him. It had only been the passing of time, his tormenter leaving him alone in agony. And maybe the blood in his eyes. Or maybe the abuse had blinded him.

How in Perdition would he get out of this? *Could* he get out? No one knew where he was—no one save for Raven, and he doubted there would be any help on that front. Jack shifted on the rug, pausing when his fingers brushed against something loose. Fibers of some sort. It took him a moment to realize they were pieces of the carpet that had been ripped from the rug during the assault.

Yes. I can work with this. He gathered them in his trembling fingers, though it was almost impossible. His hands felt like they belonged to someone else, the circulation nearly cut off from his bindings. With clumsy motions, he twisted the fibers into the semblance of a poppet. Jack knew without a doubt it wouldn't live up to his normal standards for a poppet, but in this case, anything would do. He just needed a little something to focus his magic.

Once the doll was formed, he clasped his hand around it. The fibers of the doll stuck to him, tacky with blood. That was fine.

His blood would make activating the poppet much easier. Jack called on his power, trying to send it into the doll, though it was scattershot at first. His magic shied away from him, like trying to catch a fish with his bare hands. He'd used his magic when he'd been wounded before, but never when his body had been this shattered.

Come on, Jack. Get it together. He gritted his teeth, the coppery tang of blood thick in his mouth once more. Jack fumbled with his magic, though it took another half-dozen attempts before he succeeded.

The zing of the doll's connection was almost a comfort. But activating it did precious little for his situation. He had to take a moment to catch his breath and refocus his mind from the ever-present agony surging through his body. Jack knew what he needed to do first, and he hated it because it was also one of the biggest power-drains. It was necessary, though.

He hissed out a breath, simultaneously willing a Strength working into the poppet. For a beat, Jack was certain that it, too, had failed—then he felt the telltale pull of magic being sucked from him. With a grunt, he jerked his wrists apart, gasping at the slice of rope against flesh. He ignored it, straining. Hemp fibers *twanged* as they broke, and the ropes fell away from him.

Carefully as he could manage, Jack rolled onto his back, bringing his hands to his chest. He winced, rubbing his bloody palms together, then massaged his wrists as best he could. The poppet fell onto his chest. He was going to have to get it back in hand, but first he needed to restore circulation.

Once his hands felt better, he snagged the poppet with difficulty. He still had some magic left, but nothing he could do would heal the damage that had been inflicted on him. No, the best he could do was dull the pain and hope he didn't have internal bleeding, as unlikely as that was. Clutching the poppet in his hand as if it were a lifeline, he cast a spell to take the edge off his multitude of hurts.

His vision had returned, so that was something. The surrounding room was lit by a mage-light that needed to be re-enchanted, its glow dull. Jack hissed out a long, rattling breath.

Before he could do anything else, the darkness came for him once more. As he fell into it, he hoped that he'd wake again—if only to see his wife and daughter one more time before taking the long walk to Perdition.

CHAPTER THIRTY-NINE

Meanwhile, in Fortitude...

Emmaline

The bakery wasn't as busy as when Blaise was in residence, but their patronage was steady enough to keep Emmaline, Reuben, and Hannah busy. Emmaline prided herself on running the operation as smoothly as the Breaker would have, though she knew none of them quite had his enthusiasm when it came to baking. Still, she knew they did a fine job, and he would be pleased when he finally returned to town.

Emmaline had made it her goal to keep Blaise's Bakery chugging along, if only to distract herself while her parents and friends were gone. She'd gotten into the habit of checking on them via her collection of poppets. Emmaline had one for each of her parents, and another for Blaise. She didn't think her friend knew about that, but it hadn't been particularly challenging to cobble one together in the bakery. And it made her feel better, so she figured Blaise would have been okay with that.

The poppets were anything but okay. Blaise's had resonated with pain one day, though that had quickly ended, which made her think he was fine. But then her parents' poppets had become oddly...disconnected. That was the only way she could think to describe it. As if her mother and father were no longer attached to the poppets. Had her magic finally reached the boundaries of what she could do, their distance too great? It didn't make sense—she could still detect Blaise.

With so many uncertainties, she was very, very glad for the distractions of the bakery.

<I'm here to assist with taste-testing.> Oberidon shoved his speckled head through the window, startling Reuben, who had been kneading dough nearby.

"Blasted horse!" Reuben grumbled, earning a snort from the pegasus.

Emmaline laughed. "He's here to offer his brand of help." Hannah was ringing up a customer at the front, and Emmaline slipped past her to grab a cookie that had been in the display for the longest.

The stallion gave her a dubious look. <That is not the freshest. How am I supposed to help if you're giving me day-old goods?>

"You get what you get," Emmaline said. "Take it or leave it."

<Take it, of course.> The pegasus eagerly plucked it from her palm with his delicate lips.

Emmaline grinned, wiping her hands sticky with pegasus slobber on her trouser leg. She turned to the sink, the marvel with actual running water that Jefferson had installed for Blaise. Emmaline wished she had one of these at home. So handy. Her gaze flicked to the trio of poppets perched on the windowsill over the sink. Emmaline brushed her fingertips against each poppet. Blaise's was fine. Her mother's still had that cut-off feeling. And her father's—

She doubled over as a wave of pain lashed through her.

<Emmaline!> Oberidon trumpeted.

She was dimly aware of Reuben and Hannah crouched over her. Somehow, she was on the floor with Jack's poppet clutched in her hand. The agony boiling through the poppet bled into her, so intense it was almost impossible to draw breath.

<The poppet! Get the poppet out of her hands!> Oberidon commanded.

"No," Emmaline whimpered as she felt Reuben desperately trying to claw her hand open. "Don't. *Daddy*."

"What do we do?" Hannah's voice sounded distant.

"Go get my mom," Reuben said. "She might know what to do."

The world was a confusing jumble of sound and hurt. Emmaline had the distinct sensation that her body was broken, and it came as a great surprise when Nadine arrived and sent a wave of Healer magic through her. Emmaline gasped, shaking her head once more when Nadine gently pried the poppet from her grip.

"*Breathe*," the Healer ordered.

Emmaline sucked in a gasping breath, her vision sharpening to take in the worried faces of her friends. Oberidon stared at her through the window, nostrils fluttering. <I'm sorry. I know you were helping your father, but I had to have them break the connection for a moment.>

Daddy. Tears stung Emmaline's eyes. "The poppet. I need the poppet."

"Shh." Nadine ran a hand over Emmaline's shoulders, then down her arms as she made an assessment. "You're not gonna do anyone any good if you go into magic-induced shock."

Emmaline blinked. She'd never heard that term before. "What's that?"

"The thing you were doing," Nadine murmured. "Reacting. Letting your magic call the shots." She made a soothing sound, rubbing Emmaline's back. "It's dangerous and the ticket to draining yourself dry so quickly you risk your life."

Emmaline swallowed, biting her bottom lip. Suddenly, she felt like a little girl again. Like the times after her mother had gone missing, and her father had gone off and left her in Clover's care.

Life had been uncertain and frightening, like there was nothing she could do when something terrible happened.

But that wasn't true. Not now. "Nadine, I *have* to do something. Have to use my magic. He's hurt. Real bad."

"Jack?" Nadine asked, tone neutral. Emmaline nodded. The Healer muttered something uncomplimentary about the elder Effigest beneath her breath, then fixed her gaze on Emmaline. "Can you do the same thing you did when he was shot?"

"I can try."

The Healer's lips drew taut. "You're Jack's daughter, so I know you have a stubborn streak as wide as the Untamed Territory. And even if I tell you not to, you're gonna do the thing. Do it, but this bakery needs to be closed. You don't need any additional worries while this is going on."

"But—" Reuben started.

His mother aimed a glare at him, cowing Reuben into silence. Nadine favored them with a grim look. "Reuben, you help Emmaline to her room at the Broken Horn. Let Clover know what's happened, so Emmaline doesn't waste her breath. Hannah, do whatever it is needs to be done to close up the bakery."

"Yes ma'am," Hannah said, hopping to work as Reuben offered Emmaline his arm.

"The poppet," Emmaline insisted, eyes on Nadine. The Healer had laid it on the nearby countertop.

Without a word, Nadine picked it up and dropped it into Emmaline's cupped palm. As soon as the tiny figure connected with her flesh, another lightning-bright flash of pain surged through her. Emmaline pulled on her magic, focusing it on the poppet. She sent out pleas for healing, for life.

Don't you die on me, Daddy. I'll never forgive you.

CHAPTER FORTY

Divine Approval

Vixen

The rest of the early morning was a blur for Vixen. Her memory of returning to Dawnlight was fuzzy, but she knew without a doubt the trusty unicorn had gotten her back, and somehow, she'd evaded the notice of the guards.

Vixen awoke in her bed, and a tiny part of her hoped everything had been a nightmare. But it was all too real. Raven had taken her mother—the Luminary. *Argh.*

Vixen rubbed her eyes with the heels of her hands, struggling into a sitting position. Someone had brought a meal into her room, leaving the covered tray on a nearby table. Vixen didn't like the idea that someone had come into her room, and she'd been totally unaware, but in her defense, she had been exhausted.

She dressed and ate, then went to see what awaited her.

Vixen didn't get far. A pair of men in the armor of the Lightguard stood vigil outside her door. They hadn't been there when she had returned, of that she was certain. Had they come to make sure she stayed put or to protect her? Whichever the reason, it was a clear sign that the Luminary's disappearance had become known.

Time to feel them out and see what's going on. "Hello."

The guards stared straight ahead, not meeting her eyes. Either they knew of her magic, or they were well-disciplined. Vixen figured it was the latter. "Good morning, Spark Valoria." They spoke in practiced unison. The pair must have served together for a long time to be so in tune.

"Can I leave?"

Both men tensed at the question. Neither of them shifted to look at her. "I'm afraid you can't," the guard to her left said, the apology ringing true in his voice.

"And why is that?"

The guard on the right cleared his throat before speaking, as if emotion threatened to overcome him. "The Luminary is missing, and we've been assigned the task of protecting you."

Even though Vixen knew *why*, she did her best to feign shock. She clutched the wood of the lintel, gasping. "What do you mean, missing?"

"She cannot be located. And now, Spark, we beg you to please return to your room," the left-hand guard asked.

Vixen almost relented, sympathetic to the strain in their voices. They truly were upset by events and struggling to keep their emotions behind a professional veneer. But with the Luminary missing, Vixen was the next in line. The Spark should have some control over this situation. "On whose orders am I confined to my rooms?"

"The Clergy Council issued the recommendation. They also tasked us with alerting them when you arose, as they wish to speak with you."

That sounded reasonable. Perhaps, if she spoke to them, she'd be able to gain more authority. And potentially, more freedom. She didn't want to be cooped up like an exotic creature to be protected. Vixen needed to be out there, doing something. "Let them know I'm happy to see them."

One of the men broke away from the door, leaving his fellow behind. Vixen retreated into the room to wait, replaying the events of the previous night. Was Raven working with the Quiet Ones, or had something else spurred his actions? His indignation at Juliette's words had rung true. Besides, she couldn't imagine why Raven would work for anyone in the Confederation.

Unless it was under duress. Or he had some other compelling reason.

The guard returned, this time with another female guard, to guide her to the Clergy Council. Vixen followed her out of the residence and to a waiting carriage. Before boarding, she took a moment to scrutinize the exterior. The gilded eyes of the fox-head insignia winked at her in the late morning sunlight. It appeared to be one of the official Luminary carriages. Reassured, she stepped up and settled herself inside.

The trip was relatively short. The footman came around and opened the door, helping her down, though she would have much rather jumped to the ground. But that wasn't a freedom she had at the moment, so she allowed herself to be treated as was proper for her rank.

She peered up at the towering facade of the Asaphenia, the largest cathedral dedicated to Garus on the continent. A motif of carved foxes lined the lower portions, while the architects had designed the buttress in the likeness of swooping owls. Vixen followed her escort up the stairs, sucking in a breath against the growing pressure as she entered the building.

The gods, as far as she knew, weren't magic. But they had *power*. Presence. And in a place like the Asaphenia, that very power pooled like a thick fog. The pantheon had become mostly absent from the mortal world, leaving their faithful to wonder and non-believers to doubt. The cathedral was an odd juxtaposition, a location that felt both divine and comfortable. Like coming home to family.

That single thought brought her up short in mid-stride. *Family.* If they didn't find her mother, she might be the Luminary sooner than she'd ever expected. Her mouth went dry.

Her light has not gone out, little fox.

Vixen glanced around, though the voice had reverberated in her head like when Alekon spoke to her. But it didn't have the feel of a pegasus. It had a weight to it, a pressure that made her almost reel. No one else around her seemed to notice. Vixen bit her lip and continued onward.

Her guide silently opened an ornate door, gesturing for her to enter. Vixen strode inside, finding a triumvirate gathered around the bow of a U-shaped table. The two men and one woman of the Clergy Council waited until Vixen's escort retreated before motioning for her to settle in the lonely seat waiting in the open area of the U.

"Spark Valoria, praise to Garus's wisdom for your return," the silver-haired woman said, aiming a pinched look her way. Celestine Currington, the same priestess who hadn't been pleased to see Vixen at the gala.

The Clergy Council hadn't changed, even in all the years she had been gone. Oh, they had aged, but that was it. Celestine, along with Perry Wotton and Alton Drysdale. They had risen through the ranks of the Garusian clergy through the years, eventually landing seats on the Clergy Council that oversaw much of the Phinoran government and answered only to the Luminary.

Vixen knew her mother had often clashed with her Clergy Council. She kept her chin high. "I was told you'd like to speak with me regarding my—the Luminary's disappearance."

Their glittering gazes regarded her, reminding her of the fox head from earlier. Alton leaned forward, reminding her of a praying mantis. "Indeed. While we are hesitant to elevate you as Luminary so soon, especially with the questions surrounding your return, the fact remains we *need* a Luminary."

"And that is you," Perry added, as if any of them had doubts.

Vixen swung her gaze between them. It was clear from their posture that they didn't like her. Didn't trust her. Did they know what she was? She nudged the ring in her pocket with her thumbnail. "This isn't surprising." Her mind wandered back to the earlier voice, advising that it wasn't her time. Not yet. But what could she do, if the Clergy Council declared otherwise? The only answer was to find her mother.

"We plan to hold the Reclamation Ceremony in tandem with the Elevation Ceremony," Celestine continued. "Tomorrow, so that there is no gap in our devotion to Garus."

A weight settled on Vixen, so heavy she thought it might press the air from her lungs. It was something outside herself, something otherworldly. There was disapproval in that sensation. She coughed, then shook her head. "No. That's too soon."

Their eyes snapped to her. "Spark Valoria, you may be preparing to step into the position of Luminary, but you're only here thanks to *us*," Alton told her, voice chill. "The outlaw mages sullied you. No one trusts you. There are even rumors that *you* are the one responsible for the Luminary's disappearance." His mouth widened into something almost predatory. "And as you know, the time for the Luminary Festival draws near."

A chill threaded through Vixen. It was a veiled threat, but a threat nonetheless. The Clergy Council knew what she was. Or were they simply guessing, hoping to goad her into a mistake? Indignant anger swelled within her. Bad enough that her mother had been taken. She didn't have to tolerate this.

Again, that billowing presence leaned on her, though now she was ready for it. A primal part of her mind recognized it, knew what—no, *who*—it was. And even though all her life she'd known that she would become the avatar of Garus, it had always seemed like play-acting. Not real. This presence was all *too* real.

Use your voice.

What? Vixen stilled, thinking surely that couldn't be right. Here she was, in the most sacred of places for the god of wisdom, the god who opposed the chaos of magic. Did he truly mean for her to unleash her magic?

Your voice. Your will.

Now she understood. *I'm more than my magic. More than the Spark, more than an outlaw.* The warmth of agreement flooded her, and Vixen knew she was right. Validated. She could use her magic to get what she wanted in this moment, but it would come with a cost too great to bear. It didn't mean she couldn't push back, though.

Vixen lifted her chin, meeting the gaze of each member of the Clergy Council in turn. Either they didn't know her magic, or the earlier comment had been a bluff. None of them diverted their eyes. But they were safe enough—the Persuader kept her magic tightly bound.

They were safe from her magic, but not her tongue.

"Tomorrow is too soon. A time like this requires a..." Her words faltered for a moment as she thought. *Mourning period* wasn't right, since she didn't believe her mother to be dead. But since her disappearance had been orchestrated, their enemies likely wanted her thought dead. "Reflection period. Time to remember the previous Luminary." A sense of approval from that powerful presence thrummed through her.

"That is—" Celestine started.

"That is what we will do." Vixen cut her off, the back of her neck uncomfortably warm with nerves.

Alton sputtered. "You don't—"

"I know *exactly* what I'm doing. I'm the Spark, and in this I outrank you. In this, you will bend to *my* will." Vixen wanted to tremble, but she knew that this was more serious than any hand of cards she'd played before. She couldn't crack. Couldn't fold. "Neither ceremony will be tomorrow. Three days, nothing less."

They stared at her, as if they couldn't believe that this woman who they remembered as a slip of a girl would stand up to them. Vixen crossed her arms, letting the building silence speak volumes. She wondered if the clergy felt the same divine pressure that she did. Likely not, or they would have behaved differently.

Almost as one, the Clergy Council bowed their heads. "As you say, Spark."

Good. She favored them with a smile, deciding that she might as well press for more, if she could. "Who told you to oppose my wishes?"

The trio exchanged looks. They would have made poor poker players, unable to mask their expressions well. For a moment, Vixen thought one of them would admit to their farce, but Perry shook his head. "No one, Spark. We are simply...set in our ways."

I know a load of dragonshit when I smell it. Vixen was tempted to call them on it, but she didn't want to risk her victory. Besides, Perry's statement was telling enough. Someone *did* have their claws in the Clergy Council, and she suspected it was the Quiet Ones. If not them, then someone else who had no business meddling with these affairs.

"I see. Well, I'll leave you to reflect and see to preparations for the ceremonies." She rose and swept from the chamber, feeling as if she were cloaked in righteousness.

Vixen thought more about her situation as the carriage trundled back to the residence. She hadn't bartered her way into any freedoms, but she was far from helpless now. The god of wisdom had encouraged her, hadn't turned away from her because she had magic. While Garus hadn't exactly told her to *use* it, Vixen considered it a good sign that he hadn't rejected her. That was unexpected and an ace she planned to use.

She stepped out of the carriage, surveying the grounds. The staff were going about their business as if nothing were amiss. Vixen supposed there were some things that wouldn't stop, even for the sake of a missing Luminary. She turned to head inside.

<Vixen?>

She straightened at Alekon's voice. He was distant, at the edges of his range. Vixen made a show of moving to examine the blossoms of a rosebush, touching the petals with care as she shifted to look for her pegasus. But he was nowhere to be seen. Vixen couldn't communicate with him in mind-words, as Alekon did with her, but she could send him vague ideas. She sent him her annoyance regarding Raven and fear for her mother.

<We'll figure something out. Your brother came and told us what happened. I'm at the unicorn stable.> The disdain in his mental voice was clear. <He said you wanted me close.>

Relief thrummed through her. She *did* want him close. Gods, Vixen had missed her pegasus and the freedom he represented. It strengthened her resolve to know he was near.

<Jefferson and Seledora are doing some digging of their own. Blaise will let the chicken lady know.>

That further heartened Vixen. She wasn't alone, not at all. Her friends had her back, even from a distance. Now, if only they had Jack and Kittie, they would truly be a force to be reckoned with.

CHAPTER FORTY-ONE

I Took Offense to That

Jefferson

efferson had his suspicions about who Raven might be working with. The Luminary's disappearance only confirmed that his thoughts were correct. *I hate being right.* It meant they were embroiled in a dangerous game, one in which he didn't know all the stakes—though he could guess.

He stood in the library at Hawthorne House, pleased that this book collection had stayed within his grasp. If they'd been at his home in Nera…well, the precious tomes would be long gone. But everything in this house had been willed to Blaise, which meant everything had stayed put.

Jefferson was doing his part to help Seledora find legal precedents that might offer Vixen a leg-up over the Clergy Council, the Quiet Ones, and whoever else had a thumb in this pie. Blaise had set out with Emrys to find the Maverick Underground to see if they could help. Flora had gone to skulk around, apparently hoping to find some trace of the missing outlaws.

<That one looks promising,> Seledora commented as he held a selection of three books up for her, nosing the book in the middle.

He'd opened the window so she could peer inside. She was amused that for their purpose, he was working as her aide. But Jefferson didn't mind. He enjoyed this sort of thing—and it helped to take his mind off their dire situation.

"You think so?" Jefferson discarded the other two, opening the third to its table of contents.

Seledora angled her head so she could read it. <Yes. Open it to chapter fourteen, and I'll see if there's anything useful.>

From her previous work in Izhadell, the mare had a modified easel on which they could place a book to allow her to read. She stepped back from the window to allow him room to slip the tome into position, opening it to the chapter she requested. Seledora could flip the pages with her lips if she was careful, but she had a harder time getting to the page she wanted straight away.

With his attorney settled, Jefferson turned back to the shelves. He'd already gone through half of them and had little luck so far. There were a few history texts that might—

<Look out!>

Jefferson whirled at Seledora's warning, a shadow swooping into the library. Only he knew it wasn't a shadow. It was Raven Dawson, a knife gleaming in his hand. Even with the mare's call, the Shadowstepper had the advantage of his magic, leaping to a puddle of shadow that let him come up behind Jefferson again, knife at the Dreamer's throat.

"Don't move. I'm not going to hurt—"

Tendrils of sleep wrapped around the rogue mage before Raven finished his sentence. Jefferson didn't care if the mage was going to hurt him or not. Well, he *did* care, but regardless, the Dreamer had other plans. He'd kept his magic coiled and ready ever since he'd learned the Luminary had been taken. It paid to be prepared.

The knife fell away with a sharp clatter, skittering across the floor. Raven slumped, but Jefferson grabbed his arm, easing him down to the floor. He wasn't happy with the man, but he wouldn't allow him to gash his head open with a nasty tumble, either. Besides, the hardwood floors were too beautiful to be marred by blood.

Seledora shoved her head back inside, ears pricked. <Nicely done. Now, what will you do?>

Jefferson glanced down at the slumbering Ringleader. He was fortunate Raven hadn't known of his magic—the only thing that gave him the advantage. It was tempting to hold the man in a deep sleep, as it would certainly keep him from stealing away with anyone else. But that wouldn't provide them with any answers.

"I'll pay him a visit in the dreamscape, I think. Will you keep an eye on things for me? And if I'm still out when Blaise or Flora returns, let them know?"

<I will,> the mare agreed, easing backward. Then, as if the hubbub with Raven had never happened, she stuck her nose back in the book.

Jefferson turned back to his quarry. Raven didn't look as composed as he remembered. The man's eyes were ringed with darkness, and he was gaunter than Jefferson recalled. He had clearly been through hard times, which made the situation even more curious.

"Let's find out what game you're playing, shall we?" Jefferson strode to a chaise on the other side of the room, settling down on the velvet cushions. He pulled off his shoes, then leaned back to make himself comfortable as he called on his magic to ease into the dreamscape.

This was one of those times when he was only partially asleep. When he came here with Blaise at night, Jefferson always preferred to be truly asleep. But courtesy of his magic, he no longer needed to slumber to come to the dreamscape. This would let him rouse easily if Seledora were to wake him.

The silver fog of the dreamscape swept around Jefferson, wafting around him as he stalked into his domain. He allowed the expanse to remain formless, all grey and little more. Jefferson didn't need it to be anything special, not right now. He found Raven wreathed in mist, turning in a slow circle, as if trying to figure out what had happened to him.

"I'm rather tired of being kidnapped, so as you can imagine, I took offense to that," Jefferson drawled as he approached, arms crossed.

Raven spun, giving him an assessing look. The other mage patted at his trousers, finding his knife sheath empty. No weapons in Jefferson's domain. "I'll admit, I'm impressed. I knew you were a mage, but I never thought it would be something like this." Raven gestured around them. "What sort of magic is this?"

"That isn't your concern." Jefferson's temper flared, unwilling to be patient with someone who had made himself an enemy. "I don't know what you've been up to, but here and now, you are playing by *my* rules." He tightened his fists, ready for an attack or outburst.

Instead, Raven's shoulders slumped. The man said nothing, his expression shifting to defeat.

I am not the asshole here. Annoyance surged through Jefferson at the very idea. "What are you *doing*, Raven? You've taken the Luminary, and I assume Madame Boss Clayton. Perhaps Jack and Kittie, too?"

The Ringleader glanced up at him, eyes dark with guilt. "You wouldn't understand."

"Try me. You'd be surprised at what I might understand."

Raven gave him a thoughtful look, then nodded. "I suppose if anyone would, it would be you." He shifted his weight from side to side. "I love Vixen, you know."

Jefferson canted his head. He had suspected as much. Love made a person do stupid, reckless things. Jefferson himself was a prime example of that. "And I love Blaise, but you don't see me making world leaders vanish and starting wars with my homeland."

The Shadowstepper's eyes went flinty. "But you've done things you shouldn't for someone you cared about."

Jefferson clenched his jaw. "That's different."

"Is it?" Raven challenged.

The Dreamer snorted. "Whether it is or isn't doesn't matter. From what I understand from Vixen, she doesn't feel the same for you. You should respect that and leave her alone."

Raven twitched, visibly wounded by the reminder. Then his mouth twisted into a snarl. "You're one to talk after the way I heard you pursued Blaise."

"I didn't bring you here to debate *my* shady past," Jefferson said, voice a dangerous whisper. He tried to hide the fact that Raven had scored a direct hit. Jefferson harbored many regrets about the way he'd won over Blaise. His hidden identity. Using the geasa tattoo to bind Blaise to him—even if Jefferson had only done it to block Gregor Gaitwood from doing so. It had nearly cost him Blaise's trust. Jefferson didn't want to even consider where he would be in this moment if the Breaker had rejected him. *Not doing this, certainly.* "I'm here to uncover whatever nefarious business you're embroiled in."

The Shadowstepper shook his head. "You don't understand. She's all I have. And now they're threatening her."

Jefferson paused at the note of heartbreak in Raven's voice. "*Who* is threatening Vixen?"

"One of the elite. Name's Phillip Dillon. He said…" Raven hesitated, as if he were uncertain if he should say more. The Shadowstepper seemed to steel himself, for he plowed on. "He said I had to do exactly as he told me, or I'll lose Vixen forever."

Jefferson stared at him. "That's rather melodramatic, even for my tastes. Do you realize the things you've done have put her in *more* danger?"

Raven shook his head. "Yes. But…I mean, once I…" He looked away, renewed guilt washing across his expression. "But if I succeed, if I do what they want, then she's mine."

Jefferson stepped closer until he was crowding Raven's space. It was something he was normally too polite to do, but had observed Jack pull off such a move with great success. "What do you mean she's *yours*? We've been through this. She's done with you, Raven."

The Shadowstepper had the look of a gambler who held a hand full of aces. "There's a potion that'll change that."

Fortunes of Tabris, this suddenly makes more sense. Tara Woodrow's husband was an alchemist—a damned good one, from what Jefferson understood. Perhaps on par with Marian Hawthorne. Love potions were supposed to be something for fiction, for stage plays. *Not for real life. But then again, alchemy turned Blaise into a mage. And me.*

"You would strip her will to make her love you," Jefferson said. "You would be no different from a handler with a geasa-bound mage." Inwardly, he winced at the likening. That hit a little too close to his own personal truth. *But I never sought to take away Blaise's will. To make him love me, even though I wished it with all my heart.*

"No, I would remind her of why she *does* love me!" Raven snapped.

"I don't even know where to start with how wrong you are." Jefferson crossed his arms. No doubt the Quiet Ones were leading the Shadowstepper astray, indulging a fantasy that would never come to pass. "You've turned your back on everyone in the Gutter, and for what?"

Raven shook his head. "No. The love potion...it's an added bonus. But I only did this at first to *protect* the Gutter."

Jefferson scowled. "What? You don't trust Vixen, Blaise, and I to do this?" He had been painfully aware of the Shadowstepper's disapproval during the initial meeting.

Raven looked at the fog-shrouded ground. "Dillon had been contacting me for a while. Trying to get me to their side. Sending vague threats. I ignored them, up until the time I figured out

Vixen really *was* going to come here." He sucked in a breath. "That she really was willing to leave me and her life in the Gutter." Raven's gaze flicked back up to Jefferson. "And then I realized Dillon might make good on his threats. And his promises."

"Why didn't you mention this to the other Ringleaders?" Somehow, Jefferson kept his tone neutral. *Years of practice as a politician can only do so much.* He was nearing the end of his fuse.

Raven clammed up, shaking his head. Jefferson was done, entirely frustrated with this man. He called on his magic, and a massive black tentacle reared up from the mist, snaking out to wrap around Raven before the mage could so much as blink. He yelped as the spectral tentacle hefted him upside-down over Jefferson's head.

"This is a dream," Jefferson advised Raven, "but I have my own ways of harming you here. I don't wish to, but I will if I must. *Why didn't you tell the Ringleaders?*"

Raven's face was the same ghostly white as a full moon. Jefferson was certain he was trying to use his own magic, but it failed in the dreamscape. "I couldn't tell them!"

"*Why?*"

"If I did, Vixen would die, and they promised the Gutter would be under the Confederation's thumb in less than a year."

Jefferson had the tentacle haul Raven closer. "Idiot. That's probably their plan, regardless."

Confusion crinkled Raven's brow. "What?"

"You *know* Phillip Dillon is one of the Quiet Ones." Jefferson had told all the Ringleaders of them, but now it was painfully clear he should have gone into more detail on who they were and why they were dangerous. "I suppose in the future I'll need to make elaborate presentations on our enemies, so we all stay on the same page." When Raven made no response, Jefferson crossed his arms again. "So, why did you come for *me*? I know it wasn't a social call."

The spectral tentacle set the Shadowstepper down, though it

didn't loosen around him. The mage flexed his arms, as if hoping to win free. When he realized it was useless, Raven glanced back up at Jefferson. "Dillon wants you."

"Dead or alive?" Jefferson suspected he knew, but it didn't hurt to confirm.

"Alive, as far as I know." Raven's shoulders heaved against his phantasmal restraints. "They don't treat me like a partner, though. So they may be withholding information from me."

I can guarantee that is the case. Jefferson dismissed the tentacle with a thought, secretly pleased when the Shadowstepper wobbled when it vanished. "And why Kittie? Was it because she went looking for Jack?"

Raven frowned. "At first, it was because she found me. But then..."

"What?"

The Shadowstepper's eyes squeezed shut. "I know you think I'm a traitor, and maybe I am. But I hoped Kittie might be an ace in the hole." Raven swallowed. "I thought I was doing the right thing."

Well, yes, if the right thing is handing your supposed allies over to the enemy. But I'm not bitter. Jefferson cocked his head. "I don't follow. Where is she? Where are the people you took?"

"Between the shadows. Everyone but Jack, anyway."

So, Blaise was right. Jefferson was overjoyed by his beau's insight but further confused by everything. "And how is Kittie your ace?"

Raven met his gaze. "I'm playing to win. And to win, I'm placing bets on both sides." He smiled, and it was one that spoke of the cunning Jefferson knew the man possessed. "She's my gamble against Dillon and Woodrow."

CHAPTER FORTY-TWO
As Relentless as the Sun Crossing The Sky

Kittie

"Y ou're a mage. A mage brought us here. Surely you can get us out." The Luminary crossed her arms as she frowned at Kittie. Najaria's flaming mane bathed her face in a warm glow. But in that moment, it made her look petulant and garish, like a frustrated customer demanding more sweet rolls of a shopkeeper when there were none to be had.

"Trust me, I'm trying to come up with something. I don't want to be stuck here any more than you do," Kittie replied, almost wishing that she and the aethon hadn't stumbled on the other pair stranded in the shadows. But that was unfair. Rachel Clayton was being perfectly reasonable about the mess, and Kittie couldn't fault the Luminary for wanting to leave as soon as possible.

Kittie was tired. She wanted to leave the eternal darkness, wanted to feel the kiss of the sun on her skin. And more than that, she wanted her family. Wanted Emmaline's smile lighting up the room. She longed for Jack's solid presence, the knowledge that he was there and—

Najaria wheeled with a snort, staring off into the never-ending

darkness. The move drew their attention, breaking Kittie's remi-
niscing. The red mare pawed at the ground, then ambled off.

"Where's she going?" Rachel asked.

"I wish I knew," Kittie said. "But there's only one way to find
out."

The aethon broke into a trot, and Kittie struggled to keep up.
She heard the patter of the other women behind her, along with
their confused calls. But she had no answers for them.

Najaria slowed, head high as she assessed the shadows. Was it
Kittie's imagination, or were they somehow thinning? It was like
peering through a dark fog, wisps of shadow winding around a
tree here, a lamp post there.

"What is that?" Madame Boss Clayton moved to stand beside
Kittie.

"I don't know." The Pyromancer shook her head. She didn't
have the magical education to understand what she was seeing.

"It's a liminal space," the Luminary said, voice soft. Kittie and
Rachel both turned to her, puzzled. Juliette's gaze clung to the
drifting shadows ahead. "At least, that's what I think it is."

"You'll have to explain because I don't understand," Kittie said.
She didn't like not comprehending magic, disliked not knowing
what this woman who despised mages knew. But she was
sensible enough to know that the more information she had, the
better.

"I understand it mostly in terms relating to the gods, but I
don't see why it wouldn't be the same for magic," the Luminary
mused. "After all, there is a goddess of magic, so it would make
sense for there to be overlap." She nodded, as if trying to convince
herself. "A liminal space is like a threshold, but in this sense, it's a
place of overlap between states of being."

Kittie glanced at Najaria, wondering if that was how the
aethon had found her in the shadows. Since she was both equine
and elemental, had she taken advantage of the liminal space to
travel into the shadows in search of her rider?

"States of being or realms?" Rachel put her hands on her hips as she stared into the soupy darkness.

"Both, probably. I think we're shadows right now," Kittie supplied. "That's why time feels as if it passes differently. Why we don't feel hunger or the need to sleep."

The Luminary pursed her lips. "Something like that. If we can figure out how to use the liminal space to our advantage..."

"We might find our way out," Kittie finished, meeting Juliette's gaze.

"This is way out of my depth." Rachel blew out a breath, her face pale and drawn. Kittie felt sorry for the woman—she had been ripped away from her children to a place she didn't understand, with no hope of escape without help.

Najaria nickered, shoving Kittie with her muzzle. There was something insistent about the gesture, a command for attention. She swiveled to face the mare, then followed as the aethon waded into the dark fog.

"Now what?" the Luminary called. Kittie shook her head in response.

But then the tendrils of shadow shifted, and she knew why the elemental had brought her to this veiled area. The darkness opened into a murky expanse that was bright compared to the surrounding realm. Kittie froze when she noticed the lump of a body on the ground.

"Jack!" She didn't realize she had screamed his name until Rachel rushed to her side, heedless of the shadows lurking around them. Kittie went down to her knees beside her husband, reaching out—only to discover she couldn't touch him. He wasn't in the shadows with her, but on the other side of the fog.

Jack, the man she loved even when he was infuriating, was a gruesome mess. His face was swollen and discolored; his clothing darkened with dried blood. He looked *dead*. Kittie tipped her head back, shrieking her fury, hot tears ebbing from her eyes.

She didn't know how long she knelt by her husband's still

form, sobbing. She felt the other women behind her, and the heat of Najaria's closeness as the mare stood vigil. Kittie rubbed her face, shaking her head.

"Whoever this man is, he's alive." The Luminary's voice was soft. Almost gentle. "See how his chest moves?"

She hadn't realized Juliette had shifted to crouch beside her. Rachel had a hand on her back, as if to steady the Pyromancer. Kittie wiped her eyes. "My husband. *My gods-damned idiot husband.*" Waves of anger at Jack for striking out without her warred with despair at his condition. *If only he hadn't left me behind again.*

"*Ah.*" The Luminary loaded the word with a wealth of sympathy. Then, her voice even lower, the woman added, "Garus showed you the way here for a reason."

Kittie scowled, tasting the salt of her own tears. The damned god of wisdom had done nothing. It was all Najaria. But…was it only coincidence that Kittie had come across the Luminary and Madame Boss? Had it been Raven's crafty planning? Or something more? Her head hurt almost as badly as her heart as she thought about it.

Jack's eyelids fluttered, as if he could hear them. His lips moved, his eyes barely visible through the puffiness of his face. It was almost as if he saw her. Maybe he could—she didn't know. Aside from his lips, the only other part of Jack that moved was a hand, trailing painfully across his chest before resting over his heart, patting it feebly.

At first, Kittie thought he was doing it as a gesture of love—and maybe that was a small part of it. She lifted her hand to place it over her own heart, freezing when the crumple of paper rustled in her pocket. Swallowing, she fished out the portal spell. Jack closed his eyes and went still.

She couldn't sit by Jack's side like a wraith. That wouldn't accomplish anything. She cast another worried glance at him, reaching out fingers she knew couldn't touch him. But for a moment, she could fool herself into thinking she might. Kittie sighed, recalling the feel of her hand against his muscular chest, the way she would trace the swirls of the long-dead geasa tattoo on his bicep with her index finger. The way he would look at her with his soft blue eyes, as if she were the only person in the world that mattered.

I'm coming for you, Jack Arthur Dewitt. Somehow. Kittie swallowed, weaving to her feet with renewed determination.

Rachel shot a look at Jack, then back to Kittie. "Are you going to be okay?"

"I have to be."

Juliette tilted her head, giving Kittie a look that was surprisingly empathetic. "Isn't that always the way for us women? The world falls apart around us, yet we still must press on, as relentless as the sun crossing the sky."

"Always," Kittie agreed with a whisper. What other choice did they have but to go on? She licked her lips. As upsetting as Jack's condition was, his appearance made her *think,* now that she was pulling herself back together. She wound her way back through all the conversations they'd had since their reunion. All the things he had experienced and told her about.

Jack didn't like to talk to many people, but he liked to talk to *her.* And the man knew a surprising amount about magic. She thought about the way they had combined their power to cast the portal. Her pyromancy was a far cry from his brand of ritualistic magic, but they had still worked together, based on tricks he had learned from the Breaker.

What if the gods and magic had more in common than just liminal spaces? What if the gods *were* magic—and could confer it to an avatar?

As if sensing her rider's thoughts, Najaria nickered. The mare turned, bobbing her head in the Luminary's direction.

Kittie hissed out a breath. "I'll be damned. It might be worth a try."

"What's that?" Juliette asked, suddenly aware of the way Kittie and the aethon were regarding her.

"We need another liminal space." More ideas came to Kittie as she spoke. "This one is between the shadow realm and our world. We need one between the shadows and the gods."

Both women stared at her. "Excuse me?" Rachel almost choked on the words.

"Wait," Juliette said, holding up a hand. Her eyes narrowed as she pursed her lips. "I understand what you're saying. I just don't know what you intend to do."

Kittie turned away from Jack, facing the endless darkness. "Something my husband told me to try."

CHAPTER FORTY-THREE
The Hand You're Dealt

Blaise

"Hey, I'm back. Have you—?" Blaise halted abruptly, forgetting the question that had been on his lips, when he came across his beau seated on a chaise, reading as if nothing were amiss, while Raven Dawson lay slumbering at his feet. "What's this? I mean, I know it's Raven, but…?"

Jefferson aimed a smug, devilish grin at him. "He thought he could get the drop on me."

Blaise's brows shot up at that, internally warring between worry and anger. "Raven was going to take you, too?" He moved closer, as if drawing nearer to the Shadowstepper would protect Jefferson any better than the Dreamer himself had done.

"To the Quiet Ones, yes," Jefferson confirmed, voice soft. He patted the velvet cushion beside him, an invitation. The Dreamer radiated calm confidence, as languid as a mouser cat who'd just snagged the fattest rat in town.

Blaise stepped over the sleeping Ringleader, claiming his place beside Jefferson. "How did you find out—oh. You got him into the dreamscape and asked?"

"I did." There was a layer of puzzlement in Jefferson's voice. "He says he's working with the Quiet Ones, but to *protect* Vixen and the Gutter."

Blaise blew out a breath. Vixen, he knew, would take offense to that. But by the same token, he understood why Raven might do something unthinkable. The reasons behind his actions didn't matter at the moment, though. What mattered was Jefferson had made a breakthrough in their situation. "What about Jack and Kittie? Any word on them?"

At that, Jefferson pursed his lips. "Raven is the one who took them, as we suspected. But he took Kittie for his own reasons. I suspect he's playing her like a queen in chess."

Blaise shook his head. "No, the Luminary is a captured queen. Vixen and Kittie are more like pawns about to cross the board. With Vixen in line to be the next Luminary and Kittie poised to..." He made a vague gesture.

Jefferson gave him a thoughtful look, then nodded. "Hmm. Hadn't thought of it quite that way. So she is, yes. Raven seems to think—or perhaps, hope—that Kittie will have a way to stop him. Or to help in some way I'm not privy to."

"Did Raven take Madame Boss Clayton and the Luminary, too?" Blaise asked.

The Dreamer's face lit up, as if Blaise's question had provided an answer. "Ah, yes! He did. And now I think I see the play." Jefferson became more animated as he spoke, his hands gesturing with each word. "Look, Kittie *knows* Rachel."

The Firebrand had saved the Gannish leader, in fact. The women would already have a natural trust of each other. Blaise crossed his arms, glancing down at their captive. "I don't know if that was a stroke of genius or one more thing to be mad at him about."

"It can be both," Jefferson said, his tone far too pleasant, as if he were in awe of Raven's gambit. "But now we need to figure out what to—"

There was a sharp pop and displacement of air. Flora appeared next to a bookshelf. Her mouth opened in greeting, but then her violet eyes caught sight of Raven, and she pulled her knives, crouching as if ready to pounce on an enemy. When it was clear the man wasn't moving, she twirled her knives before sheathing them. "Aw, he's breathing. I thought maybe you killed him."

"*Flora*," Blaise grumbled.

"What?" the half-knocker asked. "It was a valid thought! Or were you waiting for me? I have no problems with—"

Jefferson held up a hand before she could complete the bloody sentence. "There will be no killing of anyone in this library." Then, no doubt thinking he had better add qualifications, he tacked on, "Or anywhere in Blaise's house."

"Or on my land," Blaise hurriedly added. It was still strange to think that he had land—and in Phinora, of all places.

Flora frowned, peering at them over the rim of her glasses. "You're no fun." She came closer, poking Raven's slack arm with her toe. "I'll volunteer to torture information out of him, I guess." She shrugged, as if that were less exciting than murder.

"I already got information from him, thank you very much," Jefferson said, grinning at her dismay.

"You're going to put me out of a job," Flora complained.

"I thought you were an *aide*," Blaise pointed out.

"Sometimes I aid Jefferson by—"

"Now, now, there will be time for those discussions later," Jefferson interjected. Blaise had his suspicions about the violent ways Flora had *aided* Jefferson in the past, and he was grateful not to have to hear of them. "As I was about to say before we were interrupted, we need to plan our next step." He held up an index finger to stay Flora's imminent suggestions. "A next step that *does not* involve murder or torture."

Flora crossed her arms, her lower lip poking out in feigned annoyance.

"I think we need to let Vixen know we have him," Blaise said, jerking his chin toward Raven.

The half-knocker brightened at that. "Oh! I can do that! Especially since neither of you should leave the estate."

Blaise wasn't going to point out that he had, in fact, left the estate, and he'd been *clandestine* for once. Flora had a good point—she had expertise in moving around undetected that he and Jefferson lacked. He nodded to Jefferson.

The Dreamer sighed. "Very well. Tell Vixen about Raven and let her know that I'll bring her to the dreamscape tonight." Then his expression grew stony. "After that, I need you to do something else for me."

Flora, too, noticed the change in Jefferson's demeanor and rubbed her hands together, cackling. "Yeah?"

"Infiltrate Tara Woodrow's residence. I trust you can locate it?"

Flora gave a dismissive wave. "Yeah, piece of cake." She paused, eyeing Blaise. "Speaking of—"

"Yes, I'll make you a cake," Blaise agreed. It would be refreshing to do something normal. Cake made everything better.

"Marble cake? With buttercream frosting?" Flora batted her eyelashes at him, as if that would affect his agreement.

He waved a hand. "Yes, I have the ingredients. But only people who don't wantonly murder others get cake."

"Deal," Flora said with a prim nod. "Only justifiable murders."

Blaise sighed, though he supposed that was the best he could ask for at this point. Flora was Flora, after all.

Jefferson seemed unbothered by her words—possibly because he was sending Flora to the home of an enemy. It wouldn't be the first time a death had resulted from such a visit, Blaise assumed. "Right now, we need information. What are they planning?"

Flora gave a mock salute. "I know the routine, boss." She glanced at Raven's prone form, then back at her friends. "Be careful. If you let him wake up, I imagine he won't be happy."

"That's why I'm not letting him wake up anytime soon,"

Jefferson said, though Blaise heard the undercurrent of regret in his voice.

Flora vanished with a wave. Blaise settled a hand on Jefferson's knee. "You're only doing it because you have to."

Jefferson combed a hand through his hair. "Yes, well, I'm concerned that actions such as this will turn me into the sort of person I don't wish to be." His gaze focused on Raven, the corners of his eyes crinkling with worry.

Blaise understood. "I think half the battle is being aware. I doubt the Quiet Ones spare a moment to think of such things."

The Dreamer relaxed a hair. "You're right. I felt…" He paused, frowning. "When I have people like Gregor or Raven in the dreamscape, they're at my mercy. And sometimes I'm not a good person. I…I *liked* wielding that power over them. Enjoyed it." Jefferson gave him a sideways look, as if he feared Blaise would draw away at the confession.

But Blaise realized imperfect people surrounded him—and he was far from perfect, too. Jefferson had been raised to expect power and to wield it over others. Was it such a surprise that he fell back on old habits? But Blaise would never tell him that, knowing it was another of Jefferson's fears. He didn't want to live up to the expectations and behaviors of the Wells family. So instead, he said, "I think sometimes people are like that. Even the very best ones."

Jefferson considered his words, then nodded. "Perhaps so." He rolled his shoulders, preparing to rise. "Well, we can't sit in the library all afternoon and evening. There's no longer a full staff here to deliver meals at my leisure."

"What are we going to do with him? We shouldn't put him in the guest room or leave him here in case he wakes," Blaise pointed out.

"I'd know if he woke up, but you have a good point," Jefferson said. "We'll have to bring him along with us. I'll get his shoulders if you get his feet?"

Blaise sighed. "This is *not* how I envisioned spending my evening. Carting around a sleeping Ringleader."

Jefferson leaned over to pick up Raven, but he shot Blaise a tempting smile. "Oh, dare I ask how *you* envisioned spending the evening?"

Blaise couldn't help it—he laughed. "Probably not the way you're hoping."

The Dreamer gave a dramatic sigh. "Ah, the sting of disappointment. Now I know how Flora feels." He winked at Blaise with a grin, then stooped to grab the Shadowstepper's shoulders.

Vixen

"HE'S *WHERE?*" VIXEN STARED AT FLORA, A RANGE OF EMOTIONS flitting across her face. She still wasn't sure how the diminutive half-knocker had gotten into the residence when Vixen herself couldn't get out easily, but that was a question for later.

"In the dreamscape—" Flora began.

"No, I mean *where?* You said Jefferson has him asleep?" Vixen asked, hating that she probably sounded desperate. Raven had taken her mother—and that meant he could get her back. But could she even trust him anymore? A pang struck her as gilded memories of their time together reared up. Raven, grinning as he taught her some of his favorite tricks for knife-fighting, his body companionably close to hers. Of listening to the rich, warm sounds rising from his fiddle, Raven's dark eyes shining as she sang along.

But those times were in the past, fading like fog burned off by the sun. No, she couldn't trust him. Not anymore.

Flora was oblivious to her wool-gathering. "Oh. Shadypants tried to get the jump on Jefferson at Hawthorne House and failed. Last I saw, he was napping on a rug in the library."

Shadypants? Right, she meant Raven. Vixen would have laughed at the ridiculous name if the situation weren't so dire. She glanced at the window, then back to Flora. "So if I went there, I could talk to him?"

Flora shook her head. "Don't think so. Jefferson plans to keep him out—that's why he wanted you to have a chat in the dreamscape tonight."

Vixen sighed, rubbing her arms as she paced the room like a beast in a menagerie. "I don't know if that will be enough." As she walked, she formed a plan. It wasn't much, just a tiny seed of an idea. *Garus didn't refute me.* Anything was worth a try.

Flora nodded. "I get it. You want the personal touch—a slap in the face in the real world, not the dreamscape."

"Not exactly, but close," Vixen admitted. Slapping Raven's stupid, handsome face was tempting, yes. But ultimately, it would do nothing. And truth be told, the man deserved far more than a slap for all this.

The half-knocker tilted her head. "You need any other information from me? If not, I've got to bounce." She rubbed her hands together, as if looking forward to whatever was next on her agenda.

Vixen shook her head. "Not unless you can get me out of here."

Flora raised her bright pink eyebrows, contemplative. "I could, but since time isn't on our side, it would be louder and bloodier than you'd probably want."

That was likely true. Vixen rubbed her forehead. "Thanks anyway. I can get out if I really want to."

The half-knocker nodded in understanding, then waved. "Best of luck, then!" She vanished from the room.

Once Flora departed, Vixen closed her eyes, sighing. She couldn't stay put, not any longer. She stalked over to her closet. The tailor had stocked it with an optimistic assortment of clothing, most of it unsuitable to the life Vixen wished to lead. The outfit she had worn to the ill-fated gala was out with the laundry, so she had to do her best to cobble together clothing that would work for riding a pegasus. Dresses and flight were a poor combination, never mind the chafing against bare skin.

It took longer than she liked, but eventually, she found an old pair of black trousers meant for winter and a frilly, emerald green button-down shirt that would complement it nicely. Vixen pulled her hair back into a tail, studying herself in the mirror. She was back in that strange in-between state, somewhere between an outlaw and theocrat. She wondered if Jefferson felt this way, this odd sensation of belonging in two worlds and feeling as if she didn't fit in either.

She might not fit, but she would fake it. And for the moment, she was the Spark. Soon to be the Luminary. She took a steadying breath. *And now I'm the Persuader.*

Vixen opened her door and found the same guards from earlier posted there. They didn't look at her, but she noticed they inclined their chins deferentially. "Is there something you need, Spark Valoria?"

She exhaled a soft breath. This was it. No going back from this, either. Vixen stepped into the hallway, and both men tensed, as if prepared to physically stop her. She caught their eyes, but before she spoke, Vixen glimpsed the corner of a four of spades poking out of the guard on the right's coat. *Cards. Yeah, I can work with that.*

"Entertainment," she said briskly.

The guard with the cards nodded. "I can send for a musician or..." He faltered, no doubt trying to think of what else might divert her.

Vixen shook her head. "Nothing like that. I see you have a deck of cards. I do enjoy a good game." She aimed an amiable smile at both of them, shading her words with only a trickle of magic. Just enough to make them think this was a good idea.

Vixen felt them bridle against it. She pushed harder, encouraging them. After a moment, the guard with the cards relented, ducking his head. "We'd be honored to keep you company. Should we call for others to join the game so that no one suspects we're taking advantage of you?"

"No." Vixen nearly snapped the single word. "No, but thank you for the offer. Everyone knows your honor is beyond reproach as a part of the Lightguard." As with any group of people, there was no such assurance. But Vixen set aside that concern for the moment. Even if they intended ill for her, there was no way they would get past the persuasion she could layer on them.

They settled at a small table near a window. Really, it was designed to only comfortably fit two, but Vixen didn't care. She dragged a wingback chair over and made do.

"Thank you for joining me, gentlemen," Vixen said. "Could I ask your names?"

"I'm Walter, and he's Hubert." Walter was the one with the cards and had removed them from his coat, preparing to shuffle. "What game would you like to play? Knack or Rounce, perhaps? We can always explain the rules."

Vixen bit back a laugh. She knew how to play both games—how to cheat at them, too. In all honesty, she'd have preferred something like Wild Dragon. Now, there was a fun card game that was easy to cheat at. Small wonder it was illegal in the Confederation and frowned upon even in the Gutter. But for this to work, she had to make a bluff of her own.

"Oh, I've heard of those," Vixen said, which was true enough. They didn't need to know how much she knew. And while they were good games, they weren't quite what she wanted. "What about Foxtail? Perhaps we could try that?"

The guards traded looks. Hubert licked his lips, his words precise as he said, "We're familiar with the game. But it requires two decks."

Vixen shot them a demure smile. "Does it? We're in luck. I have my own. Walter, why don't you lay out the tableau while I grab them? I'll find some chips, too."

Neither man questioned her knowledge, instead focusing on laying out thirteen cards of the same suit from Walter's deck. Vixen snagged her deck of cards from the depths of her saddlebag, then rummaged in a drawer to find something to use as chips. She came across a small box full of buttons and decided they would do.

"I'll give this deck a shuffle," Vixen said, enjoying the solid weight of the cards in her hand. She knew this deck intimately. Once she'd completed the shuffle, Vixen discarded the top card, pausing before anyone laid out chips for their first bet. "As with any game, what we need here is stakes." She smiled brilliantly at them. "If I win, you let me out of my rooms to go about as I'd like."

Walter froze at her suggestion, eyes narrowing. "That's not something we can allow."

Vixen summoned a thread of magic. She wanted her gambling knack to give her the edge, but she wasn't too proud to use her power. "It is, because if you win, you can have something, too. Whatever you like."

They blinked at her, as if that hadn't occurred to them. Then both men nodded. "If we win, we'd like a week away. My mother is ill. I want to spend time with her," Walter said.

Hubert gave a wistful sigh. "And I see my sweetheart so infrequently. I'd take her on a trip."

Gods, their request was so simple. So heartfelt. Vixen decided that even when she won, she'd find a way for them to have that week off. Somehow. But she merely nodded. "Let's do this, then." They laid their bets, and she flipped the top two cards.

A HALF-HOUR LATER, WALTER AND HUBERT TRAILED BEHIND VIXEN as she made her way out of the residence. The ease with which she'd won the game of Foxtail had baffled them, but a bet was a bet, and they did as she asked. Well, the subtle application of

Persuader magic didn't hurt. It hadn't taken much, as they were already predisposed to serving her.

It's just a suggestion. And I'm the Spark, so they're supposed to listen to me anyway, right? Still, guilt plagued Vixen as they threaded their way toward the unicorn stables. Doubtless, everyone they passed assumed she was being escorted somewhere under orders. And it was true, in a way.

The only complication arose as they approached the stables. Flaunting her power as she was, the unicorns scented her before they could even see her, trilling cries of alarm.

<Vixen?> Alekon's mental voice quivered with excitement. <You're here?>

She sent him an affirmative, wishing she could tell him to come out to her. As it was, she was going to have to enter the stables, and at this time of day, there would be Trackers there, as well.

Sure enough, a woman with dark hair in corkscrew curls strode out of the entrance, a revolver in hand. She hesitated, uncertain at Vixen's approach with her guards. The Tracker glanced from the excited unicorns back to Vixen and her escort.

"Halt!" the Tracker cried, holding up a hand in warning. She didn't point her revolver at them, but Vixen was sure the woman would be quick to aim if needed. "There's a mage here!"

You have no idea. Vixen flashed a smile, though she kept her power quiet for the time being. "Nothing to worry about. Stand down."

Confusion flitted across the woman's face. "You're the Spark, aren't you? We were told you're to stay in residence until..." She looked at Walter and Hubert, uncertain.

The sound of boot heels drew their attention. "Valoria?" Rhys was so startled by her appearance that he seemed to have forgotten he shouldn't speak to her with such familiarity, brother or not.

Hubert strode forward in a half-dozen long strides, face stern. "You'll show respect to the Spark!"

Rhys took a step back, eyes narrowing as he felt the wash of magic and no doubt realized what Vixen had done. "I misspoke. My apologies. Carla, I can handle this." He glanced at the other Tracker, a clear dismissal. Carla scowled at being sent away, but she had the sense to retreat. When she was out of earshot, Rhys turned back to Vixen. "To what do we owe the pleasure of a visit?" His voice was as tight as a bowstring, ready to let fly, his shoulders rigid.

"You know who I'm here for," Vixen said, walking into the stables, heading for the stall where she knew she'd find Alekon.

The bay stallion watched the proceedings, ears pricked. He bobbed his head with excitement as she drew near, and Vixen couldn't help but smile at him. <Are we leaving this place? Going home to the Gutter?> There was a longing in his mental tone mixed with a fierce love for her.

I would give anything to go back to the Gutter. "We need to go to Hawthorne House," she whispered in response. His disappointment was heavy on her mind, but Alekon was also too smart to think they could leave so easily. "Raven is there."

<Is he?> Alekon's ears swept back, pinned tight to his skull.

"Let's get you tacked up," Vixen said, then belatedly realized it would look odd for the Spark to saddle her own steed.

"Allow me," Rhys said through gritted teeth, approaching with saddle and hackamore. Then, when he was at arm's length from her, he asked, "What are you doing, using your magic like that?"

"Let's just say I had a life-changing meeting with the Clergy Council," Vixen whispered. "Garus made himself known."

Rhys spread the saddle blanket on Alekon's glossy back but froze at her words. "What?"

Vixen stared at Alekon's hocks as if they were the most interesting things in the stable. "There's something going on."

"Garus spoke to you?" Her brother shook his head at that,

getting back to work. "And this? Did he approve...whatever you're doing?" He gestured to the charmed guards, disapproval in his movements.

Vixen pursed her lips. "He didn't call me an abomination for having magic, if that's what you mean."

Rhys's brow slanted. "You know I'd *never* call you that." There was hurt in his voice, enough to give Vixen pause. "I've always known what you were." His gaze flicked back to the guards. "But this? *This* is why you left—why we both knew you needed to leave. A mage capable of stripping a person's will..." The corners of his eyes creased with concern.

Vixen's gut clenched. What other choice did she have but to use the resources at her disposal? And besides... "The Confederation has no problem with stripping the will of a mage using the geasa."

Rhys winced at that. "Don't you want to be better than that?"

She did, but that seemed like an impossible burden right now. Vixen sighed. "That's not a luxury I have at the moment. And I'll have you know I didn't strip their will. That's not how my magic works."

He absently patted Alekon's shoulder. "Then what did you do?"

There was curiosity in his voice. Vixen raised her brows, considering that they'd never truly had the time to discuss her magic in depth. When it had manifested, they'd been absorbed in hiding it from their mother, and ultimately, in Vixen's escape.

"I'm called a Persuader for a reason—I can't *force* someone to do something. But I can suggest it, and make it sound like an awful tempting idea." She glanced at Hubert and Walter. "They were already assigned to protect me. It didn't take much encouragement."

He frowned. "But they knew you were under orders to not leave your room."

"They lost at cards."

Rhys's mouth dropped open. "They...what?"

Vixen reached up and made a show of pushing his jaw closed. "If we ever have some downtime, I'll show you what I did for fun in the Gutter." Then she sobered. "Now, are there any horses available for my guards? I need them to keep up with..." She nodded to Alekon.

Rhys ran a hand through his hair. "Let me see what I can do."

CHAPTER FORTY-FOUR
Between the Shadows

Flora

*I*t took some snooping, but Flora excelled in that area. In Jefferson's employ, she had scoured through records to find the right bit of information to aid whatever task he set her to. Flora had what she liked to call *people skills*, which Jefferson claimed were not the sort of *people skills* that most thought of when that term was used. Apparently, tracking down adversaries wasn't the same thing as his schmoozy charm.

She let herself into a clerk's office (because it wasn't breaking and entering if she let herself in) and rifled through the records until she uncovered what she needed. After copying the information on a scrap of paper, Flora put the files back mostly the way she found them, re-secured the office (see, common thieves didn't make it a point to re-secure the place they had let themselves into), and headed for her target.

Night had fallen by the time she found the address, but that didn't bother her. Knockers didn't care for daylight, though Flora tolerated it thanks to the glasses Jefferson had specially made for her. Something about bright light made it so the entire world was fuzzy beyond the tip of her nose. Moonlight and darkness didn't have the same effect—she could see as well in the dark as she could with her glasses by day.

She crept up to the house. It wasn't late enough for people to be abed, not yet, but that didn't stop Flora from exploring. Years of sneaking around, even before she had met Jefferson, had honed her to the task. Despite her bright hair, she naturally melted into the shadows, and her short stature made it easy to hide when needed.

After skirting a patrol of theurgists, Flora discovered an unlatched window and let herself inside. The room she entered was dark but uninhabited. It looked like a study, the sort of place she would often find a treasure trove of information. She would come back to this place later, once she had the lay of the land.

She slipped through a hallway and threaded through half a dozen more rooms before coming across a sight that brought her up short. A man lay in the middle of the floor in what looked like a parlor, the only occupant. The sharp tang of blood scented the air, and dark blotches on the rug proved to have come from the man.

"Oh, *schist*." That wasn't just any man. It was *Jack*.

Flora tiptoed over to him, afraid of what she might find. Bruises covered the visible skin, his clothing stiff with dried blood. When she drew closer, she noticed the shallow rise and fall of his chest. He was alive, somehow. The skin around both of his eyes was swollen, and she was certain if he opened them, he would have difficulty seeing.

"Jack?" Flora whispered, hoping to rouse the outlaw. When he didn't move, she gently prodded him with a finger. "Hey, asshole. Wake up. We need to get you out of here." *Somehow.*

And yet, the injured man gave no indication that he would rouse. Her heart sank. He was unconscious and badly wounded, in the hands of the enemy. Flora chewed her lower lip, thinking. Thanks to her knocker heritage, she was stronger than the average human, and in a pinch, she *could* carry him out of there. But she couldn't do that *and* fight off anyone they came across.

She cocked her head, thinking. The best plan would be to tell Jefferson and Blaise. They—

The sound of approaching footsteps and the creak of hinges interrupted her ruminations. Flora scurried out of sight, locating a low-slung table that would provide cover. In a scrape, she could use her magic to vanish from the room, but she wasn't ready to leave this place yet. Not with the Effigest unconscious on the floor.

A well-dressed pair strode into the room. She recognized them immediately: Tara Woodrow and Phillip Dillon. Flora narrowed her eyes, hunkering down to eavesdrop on their conversation.

Tara hesitated when she saw the drying blood spattered around the outlaw's prone form. "By Garus, Phillip! Did you kill him?"

The older man smiled, a cruel sort of expression that made Flora want to wipe it off his face, preferably with the blade of her knife. "No, but he probably wishes I had. See? He's breathing." He nudged Jack's leg with a toe.

"But only barely," Tara commented, crossing her arms, disapproval clear in her stance. Flora was pretty sure it wasn't from any concern over the outlaw's health, though. "Our plan won't work quite as well if he's dead."

Phillip shrugged. "I had to make sure he knew his place. He's too strong and mouthy otherwise." Flora had to admit that part was accurate. Then he laughed. "Anyway, there's no need to worry. If he died, we would just use one of the other outlaws. Really, out of all of them, Cole deserves a hanging the most, the traitor. But that won't suit my needs—you know I have plans for him."

Flora bit back a growl. She'd be damned if she'd allow them to —wait, *hang?* They were planning to hang Jack? She gritted her teeth. In a convoluted way, it made sense. They had every right to do so. Wildfire Jack Dewitt's mug was on many handbills throughout the Confederation. But if they wanted the Effigest dead, why hadn't they already done it? Why leave him in this parlor, half-dead?

"Speaking of Cole, where is he? I thought our new pet was going to deliver him, too." Tara put her hands on her waist, cocking one hip as she considered the downed outlaw. "He seemed motivated to do the work."

Phillip shook his head. "I don't know. Dawson hasn't returned, and I told him to bring Jefferson directly here. I don't know if something's happened to him or if he's jumped ship." He moved to sit in a wingback chair, which put him out of Flora's view, but as long as they spoke, it didn't matter.

"I don't think he'd abandon us—he wants the love elixir too badly," Tara said.

"Unless he doesn't care for the Spark as much as we thought," Phillip suggested.

Tara clucked her tongue, shaking her head. "Dear Phillip, you saw how lovesick that boy was. And lovesick boys do *very* stupid things." She was far too gleeful about her observation. "No, I doubt it's Dawson. More likely, Cole or his pet mage have taken our piece off the board."

And Flora was damn proud of Jefferson for doing exactly that.

Phillip made a contemplative sound. "Then I think we need to start making our move. Those blasted mages made every moment count back in Nera. They're resourceful, which makes them dangerous. If we don't keep this moving along, they'll find a way around it."

The half-knocker gritted her teeth. She was tempted to reveal herself and attack the pair of Quiet Ones, taking them out of the action for good. She'd done similar before, but usually against people who mattered much less than these two. This pair had plans upon plans, and their deaths may not be enough to end the designs already set in motion.

"You're just saying that because the sooner we move, the sooner you think you can get your hands on Cole," Tara said, and for the first time, Flora detected discord in their ranks. "This is like alchemy, Phillip. Everything must be done properly, in the right amount and time, or it will blow up in our faces."

There was a scrape as Phillip's chair shifted on the hardwood floor. "We had a deal, as you well know. That is the only reason I'm taking part in this endeavor."

Ooh. I wish I had popcorn. This could be good. Well, aside from Jack laying there near dead and all. Flora propped her elbows against the floor.

"Not the only reason." Tara's voice was sickly sweet. "But it's better to be only the two of us, rather than all the Quiet Ones here to muck things up. Too many cooks in the kitchen, as they say. This still meets the long-term goals of our organization, even as it satisfies our *personal* goals."

Personal goals? She could guess Dillon's: he wanted Jefferson. And revenge on Jack, by the looks of it. What about Tara, though? Flora certainly hoped she'd cooperate and spill her intentions. That would be handy.

"And our organization's goals are precisely why we need to keep up our momentum," Phillip said to Flora's disappointment. Well, maybe not *disappointment*, she corrected herself. This was probably important, too. "It's vital that we hit the outlaws as hard as we can while they're here."

"You took that *far* too literally," Tara commented with a laugh.

Phillip didn't even make a snort of laughter at the poor jape. "If our goal is to take the Gutter, we can't allow the outlaw mages to be at full power. They need to be demoralized; their spirits broken."

Take the Gutter? The last Flora recalled, the Quiet Ones had been pressing Jefferson to have the Gutter recognized as an independent nation. Now they wanted the Confederation to attack it?

Why? She pursed her lips, wondering if they were playing both sides.

"I still say we can take it at our own pace," Tara insisted. "What does a delay matter? The outlaws who are in Izhadell are far from home. Easy pickings, really. Word has spread like wildfire of the Luminary's unfortunate disappearance. It won't be long before the faithful of Garus are ready to tear the pretty redhead apart." She paused. "Though I suppose I see what you mean. If it comes to that, we risk losing our own prizes."

"And there you have it," Phillip agreed, sounding like the smug prick he was. "We need to move soon. Finish destabilizing the outlaw mages here. Claim our own prizes. And then we have the *real* prize: all the resources of the Gutter."

Something about the way he said it hinted to Flora that he meant more than the land. Possibly even more than the salt-iron buried deep in the ground—which she sorely hoped they didn't know about. Salt-iron had been Jefferson's original reason for visiting the Gutter, so long ago. A visit that had seemed of little consequence but altered their lives in ways she and Jefferson had never expected. There were veins of salt-iron throughout the canyons, more than in any other area of the continent. What else might they mean?

As soon as she posed the question to herself, she knew. The people. The mages. They were the ones who would die if Salt-Iron soldiers came knocking.

"I suppose you're right. Well, in the morning, I'll visit the Clergy Council again and see what we can arrange. We can have the outlaw hauled to the Asaphenia for the Reclamation Cere- mony. They'll need blood for it, anyway. May as well be his," Tara said, as nonchalantly as if she were discussing the outcome of a recent unicorn race.

"The sooner, the better." Phillip's voice was taut. "We can't take any chances. Bad enough, the Spark convinced the Clergy Council to delay. See if you can force the date up again. Three days is too long."

The pair exchanged a few more words, though they were of little importance. They exited the room, and Flora slipped out of her hiding place to crouch beside Jack again.

"Come on," she whispered. "Wake up!"

The outlaw's eyelids twitched. He made a soft, animalistic groan, as if trying to obey.

Flora wasn't exactly nurturing, but she did her best to encourage him. "That's it, you big, dumb brute. Wakey wakey. You can do it." She nudged his shoulder gently, mindful of his damaged body.

But he didn't make any other sounds or movements, lost once more to oblivion. Flora swallowed. *Damn it.* "C'mon. Wake up. Live just to spite those loads of dragonshit."

She had to give up after a few more minutes. As much as she knew Jack wanted to survive, his injuries were grave. This was going to take more than just her. She nodded to herself, resolute. *Hang on long enough for me to get back with help.*

Vixen

<I LET THE OTHERS KNOW WE'VE ARRIVED.>

Vixen patted Alekon's neck in thanks. The stallion had returned to his formerly cheerful self, although they were grounded because of the rest of their entourage. He was simply happy to have her back in the saddle—and Vixen felt likewise.

Rhys had stayed behind, but true to his word, he'd found a pair of steeds that Vixen's guards could ride. Between the men's uniforms and the gilt accents on the saddles and bridles declaring the horses as Lightguard mounts, Vixen's station was clear.

Alekon, with his cutback outlaw saddle and hackamore, didn't fit in at all. She loved him all the more for it.

Blaise and Jefferson stood on the porch, watching their approach. The other pegasi lined the fence, Zepheus the most forlorn of their group, with Jack still missing. Vixen clenched her jaw. Raven had much to answer for.

She showed her guard to the stables, where she allowed them to untack Alekon, as much as it galled her. Vixen wished she could do those simple things for herself but knew it would look odd.

With that done, Vixen hurried over to meet with her friends. Walter trailed behind, wary, as Hubert finished seeing to their mounts. Vixen didn't miss the way Blaise's eyes darted to the unfamiliar men with worry, his mouth set in a hard line.

"I will say, this isn't quite how I expected to see you," Jefferson said in greeting. The Dreamer appeared at ease, but that was often how he was—on the outside, he seemed confident in any situation. He raised a single eyebrow at her escort.

"They're loyal," Vixen said in explanation, hoping her friends would understand what she meant.

That garnered more interest from Jefferson. "Are they? How interesting. Would you like to come in?"

"Yes. You have someone I want to see," Vixen agreed, mounting the stairs. She glanced back at her guardian. "Walter, I'm among friends here. Would you and Hubert please remain outside?"

A cloud of doubt crossed Walter's face, but then he nodded. "As you wish, Spark Valoria." He ascended the stairs to the porch and took up a vigilant position by the white railing. A curious brown hen strode up with a flap of her wings, head tilting to study the Lightguard.

"Valoria," Blaise murmured with a shake of his head. "Sorry, but you'll never look like a *Valoria* to me."

Blaise's words heartened her. While she didn't despise her old life the way she'd heard Jefferson did his, she much preferred her outlaw name. She'd been born Valoria. But she'd *made* herself Vixen. "I'm happy to answer to Vixen for my friends," she told them, though she arrowed a look at Jefferson. "I want to talk to Raven."

"I assumed you would, which is why I invited you to the dreamscape tonight. Did Flora not tell you?" the Dreamer asked, turning to face her in the middle of the ornate entry.

"She did." Vixen blew out a breath. "But I need to *see* him."

Blaise shifted his weight, arms crossed in a sure sign that he was uncomfortable with her wishes. "We don't think it's a good idea to wake him. He wanted to *take* Jefferson." His voice went rough with emotion, and Vixen understood why they didn't want to risk waking the Shadowstepper. Blaise was on a cliff's edge of what he could handle at the moment. Something happening to his beau would push him over.

Vixen pulled the magic-dampening ring from her pocket. "He won't be able to take anyone, not with this."

"Ah," Jefferson murmured, considering. He glanced at Blaise. "What do you think?"

Blaise chewed his lower lip, dropping his gaze. Indecision warred on his features. "I guess it's worth trying. We know the ring works. But what if he takes it off?"

She held up the silver loop. "He'll have a difficult time. It's sized for thin fingers—and Raven's aren't." Vixen could almost feel the warmth of his fingers twining through hers as she said the words.

Jefferson winced. "Ah, yes. A ring that is too tight is *quite* unpleasant—and sometimes almost impossible—to remove."

With that decision made, she followed them to where they were holding Raven. She shouldn't have been surprised to find him in the kitchen—it was such a perfectly *Blaise* place to be. It appeared her arrival had interrupted the Breaker's baking frenzy, though he hadn't gotten very far from what she saw of the assorted pots, pans, and ingredients. But most of her attention was on Raven.

They had propped her former sweetheart up in a chair against the wall. His head lolled back. He almost appeared dead, save for the gentle rise and fall of his chest and the occasional grunt he made. Raven wasn't a quiet sleeper by any means.

Vixen crossed to him, kneeling in front of the slumbering man. He looked almost innocent in his sleep, his face younger, unhindered by the hard reality of their lives. She picked up his left hand and threaded his middle finger through the ring. As she'd suspected, it was a tight fit—he'd have a difficult time removing it.

That done, she rose, crossing her arms. "Wake him, if you don't mind."

"I mind," Blaise muttered.

"Of course you do," Jefferson said with a chuckle. He leaned over and planted a conciliatory kiss on the Breaker's cheek. "I'm safe enough with you and Vixen here." Blaise didn't appear convinced, but he nodded.

Jefferson stepped over to Raven. Vixen couldn't see what he did, but a moment later, the Shadowstepper shuddered and shook his head, eyes flashing open. He tensed in the chair, eyes on Jefferson. "*You*." It was the first time Vixen had ever heard fear in Raven's voice when speaking to the Ambassador.

"Me," Jefferson agreed amiably. "But you and I have already spoken. There's someone else who'd like a word." He stepped aside, revealing Vixen standing there with crossed arms and a scowl.

Raven swallowed. "Vixen—"

"*No*. You don't speak until I ask you to." Her voice was stern and loaded with magic. Raven had made the mistake of meeting her eyes, either foolishly thinking she'd never use her magic on him or not realizing his error. Her power curled around him, though now she felt stretched thin between the three men she was currently influencing. At least Raven did as she suggested and shut his mouth. She approached, stalking as silently as her outlaw namesake. "I hope you know how disappointed I am. I don't want to hear your excuses or whatever you think are valid reasons. You knew what I came here to do, yet you acted against me at every turn."

Raven stared down at his hands. With her magic in place, she didn't lose her grip on him when they broke eye contact. He trembled before lifting his gaze to her again. Questions lit his eyes, though he couldn't ask until she gave him permission.

"Speak," she commanded.

He made a great gasp, as if the words threatened to spill from his throat. Raven shook his head like a dog shedding water. "You used your magic on *me?*" The question was both accusation and disbelief, tempered with hurt.

"I don't have any other choice." Vixen didn't care if her words were icy. Every one of them was true.

"And why can't I use *my* magic?" he asked.

She tipped her head toward Jefferson. "Because you didn't come here on friendly terms, from what I hear. You have a ring on your finger that's throttling your magic, and you *will not* take it off until I allow it."

Raven shivered at her declaration, glancing down at the ring in question. Then he laughed, the sound of someone at their wit's end. "When *I* gave you a ring, you said no. When *you* give me a ring, I have no say in the matter."

"It's *my* ring. Don't get too attached," Jefferson corrected, his voice downright territorial.

Vixen had almost forgotten that Blaise had given the Dreamer the ring. It was more than a useful item to him. It was a symbol. *And what does it mean that I used their symbol of devotion to trap the man who said he loved me?* There was an ugly symmetry to it.

Raven sighed, seemingly aware that he was outnumbered and outmatched. "Jefferson already interrogated me. What more do you want?"

"The truth," Vixen snapped. She wanted to ask him why he had gone to such lengths, why he had betrayed his friends. She would get those answers later. "Where's my mother? Where are Jack and Kittie?"

Raven rubbed his forehead. "They're between the shadows, except for Jack."

Vixen wasn't sure if being between the shadows was a good or bad thing at this point. But that Jack wasn't with the others was notable. "Why Jack?"

The Shadowstepper's eyes darted to Jefferson. "Phillip Dillon wanted me to bring him Jack and Jefferson."

"Is that the man from the gala?" Vixen asked, rounding on Jefferson.

"Yes, one of the Quiet Ones," the Dreamer confirmed.

Pinpricks of warning raced up Vixen's arms and legs. This didn't bode well. "Why?"

Raven shook his head. "I don't know. They don't tell me things. They treat me like a tool." He glanced away. "That was why I was glad when I came across Kittie."

That was an odd thing to say. Vixen did her best not to appear too angry at him. "Again, *why*?"

A grim look touched Raven's lips. "I was told to get *rid* of the Madame Boss and Luminary. I wasn't directly told to *kill* them, which is why I left them in the shadows."

As angry as she was, his admission brought Vixen up short. Raven had killed before and certainly wasn't shy about it. He rightly could have ended both women—but he hadn't, even though that was likely what the Quiet Ones had intended. What did Kittie have to do with this? Then she realized the Firebrand knew Madame Boss Clayton. The Luminary wouldn't trust a mage, but Clayton might. Especially if that mage was Kittie.

"I don't see how that makes any of this better," Blaise cut in, sounding testier than was usual for him.

"It was the best I could do, considering I didn't have much choice," the Shadowstepper explained, though by the way his shoulders hunched, he knew it was a piss-poor answer. "If you free me, I can bring them back."

The Breaker stiffened, alarm etched on his face. "No. How can we trust you anymore?"

And that was the real question. Vixen hated that Blaise even had to ask, but he was right. There was no way to trust Raven after what he'd done. Fortunately, she was the Spark, and that meant she had options. "Blaise is right. We *can't* trust you."

"But—" Raven started.

"Don't," Vixen warned him. "Shadowsteppers aren't common, but you're not a Breaker. You won't be the only one. It's well within my right to search the mage registration records and find one." Even if she had to use her magic to brute force her way to the records, it was something she could— and *would*—do.

The lines around Raven's eyes tightened. "My father has the same magic I do. I know you don't trust a word I say, but...it's true."

There was a sharp edge of truth in his defeated words. She and Raven had never really discussed their origins, since such things were often prickly issues for the outlaws. But he had offered this, and she would take the information. "How do we find him?"

Raven studied the floor. "It shouldn't be too hard for you. He's a theurgist."

That opened a floodgate of new questions, but those would keep for another time. She nodded. "Good, we'll find him."

Vixen was about to say something more when Jefferson cut in, "There's another truth Raven hasn't revealed to you."

At that, the Shadowstepper's eyes widened. He shook his head, an outright denial of whatever the Dreamer was hoping he'd admit.

"Don't keep it hidden," Jefferson urged, his voice taking on a low, sing-song timbre. "Tell her, or I'll haul you back to the dreamscape." There was a threat in his voice Vixen couldn't recall hearing before.

"Jefferson," Blaise whispered, his eyes wide.

"This is not the time to be merciful." The Dreamer stared at Raven, who trembled beneath his intense green gaze.

Vixen swallowed. Whatever had Jefferson worked up didn't bode well. She moved over to Raven, taking his chin in her hand and forcing him to meet her eyes. "Tell me." Vixen could have poured her magic into the command, but she didn't. No, this was her final gift to the man she had once held dear.

"If I helped them, they were going to provide me with a love potion," he whispered. "For you."

She stepped back as if she'd been threatened by a rattlesnake. Betrayal stabbed at her, as sharp as any knife Raven had ever wielded. "You gods-damned—"

A soft pop interrupted her as Flora appeared in their midst. The normally jocular half-knocker's face was grim, bringing Vixen's litany to a crashing halt.

"Flora?" Jefferson asked. "What is it?"

Her violet eyes surveyed the room, probably providing the half-knocker with a slew of her own questions, but whatever she had to tell them was more pressing. "I found Jack."

Vixen breathed out a sigh of relief. "Oh, that's good news."

Flora shook her head, pink hair flying. "No, it's not."

CHAPTER FORTY-FIVE
Pawns Across the Board

Blaise

"I didn't know!" Sweat ran down Raven's face in beads under Blaise, Jefferson, Vixen, and Flora's combined glares. It wasn't often that Blaise knew hot, potent anger like this. His fists clenched at his sides, magic tingling across his palms. He lifted a hand, flexing it so that a haze of silver played across it. Raven stared at it, breathing hard. "I didn't know they'd hurt him!"

"What did you *think* they'd do with an outlaw like Jack?" Vixen snapped, her eyes narrowed and hands perched on her hips. She looked as if she were barely restraining herself, too.

At that, the Shadowstepper went silent, confirming that he'd known the Quiet Ones wouldn't have anything good in mind for the Effigest. Flora's news that Jack had been beaten so horribly only grew more sickening when she revealed their enemies planned to hang him, too. The thought of Jack hanging because another outlaw had betrayed him made Blaise's stomach twist.

"We can't allow it," Blaise said after a moment, voice deceptively soft. The fierce anger was still there, lingering just below the surface like a slumbering volcano.

<No, we cannot,> a new voice agreed. They turned and found Zepheus standing at the nearest window. <I will not stand by while my rider dies.> Fury rode each of the palomino's words.

Jefferson moved to claim a nearby chair, shoulders slumping. "I don't know what we can do. We're already suspects in the Luminary's disappearance and of corrupting the Spark." He cast a dark look at Raven. "They'll use any move we make against us. I'm sure they'd *love* for us to free the Scourge of the Untamed Territory."

Flora jabbed a finger at Jefferson. "Whether or not you do it, they win."

"I think they've outmaneuvered us at last." Jefferson closed his eyes, rubbing his forehead as if he had a headache.

Blaise cross his arms, concerned by how uncharacteristically defeatist that was for his beau. Maybe he had a point, but Blaise wouldn't let that stop them when Jack's life hung in the balance. "They haven't outplayed us yet. We need to move our pawns across the board."

At Blaise's words, Jefferson's hand dropped away from his face. "What do you mean?"

"It's our move," Blaise said, suddenly aware that all eyes were on him. Even Raven's, which he didn't particularly like. "We just need to figure out how much time we have between now and when they plan to hang Jack."

Flora was about to speak, but Vixen beat her to it. "Three days —unless they convince the Clergy Council to override my will. That's when the Reclamation Ceremony is and..." The Persuader swallowed, her silvery eyes downcast. "A sacrifice is offered, and historically it's always a mage because... Well, I imagine y'all know why."

"I don't know if Jack's got three days," Flora said, the most somber Blaise had ever heard her. She pulled out her butterfly knife, flipping it from one hand to the other in a show of nerves. "And Jack's not the only thing I discovered when I was snooping."

As much as Blaise wanted to start on a plan to free the Effigest, the half-knocker's foreboding words demanded attention. Everyone else seemed of the same mind. "What else do we need to know?" Jefferson asked.

"There's trouble in paradise with Woodrow and Dillon—they don't see eye to eye on everything. And they both had their own side projects that they're working on, besides their primary goal for the Quiet Ones." Flora's violet eyes locked on Jefferson.

"What's their goal?" Vixen hauled one of the wooden chairs closer and sat.

"The Gutter," Flora said. "They want the mages."

Jefferson made a soft sound of understanding. "Of course. The Confederation isn't happy about bleeding potential theurgists. And if they control the supply of mages..."

Blaise grimaced. It was a horrifying thought that made far too much sense. But that also raised questions. "If they want the Gutter, why are they wasting time on us?"

"Not a waste of time." Flora aimed her index finger at Jefferson. "They're glad none of you are in the Gutter right now. It'll make it easier for them." Her mouth tightened. "And the cherry on top is that they'll hit their own goals. Dillon wants Jefferson and for Jack to pay for threatening them. I'm not sure what the batty dame wants, but I figure it's not good."

Vixen arrowed a look at Raven. "Do you know what she wants?"

The Shadowstepper stared at the ring that was jammed onto his finger, reluctant to meet his old flame's gaze. "Like I said, I was a tool. They didn't bring me into their confidence."

"You certainly *were* a tool," Flora agreed in a stage whisper.

Jefferson stepped forward, drawing attention before Raven could make a retort. "If there's nothing else we need to know, then we should move on to the more pressing matter, which is freeing Jack."

"I know where he is," Raven said, attempting to curry their favor again.

"Yeah, well, so do I," Flora retorted. "I'm sure you'd love to lead us into a trap."

"You don't know about the house and their *defenses*," Raven stressed. "They're not an easy target."

"I don't know about that. I wandered in just fine," Flora pointed out.

"Not all of us are gifted with your talents," Jefferson said.

Vixen listened with her arms crossed, every line in her stance broadcasting her frustration with her former beau. "If Flora hadn't been the one to tell us about Jack in the first place, I'd also think you're eager to lead us into a trap."

Her words wounded the Shadowstepper, and he hung his head. "Everything I did was for you."

"You don't get to use that excuse. Not when we already found out *exactly* how self-serving you are," Vixen snapped. "I'm not a porcelain teacup, easily shattered. I'm like one of Clover's shot glasses. I'm tough, and I've seen a thing or two."

Blaise clamped his jaw at that. He'd personally broken those aforementioned shot glasses with his magic, though it had been on purpose. He could attest to their sturdiness.

"I say we take him along just so we can shove him into any traps that get sprung," Flora suggested. "Never hurts to have fodder."

"Or at the very least, so we know he's not out somewhere causing more trouble for us," Blaise said.

"I could trap him in the dreamscape." Jefferson's intent gaze was on Raven, a promise that there would be more nightmares than dreams.

Blaise didn't like what he saw in his love's face. Jefferson was too cold, too cruel. "No."

At his single, soft denial, Jefferson's gaze broke away from the Shadowstepper, circling back to Blaise. The skin around Jefferson's eyes crinkled, a sign that he realized he'd been slipping into something he didn't want to be. Even if it was warranted right now. He said nothing, only ducked his head and took a step back.

"He comes along," Vixen said through gritted teeth.

"If you want, I can stab him at the first sign of betrayal," Flora suggested cheerfully.

"Vixen shouldn't go," Raven protested. "These elite have theurgists in their pay. Don't you see how bad an idea that is?" His eyes raked over their group. "They'd love to have all of you. I may not be leading you into a trap, but that doesn't mean this isn't one."

Blaise hated the fact that Raven was possibly right. But by the same token... "That's why you're going with us. And you'll tell us everything you know so we can be successful."

The Shadowstepper nodded. "I said I would. When are we going? I suggest making your move at night. Tomorrow night?"

From what Flora said, Jack might not have that long—even if they didn't hang him. Blaise shook his head. "Tonight."

CHAPTER FORTY-SIX
Theatrics

Jefferson

$\mathcal{I}$n the dark of night, Seledora strode beside Emrys, a small mage-light that Blaise had brought along the only light to guide their way. Clouds hid the full moon, and a mist fell over them, not heavy enough to qualify as rain but enough to be an annoyance. Blaise and Jefferson wore oilskin coats, though their style of hats differed. The Breaker preferred his broad-brimmed hat while Jefferson had gone with an impractical top hat. Blaise's fared much better in the mist.

"I wasn't expecting you to want us to do this tonight," Jefferson said, his voice loud enough to be heard over the thud of hooves but soft enough not to draw attention.

Blaise didn't glance over at him, but the mage-light's glow revealed the tension in his silhouette. "I couldn't stay there knowing he might..." Blaise shook his head, unable to finish his sentence.

As soon as their discussion had ended, Blaise had found both Tristan and the resident chicken, hoping to get a message to the

Maverick Underground as soon as possible. Tristan had left the messenger duty to the hen.

But Blaise hadn't heard from the Maverick Underground before they needed to leave. They couldn't wait around for an answer.

"We'll do all we can to get him back," Jefferson whispered. He couldn't promise they would succeed. Not against foes like the Quiet Ones. And gods, he hated that.

He and Blaise rode ahead of the others. Vixen had come along on Alekon, accompanied by her magicked guards. Flora was there, too. And Raven, though he was tied to Zepheus's saddle as they made their way to the Quiet One's estate. The angry stallion had been quite insistent about being the one to bear the disgraced Ringleader.

Raven told them what he could, advising them on the number of guards to expect on the property. Flora couldn't confirm any of it, as she hadn't had the time to take a count. Raven seemed earnest enough, and for his sake, Jefferson hoped he was being truthful now. If not, Flora would definitely gut him, and without his magic to whisk him away, he was defenseless.

They stopped in a clearing a short distance from the boundary of the estate. Everyone dismounted except for Jefferson and Blaise. Hubert and Walter moved to flank Vixen as soon as her boots touched the ground. Flora moved to untie Raven from the saddle, and between the glinting knife in her belt and Zepheus's pinned ears, the Shadowstepper had all the incentive he needed to behave.

"The house is about a half mile from here," Raven explained, voice low as if he feared being overheard. "We'll need to split up in a quarter mile."

"Understood," Jefferson said, not even trying to hide the chill in his voice. He didn't enjoy needing to trust Raven for this, but it was necessary.

They continued on in silence before parting ways when the

Shadowstepper suggested. Vixen, her escort, Raven, and Flora went one way, while Seledora and Emrys turned to approach the front of the house. It was the sort of affair that was walled, and even though it was late, a sleepy guard manned the gatehouse.

The guard shook himself awake at the clatter of hooves. "Who's there?"

Jefferson didn't dare look back at Blaise. This was a dangerous game they were playing, and he feared for what—and who—they stood to lose. "Jefferson Cole, here to see Tara Woodrow."

The guard scratched his forehead. "It's late. Come back tomorrow."

"I suspect if you inform your mistress of my presence, she will be inclined to see me," Jefferson pushed, loading his words with every bit of arrogance and entitlement he could muster.

The guard grumbled but agreed, turning to confer with someone closer to the house. Jefferson couldn't hear any of what they said, and he debated using his magic to ease their way. But the guard returned a moment later, opening the gate and waving them through. "Mrs. Woodrow will see you. There should be a groom at the stables to mind your horses."

"We won't be staying that long," Jefferson said, tone imperious as they rode through. Besides, he hardly wanted their pegasi hindered when they may need a quick escape. "The hitching post will do." The guard shrugged, not caring the least.

Once Emrys and Seledora were loosely "secured" to the hitching post, they followed a bleary-eyed steward into the house. Blaise shifted beside Jefferson, ill at ease. Jefferson reached down and snared his beau's hand, squeezing gently. Neither of them liked this plan, but it was their best chance to rescue Jack before it was too late.

The steward showed them to a parlor. It was like the one Flora had described, though the Effigest was nowhere to be seen. Someone had laid a new rug across the hardwood floor, the pile fluffy and unworn. Jefferson narrowed his eyes as he strode across it to claim a settee.

"Mrs. Woodrow will be here shortly," the steward declared. "I'll have refreshments delivered."

"There's no need for that. It's late," Jefferson cut in. The fewer people awake in the house, the better. Once the steward retreated, he glanced at Blaise. "This is where Jack was. They replaced the rug."

"How do you know that?" Blaise's brows rose with the question.

"It feels new." Jefferson prodded it with the toe of his riding boot. He'd been in enough elite homes to know the give of a rug that had seen many a season and one that had been replaced.

"Then where's Jack?" Blaise asked.

"That's the question, isn't it?" Jefferson murmured. This was exactly why they had split up.

They had little time to confer. A moment later, the door creaked open, and Tara strode in. She was dressed as if she hadn't yet found her bed, bedecked in a bright yellow gown that would have served her well at the gala. She appeared as alert as if she'd drunk an entire carafe of coffee. Tara fixed a curious look on Jefferson, gaze sliding to Blaise as she approached.

"Mr. *Cole*, you've certainly chosen an interesting time to come calling," Tara said without preamble, flouncing to a wingback chair.

The use of his preferred name was interesting. *But this may be a new tactic.* "I've been known to keep unconventional hours," Jefferson agreed blandly. "And as you no doubt assume, I've come because of pressing matters."

Tara settled back on the cushion, greed shifting into her expression. "I prefer not to make assumptions. But you've over-looked introductions. Who did you bring with you tonight?" She smirked at Blaise.

Damn this woman. She knew very well who Jefferson had

brought along, but she was no doubt hoping to remind Jefferson of what was on the line. Especially considering their plans for Jack.

"I'm Blaise Hawthorne. The Breaker."

Jefferson hadn't expected his beau to speak up, much less to introduce himself with such confidence. All hints of the shy man had vanished, though Jefferson knew it was an act. This wasn't a simple thing for Blaise, but he was doing it. *Just when I thought I couldn't love you more.*

"Delightful," Tara murmured, and the solitary word set Jefferson on alert. There was avarice in her voice, and he didn't know why. He hoped he could play to it and perhaps keep her unbalanced. Tara continued, "It's adorable that you brought your pet. Is this a threat or a peace offering?"

It's very much a threat. Jefferson swallowed, hating what he was about to say. *But none of it's true. It's not.* Blaise wasn't the only one who'd be acting tonight. "I've reconsidered. I wish to join you."

The Quiet One was still for a moment, eyes narrowing as if she were trying to poke holes in Jefferson's words. "Truly?"

"Only if you restore the Luminary and our missing outlaw."

Tara pouted. "Missing outlaw? I haven't heard anything about that—as far as I know, the only outlaw mages in Phinora are sitting before me." She shrugged, the movement making the yellow fabric of her gown cascade. "And as for the Luminary, I don't know what you're talking about."

As the Quiet One spoke, Blaise rose from his place beside Jefferson. The Breaker made a slow circuit around the room, for all the world looking as if he were taking stock of the knick-knacks. He stopped by a shelf with decorative figurines perched on it. Blaise made a show of looking at them closely, then glanced at Tara as he said, "Are these worth much?"

The Quiet One's eyes widened. "More than *you're* worth. Mr. Cole, bring your mage into line."

"That's not really how this works," Jefferson said pleasantly as

Blaise picked up a porcelain shepherdess in a blue dress. "And you forget your own words so quickly. You're not only speaking with one mage, but *two*."

Judging by the flash of Tara's eyes, she *had* briefly forgotten Jefferson was a mage. Or perhaps, like so many others, she dismissed Jefferson's magic as paltry since he had done nothing with it. "Even so, you're on the same social standing as I, Mr. Cole. Not the baseborn Breaker."

That insult against Blaise rankled, but there was no doubt Tara intended it to get a reaction. Jefferson wasn't about to give her the satisfaction. He cocked his head, shrugging. "Oh, am I? That's a surprise, considering you and your friends did your level best to leave me with nothing."

Tara smiled. "The fortune we took away can be restored if you truly intend to join us." Then she cast a nervous look at Blaise. "But really, can you *please* put that down? It's one of a kind." Much to Jefferson's amazement, there was a layer of earnest respect in the request.

Blaise heard it, too. And though it would have been as easy as breathing for him to send a jolt of magic into the figure, he set the shepherdess back down on the shelf with her flock of porcelain sheep. Jefferson hid a smile at the silvery wash of magic that Blaise let play across his palm as he stepped away.

Tara gave a small nod of thanks, then turned back to Jefferson. "I—" She didn't finish her thought. Somewhere in the distance, a shot rang out. The Quiet One went on alert in an instant. "What was that?"

The report of another firearm sounded, followed by shouts.

Jefferson traded a glance with Blaise and rose. "Well, it seems we've overstayed our welcome. We'll see ourselves out."

Anger surged over the Quiet One's expression. "*You.* This is one of your ploys, isn't it?" Her hand rasped into the folds of her dress and an instant later she pulled something out—the glint of a muzzle caught the light.

Blaise saw it, too. Magic flared from his palms, a gossamer-thin shell of silver motes flowing in front of Jefferson like a shield. But Jefferson was ready for such a move, too. He'd kept his magic within reach, and now he imagined snaring Tara with his power. When it came to a single target, Jefferson had become quite adept. He pushed the command of *Sleep* against Tara, and the woman slumped to the floor before she could get a firm grip on the weapon. It clattered harmlessly onto the new rug.

"Goodnight," Jefferson said, not sparing the woman another glance. No, his attention was on Blaise. "What is it?"

"Hexgun," the Breaker murmured, crouching to snag the fallen contraption. Sure enough, he was right. It had been easy to mistake for a revolver in a moment of panic. "Not exactly like Jack's, though."

"Bring it along," Jefferson suggested. Then he jerked his head to the door. "We should go."

Blaise looked as if he wanted to balk at the idea of taking the hexgun, but he adjusted it so the hammer rested on an empty chamber, then shoved it into his belt. It seemed he remembered a thing or two about the strange weapon, despite limited experience with them. That done, he flexed his fingers, glancing at Jefferson. "Let's go."

CHAPTER FORTY-SEVEN

Outlaws Never Give Up

Vixen

"I doubt he's gonna be where I found him," Flora whispered as they made their way through the darkness.

Vixen appreciated having the gutsy half-knocker along with them. Between Raven's knowledge of the estate and Flora's knack for breaking and entering without leaving a trace, the unlikely group made their way in with little trouble. Walter and Hubert, on the other hand, were not enthusiastic about this endeavor, and had balked at her inclusion. When they realized their Spark wasn't going to be dissuaded, they refused to stay behind. She wished Rhys had been there to see, so that she could prove to him the guards weren't as brainwashed as he thought.

However, just because Hubert and Walter came along didn't mean they approved of the proposed actions. But since Garus hadn't struck Vixen down or otherwise showed displeasure, they followed along.

"Why not?" Vixen asked, her voice a whisper.

Flora snorted. "'Cause they had him in a fancy parlor. People like that? They're gonna take someone like Jack out with the trash. In a manner of speaking."

"So where will he be?" Vixen pressed. She glanced behind her. Walter and Hubert stood vigil over Raven beneath a dark over-hang that not only hid them but protected them from the mist.

"Gimme a minute," the half-knocker said. She pushed her glasses up on her nose, squinting as if she were thinking. "There's salt-iron in there. My guess is they'll have him near that."

Salt-iron. Like any other mage, Vixen hated the stuff, but it made sense. Odd, though. How did Flora know there was salt-iron inside? "We need to find him before we run out of time."

"Yeah. C'mon," Flora agreed, leading them around the dark-ened side of the ornate manor.

The entire way, the half-knocker stared at the inky ground. Vixen knew the short woman could see much better in the dim light than she could. After a moment, Flora held up a hand, pointing at something near the building's foundations. "Cellar door."

Vixen frowned, coming closer. It was nearly impossible for her eyes to make out, but she crouched and brushed her fingers against the treated wood. She fumbled for the handle and found it, though tugging proved it was stuck or locked.

Flora dug a hand into a pouch at her belt and pulled out some-thing dark that Vixen couldn't quite make out. It must have been lock-pick tools, since the half-knocker slid something into the lock and leaned close as she fiddled with it. Precious moments passed in which Vixen had no choice but to wait, heart thumping as she watched for trouble.

A soft click signaled Flora's success. The half-knocker was silent as she stowed her tools, then used her impressive strength to haul the heavy door open. Nothing but more darkness met them.

"There's dried blood on the top step," Flora commented,

pointing at an indistinct blotch. "Oh wait, you've got crummy human vision. Want me to go down without you?"

Vixen shook her head. "No. Give me a moment." She turned and hurried back to where the men awaited them. "Do either of you have a mage-light?"

"Don't go down there," Raven whispered, almost pleading.

She ignored him, her eyes on the shadowy forms of her Light-guards. Hubert patted his pockets and then produced one of the smallest mage-lights Vixen had ever seen. It was the size of her pinky finger, perfect for storing in a coat. He offered it to her. "Allow Walter or me to accompany you, Spark."

Vixen glanced at Raven. Even bound as he was, the Shadow-stepper was dangerous. She knew all too well what he was capable of. "I need you both to stay with him." She nodded toward Raven.

Walter shifted his weight from one foot to the other. "This mission of yours is dangerous, Spark Valoria."

"There's already too many of us here. I can't go sneaking around with an escort." She barely kept the annoyance from creeping into her voice.

"As you wish," Walter murmured.

"Let Flora go alone. Stay up here," Raven urged again, shifting closer until Walter checked him with an iron grip on his arm.

She turned to glare at him, though she supposed it wasn't very effective in the dark. "I think we've established that I trust you about as far as I can throw you. So stop trying to get me to do what you want, unless you want me to magic you into silence."

Raven swallowed. "You don't understand what these elite are like."

"But I *do*." Vixen was through arguing with him. She spun and marched back to where Flora waited at the top of the stairs leading into the depths.

Vixen tapped on the light, and together, they eased down the twisting stairs into the cool, clammy recesses of the...well, Vixen wasn't sure what it was. A cellar? Storage? A dungeon? There were so many ugly options.

With every step, Vixen wondered if Raven had been right to warn her. The cellar had a wrongness to it, something she couldn't put her finger on. But ahead, she heard a soft moan. At the sound, both women quickened their pace, though they still proceeded with caution.

The stairs led to a short hallway. Rooms without doors branched off from the corridor, their thresholds dark save for one. Vixen and Flora exchanged glances when a groan met their ears again.

It's him. It had to be Jack. Heart thundering, Vixen approached the lit room, though Flora beat her to it. The half-knocker peered around the corner. She said nothing, but she nodded and slipped inside.

Vixen followed suit. The room they entered couldn't be described as well-lit, but it was better than the interminable darkness. A single mage-light that needed a re-enchantment sat on a crate, casting a faint glow. A lump claimed the floor in the middle of the room. The lump moved, just enough to prove it was a person. Breath hitching, Vixen went down to her knees beside Jack.

"Garus help us," Vixen whispered out of reflex, startled when she felt the overwhelming presence once more. She swallowed, returning her focus to the downed Ringleader. Jack's face was a swollen mess, his eyes blackened. She couldn't even guess what color his clothing had been, it was so darkened by blood. His breath rasped, as if the act of breathing pained him. In his condition, it probably did.

Tears stung Vixen's eyes. Jack was an asshole, but he was an asshole she counted as a friend. She licked her lips, thinking.

"I'm almost afraid to move him," Flora admitted from where she crouched beside Vixen.

At their voices, Jack's eyelids flitted open. He seemed unable to focus on them, but he knew who had come. The Effigest made a rumbling sound, as if he wanted to speak, but it was beyond his abilities.

"Now, now, Mr. Dewitt, I can't have you warning my guests."

"*Schist*," Flora cursed. She whirled, moving so fast her knife was in hand by the time she faced the new threat.

Vixen turned, eyes widening. She knew the man—one of the elite who had caused such havoc at the gala. Phillip Dillon. He leaned casually against the doorframe, a revolver aimed at them. Wait, no. Not a revolver. It had a brassy cast to it and a distinct shape.

"I'll be honest. I was hoping it would be Cole coming for the outlaw, but I suppose I can make do with Spark Valoria." Dillon took a step inside.

Flora stiffened as he drew near. Vixen was certain she was going to strike. Their enemy must have thought so, too. He swiveled the muzzle of the weapon, aiming it at Flora, and pulled the trigger.

"No!" Vixen lunged toward the half-knocker, but it was too late. Her only consolation was that the weapon was a hexgun, not a true revolver. But a hexgun could cause just as many problems for them.

The pellet splattered as it struck Flora's stony skin. For a moment, Vixen hoped the half-knocker might be immune. Knockers couldn't be stabbed, as their skin was too tough. But then Flora wove on her feet, eyelids fluttering. She went down hard, asleep before her face hit the floor.

Dillon smiled, glancing down at the hexgun before settling on Vixen again. "Will you come quietly, Spark, or would you prefer to end up like your friend?"

Vixen swallowed, glancing from Flora to Jack. Damn it, if she didn't play this right, she was going to lose another friend. *If ever there's a time to use my magic, this is it.*

She raised her hands, slowly lifting her head to meet his gaze.

Did he know what type of magic she commanded? She hoped not. Vixen felt the snap of her power against him, ready to unfurl. "You're going to give me the hexgun and stand back."

She felt his mind rattle against the suggestion. He didn't want to do either of those things. Vixen pushed more magic against him, gritting her teeth. He was a stubborn one, his mind already made up. But Vixen wasn't going to give up so easily. More of her power crashed against his defenses, slowly wearing them down.

"Give me the hexgun!"

With a reluctant growl, he offered it to her, grip first. Vixen snagged it, stuffing it into the top of her trousers as he stepped back. Then she crouched down to gather up Flora. Gods, but the small woman was as heavy as a bag of rocks. Vixen grunted as she edged past the elite, heading for the stairs. She spared a single glance at Jack. "Outlaws never give up." She hoped he heard her soft words, hoped he knew it meant they were determined to rescue him. Somehow.

The climb up the cellar stairs felt like the longest in Vixen's life. Flora bobbed against her, snoring softly. Vixen's muscles complained beneath the strain of the half-knocker's considerable weight. She liked to consider herself strong and nimble, but Vixen had never needed to carry an ally out of a dangerous situation.

She reached the top of the stairs, breathing hard. Vixen emerged into the darkness, relief swelling when she saw dark shapes nearby. It took her far too long to realize they weren't friendly.

"Who are you?" a theurgist guard barked, on alert.

"That is our Spark!" Hubert bellowed. Vixen was certain he thought he was helping, but as far as she was concerned, that was about the worst thing he could have said.

"Get out of here!" This from Raven. Out of the corner of her eye, she glimpsed shining metal as the Shadowstepper wrested a gun from one of the Lightguard. She heard Walter's startled shout, followed by the blast of a revolver.

An enemy guard in front of Vixen cried out as Raven's bullet struck him. He went down, a spurt of blood spattering out like dark rain in the glow of Vixen's mage-light.

"Get her!"

Oh, no. Vixen hadn't been able to hold the Quiet One with her magic, not while negotiating the stairs. He had made it to the top, and now he glared at them with fury etched on his face.

<We're coming! We're all coming!> Alekon was frantic in her mind. She could almost feel the thunder of his wings.

"Spark Valoria! Get to safety!" Hubert cried as the enemy pulled their weapons. Some of them angled at Vixen's escort, and others trained on her. The weapons glinted with the same brassy gleam as the hexgun at her waist.

She couldn't escape, not while burdened with Flora. And the courtyard they were in was too tight for the pegasi, even for touch and goes. Their wings would snag on the nearby small trees. Vixen swallowed, glancing down at Flora. *What I need is a distraction.*

The wall to Vixen's right made an awful grating sound, as if someone were grinding its stones together. Everyone turned to stare at the wall in surprise. There were gasps all around as the mortar holding the stones split. Chunks fell with sharp pops.

She knew who was doing that. And it was the distraction she needed. Vixen turned and started to run with her heavy burden.

"Get her!" Dillon demanded again.

"No!" Vixen knew Raven's voice when she heard it.

There was a concussive pop, the telltale sound of a hexgun firing. She thought for certain it was aimed at her, but she heard Raven's soft curse followed by the solid thud of a falling body. Walter and Hubert shouted something she couldn't make out.

Vixen made it through a gap in the garden wall. Wings split the air overhead as Alekon and Zepheus appeared. Seledora and Emrys must have gone a different way for their own riders.

"Zepheus! Flora's been knocked out," she called to the golden stallion as he landed.

The palomino's nostrils flared. He didn't ask what had happened to Raven. <Sling her across my saddle.>

<Hurry! They're coming!> Alekon jigged in place, nervous.

Vixen did the best she could, but Zepheus was tall, and Flora was unwieldy. It took her longer than she liked to get the smaller woman slumped across the stallion's saddle. But then she did it and—

<Vixen!> Alekon's whistling whinny split the air.

An onyx chain snaked up from the ground, wrapping around Vixen's right ankle. She gasped as the arcane metal pulled taut, another chain whipping up to shackle her left leg. Vixen turned, spotting the Trapper mage standing apart from the crush of guards swarming the area. She was vaguely aware of Raven slumped on the ground, Walter grappling with an armed guard, and Alekon prancing nervously nearby. Zepheus thundered away, retreating with Flora.

Vixen focused on the Trapper, meeting his gaze. He smiled, confident as a cat with a mouse beneath his claws.

"Let me go." She flooded her words with magic, pressing her command against the theurgist. His resistance was like running face-first into a brick wall. She had to find a crack. Or make one.

<I'm going to go kick him in the head.> Alekon pawed at the ground, raking up a great furrow.

"No!" she told the pegasus through gritted teeth. That would put him dangerously close to the armed enemy. "I've got this!" Vixen took a deep breath, even as the chains weighed her down. She focused on the Trapper. "*Let me go.*"

But again, he withstood the assault. Was this one of those rare people who shared the Tracker immunity to magic? That was the only explanation, unless he was deaf, but she didn't think that was likely.

<I'm going to stomp him into dust!> Alekon threatened, half-rearing.

That was looking more and more like the only choice. Vixen opened her mouth to speak, right as a hexgun pellet splattered against her shoulder, the liquid gel soaking through her clothing.

<No! Stay awake!> Alekon pleaded.

Vixen wanted to. She really did, but the effect of the pellet's liquid tugged her eyelids down, and there was nothing she could do to fight off the slumber that came.

CHAPTER FORTY-EIGHT

Cinnamon Rolls Make Everything Better

Jefferson

"Well, that was yet another disaster," Jefferson groused when, at last, they reached Hawthorne House. He knew he should be grateful that some of their number had escaped. But considering the losses they'd suffered, he didn't feel as if they had much to be thankful for.

Blaise pulled off his hat and hung it by the entry, running a hand through his matted hair. He shucked off his boots, then padded toward the kitchen with a yawn. The Breaker hadn't spoken a word since they'd left the Quiet One's estate, which bothered Jefferson. Even Emrys had privately told Jefferson he was worried about his rider. Jefferson followed him, Flora bringing up the rear. The half-knocker could barely keep her eyes open.

"It was my fault," Blaise said at last. He stood before the counter, staring at a canister of sugar.

Jefferson frowned, moving to stand beside the younger man. "I hardly think it's fair to blame yourself."

Blaise closed his eyes for a moment, his face lined with defeat.

"It was my idea to go as soon as possible. Maybe if we'd waited, the Maverick Underground could have helped."

Flora rubbed her eyes. She had awoken as Zepheus carried her back to Hawthorne House, though she was still groggy. The half-knocker sat at the table, her head resting on one arm. "They were ready for us no matter when we came at them."

Jefferson glanced over his shoulder at her. She was probably right. He settled a gentle hand on his beau's shoulder, feeling the tense muscles beneath his fingers. Blaise twisted to look at him, blue eyes brimming with guilt.

"Not your fault," Jefferson whispered. "This is what they *want*. To demoralize us. To split us." And gods, they were good at it, too. Blaise relaxed the tiniest amount and went back to whatever he had gotten it in his mind to bake. Jefferson returned his attention to Flora. "What did you find? Was Jack there, at least?"

She lifted her head, blinking at them. "Yeah. Still alive but not looking good. He tried to warn us."

Blaise stooped to find the mixing bowl he wanted and paused, looking back at Flora. "He was conscious?"

"At least for as long as Vixen and I were there," she confirmed grimly. "I don't know what happened after Dillon hexed me."

Jefferson rubbed his cheek, his thoughts sluggish from stress and exhaustion. The Quiet Ones not only had Jack, but they'd reclaimed Raven and now had Vixen. He didn't think they'd harm the Persuader, not with her position as Spark, but they would do everything in their power to use her. Jefferson sighed.

"What do we do now?" Blaise's question was plaintive. Jefferson hadn't seen him measure flour, but somehow he already had it in the bowl. He added sugar and salt, then picked up a spoon to mix them together.

Jefferson yawned. "Against the Quiet Ones? I'm too tired to even think of that. I think our best option is to sleep."

Blaise nodded. "Maybe you can reach Vixen or Raven in the dreamscape."

It was a worthy thought, but Jefferson privately doubted it. If Flora had already stirred from the sleep pellet, the odds were good that they had, too. He would certainly try, though. "Yes, perhaps I can. I'll go see what I can do about that."

"I'll be up once I finish this batch of cinnamon rolls," Blaise murmured.

Jefferson smiled, leaning in to give the Breaker a kiss on the cheek. Their world might shatter around them, but at least they had cinnamon rolls to look forward to. It was a small thing, almost inconsequential, but it made Jefferson feel infinitely better.

CHAPTER FORTY-NINE
Beacon of Hope

Vixen

The burn of salt-iron on skin wasn't the sensation Vixen wanted to awake to. With a hiss, her eyelids flew open, and she struggled upright.

"Spark Valoria, you're safe." The man's voice reminded her of the slimy trail left by a snail.

She turned and saw the same Quiet One who had ambushed her and Flora in the cellar. Phillip Dillon sat in a wingback chair beside a woman dressed in a fine gown who dozed on a nearby settee. That must have been Jefferson's handiwork. Knowing that another mage had gotten the upper hand on at least one of their enemies heartened her.

"Or perhaps you prefer your outlaw name," Dillon continued. "Vixen Valerie, was it?"

The sound of her name from his mouth grated on her nerves. Vixen squared her shoulders, drawing on her composure even as the metal rattled against her wrists. She glanced downward. The bracelets were thick silver cuffs covered in ornate designs of Garus's lupine and avian representations. Flecks of black metal glinted in the eyes of the foxes and owls—no doubt the salt-iron. A quick inspection proved they truly were glorified shackles. Each one sported a tiny keyhole.

"It's Spark Valoria to *you*." She thought about demanding her release, but didn't think it would get her very far. And with the salt-iron curtailing her magic, she had no hope of overpowering him any other way. She was smart enough to know when she was outgunned. "What do you want with me?"

He gave her an appreciative nod. "I'm impressed. Not demanding your release or threatening my future."

Vixen wasn't sure if that was a compliment or not. "I'm the *Spark*, remember? Future avatar of the god of wisdom."

"So you are," he agreed. "Though I'm disinclined to consider the actions that brought you to my parlor as *wise*."

He had her there. They should have known it was a trap, but Blaise had been right. They had to try. Vixen was unwilling to acknowledge that, however. Instead, she met his eyes as she dredged up a teaching she remembered from her childhood. "Follow the path you're on, and you'll reach your destination. Divert, and you may reach your destiny."

Her words made him hesitate. "Is that a threat of some sort?"

She gave him a cool look. "It's one of the Old Teachings of Wisdom." Vixen didn't think he was a follower of Garus. He had the accent of someone from Ganland. Tabris, then. Like Jefferson.

Dillon made a noncommittal sound. "I've been a poor host. Spark Valoria, I'm Phillip Dillon." He jerked a thumb to the slumbering woman nearby. "And this is Tara Woodrow."

"Charmed," Vixen murmured, though she was anything but. "And I'll ask again: what do you want with me?" There was more she wanted to ask. Where was Raven? Were Walter and Hubert okay? And what had happened to the rest of her friends?

Dillon smiled. "I do like how you get straight to business. I'll lay it out for you, Spark Valoria. We know exactly what you are. Not only the Spark but also a mage." He waited, as if expecting her to deny it, but Vixen remained quiet, deciding it was best not to react. "Am I right in thinking that particular dirty secret is why you fled so long ago, leaving your poor mother to give you up for dead?"

Vixen narrowed her eyes. "There's nothing dirty about magic."

He scoffed. "I'll be the first to disagree, but that's not what we're discussing. Back to the point. You only returned when word reached your ears that the Gutter might face a Salt-Iron army soon. For the second time in as many years." Dillon steepled his fingers before him. "The long-lost Spark returns in a desperate bid to save her friends and the land she's grown to love, is that it?"

Vixen seethed. He certainly had a way of wrapping everything up into a nice package. "Again, what do you want with me?"

Dillon cocked his head. "Hit a nerve, did I?" He leaned forward in his seat as the woman stirred. "Your secrets are safe with us. For a price."

Of course, there's a price. "And that is?"

"Work with us. Follow our directives. The Clergy Council is prepared to support you in this."

Vixen froze, shaking her head. "No. I won't. Not when you're actively working against the mages." Her heart raced. If she became the Luminary, she would be one of the most influential leaders in the Confederation. And she would be a puppet to the whims of the Quiet Ones.

Dillon sighed, affecting a look of utmost patience, as if he were speaking to an unruly child. "We want mages, yes. But we don't want the Confederation to attack the Gutter any more than you do." He spread his hands. "Surely we can agree on that. The outlaw mages are better off alive than crushed beneath the Confederation's might."

But at what cost? His words were true, though. And her entire point in coming here had been to stave off a war. Vixen swallowed. "What do you intend?"

Dillon leaned forward, eager now that she seemed receptive.

"You were an outlaw mage—they'll listen to you. Ask the mages who fled to return home to the Confederation. They'll look to you like a beacon of hope."

And just as quickly, you'll turn me into a snare. Dillon didn't say it, but they both knew it for a truth. Jefferson had mentioned this group was playing a long game. Well, so could she. "If I agree, you'll leave Blaise Hawthorne and Jefferson Cole alone."

He frowned. "Unfortunately, you're not in a position to barter, Spark Valoria. You'll agree, or your secrets will come to light. And in that case, Jack Dewitt won't be the only outlaw to hang."

Vixen swallowed, her heart thundering. She considered snapping back at him for daring to threaten her, but that same solid presence she'd felt earlier stayed her hand. Garus. She knew it had to be. The god had reason for her to capitulate. She hoped he didn't intend for her to serve these men.

A muscle in her jaw ticked. "I'll work with you."

At her agreement, Dillon smiled. "Excellent. I was hoping we wouldn't have to call an Inker in."

That was why Garus wanted me to hold back. A trill of worry shot through her. A Spark or Luminary, bound to a handler? That was unthinkable. And this group would do it, too. She released a ragged breath. "You can't hold me here forever. The Lightguard is surely looking for me." And Rhys. Maybe she could get him to help somehow.

Dillon nodded. "Indeed. How fortunate it is that we could rescue you from the outlaw mages who were trying to steal you away again. Your devoted guards have already agreed to the story, lest they face...retribution."

Vixen's gut clenched. There it was. He was determined to go after her friends in every possible way.

He smiled. "Is that better or worse than the accusation that they tried to break into an elite's home? They attacked my associate." Dillon waved a hand to Tara, who rose, groggy. "With *magic*."

The awful thing was, he was right. Jefferson and Blaise would be in trouble for either charge. "I'll do whatever you say as long as neither of those accusations see the light of day."

Dillon chuckled, and for a frightening moment, she feared he'd deny her. Then he nodded. "If it will win your loyalty, then you have a deal."

Vixen slumped against the chair, exhausted from the night she'd had and the conversation. She wanted to walk into an empty field and scream at the injustices that were being done.

The Quiet One rose from his seat. "I'll call for a coach, and you and your loyal guards can make your way back to your residence. We'll be in touch soon, Spark Valoria."

CHAPTER FIFTY
Mutton Underpants

Blaise

Once Blaise claimed his warm spot in the bed beside Jefferson, he slept for longer than he'd thought he might. It had been a blessedly dreamless sleep, not even Jefferson's dreamscape encroaching on the needed oblivion.

Jefferson's arm was slung over Blaise's side, the Dreamer's breath gentle as he dozed. Blaise shifted out from beneath it, carefully rising to sit on the edge of the bed—then he saw Flora perched in the armchair in the corner, watching them.

"Um." Blaise rubbed the back of his head as the half-knocker cackled.

At his voice and the laughter, Jefferson stirred, eyes flashing open. Normally, it took him longer to rouse, much less bother sitting up, but he launched upright. He stilled when he saw Flora. "Oh, it's just you."

She waved at them. "I decided to keep tabs on you two since Raven's out there somewhere. Not taking any chances, you know?" Then she leered at them. "But you two were so tired.

You're very boring when the most interesting thing you do is sleep."

Blaise glowered at her. "We're fine. You can go now."

She huffed. "Why? You're fully dressed."

He was, as was Jefferson, but it was the principle of the thing. Blaise would rather not have Flora randomly appear in their bedchamber, even if she had good intentions. But he knew that was unlikely to deter her, especially with all that had transpired. Blaise sighed. "Any news while we were sleeping?"

"An extremely good-looking man with a unicorn is outside waiting for you to wake up. And a chicken came with a note tied to it. Like a poor man's messenger pigeon. This place is *so* much more interesting than it used to be. I love it."

Rhys was here? And they'd received a note? "What did the note say?"

Flora produced the small curl of paper from a pocket. "'MU will help.' I hope that means something to you. I've spent the better part of an hour trying to figure out what MU is. Mulish Uncle? Maniacal Unicorn? Mutton Underpants?"

"Maverick Underground," Jefferson clarified, clearly hoping it would make her stop.

Hope surged in Blaise, and he traded looks with Jefferson. "We won't be on our own." Then he recalled what else Flora had said. He got up, moving to the window and peeking through the blinds. Sure enough, he recognized the unicorn grazing on the lawn. "It's Rhys. And I can't imagine he's going to be happy."

"No, I imagine not," Jefferson agreed with a sigh. "Let's go face the music."

Jefferson sent Flora to fetch the Tracker. Meanwhile, Blaise made the strategic decision to meet with him in the kitchen. It was hard to be mad around breakfast pastries, or so he hoped. At the very least, it would make *him* feel better.

Jefferson carried over two mugs of coffee, setting them on the table before taking his seat beside Blaise. He had just taken a sip when Flora showed the Tracker in.

"I should haul you both to the Golden Citadel!" Rhys stormed into the room, his shoulders rigid and fists clenched.

Blaise froze at the mention of the Golden Citadel, his mouth going dry as his world contracted to those words. He squeezed his eyes shut, heart racing. If anyone had the authority to take him there, it was a Tracker—

A hand grasped his, fingers massaging his palm. Blaise almost sent a volley of magic in retaliation. Only the hand was familiar. And someone was speaking to him, voice soft and pleading.

"You're safe. He didn't mean it, Blaise. He's upset. You're not there. You're *safe*." Jefferson repeated a variation of those words over and over, desperate. Distantly, Blaise heard Flora angrily berating the Tracker.

With a shuddering breath, Blaise opened his eyes. He rubbed at his forehead with his free hand, wincing when he realized his skin was clammy with nervous sweat.

"I'm okay." He wasn't, not really. But he had to pretend. Rhys was right to be angry with them. He couldn't truly fault the Tracker for his words, even if they had spurred him into a panic. Blaise hadn't realized how close he'd been to succumbing to his old fears over the past day. He was ashamed that it only took three words to undo him.

"You're a terrible liar, and I love you very much," Jefferson whispered. His hand clutched Blaise's like a lifeline, as if he were afraid releasing it would mean losing Blaise forever. "In this moment, you're safe."

Blaise swallowed, nodding. Jefferson had chosen his words with care—he couldn't promise future safety as much as he might wish to. But here and now, he could. That would have to be enough.

"He's going to sit down, stuff a cinnamon roll in his face, and behave. Trust me when I say what I lack in height, I make up for in rage," Flora declared, jabbing Rhys in the arm. The Tracker winced. Flora made good on her threat, stalking over to the batch of cinnamon rolls and snatching one up, dropping it onto a plate. She pointed to a chair, leaving Rhys no choice but to sit obediently and accept the fated cinnamon roll.

Rhys stared at the pastry, bemused. "What am I supposed to think when the Spark is returned by the very elite who sowed rumors about her reappearance? I know it means whatever scheme she was up to with all of *you* went wrong."

"Vix—Valoria Kildare is a grown woman," Jefferson reminded the Tracker. "*She* decided to accompany us. No one forced her." He massaged his thumb into Blaise's palm, a gentle reassurance. "But if she made it back to Dawnlight, that seems like a good sign, at least."

Blaise thought so, too. It meant they weren't holding her, which was promising.

"Whatever's going on, she's moved the Reclamation Ceremony up. It's shifted to tomorrow," Rhys said, spreading his hands. "If the Luminary really is out there like Valoria thinks, we're running out of time."

Blaise swallowed, looking at Jefferson. "We're not the only ones running out of time, in that case." How would they ever free Jack now?

"What do you mean?" Rhys asked. He took a tentative bite of cinnamon roll, his expression shifting to one of momentary delight at the burst of flavor. Then his shoulders relaxed as he bit off another chunk. Blaise's own tension ebbed a fraction.

"The elite who had the Spark also have someone we know," Jefferson explained. "We're fairly confident he's the one slated to be offered as a mage sacrifice."

The Tracker was quiet for a moment, thinking. "She was trying to free the mage, wasn't she?" When Jefferson nodded, Rhys blew out a breath. "If they have your friend earmarked for the ceremony, he's as good as lost. You attack that ceremony, and it will be a bloodbath."

Rhys was right, but Blaise was never one to go on the offensive. He recognized there was a time for direct assault, but this wasn't it. As he thought about that, an idea came to him. "We won't attack the ceremony, not exactly." He took a steadying breath as their curious eyes fell on him.

"Not exactly?" Flora asked. "What's going on in that noggin of yours? Spill it."

Blaise worried at his lower lip, though the more he thought about it, the more plausible his idea became. "We'll let them think they've won."

"They already think that," Jefferson mused.

The half-knocker crossed her arms, kicking her feet in a rhythmic motion. "Hmm. If anything, they're going to think we'll make one more bid before that goes down." Her violet eyes narrowed. "This is gonna cut it close for Jack, though."

That thought made Blaise's stomach churn. But he had a plan. He didn't know if it was a good plan, but it was all he had left that didn't involve using his magic to turn the cathedral into rubble. "At this point, I'm trusting that Emmaline's keeping him stable, and we can get him in time." Based on Flora's report, the young Effigest's magic might be the only thing keeping Jack in the world of the living. She'd done it before…he had to hope she was doing so now. Blaise looked at Rhys. "If you had to work with maverick mages, would you?"

Rhys frowned at the question. "I don't follow."

"To help Vixen, and hopefully stop whatever the elite are plotting, would you work with mavericks?" Blaise pressed. He wouldn't be able to coordinate with the Maverick Underground, and he needed someone with connections. Someone like Rhys.

The Tracker licked a glob of frosting from his lower lip, then gave a hesitant nod. "I…yes. I would."

That was progress. Blaise felt as if a weight were slowly lifting from his shoulders. "Good. There's a chicken I need you to talk to."

Rhys stared at them, bewildered. "A what?"

Flora flapped a hand. "Just go with it. If Blaise says you gotta talk to a chicken, he means it." She grinned, clearly enjoying the chaos.

Jefferson squeezed his hand. "Blaise, you have a plan?"

Of all the questions anyone ever asked, that was always his least favorite. What if he failed again? But Jefferson and Flora watched him with such confidence that it was hard to deflate beneath their gazes. "Sort of. Flora, can you get uniforms for Jefferson and me?"

She twirled a finger in a circle. "Probably. Depends what kind you need."

Blaise swallowed. "The same as will be worn by the people taking Jack to the cathedral." He looked at Rhys, hoping he might have answers.

The Tracker tilted his head, skeptical. "Do I even want to know?"

Flora cackled. "Just answer the question, sweet cheeks."

Rhys glowered. "Salt-Iron Confederation, since they'll be handling a mage."

The half-knocker gave a nod, aiming finger guns at Blaise. "Got you covered. Anything else?"

Blaise turned to the Tracker. "Can you help me and Jefferson get in with the ones serving as the escort?"

Rhys pursed his lips, his eyes troubled. "If I help you, I'll be called a traitor if this goes wrong. I'll lose my position."

"As a traitor who lost my position, I understand," Jefferson said. "But sometimes, to do the right thing, it's worth it."

"And this outlaw is worth it?" Rhys asked.

Jack. The most infuriating, ruthless, and arrogant man Blaise had ever come across. He'd done horrible things—but gods, when he was a friend, he was loyal. And he had loved ones who would

feel the aching hole in their lives. Blaise couldn't imagine Fortitude without Jack. "Yeah, he's worth it."

Rhys huffed out a breath. "Then I can help you get as close as
possible to your mage. But I don't know how you intend to do so
—the Lightguard present at the Asaphenia will know the both of
you from the gala."

"I've got an idea." Blaise stood, lifting a finger in silent supplication for them to wait. He headed upstairs to the master
bedroom, going straight to the dresser where he'd stowed the
alchemical potions his mother had insisted on sending along with
him. Blaise stuck a hand into the bag and pulled out a linen-
wrapped flask to reassure himself it was still there. Then he took
the bag back to the kitchen, hefting it like a trophy.

Jefferson knew what he had. The Dreamer grinned.

CHAPTER FIFTY-ONE
Fear Doesn't Win

Blaise

"I said it before and I'll say it again, you look *good* in a uniform," Flora crowed as Blaise stared at his reflection, pulse racing. He stood in the master bedroom at Hawthorne House, clad in the scarlet uniform of a Salt-Iron Confederation soldier.

"Flora," Jefferson said, voice a soft warning. The Dreamer laid a hand on Blaise's shoulder, a steadying presence. "This is not the same, Blaise."

Blaise nodded, turning away from the mirror. Earlier, after Flora and Rhys parted ways to handle their details, Blaise had admitted to Jefferson he feared blundering their mission from panic. It was suddenly too much like the plan for Fort Courage, and that had ended badly for Blaise. So badly that he trembled just thinking about it.

Maybe he shouldn't do this. He could send Flora with Jefferson—surely they had the means to help Jack. But this was *his* idea, and belatedly Blaise realized he'd based it on Fort Courage for a reason: because they *had* succeeded at freeing the trapped mages. And maybe, just maybe, this time he'd have a better ending and could finally put the demons of Fort Courage to rest.

"I know. I'll be okay," he whispered.

Jefferson studied him so intently that Blaise was certain he'd call him on the lie. The Dreamer reached up and touched his cheek. "I know you don't consider yourself brave, but you are. You possess an incredible amount of courage to take action despite your fear."

Some of Blaise's nerves melted away at Jefferson's words. "My courage isn't stronger than fear, but my love is."

"And that, my dear, is where the *real p*ower lies." The Dreamer's smile was like basking in the sun on a late autumn day, warming Blaise through to his core.

"Are you done being mushy and introspective?" Flora asked.

Jefferson's gaze slid to her, though he didn't face away from Blaise. "We were having a moment. Did you not see us having a moment?"

"Tick-tock." The half-knocker crossed her arms, reminding them of their tight schedule.

Blaise swallowed. Flora was right—they didn't have time to waste. And maybe, just maybe, if Blaise kept his forward momentum, he wouldn't have time to think too much and panic. He nodded. "We should, um, get going probably. Flora, you're going to check that everyone is where we need them?"

The half-knocker grinned and tapped two fingers to her forehead in a salute. "Yep. I'm still planning to help Rhys meet up with the Mutton Underpants." Flora had decided Maverick Underground was too boring and had gone with one of her variations. "Then I'm gonna hustle to the top of the Asaphenia and hang a few mirrors so the pegasi can use 'em to navigate and know where to go."

When Blaise had laid out the plan, Emrys had overheard and wasn't having any of it. The black stallion raised such a fuss that Seledora and Zepheus had agreed they wouldn't be left out—not when their riders were at risk. But that had added a new complication: none of the pegasi were familiar with the city from an aerial view, and it would be a slow and dangerous process seeking their riders with telepathy from overhead. Flora's brilliant solution was to hang mirrors that would reflect the sunlight, creating a beacon for the equines.

<And we will be overhead once Flora has the mirrors in place to let us know the ceremony has begun,> Zepheus added.

Blaise sighed. It seemed the pegasi were eavesdropping once again. He slipped over to the window and peeked through the curtain, discovering that the trio were right outside the window. At least they were using their ears and not their magic.

"Shall we?" Jefferson asked, eyebrows raised.

Blaise pulled out his pocket watch, checking the time and then snapping it closed. If they delayed much longer, they'd miss their opportunity to join the forces bringing in their prisoner. "Let's go."

After checking that the alchemical potions were safely in the pouch nestled at Blaise's side, they boarded the carriage, driven by Tristan. The teen would deliver them to the location Rhys had recommended, where they would meet up with the rest of the Confederation contingent. Flora had used her talents to get Blaise and Jefferson assigned as the pair who would personally handle the outlaw. Blaise had started to ask how she managed it, but Jefferson assured him he probably wouldn't like the answer.

Their carriage drew to a stop and Tristan pounded his fist against the side, announcing they had reached the end of their route. Blaise swallowed, pulling the potions from his pouch. He handed one to Jefferson.

The Dreamer accepted it with a nod of thanks before uncorking it. "Cheers." He took a sip as if it were a fine champagne, though his lips curled when he encountered a taste that disagreed with his palate.

And then he changed. His features melted into those of

someone else, much like when he used his cabochon ring. Jefferson's hair darkened, and for a moment Blaise feared he might look too much like Malcolm. But then a thick black beard sprouted along his chin, shaggier than Blaise's, and all resemblance to the former Doyen was lost.

"Ah, I much prefer facial hair on you," Jefferson lamented, touching his chin. "Oh. This feels as real as my glamor. Quite impressive."

Blaise couldn't help but smile at Jefferson's observations. "You should try a beard sometime. You could pull it off." Though Jefferson would find a way to make a burlap sack look fashionable.

"Not a beard, but I *have* considered growing out my hair. You know, sort of a ne'er-do-well, roguish look." Jefferson tilted his head. "Now let's see you."

Blaise opened his own potion, wrinkling his nose. He took a sip, surprised when he didn't feel any great change sweep over him. In fact, he almost thought it hadn't worked until Jefferson heaved a dramatic sigh.

"It gave me a beard and took yours away. That's downright cruel."

Blaise reached up and gingerly stroked his too-smooth chin. It was an unnerving sensation, knowing that his beard *should* have been there, but wasn't. "If that's the worst of it, I'll take it." He stoppered the remaining potion. He had some of his mother's healing potions in the pouch as well, but he didn't think they would do much for Jack. Maybe he *should* have brought along Chill of Death. As awful as the potion was, it would have kept the Effigest from death. Well, that wasn't something he could dwell on now. "You know what to do?"

Jefferson squeezed Blaise's shoulder. "Make sure we both stay near Jack. And, most importantly, ensure that you have a chance at the rope."

Blaise nodded, then leaned over to open the carriage door. As light poured in, a wave of panic swept over him. Visions of them being found out before they could get to Jack. Of being thrown back into the Cit—

"Don't let your fear win." Jefferson was suddenly much closer than Blaise recalled. "We can do this. I'm here."

Blaise swallowed, sucking in a steadying breath. He met Jefferson's eyes—no longer green, but more of a muddy brown. But still filled with love and determination. *I'm not alone.* "Fear doesn't win. Love wins."

"And it always will," Jefferson whispered.

CHAPTER FIFTY-TWO

Fowl Intercession

Jack

Thinking hurt. Moving hurt. Jack's body felt like one enormous bruise. The pain-numbing working from his poppet had ebbed during his unconsciousness, the doll tumbling from his grip when his captors had moved him.

There was a time when he thought help had come. Jack had heard familiar voices, had been sure it was Vixen and Flora. They couldn't be here. He knew that much, and he'd tried to warn them. Only he was no longer sure if they'd ever been there or if they were figments of his imagination.

And Kittie. Had he seen her, too? He certainly felt like he had, but maybe that was only his longing to be with his wife one more time. To tell her how he loved her more than all the stars in the sky. Her presence had felt so real, but Jack vaguely thought it seemed like she'd been trapped. But that made little sense. Nothing did.

Jack hoped rescue would come, but that didn't seem to be in the cards. In between the bouts of darkness, he tried to come up with an idea to save himself. But every plan required him to be whole. And right now, he was a broken thing. Even if help came, he might be too far gone.

More time passed. He was vaguely aware of hands grasping him, picking him up. His eyes fluttered open, but the world around him was a confusing riot of color and shadow. The light stung his eyes, making them water. All around him, men and women were talking, going about their tasks as if it were any other day. He tried to decipher their words, but he couldn't.

He groaned as they dumped him into...something. The rough wood beneath him and the nearby sound of horses or mules suggested it might be a wagon. Jack struggled to open his eyes again, wincing in the light. It was, in fact, a wagon, which a moment later jerked into motion, the wood rattling beneath him so hard it made every injury flare to life with a shining corona of agony.

Jack didn't know how long he was in the wagon. He was pretty sure he lost consciousness again. He only awoke when he felt a light touch against his bare arm and what he thought was a familiar chorus of voices. But it couldn't be. He tried to lift his head to see, but the effort was too much. Jack's head fell back against the wood with a painful thud.

Hands tugged at him, pulling him upright. Heart thundering, a surge of adrenaline pulsed through him. Jack tried to shake them away, tried to curse his outrage. But he was about as effective as a day-old kitten. The hands dragged him forward, marching him somewhere he couldn't see before pinning him in place.

"Devoted of Garus, our sacrifice has arrived to consecrate our returned Spark, soon to be the next revered Luminary."

The voice rang loud and clear, the first Jack had truly made out since he'd been beaten. He didn't know the speaker, but with a sinking feeling, he knew what was happening. Dillon had said they would hang him, and the Quiet One was making good on his promise. With effort, he cracked his eyes open once more. His vision blurred, but he saw enough to recognize the exterior of the

Asaphenia. Garus's bloody ceremony required a death, which meant they were holding it in the courtyard located beside the cathedral.

"This is not just any sacrifice." This voice, Jack recognized. Tara Woodrow, Dillon's crony. The priest must have invited her to speak. "Spark Valoria will be brought to power by the lifeblood of one of the most feared outlaws, the Scourge of the Untamed Territory. Wildfire Jack Dewitt." There was a pause as the crowd murmured, and then Woodrow continued. "Not only has this wicked mage robbed and killed countless innocent merchants, but he's the cold-blooded murderer of Doyen Gregor Gaitwood and Commander Lamar Gaitwood."

At least they got my damn accolades right. That was little consolation, though, as the crowd's rumble grew at the revelations of all Jack had done in his life. He'd known that his enemies would come calling for his sins. Kittie had tried to warn him, and he'd been the fool who thought nothing could touch him. *I should have listened to her.* Jack had always known this might be his end—he just wished it wasn't now.

The crowd grew more vocal, calling him every name under the sun. But they quieted after a moment, and Jack figured the priest must have made some gesture to continue the ceremony.

"Spark Valoria, do you vow to allow the wisdom of Garus to light your path, unto the end of your days?" the priest intoned.

"I have, and I will." Sure enough, that was Vixen's voice, though there was a hitch in it. What was she thinking, standing on a dais as her life was about to change—his blood the very impetus for that change? He wondered if both of their lives were about to end, only in very different ways. She would no longer be an outlaw.

"Let the chaos of magic be doused so that wisdom may flow forth," the priest declared, his voice sweeping pin-pricks of dread across Jack's body.

No. This couldn't be it. It took great effort, but he squinted and made out Vixen's hazy form. She wasn't looking at him. Her gaze was turned away, as if she couldn't bear to see him. There would be no rescue from her. It shouldn't have been the gut punch it was. Vixen was sacrificing herself for the Gutter in her own way.

Hands gripped his shoulders, guiding him forward. Jack wanted to fight, wanted to do something. Maybe he could trip his escort? But then what? A one-legged donkey could apprehend him in his current state.

"Stairs," a masculine voice advised him.

That voice. But it can't be... Suddenly, he didn't have time to focus on the voice that was so familiar it shot an arrow of hope through him. With help, he staggered up the stairs that led to the gallows. The acrid scent of varnish was strong in the air, proof that they'd treated the wood recently to protect it from the elements in the courtyard.

Hands tugged at his shoulders again, getting him into position atop the platform. Jack's breath came short and hard from the effort of the stairs. Yeah, and he'd thought he could fight? All he was fit for was the long walk to Perdition. This was it. The end of the trail for the Scourge of the Untamed Territory.

The rough coil of rope slipped around his throat, grating against his skin. The hangman fiddled with the noose, adjusting the loop until it was uncomfortably taut.

"Don't I get any last words?" Jack rasped. Gods, it had taken far too much effort to ask. Every syllable scraped against his tongue, unwieldy and awkward.

"That is not a part of the ceremony." The priest had the gall to sound apologetic. "May Garus grant you rest in Perdition."

"You and your god can go hump a flatulent dragon." Jack's lips were so chapped they felt like sandstone, and the effort of speaking burned his throat, but damn, the mortified gasps his suggestion received made it worthwhile.

"His life for the Spark," the priest declared, ignoring Jack's pettiness.

The trapdoor opened beneath Jack's feet with a clatter.
He fell.

———

Blaise

OH GODS, WHAT IF THIS DOESN'T WORK? I'M SO SORRY, JACK.

The crowd cheered as Jack fell, eager for the sudden stop as he
reached the end of the rope. It was like watching wolves preparing
to rip apart a rabbit. Instead, when the outlaw hit the end, frayed
strands snapped, releasing him from the deadly noose. He
tumbled into an unceremonious, groaning heap beneath the
gallows.

Blaise winced, peering down at the Effigest. His magic had
worked on the rope as he'd hoped, but that drop was enough to do
considerable damage. The fingers of Jack's right hand twitched
into an agonized fist. Blaise imagined his friend was in a world of
pain, but it was preferable to the alternative. Now he just had to
hope they made it through the next few moments.

"What is the meaning of this?" The priest turned to stare at
them, shock etching his pale face. He was flustered, unable to
comprehend that the ceremony had gone off the rails.

Tara Woodrow, who had been enjoying the show from the
front row, stormed over to the gallows. She was dressed in finery
that suggested she was attending the social event of the year—
the dress bedecked with tiny crystals that caught the light as
effectively as the mirrors Flora was supposed to hang in the
cathedral. "You're the most incompetent hangman in all of
history!"

Blaise crossed his arms as he peered down at the Quiet One.
"Maybe. But I'm a pretty damn competent Breaker." He called on
his magic again, touching a finger to his own arm as he sent a
ripple of power out to remove the effects of the incognito potion.

It tried to cling to him, like grease reluctant to be scrubbed from a pan, but after a moment, it washed away.

Tara's face clouded with a medley of frustration and sly avarice. Behind her, the crowd grew louder. "Oh, fancy seeing *you* here. I suppose Jefferson can't be far. I'm certain we can replace one sacrificial mage with another."

"Really? Is that what we're doing? How tiresome," Jefferson said, holding out his hand. Blaise took it, sending a gentle wave of magic over his beau to dispel his potion. He had to be careful, lest he also strip the glamor powered by the cabochon ring. Removing the potion from Jefferson was a bit like peeling an apple. "Now, I may not be a follower of Garus, but if something like this were to interrupt a very important ceremony, it might be seen as a sign." Jefferson smiled.

As if to emphasize his point, Emrys, Seledora, and Zepheus made a pass overhead, their huge shadows racing over the crowd. Blaise felt the brush of Emrys's mind against his own, the stallion smug at the cleverness of his rider and content that he was currently safe. From her vantage point on the dais, Vixen barely contained a grin at the disruption.

"Garus does not abide mages." The priest sounded certain of this, a promise of retribution in his voice. He drew himself up, as if deciding this was the time to regain control of the proceedings. "Lightguard, gather up all the mages and—"

"*All* the mages?" a new voice interrupted. Blaise followed the sound to the back of the courtyard. At first, it was hard to see Rhys through the throng. The dark shape of his unicorn loitered just outside the stone entryway. The Tracker strode forward with such a swagger he could have been an outlaw. Rhys had dressed in what Blaise guessed might be a ceremonial uniform, but he was still armed and ready for action. He halted before the dais where Vixen stood. She stared down at her twin, her silver eyes unreadable. "Because you'll have to start with her." He nodded to Vixen.

The Tracker made the accusation with such gravity, Blaise

would have suspected another betrayal if he hadn't been the one to make the suggestion. Jefferson would probably consider Rhys a serviceable actor. The Tracker stood rigid, his expression stern, without so much as an amused twist to his lips. The assembled mass went into an uproar, some calling that it was impossible and others declaring they had known it to be true.

Members of the Lightguard filed in, though they paused at the outskirts, uncertain. They didn't know what to do, and they appeared reluctant to approach Blaise and Jefferson, which was a wise decision. Blaise didn't want to use his magic right now, but if it came down to their lives and freedom, he would become a force to be reckoned with.

Rhys held up a hand, keeping the attention on himself. "And they're not alone."

At his declaration, magic swelled. A cacophony sounded in the distance, and seconds later, a dark cloud of birds alighted in the courtyard. Mostly pigeons, by the looks of it—so many they were forced to land for a beat before taking off again. Men and women screamed as pigeons used their heads as temporary perches, many attendees fleeing to avoid the avian invasion.

"They came," Blaise whispered. He hadn't realized he'd been holding his breath, waiting to see if the Maverick Underground would work with Rhys as he'd asked.

Jefferson nudged him with an elbow. "Of course they did. Look, there's the Birdcaller." Blaise followed Jefferson's gaze and recognized Holly, clutching her rooster off to Rhys's right.

"Garus *does* abide mages," Vixen declared, her voice ringing out even over the clamor of the birds. As if to allow her a chance to be heard, half of the pigeons thundered away to roost on the architecture of the looming cathedral, staring down at them like tiny, feathered gargoyles. She held up her wrists, showing the gleaming salt-iron cuffs that dangled from them. Someone had crafted them to look like jewelry, but there was no hiding their purpose. "He knows of my magic and never turned his back on me."

"Liar!" A silver-haired woman dressed in the regalia of a priest rose and stormed toward the dais, crooking a finger at Vixen. "You'll hang for deceiving the god of wisdom!" She turned to the Lightguard. "Capture the pretender."

"Damn, Vixen's in trouble. She can't use her magic," Jefferson whispered.

"She can if I get to her." Blaise glanced down at Jack again. The outlaw had gone still, but his chest rose and fell as proof that he clung to life.

"Go on. Do your thing." Jefferson smiled at him. "I'll see to Jack. I'll know he's okay if he starts cursing at me." Then, before Blaise could say anything else, the Dreamer dropped over the side of the gallows, landing in a crouch beside Jack. Jefferson made the whole thing look effortless and heroic.

He's much more agile than I am. Blaise knew if he tried the same trick, he'd probably fall on his face or end up with a broken leg, neither of which would help their cause. So, while it ate precious seconds and didn't make him look all that heroic, he took the stairs.

The Lightguard moved to intercept him, but as soon as they did, the birds swooped in. Pigeons and sparrows harried them from above while a handful of geese hissed in rage, mantling their wings as they drove the guards back. Fortunately for the birds, the Lightguard were stunned by the fowl intercession and allowed themselves to be herded rather than attack.

Blaise crossed to the dais, but halfway there, the gold braiding of his borrowed Salt-Iron Confederation uniform caught his eye. The fleeting glance tapped an old memory, squeezing the breath from his lungs. Blaise froze, his pulse quickening. His eyes teared as he closed them, trembling where he stood.

The deck of the airship listed beneath his feet. Emrys flew in a frantic circle overhead as the airship stuttered, first shifting to the left before dipping wildly to the right. Blaise's hands pressed flat against the vibrating wood, head bowed. He couldn't do this again.

"Blaise! Look at me!"

Vixen's voice. An anchor of familiarity amid the storm-tossed sea of panic. With effort, Blaise opened his eyes, taking a ragged breath as he stared at his friend on the dais, waiting for him. He had to make it there, but he didn't know if he could. His feet were rooted in place not by magic, but by memories he had thought he could defeat. *I was wrong.*

He met her silver-eyed gaze. Blaise desperately wished she had her magic. She'd used it on him before, long ago. The memory of that time swam up, banishing the airship. Blaise had just fled his home, lost and alone, except for Emrys. He hadn't known it was magic back then, but her power had wrapped around him like a comfortable blanket, lulling him into calmness as he'd revealed his plight. Blaise focused on that, latching onto the memory of calm. Of momentary peace. His labored breathing slowed.

"Come on, Blaise. You can do this." Vixen's voice was soft, so soft it was amazing that he heard it. If not for the salt-iron stifling her, Blaise would have thought it was her magic. But it wasn't. It was her friendship, her unerring belief in him.

He swallowed and took a step forward.

CHAPTER FIFTY-THREE

From Darkness to Light

Kittie

"When I get back to Nera, I swear to Tabris I'm going to have gas lamps installed everywhere. I'm so tired of the dark," Rachel murmured as she trailed at Kittie's elbow.

"I'd suggest you have a care for swearing to any gods where we're going," the Luminary cautioned, breezing past the Madame Boss.

Kittie had sent Najaria on the hunt for more liminal spaces, hoping to find more thresholds that would tie the shadows with both the divine and the living world. The aethon seemed to be sensitive to them. They'd found others as they walked, though none of them suited their purpose. They lacked the divinity Kittie suspected was necessary to make her idea work.

That had all changed about a half-hour ago, according to Rachel's watch. Juliette had frozen, her eyes going wide. Kittie had thought the woman was startled at first, but something had passed over her countenance. A subtle change, almost impossible to pinpoint. If Kittie hadn't been watching, she'd never have noticed.

"I know where to go," the Luminary had declared. There was something different about her voice—a strange resonance, almost as if she were speaking in tandem with someone else. She'd been leading the way ever since.

"All I'm saying is that if invoking Tabris's name gets me back home, I'm all for it. I pay my tithe to the sacellum each month." The Madame Boss glanced over her shoulder, as if expecting to find her deity sneaking up on them.

The Luminary ignored the comment, continuing on. She strode into the darkness ahead of Najaria's halo of light, her steps as certain as if it were daylight.

Rachel moved closer to Kittie, pitching her voice low. "I'm going to be honest: I like the Luminary, but right now, she's creeping me out."

Kittie hid a smile. "Do you believe in the gods, Rachel?"

The Gannish leader raised her brows. "Of course. Don't you?"

Kittie didn't have a ready answer for that. It was complicated. Jack believed in them, but she'd never known what to think of deities who played favorites. Oh, each deity and their followers professed all the reasons they were good and worthy, but Kittie understood none of it. How could Garus be so wise if he allowed such atrocities against mages? Likewise, how could Faedra, the goddess of magic, allow for such wrongs to be done to the mystic races? It made no sense. Greater powers might exist, but she supposed they were as fickle and imperfect as the creatures of the land, sea, and sky.

Rather than give an answer, Kittie deflected. "If you believe in the gods, then Juliette truly is the Luminary, the avatar of Garus. In that case, I'm hoping her god is leading us where we need to go."

Rachel nodded at that. "Makes as much sense as anything else in the shadow realm."

Ahead, Juliette drew to a halt. She pivoted to face them. "All the gods have been absent, not just Garus. His communication with me had been limited—until now." Her eyes shone, not with tears but with a golden gleam. Gooseflesh pebbled over Kittie's skin at the spectacle. "You were right about the liminal space. There's one ahead, and it combines the shadows, the divine, and our physical world."

Kittie swallowed. Najaria snorted before taking another step forward, casting her glow further. A structure rose out of the twisting shadows, something about it familiar. For a heart-stopping instant, she feared it was the Golden Citadel—but it wasn't. It was a building that belonged in Izhadell, though. Kittie had seen the architecture before from a distance.

"Where are we?" Rachel asked.

The Luminary smiled, the expression radiant. Even her golden red hair seemed luminous. "Just outside the Asaphenia, the most revered cathedral of Garus."

Well, that made sense. Of course, a place of worship would thin the veil. A chill of anticipation raced through Kittie's muscles. As eager as she was to begin the spell and see if her idea—the idea Jack had given her—might work, she also experienced a frisson of fear. It might not work. It might end in their deaths. Or it might result in angering beings capable of destroying her without a second thought.

The Luminary peered at her, and Kittie had the disconcerting sensation that someone or something *more* was assessing her, too. "What is your plan to lead us from darkness to light, Firebrand?"

Even Najaria startled at the voice. It was Juliette's but overlaid with another that was deep and rich. Like listening to a distant rumble of thunder. There was more to the Luminary than met the eye. Kittie couldn't falter, not now. She took a breath. *I have to do this not only for us but for everyone.* Her fingers trembled as she retrieved the folded paper from her pocket.

Kittie met the Luminary's golden gaze, unflinching. One

wrong word and she might find herself in Perdition. "I petition the god of wisdom to work with a mage."

The surrounding darkness became stifling as she waited for an answer. Juliette stared at her, and for too long, Kittie feared she would receive no response. That all was lost. Then the avatar spoke. "Do you know, little flame, that I have *never* harbored hatred against you and yours? Wisdom has no room for hate."

Kittie's mouth went dry, her tongue threatening to stick to the roof of her mouth. She might have entertained doubts about the gods earlier, but those fled in the face of the Luminary. A primal urge deep within Kittie pressured her to flee, but she stood her ground. "That's not my experience."

"Hear me now. Humans—even this avatar—don their hate like armor and wield fear as a weapon. But the strongest armor can crack, and there are defenses against even a well-forged weapon." The Luminary turned to stare into the shadowy distance. "Hope pierces armor, and love turns away the edge of fear."

Juliette blinked, her eye color flashing between luminescent gold and cool grey. The woman shivered, turning to Kittie with her jaw clenched. As if she'd experienced something that had changed her life. "We were wrong about mages. *I* was wrong about mages." She lifted her chin, accepting her own mistakes. "How do we do this, Kittie?"

She used my name. There was something remarkable in that simple word, an acknowledgment that held weight she couldn't explain. Kittie opened the slip of paper, gaze raking over the spell to familiarize herself with it once more. Gods, they were missing so many of the items recommended for success. No stones, no physical doorway to use as a guide.

The aethon snorted at her, shaking her mane. Kittie bit her lip and murmured, "You're right. Who needs that when I'm working with an avatar?" She took another deep breath to steady herself. "The spell I'm going to cast is made for wizards, and I'm just a mage. I'm going to need all the power you can give me."

"You're not just a mage; you're the *Firebrand*," Rachel cut in. "Give yourself more credit."

The Luminary nodded. "The Madame Boss is right. You're more than you think you are." Juliette stepped closer, holding out a hand that glistened with dancing golden motes, like rays of sunshine filtering through a cloud.

I don't know about that. But Kittie wasn't about to argue. She took the offered hand, gasping at the warm surge of unfamiliar power. She bent her head against the growing tide. They were right. She was a Pyromancer. The Firebrand. The Dragon. Flames danced between her and the Luminary. Rachel yelped in surprise, but Kittie kept her focus on the spell. The fire swelled to surround them, tongues feasting on the darkness. None of it harmed them —Kittie had impeccable control over her summoned element. The flames crackled, their intensity and magic growing as the Luminary fed the inferno with power from the god of wisdom.

Flames clawed at the shadows, burning a portal through the liminal space.

"Tabris's sweet gilded buttcheeks," Rachel whispered.

CHAPTER FIFTY-FOUR
Force of Nature

Vixen

Vixen hadn't expected Blaise to falter. It was easy to forget he was grappling with old wounds that hadn't healed—that might never heal. But she had been at Fort Courage, too, and understood. Vixen didn't particularly like using her power on friends, but in that moment, she would have—if only to help him through. But with her power chained, all she could do was hope her heartfelt words would break him free from the horrors of his mind.

Blaise's steps grew more certain as he approached and mounted the dais. The priest shied away from the Breaker's approach, as if he were a looming threat. Blaise ignored the man, aiming a weak smile at Vixen. Sweat beaded on his forehead. "Thanks."

Her shoulders relaxed, relief surging. He had made it, and not only that, he was back in the present. "You'd do the same for me, right?" She held up her wrists meaningfully.

"Always," he agreed, his voice low. As Vixen flexed her wrist, Blaise frowned at the welts revealed by the shifting plates of silver and salt-iron. He wrapped his hands around the cuffs, his grip loose. Blaise didn't even flinch at the sting of salt-iron against his flesh, only focused his devastating power on the metal. Vixen felt the feather-light brush of his magic, and not for the first time, she marveled at the control he'd learned. When she had first sought to help him learn how to harness his magic, Blaise would have shied away from a task such as this. Now he met it head-on with methodical determination. The jewelry made an unearthly grating sound, then started to crack. The links shattered, the metal falling away as flakes rained to the dais below.

She rubbed her wrists. "Much better. That's not quite my taste in jewelry."

Blaise nodded, though he had shifted to study the surrounding pandemonium, gaze flicking from Jefferson and Jack to Woodrow and then to the riled crowd. "I think whatever comes next is on you."

Vixen swallowed. He was right. She was the Spark and would be the Luminary if they didn't find her mother soon. "The bracelets sapped me dry. I don't think I can do much." Exhaustion dogged her. Oh, what she wouldn't give to curl up somewhere to sleep and recover.

"Good thing you're not alone then," Blaise said, though his gaze had dropped back to the crowd, tracking Tara Woodrow as she squeezed through the masses to head for the exit.

Vixen thought Blaise was going to use his power, but instead he lifted his right hand, as if to gain someone's attention, then nodded. Tara's forward momentum came to a sudden halt, her face twisting in frustration as she hefted her skirts to locate the problem. Huge roots had ripped up from the ground, lashing around her ankles and calves to anchor her in place.

"That one of your Maverick Underground?" Vixen asked the Breaker.

"Yep," he murmured. "I don't see the other man. Phillip Dillon."

Vixen had scanned the crowd earlier and hadn't seen him,

either. She didn't know what that boded for them. The maverick had stopped Tara in her tracks, so they could deal with her later—and perhaps uncover Dillon's whereabouts. Vixen's mind whirled as she tried to think of what to do next. *Continue with the ceremony. Seal my legitimacy.* She gave Blaise an appreciative smile. "Thanks, I've got this from here."

Vixen turned toward the priest and was about to speak when a sudden whoosh of flames erupted out of the flagstones ten feet from the dais, making her stumble backward. Even the geese retreated, necks outstretched as they honked their alarm. The remaining audience screamed, nearly causing a stampede in their haste to leave. Others pressed against the walls but stayed, giving in to their potentially ill-advised curiosity.

Blaise stared at the growing wreath of flames, making a soft sound of surprise.

"What is it?" Vixen asked, voice gentle. Blaise hadn't tensed, but whatever he suspected was going on hadn't stirred his usual anxiety.

He didn't answer, but he didn't have to. The flames swirled to form a portal that led to a world of darkness. *No*, Vixen corrected herself. *A world of shadows.* For a moment, she thought it might be Raven, but that made little sense. Not considering the fire.

With a haunting cry, a glossy chestnut equine tore through the portal, coming to a stiff-legged halt in the middle of the courtyard. Vixen knew that mare. She hadn't realized the aethon had come to Izhadell, but it had to be...

Kittie Dewitt stepped through, smoke wreathing at her back like dark wings. The Firebrand paused as soon as her boots hit the flagstones of the courtyard. Her gaze raked over the scene. Pigeons still flapped overhead and geese honked, their long necks snaking at anyone who came too close, bills snapping. She found Blaise and Vixen on the stage. The mage turned as if she were speaking to someone behind her, then strode forward to make room.

A woman with mussed hair stepped out next. Her face was ashen, and she looked as if she were trying to compose herself as she appeared in the unfamiliar area.

"Rachel Clayton," Blaise whispered.

To their left, a high-pitched voice yelped, "There you are!" A moment later, Flora vaulted onto the scene, her pink hair bobbing in pigtails as she pulled out her knives, as if preparing to take on the world. The half-knocker crouched beside the Gannish leader. Vixen hadn't even known the diminutive woman was there, but then again, Flora excelled at not being seen.

But wait...the Madame Boss of Ganland? Did Vixen dare to hope...?

Juliette Kildare stepped out of the shadows.

Celestine Currington of the Clergy Council saw her, too. "The might of Garus has returned the Luminary to us!"

The Luminary surveyed her surroundings, hands on her hips. She still wore the same golden garb as the night of the gala. Her gaze snapped to Vixen, her lips curving into a smile. There was new acceptance in her expression, as if she had come to terms with what her daughter was and approved.

"I'll leave you to it," Blaise murmured, dropping from the dais.

Juliette Kildare stalked to the dais and peered at her daughter before stepping up to join her. "The ones behind this were hoping to give me up for dead, were they?"

"They were," Vixen confirmed.

The Luminary smiled, though it was an expression that promised vengeance. "Foolish of them to discount the wisdom of Garus."

Kittie

KITTIE IMMEDIATELY RECOGNIZED THE LUMP CRUMPLED BENEATH the gallows. Jack's still form was too painfully close to what she'd seen in the liminal space of the shadow realm. He wasn't moving, and Kittie didn't know why he was on the ground, but...her eyes drifted up to the frayed rope.

They were going to hang him.

But they had failed. She took a breath, repeating it in her mind like a mantra. *They failed. They failed.* If they hadn't, her husband would be hanging from the noose, his neck broken. It wasn't much solace, though. Not when she recalled how awful he had looked.

Kittie dispelled the portal with a snap of her fingers, gritting her teeth against the rebound of magic. She was tired, but not the boneless exhaustion she'd suffered after portaling with Jack. Garus had provided quite the power boost. Kittie raced over to her husband, ignoring the assortment of birds and the shouts of confusion. None of that mattered. She went down to her knees beside him, aware of Jefferson shifting to make room.

"Who did this to you?" Kittie whispered, her voice breaking. She touched his arm, gut clenching at the bruises that dappled his skin. Someone had to pay for this. Jefferson spoke to her, but she refused to hear him. Not right now. She needed to find the one who had hurt Jack. The ones who wanted him to hang. Her gaze roved over the crowd, the fire within her heart ready to unleash an inferno on *everyone*.

"No," Jack rasped, his voice so faint she almost didn't hear. "Don't."

His voice brought her back to him. Kittie trembled, body quaking from the expense of power and the shock of finding her husband almost dead.

"He's right," Jefferson whispered, voice apologetic. Kittie hated that Jefferson could sound so composed when her world was crumbling. This was a time for unfettered rage, for a wildfire that would turn the city to crumbling ash. "You're surrounded by the

Confederation right now, Kittie. And you have every right to be angry. But if you kill anyone, even someone who deserves it, you won't leave here."

"Don't," Jack insisted, the word like grating rocks.

Kittie took a gasping breath, hot tears burning her eyes. "I don't know how else to help him."

"We need a Healer," Jefferson said, his voice calm and far too reasonable. Kittie wanted to lash out at him, to erupt with anger, but he was right.

Movement nearby caught Kittie's eye. Her hands curled into claws, cradling a flame—which she quenched when she realized it was Blaise. He wasn't alone. A woman carrying a huge, brown rooster trailed him, along with a balding man.

"I know of a Healer, but it will take time for him to get here," the woman said, her face grave.

"No," Kittie said with a shake of her head. A lock of hair fell into her eyes, and she tucked it back behind her ear. "There's no one in all of Phinora I'd trust with him." Not only because of his injuries but also his status as a wanted outlaw. The price on his head would be too great a temptation.

"We have to do something for him," Blaise argued. "We can trust these mages, Kittie. I promise."

As much as Kittie wanted to share Blaise's faith in others, she couldn't. Kittie shook her head, insistent. Overhead, the birds parted in a riot of cries as huge, dark forms appeared. She glanced skyward and found the pegasi circling overhead. They swooped lower and lower, taking the measure of the courtyard to find an angle for landing. The majority seemed to think better of it, but a lone pegasus made the descent.

Zepheus came down hard, throwing up a scatter of dust as his hooves crashed against stone, wings braking. The stallion whirled, tail flying like a gossamer banner as he folded his wings. His dark, intelligent eyes homed in on Jack, and he trotted over, neck arched.

<My rider.> Zepheus dipped his muzzle low, blowing out a soft breath that ruffled Jack's hair. *<Do not cross to Perdition without me.>*

"He's *not going* to Perdition," Kittie whispered, choking out the words.

<He has one foot on the path already.> The stallion jerked his head up, the whites of his eyes showing.

Tears brimmed in Kittie's eyes. "He needs Nadine." Kittie didn't get along with Fortitude's most skilled Healer, but the woman knew her job and did it well. But Nadine was half a continent away.

Except half a continent wasn't so far, not with the magic Kittie had just wielded. She had trod dangerously close to the realm of the gods. She could do it again, though this time, she wouldn't have power fed to her from an avatar. But to save Jack, to give him a chance, she would burn herself to ashes if she must.

She looked at Zepheus. "We need Nadine. Now."

The stallion bobbed his head, dancing in place. *<But she's too far. Not even the swiftest pegasus could get there and back in time, and there are no Walkers here.>*

Kittie shook her head. "We don't need a Walker. We need a portal." The spell was fresh in her mind, almost burned into her brain after the effort with the avatar. She could cast it without worry—except for the sheer power required to make it successful.

Blaise rose from his crouch, the normally reserved Breaker almost effervescent with determination and the need to do something. "Kittie, you shouldn't try another so soon. Especially without help."

"I had the help of a *god*," Kittie shot back, frustrated that anyone would naysay her. She gestured to Jack. "And he..."

"Is going to be pissed if you kill yourself to save him," Blaise supplied. "Let me."

Kittie's first instinct was to deny the offer, but Najaria bumped her forehead into the Pyromancer's shoulder, as if to clear her mind. She nodded. "But I want to help." Kittie unfolded the spell and held it out.

Blaise took it, gaze flicking over the words. Jefferson had shifted to look over the Breaker's shoulder. "We don't have the reagents it suggests," the Dreamer pointed out.

"No, but you can use sheer power to overcome it," Kittie said.

"Guess we'll test my mother's theory," Blaise murmured, leaving Kittie to wonder what he meant. Jefferson made a soft sound, the lines around his eyes telegraphing his concern.

Blaise smiled, and even though the expression lit his face, Kittie already saw the exhaustion in his eyes—not from the use of his power, but from everything else. The Breaker ignored it, spine straightening as he turned to face Kittie. "Every bit of magic I have is yours." He held out a hand, fingers trembling.

Kittie took his hand. The flesh of his palm almost tingled, as if his magic lay just beneath the surface, like a pond beneath a layer of ice. How much was buried below? Jack had told her Blaise was unlike any other mage he'd ever come across.

"Thank you," she whispered, hoping he understood she meant not only for the magic but for his willingness.

He nodded, staring straight ahead. "I don't think Jack would survive going through the portal. Who can go through to get Nadine?"

<I will.> Zepheus stomped a forehoof against the flagstones, a sharp clatter that startled the nearby pigeons into flight.

"We'll hold it open as long as we can, but I don't know how long that will be," Kittie told the pegasus. In answer, the palomino pranced in place, the muscles in his hindquarters bunched in anticipation. He was ready to bolt forward like a golden bullet.

Blaise had folded the spell back into a square, stuffing it inside the pocket of his—wait, he and Jefferson were both wearing Salt-Iron Confederation uniforms. Kittie had been too distracted to notice. Blaise's hand shifted beneath hers. "Since you've cast this spell more than I have, I'll let you take the lead. But you've got all my magic."

"Right," Kittie murmured. "Let's do this."

She began the working, feeling the ache and burn as the formation tapped her personal reservoir. Without the reagents, it would drain like a bucket shot through with holes. But then the Breaker's power came, roaring up like a hurricane. To say Blaise was *powerful* or *unique* wasn't enough. It was the difference between hearing about what a tornado could do and witnessing the force of nature ripping apart a barn. *Now I understand why everyone wants the Breaker.*

Swallowing, she harnessed his river of magic, feeding it with care into the working before it had the chance to drain her dry. If she exhausted her resources, she would be too weak to continue the spell, and the portal would collapse. The Breaker magic served as a buttress for her own, and seconds later, the burning frame of the portal snapped into place.

CHAPTER FIFTY-FIVE
Not Here to Make It Right

Vixen

As much as she wanted to join her outlaw friends surrounding Jack, Vixen knew that she couldn't. The maverick had released Tara from the roots, but that hadn't meant she got away. No, a flock of hissing geese had moved to flank her, wings spread as they harried her over to the dais.

Tara shrieked as their wicked bills snapped at the glistening fabric of her dress. She looked up with surprise when she nearly ran into the dais. The geese kept their distance, no longer herding her. But the waterfowl made no moves to retreat.

"Well, now I've seen everything," Juliette remarked, her gaze locked on the woman. "Tara Woodrow, have you been plotting against me?"

"I most certainly *haven't*," the cornered elite woman sniffed. "A mage took you, Luminary. And even now, they conspire against you." Tara gestured to Vixen, pitching her voice so that others might hear. "She even ensorcelled her guards. *You* may be next."

Vixen narrowed her eyes. Walter and Hubert. They had escorted her back to Dawnlight after the ill-fated attempt to rescue Jack, but by then she'd been cuffed with the delicate salt-iron bracelets. And the guards had been yoked with threats of their own—if Vixen had to guess, likely against the loved ones the men had mentioned to her.

But she *had* nudged them with her magic, so she couldn't dispute the truth. Not here in front of Garus.

"The Spark would *never*," Juliette declared.

"Oh?" Tara asked, arms swinging at her side until a nearby goose hissed to keep her in line. "But she *was* ready to replace you. Why else would she come armed with the Breaker, and the Scourge of the Untamed Territory skulking about? The mages plot against you and all the Confederation."

Vixen clenched her teeth. With Tara's spin, every one of her points made sense—even though they were lies. The Luminary hated mages. Everyone knew that, and Tara Woodrow was weaponizing that hate.

The Luminary's mouth drew into a thin line. "Garus's wisdom exceeds your own, and he chose a mage to lead me from the darkness." Her eyes flicked to Kittie, who appeared to be casting another portal. "And he has placed a mage I trust beyond all measure at my side right now, when I need her."

Vixen startled at that, glancing at her mother. Juliette kept her steely gaze on Woodrow. Something had changed in the time between when they'd spoken after the gala and the Luminary's reappearance. She suspected that not only had Kittie been key, but the god of wisdom, as well.

The Luminary gave Vixen a contemplative look. "I don't know exactly what magic you wield, but I have my suspicions. Can you make her answer my questions truthfully? Here in the Asaphenia, Garus's hallowed halls?"

Vixen pursed her lips. Her mother was asking in a roundabout way if their god would allow her power to serve. "Yes." Tara's eyes widened at her admission.

Juliette smiled, a grim expression. "Were Madame Boss Clayton and I meant to only be kidnapped or killed?"

Tara's lips twisted, as if she were trying to choke back her answer. Vixen weighed her magic upon the woman, once more feeling Garus's presence over her. The Quiet One twitched and tried to fight, but Vixen was too much for her. "The mage had orders to get rid of you! How was I to know he was too stupid to realize we meant for you to die?" Tara's voice was a frustrated wail.

Raven wasn't stupid, he was clever. He was also misguided, but even then, he'd tried to mitigate the damage. Vixen didn't know how to feel about that.

Juliette narrowed her eyes. "I've heard enough. This is treason."

"No more treasonous than birthing a mage!"

"My child was not a mistake," Juliette said, her voice a low husk that only those nearest the platform could hear. But it was enough for Vixen. It was what she had needed to hear all along. "And she's been truer to me than you, who call yourself one of the elite." She turned, surveying the remaining crowd. "Where are my Lightguard? We're conveniently close to the Golden Citadel. Take this woman away."

The guard swept in to obey, converging on the Quiet One like a pack of hounds rushing a rabbit. In short order, they marched Tara toward the exit. Vixen followed their progress, but then the sight of her brother striding in caught her eye.

Something dark leaped from the shadows beside him. As soon as the edge of the raised knife caught the light, Vixen knew who it was.

"*Raven, stop!*" she screamed, pouring magic into the command.

But Raven wasn't looking at her, and he didn't hesitate. For a sickening instant, Vixen was sure her former beau was here to kill Rhys. But as he pivoted, the arc of his arm descending, she knew she was wrong. Raven plunged the knife into Tara Woodrow's chest, burying it to the hilt. The Lightguard escort didn't have time to respond as Raven slashed with the knife he held in his other hand, ripping it across Tara's throat. A burst of scarlet sprayed into the air.

Rhys shouted and tackled the Shadowstepper. Raven crumpled beneath him, the pair cascading to the flagstones. The Lightguard had finally recovered, doing their best to lay the bleeding elite down to render aid.

The Luminary clasped a hand to her mouth, eyes wide. "That's the mage who took me."

Rhys had Raven firmly in hand, dragging him upright. The Shadowstepper didn't struggle against the Tracker's grip. Raven's face and hair were spattered with blood, but he seemed otherwise uninjured as Rhys brought him under control.

A mix of terror and rage flooded through Vixen. She stepped down from the dais, running over to the pair. She spared a furtive glance at Tara, heart thundering at the vivid ribbons of scarlet trailing down the woman's fine taffeta gown. Blood dotted her sleeves like rubies. There was so much blood, she wouldn't last long. If Raven wanted someone dead, it was going to happen.

"What did you do?" Vixen demanded as she stormed over, face flushed with anger and confusion.

"She lied to me. You'll never love me." Raven's dark eyes were on the fallen elite woman.

"Gods damn it, I already told you that, you selfish piss-goblin," Vixen growled, her voice carrying farther than she intended. Listeners gasped at her choice of words, but she didn't give a damn. All bets were off.

Raven didn't meet her eyes. "She deserved what she got."

Yeah, maybe Tara did—but that didn't make it right. Or helpful. She seethed. If Tara lived, Vixen could use her magic to force the woman to reveal more about the Quiet Ones—if her mother allowed her to do so, at any rate. Now they'd lost the opportunity, their best hope bleeding out on the ground ten paces from them.

The Shadowstepper's gaze shifted to the outlaws huddled over

Jack. Wait, was *that* why Raven had made such a public display of killing the woman? Otherwise, he could have done the deed somewhere quiet. Raven had betrayed the outlaw mages and the Gutter, which in their eyes was the worst thing possible. If Jack lived, he would hunt Raven down. Although, maybe he wouldn't need to, if he had a poppet of the man. But in the Confederation's custody, Raven would be held in the Golden Citadel, which would make it difficult for magic to touch him or for an outlaw to visit retribution upon him.

If he wanted to live to see another day, it wasn't the worst idea —unless the Confederation hung him.

And as angry as she was with him, Vixen wouldn't allow that to happen. Raven had manipulated them at every twist and turn.

"For what it's worth, I'm sorry." Raven's voice was little more than a murmur.

Vixen knew he wasn't apologizing for the murder he'd just committed. Not even for taking the Luminary, Jack, and Kittie. Somehow, he had seen those actions as necessary. "It's too late to make it right."

"I'm not here to make it right. I'm here to pay for my sins." Raven swung his gaze back to her, clearing his throat. "In case you're wondering about the ring you gave me, it's in my pocket." He dipped his chin toward the pocket at his chest.

"I'll get it," Rhys said before Vixen could step closer. The fingers of his left hand dug into Raven's upper arm as he used his free hand to retrieve the ring. He pulled it out, examining it for a moment before offering it to Vixen.

She accepted the ring, turning it over to check it before pocketing it. Vixen wondered how he'd gotten it off in the first place, but this wasn't the time to ask. In the end, what did it matter? He'd gotten it off.

Vixen swallowed a lump, part of her heart aching, wishing things had gone differently. There was no room to forgive Raven for any of the things he'd done, even if he'd thought he'd acted to help her. Perhaps especially if he'd done them for her. "Take outlaw Raven Dawson to the Golden Citadel to await trial for his crimes."

A handful of additional guards appeared, along with a duo of Trackers. Rhys hailed them, and they strode over. One Tracker had a set of salt-iron manacles, and a moment later, the mage shuffled off, bound by the metal.

"Are you okay?" Vixen asked her brother, as Raven vanished around the corner.

Rhys straightened his uniform. "He didn't even try to fight me." There was a veneer of puzzlement to his words. Vixen knew that most mages would have struggled. Maybe later, she'd explain her suspicions to him.

"Mother's back." Rhys's voice was a reverent, grateful whisper. Then, louder, "The Luminary has returned." He turned to march up to her, every muscle in his body intent on reaching the dais.

"Thank Garus and the mages for that," Juliette agreed, smiling down at him.

His brows hiked at that. "What?"

The Luminary smiled. "Explanations later." She glanced at her daughter. "You handled that well. But you should also know that you don't have to do this."

Vixen blinked in momentary confusion. "What?"

Juliette didn't get the chance to explain. Instead, something huge and golden coalesced over Rhys's head, great wings billowing. At first, Vixen thought it was an approaching pegasus, but it was all wrong. It shined with impossible gilded light, enormous eyes bright. An owl, the other animal representation of Garus. The Tracker sucked in a breath but didn't flinch, his expression growing intent, as if he were listening to something. Or to someone.

"This one will serve." The spectral owl's voice made the air vibrate like a thunderclap. Its gaze swung to Vixen. "And you? You were always meant to be free, little fox."

Vixen swallowed. "Why?" *Because I'm a mage?* Had her use of magic here, so close to the Asaphenia, finally made Garus see her for what she was?

The owl shrank into a golden-red fox, paws striking the ground in silence. "Because your path leads elsewhere." The celestial fox spun to regard Rhys. "And his has always led to this moment. You will serve as the sword of my truth and the shield of my wisdom, Rhys Kildare."

Rhys had gone down to his knees, almost overwhelmed by the news. He looked up, trembling, but nodded. "I will."

Vixen wanted to demand more answers, wanted to understand why—but before she could do so, the fox faded away. Tears stung her eyes. She felt as if she'd been cast out. She had come willingly, ready to give up everything to help her friends and the Gutter. Now everything was lost. "Why?"

Her mother took her hand, her fingers warm. "Did you really come back to reclaim your place as the Spark? To someday become the Luminary?"

Vixen met her eyes, hating that it was the perfect question. She had come back. Wasn't that enough? She could use her magic, convince her mother that, of course, that was her intent. But why? Garus had claimed her brother before the Clergy Council and the citizens who hadn't yet fled. News would spread. Vixen's only choice would be to seek the position by force—and that would be impossible without her heart in it.

"I came because most of the people I care about are mages. The land I love is under threat. And I'd do anything to keep them safe."

"Even sacrifice yourself to be something you never wanted to be." Juliette's voice was neutral.

Vixen nodded. "You never asked for it, either."

Juliette squeezed her hand. "That doesn't mean I want the same fate for you. Not when there's someone else willing." She smiled at Rhys. "And you. Is this a life you want?"

Rhys glanced from Vixen to their mother, then nodded.

"Always." His gaze flicked to the cluster of mages. "I'll do my best for all the people of Phinora, including the mages."

Juliette put an arm around Vixen. "The Gutter will not suffer another attack by Phinora. Not while I draw breath."

Vixen froze. Now she understood why Garus had chosen Rhys. While he had approved of her magic, placing a mage in the position of Luminary would cause upheaval and strife. But Rhys? He was a Tracker, with not only the skills to handle a mage but magical immunity. He could interact with mages, free of the fear that they might turn their power against him. It was a small step toward showing the populace at large that mages could be trusted. "Oh."

Her mother didn't ask about her revelation, only smiled as if it was something she had figured out some time ago. And perhaps she had. She turned to Rhys. "Then let's make this official. I'll make certain the Reclamation Ceremony continues without a sacrifice, since we're making changes." She smiled at Vixen before rolling her shoulders and assuming the persona of the avatar.

"Faithful of Garus!" the Luminary declared, her voice rolling through the courtyard. The crowd that remained grew quiet, though admittedly, there were few left. Vixen knew those who had stayed were about to witness something they'd brag about for years. "I present to you Spark Rhys Kildare."

A murmur began that grew into a cheer. Rhys stood tall, his shoulders rigid as a burst of light appeared over his head, the spectral owl a flash and then gone once more. Vixen felt the familiar pressure of Garus in her mind, though this time, it was a reassurance. He wasn't turning his back on her—he was giving her what she'd always wanted.

CHAPTER FIFTY-SIX
Not the Voice of an Angel

Emmaline

*H*er father was dying, and there wasn't a damn thing she could do about it. Emmaline had already poured all she had into the poppet, but it wasn't enough. If only she were *stronger*.

She curled up in her bed, her parents' poppets cradled against her chest. She knew she looked a fright—hair tangled and unkempt, her face stained with tears. Emmaline didn't care. Her days and nights had turned into a cycle of willing for her father to live until she dropped into an exhausted sleep to allow her magic a chance to replenish.

"You are burning yourself out like a candle with little wick left," Clover said, her hooves ringing on the floorboards. Emmaline hadn't even heard her knock, hadn't heard the creak of the door opening. The Knossan carried a wooden tray in her hands, setting it down on the table beside Emmaline's bed.

She was staying with Clover while her parents were gone, which was for the best with how she felt at the moment. Emmaline eyed the food, though she had no appetite.

"Mindy said you need this." Clover waved a rough hand over the tray. "You won't do Jack any good if you faint."

Clover had a point. Emmaline sat up, nestling the poppets against her pillow before picking up a peach turnover. It was something she could have made herself if she'd felt up to working in the bakery. As far as she knew, Reuben and Hannah had shuttered it for the time being. That meant Celeste had probably made the turnover. She was a good cook, but no one in Fortitude was a match for Blaise when it came to baking. Emmaline nibbled a corner.

"I can't stop. What if I do and he...?" She swallowed the turnover, though it was little more than a flavorless lump. Not because it had been poorly made but because nothing tasted appealing at the moment.

"He knows what you can do, and he will know you have done all you can," Clover said, reaching down to pat Emmaline's knee. But there was stark sadness in her words, too. The last time Jack had been so badly injured, he had been close enough for them to help. That wasn't the case now. Emmaline knew Clover had to feel even more helpless than she did.

<Em! Zepheus is here!> Oberidon's call broke through her thoughts.

Emmaline dropped the peach turnover onto the tray, buttery crust flaking from the impact. Zepheus? What did that mean for her father? Did that mean he was...? No. Surely she would know if he had died. To be sure, Emmaline's fingers fumbled for the poppet. It was warm to her touch, still laced with pain. Still alive.

"I need to go see why Zeph is back," Emmaline murmured, rising unsteadily. Gods, Clover was right—she was exhausted. But if she made it to the saloon entrance, Oberidon would be there, waiting for her.

"I will go with you," the Knossan said. They both knew it was to make sure Emmaline made it all the way down the stairs.

By the time Emmaline made it to the door, her spotted pegasus

was there, waiting for her. But not only that, she had a prime view
of Zepheus dragging Nadine out of the clinic, his teeth clamped to
the loose fabric of her shirt.

"Let go of me, you bossy broomtail!" Nadine tried to jerk free
without ripping her clothing, which looked to be a losing battle.
Her own pegasus, a red roan, followed, though he didn't seem
inclined to intervene.

<No. You will come. You will heal Jack.> Zepheus had dragged
her out into the street, tail swishing with determination.

"Oh," Clover whispered, her eyes widening.

Heal? That meant... Emmaline swallowed as she saw the fiery
portal swirling at the end of the street. Curious citizens gave it a
wide berth. The portal rippled like the surface of a pond, revealing
a faraway courtyard scene framed by Confederation architecture.
A dove flew through the portal and landed on the clinic roof,
cooing.

"I'm coming, too!" Emmaline called.

"You will not!" Clover protested. "You can hardly stand. Going
through a portal will do you in."

"Clover's right. Don't give me someone else to tend." Nadine
gave her a sour look. "Could one of you go inside the clinic and
grab my black medical bag? I doubt this stud will let me go."

<I will release you when we get to Phinora,> Zepheus
promised.

"You'd better, or you'll end up a gelding," the Healer groused,
earning a derisive snort from the palomino.

Emmaline swallowed, pulling out her own poppet. She didn't
want to be left behind, not when her parents might need her. All
she had to do was grant herself a little perseverance, hang on just
a little longer...

Oberidon pinned his ears, realizing what she was doing.
<You're going to do yourself in. Stay here.> He pawed the ground
to make his point, then trotted toward the clinic before Emmaline
could ask what he was doing.

"No pegasi in the clinic!" Nadine hollered. Oberidon, of course, ignored her as he used his dextrous lips to open the door.

Zepheus might not be the only one who ends up gelded. Emmaline shook her head as the spotted pegasus emerged a moment later, clutching the wooden handles of Nadine's medical bag between his teeth. It swayed with each stride as he delivered the bag to Nadine.

With his task completed, the spotted stallion swung around to face his rider. It was strange to see her normally mischievous pegasus so stern. He stomped the ground with a forehoof, kicking up a puff of dust. <You have done what you can. Now do your part by *staying.*>

Emmaline sighed. She hated to admit it, but the stallion and Clover were right. She released her magic from the poppet, watching as the portal closed behind Nadine and Zepheus.

Jack

A RADIANT GOLDEN ANGEL STOOD OVER HIM, BECKONING HIM toward the dusty road that led to Perdition. Jack squinted through his crusty eyelashes, perplexed since he was certain the demons rumored to call Perdition home would have been the more likely guides for his trip to whatever awaited him beyond the living world. Blazes, the feared Ghost Riders would be better picks to drag him to Perdition than an angel.

"Come on, you stubborn asshole, you've survived this long, so get your shit together."

That was most decidedly *not* the voice of an angel. Jack tried to place the voice, but thinking that hard made his brain hurt. He knew it wasn't Kittie. Jack vaguely remembered seeing and hearing his wife, cautioning her not to do something she'd regret, but then he'd slipped back into the depths of unconsciousness again. The fall he'd taken from the gallows hadn't done him any favors. Might have just delayed his death.

Jack felt hands on him, the touches only aggravating the myriad aches and pains of his body. He wished for the embrace of unconsciousness again—at least then he felt nothing.

Suddenly, a warmth flooded him, and Jack knew exactly what it was. The power of a Healer. He wanted to grit his teeth, wished he could brace himself, because few Healers he encountered had a gentle touch when it came to treating someone as badly off as he was. Often a patient felt as if they'd been trampled by a horse and then dropped from a cliff, which weren't currently high on the list of things he wanted to feel.

But whoever this was, they were *good*. There were no slipshod attempts at repairing broken bones, no ramming of blood vessels to stop bleeding. Jack didn't know how long he lay there, but the next thing he recalled, his eyes worked well enough for him to see clearly for the first time in...he didn't know how long.

The golden angel's wings spread wide. Then an equine head dipped low, muzzle close to his face. "Zeph?" Jack croaked. Yeah, the stud would like the idea of his rider thinking he was a golden angel. Maybe Jack would even tell the pegasus later if he pulled through.

Zepheus said nothing, instead sending Jack a rush of emotions. Fear. Grief. A profound sense of missing a part of himself. The pegasus brushed his nose against Jack's cheek, then blew a soft breath against his blood-caked hair. *Yeah, you're my ride-or-die, too.* Jack's face hurt too much to smile.

"About time you got your shit together." Nadine peered down at him, but the glint of worry in her eyes belied her stern tone. "I was going to be pissed if I drained myself and you still decided to up and die."

Good ol' Nadine. "Feels like that's still on the table." Jack winced. Yeah, talking hurt. Wasn't a good idea.

"*Jack.*" Kittie dropped to her knees at his side. Jack wasn't sure where they were, but didn't care. All that mattered was that *she* was there. Kittie lifted a hand and looked as if she wanted to touch him, but there wasn't a part of him that didn't have some kind of injury. At least, that was how it felt. She settled for touching his hair where Zepheus had nuzzled. "We're going to talk later, you and I. When you're up to it."

Well, damn. How could words be both foreboding and heartening? But yeah, he probably had this reckoning coming. And at least he'd be around for it.

CHAPTER FIFTY-SEVEN
Stronger Than Salt-Iron

Blaise

Hawthorne House was abuzz with guests. Everything had been chaotic in the day that passed after the interrupted Reclamation Ceremony. There was a disconcerting mix of people from the Luminary's office, mages with the Maverick Underground, and others Blaise didn't know. He made it a point to not stick around in the locations others populated for too long.

They had saved Jack and so far, everything had worked out. But Blaise couldn't help but feel as if something were going to happen. That he wouldn't get out of this unscathed. There were too many people he didn't know around the house. He ended up spending the daylight hours in the barn.

Blaise picked up one of Emrys's massive hooves, checking the health of the frog and other important parts of the foot.

<This is the third time you've checked my hooves today, and I haven't left my stall,> Emrys observed, craning his head around to nudge Blaise's back. <You know if I picked up a stone, I'd tell you.>

Blaise sighed, setting the hoof back down. "Sorry. I don't know what to do with myself."

The black pegasus snorted, ears swiveling. Earlier, the stallion had suggested Blaise spend his nervous energy baking—until Blaise had told him the comforting kitchen was playing host to unfamiliar people, too.

<We could go for a ride. Stay in the pasture,> Emrys suggested. <Or we could go to the market.>

The market was tempting, despite Blaise's ill-fated trip there. It had been such a small, mundane thing. He scratched Emrys's neck. "Actually, I'd like to go there again before we leave. But not today. I can't handle it yet."

<I bet Jefferson and Seledora would come along.>

Blaise smiled, resting his forehead against the stallion. "I like the sound of that."

Emrys's ears flicked, and a moment later Blaise heard new footsteps crunching against the ground. He thought it might be Tristan coming to take care of the horses, but instead he saw Nadine stalk into the barn like an old wildcat on the prowl. There was a little stiffness and fatigue to her movements, but that clearly wasn't stopping her. Her gaze snapped to him and a grim smile touched her lips as she made her way over.

"There you are. Been looking for you." Nadine leaned her arms against the wood of the stall partition.

"How's Jack?" Blaise asked. He knew why Nadine had come out here, and he didn't really want to discuss it.

"The ornery cuss is firmly this side of Perdition."

Blaise released a long breath. "Can he have visitors?"

The Healer eyed him. "How are *you*?"

"Tired of people answering my questions with a question," Blaise muttered, earning a deep scowl from Nadine. He rubbed his forehead. "I wasn't hurt." That in itself was remarkable. Blaise had the worst luck when it came to injuries. "And you already know about my magical reserves." Nadine knew he had an inexhaustible supply of magic. She'd been one of the first interested in it.

Nadine shook her head. "That's not what I mean. You came to *Phinora*." She didn't need to explain why she emphasized the word. They both knew.

Blaise turned to stare at Emrys, brushing a nonexistent speck of dust from the stallion's shoulder. "It's been hard. I'm not as strong as I thought I was."

Nadine scoffed. "Do you hear what you're saying? You're stronger than salt-iron, Blaise. You came back to a place that holds painful memories. Not only that, you had to overcome other obstacles, other attacks, while doing that." She heaved out a breath. "I wouldn't be surprised if you'd been further harmed by that."

"Oh." He hadn't thought about that. Blaise had only known he was walking a narrow line between keeping it together and breaking. And he had broken, repeatedly. He rubbed the bridge of his nose.

"Blaise, you don't have to be invincible," Nadine said, her tone firm. As if she knew the thoughts brewing in his mind.

He nodded, unsure what to say to that. Instead, he changed the subject. "Thanks for coming to heal Jack."

Nadine grunted. "Not as if that pesky golden stud gave me a choice. No one is allowed to so much as stub their toe for the next week. Faedra knows it'll take me that long to recover." She pushed away from the stall partition, then paused to arrow a look at him. "Except you. If you need to see me, let me know. And yes, Jack can have visitors. Don't stay too long."

Blaise waited until she left before slipping out of Emrys's stall and heading back to the house. He steeled himself and entered, striding past those he came across with single-minded determination as he headed for the parlor where Jack had been taken to heal.

The room was dark, the only light filtering in from a single window with the curtains pulled open. Jack lay on the lounge, pillows propped beneath him. His eyes were open, blue eyes tracking Blaise as he made his way across the room. The swelling had gone down on the outlaw's face, though he still looked a far cry from well.

"You gonna say I told you so?" the Effigest rasped.

Blaise pulled a chair over. He was impressed that the injured man felt well enough to say anything at all. "I was thinking I'd leave that for Kittie."

Jack snorted, then winced as if the action pained him. "If I'm lucky, I'll look suitably pitiful to avoid that for a while."

"You do look pretty awful," Blaise agreed. There was no way around it. But at least he was alive. "How do you feel?"

"Like a dragon chewed me up and spat me out. That was a ballsy move, what you did at the gallows." Jack adjusted himself on his throne of pillows.

Blaise shifted in his seat. There were so many things that could have gone wrong. That almost did go wrong. "Didn't have a lot of options."

"You could have let me hang," Jack pointed out, tone painfully neutral. He lifted a bandaged hand to scratch his nose, grimacing. "How in Perdition did you pull that off? I heard your voice, but I didn't think it could be you."

"Remember how we…?" Blaise paused as he struggled with the next words. "Like Fort Courage. Flora found uniforms for Jefferson and me to use."

Jack whistled, though it didn't sound quite right. "Damn, Breaker. But wouldn't they know your faces? The peacock's, at the very least."

Blaise allowed himself a small smile, warmed that his plan impressed the outlaw. "Alchemy."

"You gonna explain?"

Blaise shook his head. "Maybe later." He didn't know how to

explain that talking too much about what had happened threatened to send him over the brink again.

He had expected Jack to push, but maybe the Effigest had learned not to. At least when it came to Blaise. He raised his brows, a move that had to be agonizing with the bruises on his face. With a groan, he rubbed at his cheek. "What happened with Vixen? And where's your peacock?"

That was a safe topic. The scene that had occurred while Zepheus was fetching Nadine was fresh in Blaise's mind. "Um, you missed seeing a god manifest. A big glowing owl named Rhys as the Spark and a fox said Vixen was free." Jack's jaw dropped open, but Blaise plowed on. "I'm going to be honest, I didn't really follow all that was happening because it was a lot. But now Vixen and Jefferson are meeting with the Luminary and new Spark."

"You saw a gods-damned god manifest?" the outlaw repeated, either oblivious to the blasphemy or not caring. Blaise figured probably the latter. A frown creased Jack's face. "Meeting about what?"

"The Gutter and mages."

Jack grunted. "You think anything will come of it?"

Blaise nodded, feeling a wave of relief ease his formerly tense shoulders. "Yeah, I do, actually. And that's why we came, after all." He blew out a breath. "Something worthwhile will come from all of this."

"Not sure I'll ever believe that," Jack rumbled. "But I sure as Perdition hope you're right." He shifted, wincing with the effort. "So. Your Maverick Underground. What's to become of them?"

Blaise scrunched his nose. He wanted to deny that they were *his*, but he kept thinking about the stories they had told him. How he had given them the courage to do what they did. Awkward as always, he rubbed the back of his neck. "Holly—the one with the chickens and geese—is meeting with the Luminary, too. That's why I think we have a chance. They're talking to the local mages like they're people." He swallowed. Jefferson had told him once that he had been the first mage in decades to be treated like a person and not a second-class citizen in Phinora. Blaise knew how important this was.

Jack made a sound that could have been a grunt of pain, but Blaise figured it meant he was listening and found what Blaise had said of interest.

"And since the Quiet Ones chased off most of the skeleton staff here, I've asked if any of the Maverick Underground would like to work at Hawthorne House." Blaise blew out a breath. "So, now I guess I have a bunch of mages working for me." That was *weird*.

"You don't say?" Jack gave him a keen look, which was a little intimidating with his bruising and the web of broken blood vessels in his right eye. "You telling me there's a network of mage spies in your pay now?"

Blaise groaned. "Jefferson told me you'd say something like that."

"The peacock's smart sometimes."

Blaise crossed his arms. "They're just taking care of the house and the grounds. That's all there is to it!" But Jack only laughed at his insistence. The outlaw's laughter sounded like a goose being strangled.

Jack was about to speak again when a single knock sounded on the door, and then Kittie let herself in. She stood framed in the doorway, hands on her hips as she glared at her husband. "Jack Arthur Dewitt, where do I even begin with you?"

Blaise cleared his throat, rising from his seat. "I should, um, probably go."

"Coward," Jack growled.

"I'm not the one who just had my full name used." Blaise made a beeline for the door, leaving the outlaw to his fate.

CHAPTER FIFTY-EIGHT
Living Nightmare

Jefferson

A plume of smoke from the waiting locomotive curled into the air ahead. Rachel Clayton stepped down from the coach that had brought her from Dawnlight to the station. After her reappearance at the Asaphenia, the Luminary had treated the Madame Boss as an impromptu guest. Jefferson regretted his inability to spend time catching up with her immediately after the events, but he'd made it a point to accompany her to the station.

"Are you sure you want Flora to stay with me?" Rachel asked, glancing at the half-knocker. Flora stood beside her, swaying on her heels. "The Confederation has agreed to send a guard with me on the train."

Jefferson's gaze fell to his oldest and dearest friend. Flora peered up at him, grinning. "They won't do half as good a job keeping tabs on you as I will."

And Jefferson had to agree. Flora, for all of her idiosyncrasies, was unmatched. She would safeguard the Madame Boss better than anyone else. He would miss her, but he was no longer the defenseless elite he'd been when they first met. And he no longer had business affairs for her to help him keep tabs on. Jefferson's world had changed, and while he hated to part ways with her, it was for the best. Besides, he reassured himself, it was only temporary.

"She's a part of my office as ambassador," Jefferson said after a moment. That was the best way to do it. Then he wouldn't lose Flora, not really. She could serve as a vital source of intelligence for the Gutter and still be his friend.

He stepped aside to speak with the pink-haired woman, sitting on a nearby bench so their height difference was minimized. "I'm going to miss you."

She rolled her eyes. "You're not rid of me yet." She patted his cheek for good measure. "Stay out of trouble. I won't be around to save you anymore."

He chuckled. "I'll try."

<At the very least, he has his attorney,> Seledora commented from nearby.

Jefferson watched as Rachel boarded the train, followed by Flora. He stayed on the platform until the locomotive pulled out from the station. With that task complete, he strode back to Seledora.

<Are you still determined to see to the next errand?> the mare asked, disapproval in her voice.

"Yes." He put a foot in the stirrup and swung into the saddle.

<Minutes after literally telling Flora you'd stay out of trouble?>

"In my defense, I said I'd *try*. I never said I'd be good at it."

Seledora blew out an annoyed snort.

"And it's not as if I'm going alone," Jefferson reasoned as she broke into a trot. "I'm taking you along, aren't I?"

<The only smart thing about this, if we're being honest.>

He ignored the dig.

They travelled in silence as Seledora opened up into a canter once the road cleared. If he'd been heading for Hawthorne House, they would have chanced taking flight, but not for this errand. No, Jefferson intended to keep a low profile, at least for the moment.

The Quiet One estate was just as he remembered it, though there was a notable lack of mercenary forces and theurgists compared to the last time they'd come. Most of them had flown the coop with Tara's death, he supposed. Good. That worked in Jefferson's favor.

He left Seledora loose in the driveway, a perplexed groom debating whether he should approach the pegasus. Jefferson strode to the entry with his head high and shoulders squared. A steward was quick to open the door and show him inside, leading him to a study where Phillip Dillon awaited him.

The Quiet One had claimed a wingback chair and sat like a monarch holding court. A half-full glass of an amber-colored beverage sat on the small table beside the chair. He nodded to a nearby settee. "Would you like my staff to bring you anything to drink? Refreshments of any sort?"

This was elite behavior. Jefferson noted the difference from the last time Dillon had spoken to him. There was a level of grudging respect now. "No, thank you." He wouldn't trust any food or drink in this house. Jefferson settled on the plush settee.

"You wouldn't happen to know anything about the disaster that befell the slaughterhouse west of Izhadell, would you?" Phillip asked. "Seems there was a terrible fire there last night." He motioned for the maid, who entered to set a bowl of grapes on the table beside him.

"How unfortunate," Jefferson murmured. He might know a thing or two about it, but he wouldn't reveal anything. From what he understood, Jack and Kittie hadn't liked what they'd seen there. The Effigest wasn't well enough to cause trouble, so Jefferson assumed Kittie had struck out to do something about it. "Was it one owned by the Blakely family?" Russell Blakely of Canen was another of the Quiet Ones, his family making their fortune from slaughterhouses. While he hadn't crossed Jefferson directly, Jefferson was predisposed to dislike all of the cabal at this point.

"No, it was owned by Smithstone."

Jefferson's brows lifted. So Cinna, his former fiancée, had a hand in this, too, albeit indirectly. He wasn't surprised. He gave a single-shoulder shrug. "These things happen."

The maid left a plate of cheeses before hurrying from the room. When she was gone, Phillip fixed a dour look on Jefferson. "Come to gloat, have you?"

Ah, there it was. And while it was an extremely tempting prospect, that wasn't it. While both men knew this visit was a power play on Jefferson's part, coming back to this estate after their last foray had gone so wrong was audacious, to say the least. "I noticed you weren't at the Reclamation Ceremony. You missed quite an event."

Phillip took a sip of his beverage, savoring it before setting the glass down again. "I have no interest in the workings of the Phinoran god."

That was a lie. He'd been interested enough to attend the gala. No, Jefferson suspected Phillip had served as the puppet master from afar. "A pity. It was quite a historic moment." Jefferson couldn't help but smile. "You asked why I came. I have questions."

Dillon took another sip of his drink. "What makes you think I'll answer them?"

Jefferson leaned forward. "While Tara may rot in the ground, let me assure you there are far worse fates."

Phillip's glass rattled against the table as he set it down again, frowning. "You've been around the outlaws for too long. Their petty threats have rubbed off on you."

Jefferson studied the other man for a long moment before speaking. "Let me assure you that there's nothing petty about my threat." And then he pulled on his magic, enveloping Dillon and dragging him into the dreamscape.

Jefferson had debated long and hard about this move. It tipped the hand of his magic to an enemy and left him vulnerable in an unfriendly location, but sometimes it was best to let others know what they were risking. Even a rattlesnake gave warning before a strike.

He was close on Dillon's heels, following the Quiet One into the dreamscape. The older man gasped, stumbling as he arrived. He stared, bewildered, as Jefferson drew a veil of storm clouds around them. Lightning pulsed and thunder growled.

"What *are* you?" Dillon asked, taking a step backward.

"Tired of your games," Jefferson snapped. "You think you've stripped me of my power by taking my wealth? You're wrong. Who needs money when they have *magic?*"

Phillip turned and tried to run, but as so often happened in dreams, his legs refused to follow through. He staggered as Jefferson further twisted the dreamscape so that he was falling, falling, *falling*. Dillon screamed, a sound of full-throated horror as he tumbled before thudding against a formless black void.

The Quiet One rolled onto his back, staring up at Jefferson's approach. "Ask your questions." He nearly panted the words. Phillip warbled as, one by one, his teeth fell out, clattering around him like ivory hail.

Jefferson hadn't realized until that moment that he was shaking with rage. He'd never been this cruel to someone so quickly in his dreams, not even Gregor Gaitwood. "I know you and Tara had other goals besides the mess with the Luminary and claiming the Gutter. What are they?"

Phillip picked up one of his front teeth, trying to force it back into the empty socket in his mouth. The man began to sob as he tried and failed to replace his teeth. That wouldn't do. The dental nightmare was far too distracting. With a frustrated sigh, Jefferson waved a hand, restoring the man's teeth.

Dillon stared up at him, swallowing. "Tara...she wanted the Breaker. She could hardly believe her luck when he came with you."

Blaise. That wretched woman had wanted Blaise. *But Tara is dead. She can't get him now.* Jefferson took a calming breath, lest he inflict a new torture on Phillip. "Why?"

Phillip clumsily stumbled to his feet, no longer the cultured elite. The dreamscape had turned him into a trembling man, a shell of himself. *No, I did that. Me and my cruelty.*

For a moment, Jefferson thought the other man would refuse to answer. But then, with a grimace, Phillip asked, "Have you forgotten what her husband is?"

Jefferson's mouth went dry. An alchemist. Tara's spouse was an alchemist, a brilliant one on a par with Marian Hawthorne. Of course, they would be eager for Blaise. They probably knew he was an alchemical mage, and not born into power.

"That's why he was almost captured at the market," Jefferson murmured, understanding dawning.

"Yes," Phillip agreed, tone neutral. "That was part of Tara's gambit."

Jefferson clamped his jaw. Fury swelled within, but Tara was dead. She couldn't hunt Blaise anymore. That didn't mean the Breaker was safe, though. He never would be, and that was perhaps the most distressing part of this entire mess. Jefferson blew out a breath. "And you. What was your goal?"

"It's as I told you in the Golden Citadel. Because of all the people in the world, you might be able to get Alice back."

My sister. He does indeed have a one-track mind when it comes to her. Interesting. "Why would I do that?" Jefferson asked. He wanted to add comments like *"She seemed to hate you"* and *"I'm sure she's better off without you,"* but he kept those to himself.

Phillip lowered his head, chin against his chest. He suddenly looked older than his years. So much older than Alice. "Because losing her and our son was my worst nightmare."

Wait, I have a nephew? Gods, I never knew. Jefferson schooled his features. "She *left* you."

Dillon's shoulders drooped. "I know. She deserved better than the way I treated her. And you probably don't believe me, but I love our son." He had a faraway look in his eyes, as if recalling a fond memory.

Jefferson took advantage of it and allowed the other man's mind to influence the dreamscape. The ghostly visage of a young woman with a waterfall of dark hair appeared, her hands resting on the shoulders of a small boy. Phillip startled at their appearance, but then tears sprang to his eyes as he knelt before the child. The boy turned away, clinging to his mother as if he were shy.

"I didn't love Alice when we married. I did it purely for the power. To join the Dillon line with the Wells, with a dash of magic." Phillip stared at the memories. "I had planned to keep her the same way that I kept the Herald."

The Herald? Jefferson's brow furrowed as he tried to recall how he knew that name. *Oh.* The Wallwalker that had taken Blaise all the way from Thorn to Nera the first time the Quiet Ones had tried to coerce Jefferson to their cause. Phillip and the other Quiet Ones kept mages as pets and employed them for their purposes. Jefferson wasn't surprised Phillip had sought to do the same with Alice. "The Herald was your lover."

"That, and more," Phillip agreed. "She was useful."

A tool. That's what she had been. And that was what he'd wanted to do to Alice, too. "Why would you even entertain the notion that I might bring Alice back to you?"

"Because while I know she will never love me, I love our son," Phillip said, his voice plaintive. "This is what happened to Gregor, isn't it?" Phillip asked as Jefferson digested the revelation that Phillip cared for someone other than himself. "It would explain why he was so...unstable." He shuddered.

Jefferson smiled, unable to rein in his glee that finally, Phillip Dillon would see him for the threat he truly was. "He dared to harm someone I love," he whispered. "And so I made his life a living nightmare." Jefferson shifted his hands behind his back, threading the fingers together. "I thank you for the answers.

They've been most enlightening." Before Dillon could say anything else, Jefferson shoved the man out of the dreamscape.

Jefferson roused before Phillip, an advantage he had as a Dreamer. He was already leaning forward on his velvet settee when the Quiet One awoke with a sharp, terrified gasp, eyes bulging as he stared at Jefferson.

"I trust we understand one another now?" Jefferson asked icily as he rose.

"Wait." Dillon stared up at him, face desolate, like a man who had lost everything. Jefferson knew the feeling only too well. "What would it take for you to help me with Alice? Restore your fortune? I can do that."

Tempting. Gods, that is so tempting. Jefferson shook his head. "It's not about me, Phillip. It's about my sister and nephew, and what is best for them." He shifted, thinking about himself. About the series of events that had led the son of a cruel elite down a path that had molded him into something different. Blaise wouldn't have loved him if he had become Stafford Wells's shadow. "You would have to *change*, and even that might not be enough."

Phillip swallowed. "I can change."

"Can you, though?" Jefferson strode in a circle around the wingback chair, a big cat on the prowl. "To have a chance, even the *slightest* chance, you would need to adjust your mind and behaviors. And I'm not convinced you can." Tabris knew Jefferson grappled with his own streak of cruelty. And he was far kinder than Dillon.

The Quiet One wilted. "I can't stop being what I am. That's like asking me to stop breathing."

"Then they're lost to you," Jefferson said, starting for the door.

CHAPTER FIFTY-NINE

I See You Have Cake

Vixen

The last few days had been a surreal blur. Vixen still had to pinch herself, hardly believing the events at the Asaphenia could possibly have been real. But they were. The very fact that her mother walked alongside her served as proof.

"You really don't mind that I want to go back to the Gutter?" she asked, pushing her glasses up the bridge of her nose. Vixen had taken to wearing them again as a vestige of her outlaw side.

Juliette continued walking, though she hazarded a glance at her daughter. They were ambling along the path that led to the unicorn stables. Vixen had forgotten that her mother loved to take walks, and venturing around the stables had been a particular favorite as she could watch the majestic unicorns graze. "Would I prefer for you to stay in Izhadell? Of course. You were only recently returned to me." She slowed, turning to face Vixen. "But now I know that you're alive. And not only that, you're..." Juliette made a circuitous gesture to encompass all of Vixen.

Vixen tilted her head. "I'll be honest, I'm not entirely sure what you mean by that."

Juliette laughed, shaking her head. "Amazing. That's what I mean."

Amazing? Vixen felt a lump form in her throat. "I was always afraid you'd hate me."

Her mother's face crumpled, but she nodded. "I wish I could say I'd have behaved differently, but I can't." She released a long breath. "That's not how I feel now, though. And it's going to be a long, hard road before other Phinorans feel the same, but I hope that in time, we'll get there."

They continued walking, with Vixen wondering if there would ever be a widespread acceptance in her lifetime. Her mother and Rhys were certainly willing to plant the seeds, which was a start.

They rounded a bend, the paddocks visible before them. Vixen paused, raising her brows at a sight she would never have expected. Alekon was in the paddock with Darby, the pair head-to-tail as they groomed one another like old friends. The unicorn nibbled gently at the feathers at the pegasus's shoulder, his horn catching the light with his deft movements.

"Now I've seen everything," Vixen murmured, breaking into a jog.

Rhys lounged against the fence, looking more like a glorified stable boy than a man who had been bestowed the title of Spark. He turned at the sound of her footsteps, grinning.

"They're playing nice?" Vixen asked when she reached the fence. Alekon hadn't so much as glanced her way, too absorbed in the delicious sensations.

"So far. That's why I'm keeping an eye on them."

"Whose idea was it?" Vixen asked.

Juliette had caught up and climbed the fence, sitting on the top rail. Vixen followed suit. If the Luminary could climb a fence, then so could an outlaw.

<Both of ours,> Alekon announced, clearly addressing all of them. He hadn't stopped grooming the unicorn. <We thought we'd set a good example for you humans.>

Rhys's brow furrowed. "You can understand Darby?"

<I'm fluent in equine, bovine, and caprine.> Alekon paused his grooming to flex his neck, the glossy hide shining.

Vixen blinked in surprise. "How come this is the first I've heard of it? You can talk to goats?"

<You never asked.> The bay stallion flicked his tail. <By the way, Darby wants to try Blaise's cookies before we leave. He never had the chance before.>

Juliette's eyes narrowed in confusion. "What?"

Vixen waved a hand. "Long story. But we'll make it happen, Darby." The unicorn stuck out his tongue and then began to smack his lips, as if he were already anticipating the sweetness of the impending delicacies. She looked at Rhys. "We're leaving tomorrow."

Her brother glanced at their mother. "Did you ask her yet?"

Vixen frowned. "Ask me what?"

Juliette shook her head. "I was waiting until we met with you."

"What do you want to ask me?" Vixen demanded, almost releasing a tendril of her magic but drawing it back at the last second.

Rhys grimaced, as if he'd felt an echo of her power. Juliette didn't notice. "We thought you might serve as an envoy."

Of all the things her mother might have proposed, this wasn't what Vixen had expected. Ever. "Huh?" She swallowed as the full import hit her. "Me? I'm..." What was she? No longer the Spark, not really. Was she still a Ringleader? Her stomach sank at the idea that might be taken from her. She didn't want to give that up. "An outlaw mage."

"And so is Jefferson Cole," Rhys agreed patiently.

"I'm not..." Vixen knew she was gaping like a fish out of water. Her mother was doing a poor job of hiding an amused smile. "Why?"

"Because Garus still counts you as his. You have your boots in two worlds," Juliette said. "Beloved of Garus. Outlaw mage. There's no one more qualified."

"I can't."

Juliette's eyebrows hiked up in surprise. "Why not?"

Vixen glanced at Alekon. The bay stallion had turned to watch with interest. "I've already got a position in Fortitude. I'm a Ring-leader." And she had her tailoring shop, if any outlaws would buy from a former Garusian Spark. "It means I'm kinda part of the group of leaders already."

Her mother and brother exchanged glances, then Juliette nodded. "I shouldn't be surprised that you've been a leader all this time."

Vixen's face warmed with pleasure. "Sorry I have to turn down your offer. I hope it won't impact relations with the mages."

"It won't," Rhys promised.

Juliette nodded agreement, then hopped down from the fence to land beside Vixen. She made the movement look graceful and almost otherworldly, but her smile was all human, motherly and warm. "Now let's stop talking Luminary business and enjoy the time we have left together. Rhys, do you have a unicorn or horse I could ride?"

Vixen could hardly believe her ears. "We're going for a ride?"

<Darby says Vixen can ride him. The Luminary should try a pegasus.> Alekon's dark eyes gleamed.

Today, it seemed, was a day for surprises.

Blaise

"Do you think the chicken is a spy?" Jefferson asked, watching as the newest member of their cobbled-together family pecked at the dirt behind the bakery.

They'd returned to Fortitude two days ago after a train ride that had been as uneventful as their first. Though this time Blaise had spent most of the trip in their room, unwilling to tempt fate. Jack, who was still convalescing, had suggested they try a portal back. Despite wanting to get back to Fortitude, Nadine had nipped that idea in the bud, declaring that it wouldn't hurt any of them to rest for the time it took to travel from Izhadell to Ondin.

Blaise chuckled at the idea. "I guess it's possible, but I don't think so." Holly Lewis had given the hen to him as a parting gift. Before they had left Phinora, the Maverick Underground had met with Rhys to discuss the concerns of the maverick mages. According to Holly, it had gone well, and there was truly hope for the future.

It didn't hurt that Jefferson and Vixen had brokered a peace of their own with the Luminary. Vixen's mother vowed she would work with Rachel Clayton to make sure the Confederation stood down and didn't attack the Gutter. It sounded as if Phinora might even be prepared to recognize the Gutter as a nation, though Jefferson had privately told Blaise the elite may see that as a step too far, too quickly. Far better for the Maverick Underground to work with Rhys to improve conditions for Phinoran mages first.

"I suppose it means fewer eggs for you to buy," Jefferson said. "Should we get more chickens, do you think?"

Blaise raised his brows. "You're interested in chickens?"

Jefferson shrugged. "Only because Mother Clucker might be lonely."

"I'm not letting you name any more family members, by the way."

"It's an amazing name, and you know it." Jefferson grinned. Then he paused, as if he'd just dissected the words Blaise had used. "Wait, what do you mean?"

Swallowing, Blaise turned to Jefferson, digging a hand into his pocket. Things were going to get awkward real fast if—oh good, there it was. His fingers closed around the ring, the pegasus-etched piece he'd picked up at the market what felt like ages ago. Everything had been so chaotic, he'd forgotten about it until Vixen had returned the nullifying ring to him. He took a steadying breath as he fished it out.

"What I mean is, you are the frosting for my cake. The crust of my pie. An ingredient in my life so important, I'm not the same without you." Blaise hoped he wasn't trembling too badly. He was afraid that despite everything, Jefferson might not feel the same. Even though Emrys and Seledora had assured him that was foolish. He held out the ring, the engraved pegasi catching the light. "Will you be a part of my life forever?"

The Dreamer stared at him, green eyes narrowing a smidge as if he were making certain he understood what Blaise had said. "Is this a proposal?" His voice was husky.

Blaise glanced down at the ring. Jefferson was giving him an out, a chance to take back his words if he needed to. But he didn't need to. His breath hitched. "Yes."

"Oh gods," Jefferson whispered, closing the distance between them. He wrapped his arms around Blaise, drawing him close. "I... Blaise, you're the best part of my life." Heartfelt tears glimmered in the corners of his eyes.

"So, is that a yes?"

"Yes."

Warmth bloomed in Blaise's chest as he leaned in, lips brushing Jefferson's. The Dreamer exhaled softly as they met, his fingers digging into Blaise's shoulders and back, a gentle possessiveness. Butterflies fluttered in Blaise's stomach. He'd been so worried Jefferson would say no, had grappled with the potential heartbreak for most of the train ride. Now all of those worries melted like sugar in water, replaced by the delectable euphoria of this love they shared.

When they parted, Jefferson rested his forehead against Blaise's. "When did you decide this?"

"After they arrested you." Blaise swallowed at the memory.

"That was when I knew without a doubt that you made my life better." It was something he'd almost taken for granted.

Jefferson reached up to touch Blaise's face, fingertips scrubbing against his beard. "You were worried about asking me, weren't you?"

"A little." Blaise paused. "Okay, a lot."

"You didn't need to worry. You dreamed about this sometimes, you know." Jefferson pressed his lips together as if he were hiding amusement.

Blaise stared at him. "I *what?*"

"On the train ride home. Sometimes, when I fetched you to the dreamscape, I'd find you dreaming about this," Jefferson said, voice gentle. "I knew it would embarrass you if you thought I'd discovered it, so I never mentioned it."

Blaise didn't know if that was better or worse. "You knew all along that I'd ask you?"

Jefferson shook his head. "No, I knew you *wanted* to ask. But you were afraid. And I don't like when you're afraid—I never want to be the source of your fear. So, I set that knowledge aside, hoping that some day you might."

Blaise swallowed the lump in his throat. Jefferson had known but had patiently waited for something that might never come. And he'd never forced the issue, instead making himself happy with what Blaise offered. "Well, today's the day."

Jefferson's eyes gleamed. "And it only gets better from here."

"It does," Blaise agreed, turning to a tray resting behind him. It had a tin cover, and he removed it to reveal two slices of yellow cake with chocolate buttercream frosting—one of Jefferson's favorites. Blaise picked up a plate, offering a slice to the man he loved.

"You weren't kidding," Jefferson murmured as he dug his fork into the cake, uttering a blissful sigh.

Emrys angled his dark head through the bakery window,

nostrils flaring as he drank in the sweet scents. <I see you have cake. I, too, enjoy cake.>

<You're supposed to say *congratulations*,> Seledora chided the black pegasus, nipping at his neck.

<Congratulations. Now can I have cake?> Emrys eyed the plate in his rider's hands.

Blaise couldn't help but laugh. He'd known the pegasi had lingered outside, waiting. Blaise set his own plate aside, moving to a glass stand that held the rest of the cake. He knew his pegasus's sweet inclinations and had planned accordingly. Blaise cut the rest of the cake in half, dumping the sides into a pair of pie tins and carrying them over to the window. He placed them in front of each pegasus. "We're happy to have you celebrate with us."

Emrys dug in immediately, smearing his muzzle with chocolate. Seledora took a more delicate approach, first licking the buttercream before taking a hearty bite.

"So when do we tell your family?" Jefferson asked, eyes twinkling. "I'm curious how they'll react."

Blaise chuckled. "Not yet. I need a few days of normal before stirring them up." He pursed his lips. "Are you sure about this, though? About me?"

Jefferson's green gaze fell on him, a satisfied smile curling his lips. "Blaise Hawthorne, I have never been more certain of anything in my life."

Stay In the Know!

Sign up for my newsletter to receive a free short story plus sneak peeks, exclusive short stories, and more!
www.amycampbell.info

And if you enjoyed *Persuader*, please take a moment to leave a review on the platform of your choice! Reviews help authors like me gain a foothold in the wild world of publishing. It's a small thing that means a lot!

Soundtrack

Try - Dolly Parton
Landslide - The Chicks
Where I Belong - Saint Chaos
Let It Go - Tim McGraw
Shatter Me - Lindsey Stirling
Whisper - Evanescence
Weapons - Ava Max
Use My Voice - Evanescence
OMG What's Happening - Ava Max
Not Ready to Make Nice - The Chicks
Flowers - Miley Cyrus

Acknowledgments

I wouldn't be where I am without my readers, so if you made it this far—thank you. I appreciate you giving the outlaw mages a place in your reading world. There are so many good books out there, I'm honored that you've read mine.

Huge thanks to my editor, Vicky Brewster, who finds all the weird plot issues I want to ignore and makes my commas go in the right places. And to my cover artist, Anna, for always making my covers true works of art that catch the eye! I also want to thank my dedicated beta readers, who help make this book all the better: Catherine, Eline, Jen, Percy, Raina, and Sumi.

CPSIA information can be obtained
at www.ICGtesting.com
Printed in the USA
BVHW071921210423
662821BV00013B/206

9 781736 141878